PRAISE FOR

CASTE IN THE STARS

"Every once in a while, you read a romance filled with so much heart that your own heart grows a few sizes. *Caste in the Stars* bursts with the beauty of human connection, the courage of reaching for dreams, and the pure healing power of family. Swoony, sexy, and fearless—I absolutely loved it!"

—Sonali Dev, bestselling author of *There's Something About Mira*

"Love conquers all in this sharp, witty, and humorous tale of two people who find love in the most unexpected of circumstances. Leylah Attar has, once again, captivated our emotions in this second-chance story where cultural expectations and conflicting backgrounds are no match against the unifying power of the human heart."

—Anna Gomez, bestselling author of *Moments Like This* and *In This Life*

"I binge-read this! Heartfelt and hopeful—*Caste in the Stars* is a sexy, swoony story about second chances, finding your place in the world, and the wonder of falling in love."

—Bailey Hannah, *USA Today* bestselling author of *Alive and Wells*

"*Caste in the Stars* is both swoon-worthy and thought-provoking. This childhood-crush, movie-star romance is filled with heartfelt moments, memorable characters, and sizzling connections."

—Farah Heron, author of *Accidentally Engaged* and *Just Playing House*

CASTE IN THE STARS

ALSO BY LEYLAH ATTAR

The Night Blossoms
Moti on the Water
Mists of the Serengeti
The Paper Swan
53 Letters for My Lover

Caste in the Stars

LEYLAH ATTAR

A Novel

DOUBLEDAY CANADA

PUBLISHED IN 2025 BY DOUBLEDAY CANADA

Doubleday Canada, an imprint of Penguin Random House Canada Limited,
320 Front Street West, Suite 1400,
Toronto, Ontario, M5V 3B6, Canada
penguinrandomhouse.ca

Library and Archives Canada Cataloguing in Publication

Title: Caste in the stars: a novel / Leylah Attar.
Names: Attar, Leylah, author
Identifiers: Canadiana (print) 20250154412 | Canadiana (ebook) 20250154420 |
ISBN 9780385702270 (softcover) | ISBN 9780385702287 (EPUB)
Subjects: LCGFT: Romance fiction. | LCGFT: Novels.
Classification: LCC PS8601.T72 C37 2025 | DDC C813/.6—dc23

Cover and book design by Talia Abramson
Cover images: (paisley) malkani, (stars) OpenDesigner,
(marigolds) lunika / Adobe Stock
Typeset in Adobe Garamond by Sean Tai

Printed in Canada

2 4 6 8 9 7 5 3 1

For my brothers—
who taught me how to listen with my heart

PLAYLIST

Reading with the right soundtrack just makes everything feel more alive. These songs helped me tap into the mood of the story while I was writing. I hope they bring a little extra magic to your reading too!

1 **Stars** Simply Red

2 **Fire for You** Cannons

3 **Crush** Jennifer Paige

4 **Kamariya** Darshan Raval;
Chogada Darshan Raval & Asees Kaur

5 **Thunderstruck** AC/DC

6 **Night Changes** One Direction

7 **Marigold** Jelani Aryeh

8 **Closer** Tegan and Sara

9 **Electric** Alina Baraz ft. Khalid

10 **Hold On, We're Going Home** Drake ft. Majid Jordan

11 **Birds of a Feather** Billie Eilish

12 **Home** Michael Bublé

13 **Kiss Me** Sixpence None the Richer

14 **Have You Ever** Brandy

15 **Adore You** Harry Styles

16 **Darkhaast** Arijit Singh & Sunidhi Chauhan

17 **Love Me Now** John Legend;
Dusk Till Dawn ZAYN ft. Sia

18 **Love on the Brain** Rihanna

19 **Sex on Fire** Kings of Leon;
Dreams The Cranberries

20 **Technicolour Beat** Oh Wonder

21 **Golden Hour** JVKE

22 **Rewrite the Stars** Zac Efron & Zendaya

23 **Blinding Lights** The Weeknd

24 **Stand by Me** Ben E. King

25 **Let's Stay Together** Al Green;
Sparks Coldplay

26 **Falling** Harry Styles

27 **Somebody Else** The 1975

28 **Spirit in the Sky** Norman Greenbaum

29 **Read All About It, Pt. III** Emeli Sandé

30 **Roar** Katy Perry

31 **Girl on Fire** Alicia Keys

32 **It Must Have Been Love** Roxette

33 **Stars Dance** Selena Gomez

34 **Bad Dreams** Teddy Swims

35 **Die with a Smile** Lady Gaga & Bruno Mars;
Titanium David Guetta ft. Sia

36 **Physical** Dua Lipa

37 **Chaleya** Arijit Singh & Shilpa Rao;
You're the Inspiration Chicago

38 **Sweet Disposition** The Temper Trap

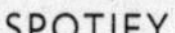

SPOTIFY

YOUTUBE

One

THE BAGGAGE CAROUSEL at Toronto's Pearson International Airport clunked to life, and Priya Solanki stood back, watching suitcase after suitcase glide past until hers came into view. Two bags were all it took to hold ten years of her life—a failed marriage, a business she had walked away from, and the freedom she had built for herself. All now completely gone. She'd promised herself she'd never return, yet here she was, out of options.

After dragging her luggage through the terminal, she stepped outside and slid into the back of a waiting cab.

"Where to?" The driver met her eyes in the rearview mirror.

"Moksha Funeral Home," Priya replied. "In Ajax."

"Lucky you're not heading downtown today," he said as they merged into traffic. "I just returned from a drop-off there, and it was brutal. Bumper to bumper the whole way."

"Construction?" Priya asked, peering out the window. It was late April, which in Toronto translated to the start of roadwork season.

"Not this time," he replied. "There was a celebrity sighting at the Hazelton. Some big star from out of town. Turned the whole area into a total gridlock. Traffic was backed up all the way to the highway, nobody moving an inch."

Priya leaned back, only half listening. A traffic jam over a celebrity sipping an overpriced latte was both absurd and entirely expected. She'd spent the last ten years in Calgary, where the rhythm of life was slower. Here, even at a standstill, the city buzzed with urgency.

The drive to Ajax, a suburb east of Toronto, took a little under an hour. Clusters of daffodils and crocuses bloomed along the edges of the roadside. As they approached her old neighborhood, familiar sights greeted Priya like pages from an old diary: the community center where she first learned to swim, the No Frills grocery store where her family did their weekly shopping, the library where she met up with her friend Brooke, though they usually ended up at the McDonald's across the street. Every place was exactly as she remembered, yet within Priya, everything had shifted.

When the cab finally turned into the parking lot of the funeral home, Priya straightened, her eyes locking on the building. The weight of what lay ahead twisted in her chest.

"Go around the back, please." Priya gestured toward the rear lot.

She winced at the fare on the meter, mindful of her dwindling savings. Then she spotted a photo of the cabbie's children smiling from the dashboard and gave him a generous tip anyway.

Sucker, her thrifty Gujarati ancestors scolded from beyond the grave.

The driver heaved her suitcases out of the trunk, chuckling as he read the tag on one: "You can't handle my baggage."

Priya felt a pang of guilt as he set the bag down with a huff. The joke was a little too on the nose. Her baggage, literal and otherwise, was ridiculously heavy.

As the cab drove away, Priya turned toward the building, standing in the very spot where bodies were delivered from the morgue. A shiver ran down her spine. Death was inevitable, and for her, so was this place. She thought she had escaped it, but as she stared at the side door to her parents' second-floor apartment, her certainty crumbled.

She lugged her suitcases up the narrow stairs, each step groaning under her weight. The wood was worn and uneven, some planks smoothed by years of use, others jagged with splinters, the paint peeling on every one. She hesitated at the top step, the duct tape still holding it together after all these years. Despite herself, she smiled. Her father's handiwork had somehow stubbornly stood the test of time.

Standing by the door, Priya took a deep breath, and almost immediately the rich, smoky scent of *rotlis* transported her back in time. Over the years, her annual visits had been brief and dutiful, but some things never changed, like the way her mother's cooking clung to the walls, familiar and comforting. She could almost taste the soft, warm flatbreads, and she hadn't even stepped inside. As she lifted her hand to knock, the door burst open, and her mother stood there, arms outstretched.

"I knew it!" Her mother beamed, eyes shining. "I can recognize your footsteps anywhere. My Priya baby is home!"

"Mumma." As Priya stepped into her mother's embrace, her body relaxed. Ever since her divorce, she had carried the weight of letting them down, of returning as someone who hadn't made it, but that feeling lifted, replaced by the quiet comfort of home.

"What Mumma-Mumma?" Her mother pulled back with a pout. "You forgot Mumma. You don't call Mumma, don't ask Mumma, don't love Mumma."

Priya chuckled at her mother's lightning-fast transition from a warm welcome to a full-on guilt trip. Mumma had mastered the art of emotional drama, keeping the whole family on their toes.

"Enough, Seema," her father intervened, appearing behind his wife. "She's only just arrived, and you've already started. Let her relax and eat something. Then we'll *both* gang up on her."

Priya laughed, but tears stung the corners of her eyes as she hugged him. She hadn't known what kind of welcome to expect, but this warmth, this lightness, filled her with relief and gratitude. Pulling both her parents close, she buried her face between them.

"I love you very much," she said.

For a moment, the three of them remained locked together. Then, as if realizing they'd lingered too long, her parents pulled away. Seema and Rakesh Solanki dispensed affection in appropriate doses, but verbal declarations of love to each other or the kids? *Na, baba, na.*

Mumma smoothed her nightgown to dispel the awkwardness. Priya couldn't remember her wearing anything other than button-down nightgowns around the house. When they grew flimsy, Mumma tore them into scraps and used them as a *potu* to mop the floor.

"Is this everything?" Puppa asked, reaching for Priya's suitcases.

"This is it." Priya forced a cheerful smile, hoping it would hide the ache beneath it. Coming home after years of trying to build a life of her own felt like proof that she had failed. She trailed behind her parents, stepping into the familiar living room of their modest apartment.

"So, tell me . . ." Puppa settled into his usual spot at the dining table and motioned Priya to join him.

But Priya wasn't ready. Not yet. She slipped into the kitchen instead, where her mother was already busy making chai.

"Let me help." She opened the cupboard next to the sink and reached for the cups, hoping to stall the conversation that lay ahead—and her parents' inevitable autopsy of her marriage.

"Priya," her father called her back, firm and steady.

Priya sighed and carried the cups and sugar bowl over to the table, bracing herself as she sat beside him. Even though she was twenty-eight, her heart still raced whenever her father wanted to "talk," and a familiar fight-or-flight response took over her body. In the past, she had fled, because fighting was disrespectful, but now she had nowhere to run. Her parents held all the power.

Puppa leaned forward, clasping his hands on the table, and fixed his gaze on Priya. "How much did you pay for the taxi?"

Priya's shoulders relaxed. This she could handle. Rakesh Solanki was a frugal man who took great pride in imparting his money-saving habits. Priya divided the fare in half and gave him the number.

"*Hey Bhagwan.*" Dear Lord. "Seema, did you hear?"

"I heard. I heard," Mumma replied from the kitchen. "Priya, you know Ramila *ben no jamai no kaka no nano babu*?"

"Do I know your friend's son-in-law's dad's brother's younger son? I don't think so."

"Yes, you do. Jignesh. You know. *Jignesh*."

"Ah, Jignesh." Priya had no idea who Jignesh was, but it was easier to let Mumma assume she knew every Gujarati person in the Greater Toronto Area than to suffer a long-winded explanation.

"He gives people a ride to the airport for only ten dollars." Mumma added ginger and cardamom to the tea before glancing at Priya through the archway that joined the kitchen to the dining area.

"Ten dollars doesn't even cover the gas, Mumma," Priya muttered, shaking her head.

"He doesn't do it for the money. It's *seva* for our community. He's creating good karma. He will reap the rewards one day."

"So, Jignesh is currying favor with Bhagwanji. Good business strategy. Investing now in the hopes of future gains."

"Don't be cheeky." Mumma stepped out of the kitchen and plopped a plate of hot rotlis on the table. "Why didn't you come home sooner? A whole year in Calgary, living on your own after you separated from Manoj. What were you thinking?"

Priya smiled faintly, tearing off a piece of rotli and dusting it with sugar. "It's not like I was the only woman in Calgary living on my own. A lot of my girlfriends live alone too."

"That's different." Mumma poured chai into three cups and took her seat. "You're our daughter. You don't need to struggle by yourself when you have a family right here."

"I know. But I put so much work into building the company Manoj and I started," Priya said, her voice softening as she looked at Mumma. "I thought we could still work together, but we didn't see eye to eye on the business either, so I decided to leave." She lifted her cup and took a slow sip. None of this was a lie, but it wasn't the full truth either. The truth was that Calgary had given her the kind of independence she could never have here, the freedom to live life away from her parents' well-meaning but constant interference—even if it came with loneliness. Losing her marriage had been painful, but losing her career had shattered what was left of her life out west. Without a partner or a paycheck, coming home had been her only option.

"You did the right thing." Puppa tipped his tea into a saucer, blew on it, and took a loud, slurping sip. "A daughter's place is with her parents until she marries or . . ." He hesitated, his voice trailing off.

"Or what, Puppa?" Priya placed her cup down and met his gaze. "Go on, say it." When he remained silent, she sighed. "Divorce. It's not a bad word, you know."

"Of course not, *beta*." Puppa patted her hand. "When we came to Canada thirty years ago, no one spoke about these things openly, especially not in our community. But times have changed. This isn't the future we wanted for you, but your happiness is all that matters. So, tell us . . ." He leaned back in his chair. "After five years together, what really happened between you and Manoj? You've said so little."

The lights suddenly flickered overhead, throwing brief shadows around them, but Priya barely reacted. Growing up at Moksha, she was used to its oddities—the strange groans of the pipes, the unexplained drafts, the way certain rooms always felt colder than the rest.

"There's not much to tell," she said before popping the last piece of her rotli in her mouth. She gave herself a moment to swallow before answering. "We just wanted different things in life."

"But you had so much in common." Puppa's voice tinged with disbelief. "Same caste, same background, same profession. He didn't drink, didn't gamble. A good boy from a good family. You know we would never have approved otherwise."

And that's exactly why I married him, Priya thought. *Not because I loved him, but because it made* sense. *Marrying a man who checked all your boxes was the only way to claim my freedom. It was my permission slip to stay in Calgary after university and build a life of my own.* But these were words she'd never say aloud to her parents.

"Did he mistreat you?" Mumma asked. "Did you fight? Argue?"

"No, and we didn't really fight. Just the normal ups and downs."

Mumma flung her hands up. "Then what?"

Priya sighed. "Not fighting doesn't mean a marriage is happy."

"But it's a start." Mumma placed another rotli on her daughter's plate. "A peaceful home is a good home."

Priya nodded, tracing the edge of the rotli with her fingers. If her parents knew the truth of their "good home," the gossip would spread like wildfire, and she didn't want Manoj to shoulder all the blame. His affair had ended the marriage, yes, but it wasn't the cause of their problems. It was a symptom of what had been missing all along.

"Well, everything happens for a good reason," Puppa declared, clapping his hands together as though closing the matter.

Once again, the lights flickered overhead.

"It's getting worse," Mumma said, turning to Puppa. "You still haven't heard from the bank?"

"They called yesterday."

"And?" Mumma pressed.

"We can talk about it later," he said, patting her hand. "Let's not ruin Priya's homecoming."

"What's going on?" Priya glanced between her parents.

"We live in an old building," Puppa explained. "It's always one thing or another. Nothing to worry yourself about."

"Then why is the bank involved?"

Puppa looked away, and Mumma fidgeted in her seat.

"Well?" Priya prompted.

"The wiring is outdated," her father finally said with a sigh. "The fuse boxes keep shorting. We have to replace everything to bring Moksha up to code—new wiring, outlets, circuit breakers . . . The entire electrical system. It's a big job, so I applied for a loan."

Priya's stomach dropped. The look on Puppa's face said it all. The loan hadn't been approved. He took a deep breath before speaking. "If we don't make these upgrades, we won't be able to keep the business running."

"You'll lose the funeral home?" Priya felt as though the wind had been knocked out of her. As much as she'd always wanted to escape Moksha, she knew the significance it held for her parents. It wasn't just their home—it was the heart of who they were and what they stood for.

"We have three months to make the repairs," Puppa said. "We'll find a way."

"Why didn't you tell me before?" she asked.

"We were hoping the loan would come through," Mumma said quietly. "We didn't want to worry you or your sisters for no reason."

A pang of regret twisted in Priya's stomach. She'd been so caught up in her own problems that she hadn't known what her parents were going through.

"I have some savings," she said. "It's not much, but Manoj is buying me out of the company, so I'll have more once that's finalized. I've also picked up some freelance work. I can help you bridge the financing—"

"Out of the question," Puppa interrupted, placing his hand over Priya's. "Thank you, but we don't need your money, beta. You have come home for a bigger purpose. Don't you see? The timing is no coincidence. Moksha has a way of calling those it needs. This is your time to step in, to start taking over some of the responsibilities, so you can take over one day."

Priya stared at her parents, her hand frozen beneath Puppa's. "Are you serious? You think I've come home just to drop everything and step into this . . . *role* you've carved out for me?"

"We're not asking you to drop anything, Priya," Mumma said gently. "But you have nothing tying you down right now. This is your chance to start over, to find purpose and do something meaningful."

"Meaningful to who?" Priya pulled her hand out from under her father's. "Just because I'm divorced, between jobs, and don't have any kids doesn't mean my life is without meaning." Her words tumbled out, faster and sharper. "I haven't even unpacked, and you're already dragging me into the business. I didn't come home to be a cog in a wheel that's been turning in our family for generations—the same damn wheel that's been grinding me down my whole life. I'm not going to let it crush me too!"

"*Ey!*" Puppa wagged his finger in warning.

It didn't matter what came after *Ey*. Puppa's *Ey* was enough to bring Priya to a screeching halt.

"We are Dalit, Priya. The funeral home is not just our generational occupation. It is our karmic undertaking and duty."

"Those are *your* beliefs, Puppa. You and Mumma have built your entire lives around them, and I respect that, but you can't force them on me." Priya tried to control the volume of her voice. "To me, Moksha is a *business*, not a divine mission. It needs money, resources, time, attention. Even if I agree to take over, what happens when we can't pay for the repairs it so obviously needs?"

Her parents shared a glance across the table before Puppa pushed his chair back and stood. Retrieving his address book from the drawer next to the sofa, he pulled out an envelope from its pages and handed her the papers inside.

Priya's eyes widened as she scanned the document. "An offer from a land developer to buy the funeral home?" She glanced at her parents. "This is a lot of money. You wouldn't need a loan to keep Moksha running." Her heart began to race. "You could sell, retire, and never have to worry about finances again," she said, her voice bright with excitement.

"Read it properly," Puppa urged. "They want to build condominiums here."

"So?" Priya's brows furrowed. "I don't see what that has to do with anything."

Puppa shook his head. "Moksha is the only funeral home in the area run by a Hindu family, Priya. We welcome people of all faiths, but it's our duty to provide the last rites and rituals for our *community*. When I was a boy in Gujarat, my father upheld that responsibility, and my grandfather did the same before him. Your mother and I may have moved to another country, but we can't shed our caste or the responsibility that goes with it."

Priya drew in a measured breath. "It always comes down to that. Tradition, duty, obligation . . ." Her gaze shot to her father, eyebrows raised. "Don't tell me you rejected it?" She nodded toward the offer.

"Not yet, but I will do whatever I can to keep Moksha going."

"And you're okay with this?" Priya turned to her mother.

"Of course. Your father is right. It's one thing if we had no other option, but we still have time to find a solution. We can't just run from our karma. And neither can you. You're part of the same lineage, Priya, and no matter how far you run, fate will always pull you back."

"And Meghna and Deepa?" Priya countered. "Are you saying they're going to end up here too?"

"Your sisters will always be tied to this place. It's in their blood, same as you." Mumma's words carried a quiet certainty.

A heavy sigh built in Priya's chest. Her parents still saw the world through the lens of a caste system that had been abolished over seventy-five years ago. To them, caste dictated everything from what kind of work you were expected to do to who you could marry to your place in the world. And because their family was Dalit—considered so low they weren't even counted within the hierarchy—Priya's parents made sure their daughters understood it from an early age.

Don't reach too high.

Don't think too big.

Don't dream beyond your station.

But Priya had always wanted more. More than quiet obedience. More than a future shaped by the past. She wanted to break the cycle—for herself and for her sisters. A life beyond inherited limits. A life where they weren't just surviving but growing, flourishing, *thriving*. But now, sitting around the table with her parents, she held her tongue. This was not a war of words; it was a clash of perspectives, both sides digging in with no intention of waving a white flag.

As she sipped her tea, a notification flashed on her phone. "It's Brooke," she announced, reading the message. "And she's on her way over."

"Here? Right now?" Mumma exclaimed. "What will we feed her?"

Hosting guests was a point of pride for the Solankis. Even a casual visit called for an entire spread of *dhoklas, khakhras, bhajiyas, patras*—each lovingly prepared and served with a side of warm hospitality.

"Tell her you're tired from your flight and ask her to come tomorrow," Puppa said.

"She's flying out herself tonight and won't be back until summer," Priya replied. "Don't worry, she's just popping in for a quick hello. I haven't seen her in ages."

Mumma shot to her feet and went into full panic mode. "*Hai Ram!* Rakesh, get the cushions!"

Puppa hurried to the closet, resurrecting every cushion stored away in the closet.

"You should have told us she was planning to drop in, Priya." Mumma lit a candle, waving a kitchen towel in the air to dispel the smell of rotlis.

"I didn't know!" Priya said, throwing her hands up. "I told her I'd be arriving today, but I had no idea she was *leaving* today."

"Does she drink tea?" Mumma called from the kitchen. "Do we have soft drinks? Oh, orange juice! We have orange juice," she declared, peering into the refrigerator.

"It's just Brooke, you guys. Relax."

"Just Brooke," Mumma muttered, gathering her prized dinnerware from the cabinet. "She may be 'just Brooke' to you, but she's from a rich family. *Mota loko chhe.*"

"Big people," Puppa echoed, sweeping the clutter off the kitchen counter and shoving it into the oven.

Mumma raced ahead of Priya toward the bathroom. "Out of the way, beta. You can freshen up in a minute." She ducked in through the door and immediately called out, "*Hai Ram.* Is that hair on the soap dispenser?"

Priya sighed and wheeled her luggage down the hallway to her room. As she stood gazing at the twin bed pressed against the wall, she was flooded with recollections of the past—journaling at her desk when she was too overwhelmed to talk to anyone; sprawling across the bed with Brooke, their giggles filling the room. Dropping her bags, Priya collapsed on the bed with a sigh. Her room was just as she had left it: lavender walls, her old backpack and computer collecting dust under the desk, the scent of budget-friendly detergent still clinging to the sheets.

Priya's eyes drifted to the corkboard above the desk, decorated with medals from summers at computer camp. She remembered the thrill of earning her first one, and then, immediately, the sadness that followed. Her eyes prickled with tears, but she pushed the memory aside, drew in a deep breath, and rose to her feet.

She could still hear her parents frantically tidying down the hall. Unzipping her old backpack, she idly rummaged through it and pulled out a worn textbook. Flipping it open, she stared at the outdated diagrams. But her mind wasn't on the pages—it was on an earlier conversation.

The offer to buy Moksha.

The funeral home had consumed Priya's parents for as long as she could remember, draining them of their energy, their finances, and their joy. Selling it would give them a chance to breathe, to slow things down and experience life beyond its walls. It would also mean freedom for her and her sisters—freedom from the duty that always loomed over them, freedom to live the lives they wanted. Selling Moksha wasn't just a good idea. It was the only way out. If her parents didn't accept the offer, they'd all be stuck in an endless cycle.

"This ends now," Priya muttered, slamming the textbook shut. "I have to convince them to sell it. If I show them what it costs to . . ."

But then it hit her—a quiet, unexpected thought that stopped her cold.

Maybe I don't need to convince them at all.

The loan hadn't come through. Her parents couldn't fix what they couldn't afford. Once the renovation deadline passed and the required upgrades weren't met, they would have no choice but to shut down. Whether she pushed or not, her parents would end up facing the truth on their own.

Priya let out a slow exhale, the fight to fix things draining from her. She rubbed her eyes, surrendering to the fatigue she'd been too restless to feel until now. After fishing out her contact lens kit from her bag, she removed her lenses and slipped on her glasses. Shrugging out of her travel-worn clothes, she dug through her closet until she found an old high school sweatshirt and a pair of faded sweatpants. It wasn't the most flattering outfit, but it felt comfortable and familiar.

Welcome home, her reflection seemed to whisper as she stared into the mirror, seeing traces of the teenage girl she used to be. A pang of bittersweet emotion shot through Priya's heart, but she ignored it. Securing her hair into a loose bun, she made her way to the bathroom.

"Are you done, Mumma?" she asked.

"In a minute," Mumma replied, rummaging through the medicine cabinet. "Last time Hema *ben* was here, she saw a tube of cream for your dad's toenail infection and thought I had a feminine infection."

Priya wrinkled her nose. "Okay, that's weird." She leaned against the wall in the hallway, waiting for her mother to finish. The apartment felt quiet without Meghna and Deepa. Growing up, she never imagined she'd miss the bickering and chaos; now Priya found herself wishing for her sisters' presence.

She wandered into Meghna's room—pale green walls, a simple bed, river stones resting on a faded magazine on the nightstand, everything perfectly in its place. Deepa's room, by contrast, looked like a teenage fever dream—pink faux-fur pillows, a metallic banner with her name, indie band posters taped haphazardly to every wall. Priya's eyes landed on Deepa's celebrity collage, and her breath caught in her throat.

Ethan Knight.

The past crashed into her, sharp and unexpected, as if he had swept into the room himself. His voice curled at the edges of her mind, the heat of his body seeping through layers of fabric. Priya recalled the smell of the earth that night, fresh from a rainstorm. Headlights cut through the slick road ahead. Fields stretched endlessly into the darkness. The air was cool and damp, but Priya's skin burned with exhilaration. She had never felt more alive, clinging to his back as the motorcycle roared beneath them.

The doorbell rang through the apartment. "Brooke's here!" Mumma called.

Shaking off the memory, Priya headed down the narrow stairs and swung open the front door. There stood Brooke, a vision from the runways of Milan. Her sun-kissed skin exuded jet-set luxury, mojitos in Saint-Tropez, skiing down the Alps. Though life had pulled them in different directions and different cities, she was still Priya's childhood best friend.

Brooke beamed as she enveloped Priya in a hug. "Pri, I can't believe it's been so long! You've forgotten the girl next door."

Priya pulled back and tugged at Brooke's hair. "We may be neighbors, but you'll never be the girl next door," she teased. "Look at you!"

"Isn't it fabulous?" Brooke grinned, spinning to flaunt her dress. "I'm off to Tulum, then heading straight to Bali, but I couldn't leave without stopping by."

Priya smiled as she admired the dress—airy and vibrant, as if it was made for dancing barefoot on the beach. Brooke truly had an outfit to match every occasion.

"Guess who I brought along?" Brooke said cheerily, nodding to the left of her, just beyond Priya's view.

Priya craned her neck and looked to the ground, expecting to see Lady Whiskerbottom, Brooke's famous cat—a feline influencer who had traveled to more countries than Priya could ever hope to visit. But instead of Lady Whiskerbottom's carrier, her gaze landed on a pair of sneakers, sleek and effortlessly cool. Her eyes drifted upward, trailing the length of well-worn denim that clung in all the right places, over a lean, sculpted torso, and shoulders broad enough to carry the world.

A jolt of recognition surged through Priya before she even saw his face. The lazy confidence, the easy swagger—a silhouette etched deep in her memory. As she took in the rugged angles of his jaw, Priya's breath dissolved into an elusive wisp.

Ethan Knight stood before her, his presence crackling like stardust in the center of a storm. There was a weight to him, not just of fame but something deeper, something impossible to ignore. The air bristled with his energy, and for a second, Priya swore she could feel the static dance along her skin. Then, just as her pulse started to trip over itself, his lips quirked into an easy, devastating smile.

"Hello, Priya," he said, his voice deep and smooth. "It's been a while."

Two

PRIYA WANTED TO reach back in time and shake her younger self. Why couldn't her first crush have been Rahul, the math whiz, or Raj, the cricket champ, or Lorenzo, who played the accordion at the farmers market? No, she had gone straight for the most impossible option of all. Ethan Larger-Than-Life Knight.

"Priya?" Ethan said, removing his baseball cap as if offering a silent eulogy for her teenage delusions.

Priya scanned his face, taking in the transformation from boyish charm to raw, rugged appeal. She had seen that face on countless posters and billboards, but nothing prepared her for the electric jolt of his attention. His steel-gray eyes swept over her, and suddenly, she was untethered, like a comet ripped from its trajectory. Ethan Knight wasn't just a *star*. He was heat and gravity, a supernova pulling everything toward him. She had to distance herself or she'd end up spiraling right back into his orbit.

"Ethan," she said with a curt nod.

Without breaking eye contact, Ethan extended his hand out to Brooke. "I win."

Brooke groaned, then reluctantly slapped a ten-dollar bill into his palm.

"I told you, Brooke." Ethan's mouth curved into a half smile as he spoke to his sister. "Priya Solanki isn't one to swoon. Never has been and never will be."

"Damn it, Priya." Brooke snapped the clasp of her handbag shut. "You could have at least shown a *hint* of awe. A burst of starstruck silence. It's been, what? Twelve years since you last saw each other?" Her eyes flickered between her friend and brother.

Twelve years, eight months, and I'm-glad-I-don't-remember-how-many days because that would make me truly pathetic. "That's what you get for making a bet without consulting me." Priya gave Ethan a dismissive shrug before turning to Brooke. "We could have split that tenner."

"Hell, I would have even autographed it for you," Ethan teased. "For old times' sake."

His words made Priya's heart lurch. *For old times' sake.* Once, they had shared a connection, quiet and unspoken, something that even Brooke had never caught on to. But Priya had been just a kid back then, starry-eyed over her best friend's older brother, long before fame swept him away.

"So, what brings you back to Toronto?" Priya asked, trying to sound breezy.

"I need to get into the right headspace for my next project," Ethan replied. "Plus, it was a good excuse to see Brooke before she sailed off again. And you? Brooke said you just moved back."

His eyes lingered, steady and curious, and Priya felt her stomach tighten. She glanced at Brooke, who grimaced apologetically and gave her an awkward smile.

Ah. So, he knows. Priya swallowed the wave of embarrassment creeping up her throat. *Great. Now he thinks I'm some sad divorcée limping back home.*

"Yeah, it just felt like the time was right for a fresh start," Priya said, keeping it light and casual. *As if Ethan Knight would ever want to hear about my train wreck of a life.*

"That's great. And what's keeping you busy these days?" His presence was even more intense than she remembered.

Priya scrambled for words. "Figuring out my life" was not an option.

"I, uh, just stepped away from the company I cofounded," she said. "We built and managed websites, but I'm also starting to branch into app development now." As she spoke, a well-worn fantasy flickered to life in Priya's mind. She had imagined running into Ethan many times over the years—always on a red carpet, wearing a stunning gown, her hair cascading down her back, makeup done to perfection. The setting: Oscar night for non-celebrities, because the world had come to realize that ordinary people deserved awards, too, for their convincing performances in life.

The paparazzi trip over each other, hollering her name. Priya sashays down the carpet, radiant in her confidence, her smile bewitching as she poses—left, right, center. Well, maybe not right. Not her best side.

Ahead, Ethan Knight is surrounded by a swarm of reporters. As he answers their questions, he catches a glimpse of her. His words falter, his jaw slackens, his eyes widen. He is mesmerized by the enchanting woman before him, the woman he's overlooked all these years. He takes her hand, draws her close, and confesses she's the only one he's ever truly wanted. Cameras flash. The crowd erupts as they embrace in a passionate kiss—

"Earth to Priya." Brooke waved her hand before Priya's face.

"Sorry. What was that?" Priya blinked, jolted back to reality as if someone had dumped a bucket of ice over her daydream.

There was no red carpet, no perfect makeup, no grand and fiery declarations of love. Just her, standing in front of Ethan in shapeless sweatpants and glasses, feeling about as glamorous as a forgotten sock at the bottom of the laundry basket.

"I said maybe we should go inside." Brooke tilted her head toward her brother.

"Of course." Priya's eyes darted to the street. She had been so caught up in the whirlwind of seeing Ethan again that she'd forgotten he wasn't just Ethan anymore—he was someone the world watched closely.

As she led Brooke and Ethan up the apartment stairs, Priya cringed internally. The peeling paint and sagging banister seemed impossibly worse in their presence, and the dim lighting screamed low-budget horror movie. Priya hesitated at the door. Her parents would freak out upon seeing Ethan, but it was too late to warn them. She let Brooke inside, then barred the way. Mindful that Priya's family removed their shoes upon entering, Brooke slipped her shoes off.

"Hello, hello," Puppa greeted her with his standard handshake and half bow. "It's been a while. The last time we met, you and Priya were . . ." He trailed off as he caught sight of Ethan. "You were . . . um . . ." His eyes widened before flicking around the room in urgent search of Mumma. Failing to locate her, he cleared his throat and edged past Priya to welcome Ethan.

"Mr. Ethan." Handshake, half bow.

It was customary for the Solankis to add *-ji* at the end of a person's name as a sign of respect, but Puppa adjusted for Ethan's Canadian roots, settling on "Mr. Ethan" instead of "Mr. Knight." He held on to Ethan's hand and gave him another half bow.

"Please, call me Ethan." Ethan reciprocated with a slight bow of his own. But Puppa, a seasoned player in the game of deference, had to have the final say and slipped in one more bow before releasing his grip.

Ethan bent to unlace his shoes, and the sight of a superstar at his feet—a gesture traditionally meant to seek blessings from an elder—sent Puppa into a tailspin. He defaulted to another half bow as Ethan straightened. Their heads bumped, colliding like two coconuts in a monsoon rainstorm. Priya winced, her face heating up as she fought the urge to bury her head in her hands. *Perfect. Just perfect.*

"Are you all right?" Ethan steadied Puppa as he staggered back.

From the corner of her eye, Priya caught Mumma enter the living room. She froze at the sight of their unexpected guest before quickly retreating into the hallway.

"Please come inside," Puppa offered, wiping his brow; he was sweating like he'd just jogged up three flights of stairs. "You, too, Brooke. Have a seat."

As Brooke and Ethan settled on the couch, Puppa gave Priya a look so sour it could curdle milk, silently scolding her for not giving him a heads-up about their famous guest. But then, attempting to regain his composure, he sat and smiled, first at Brooke, then at Ethan, fingers tapping nervously on his knees.

"Seema," he called with forced cheeriness. "Look who is here." Beneath the calm façade, he was sending silent SOS signals to his wife.

Mumma did not reply.

A moment later, Priya's phone buzzed with a text from her mother.

You brought Ethan Knight upstairs?? We can't host him here! Take him and Brooke to the lobby.

They're already here, Priya texted back. *I can't take them back down.* She shot Ethan an apologetic smile, embarrassment crawling beneath her skin. Of course this would happen. Awkwardness and drama, right on cue.

His reaction only made it worse. A faint smile tugged at his lips, like he'd seen it all before—people stumbling over themselves in his presence.

"Priya," Mumma called sweetly, her voice wafting from the hallway.

Priya excused herself and knocked on the bathroom door.

"I am not greeting Ethan Knight in my nightgown," Mumma hissed through the crack.

"It's not as if I'm dressed any better," Priya muttered. Even her travel-worn clothes would have been better than the grungy outfit she had on. "At least you can change before you greet him."

"I can't," Mumma said. "He can see me from where he's sitting!"

Suppressing a sigh, Priya marched to Mumma's closet. She rummaged through her clothes and picked out a green salwar khameez. Heading back to the bathroom, she slid the outfit into her mother's waiting grasp.

"Not so fast." Mumma grabbed her wrist and listed her demands. "I need lipstick. The *laal* one. And my gold bangles. And earrings. And perfume."

Priya collected the items, including the red lipstick, from her mother's dresser and then slipped them through the door before returning to the living room.

"Priya, beta," Mumma cooed from the bathroom as soon as Priya sat next to Brooke on the love seat.

"Sorry," Priya mouthed to Brooke and Ethan before rising and marching back to her mother.

"My bra," Mumma said in a low voice.

"Mumma . . ." Priya's voice tightened, but she went back to her parents' room and riffled through her mother's underwear drawer. Bypassing the collection of vintage twin-peaks bras, she picked the least ferocious option. Mumma's bra could house a brood of sparrows, so Priya rolled it tight before passing it to her through the crack in the door.

"Anything else?" she asked.

"*Tu ja*," Mumma retorted. "*Maru mathu nai kha*." Go away. Don't eat my head.

"Everything all right?" Brooke asked when Priya returned.

"Mumma forgot her towel. She'll be right out," Priya replied, earning an appreciative glance from Puppa. Lying was dishonorable, but lying to save your family's honor was wholeheartedly approved.

A moment later, Mumma swept into the room in a scented cloud of jasmine and rosewater.

"Brooke, beta." She strode over to Brooke, arms wide and welcoming. As she released Brooke from her tight hug, her eyes fell on Ethan, and she mustered a look of surprise that would give veteran soap opera stars a run for their money.

"Heavens! Ethan Knight. In our home?" She turned to Puppa, as if to confirm she wasn't dreaming. "Please forgive me. I'm so starstruck!"

Priya stifled a snort. That part was one hundred percent genuine.

"It's nice to see you again, Mrs. Solanki," Ethan replied politely.

"You remember my name." Mumma got so giddy, she could barely contain herself. "And you know what? I remember your favorite snack. Every time I packed some for Brooke, she complained that you gobbled it all up." She beamed at him. "Sit, sit. Please. Everybody sit and talk. I will whip it up in a flash."

"Please don't go to any trouble," Ethan said, but Mumma had

already darted off into the kitchen, leaving no room for debate. Now that she was around, Puppa was more at ease.

"You know, I have not missed a single one of your films," he said to Ethan. "Every time we go to the movies, I tell them you grew up right next to us. I still remember you tearing down these streets on your motorcycle. That was before all the houses and shops came to the area."

"I must've been a real pain," Ethan said with a chuckle. "Enough for you to talk to my dad about it."

"Oh, no, no," Puppa said, flushing with embarrassment. "Nothing like that. We just had to make sure the funeral home was peaceful and quiet."

With Ethan and Puppa fully engaged in a conversation, Brooke leaned closer to Priya and lowered her voice. "How are your parents handling things? I mean, with the divorce and all."

Priya shrugged. "They're not exactly thrilled, but they've had some time to adjust. Now they're on me to join the family business." She rolled her eyes.

"Ugh. Not the family business pitch." Brooke's lips twisted, her eyes darting to Ethan.

"Right?" Priya replied. "I'd barely come through the door before they started. But enough about me. Are you still with that guy from Istanbul?"

"I've moved on to Helsinki, with a healthy side of Montreal."

"What happened to Istanbul?"

Brooke dropped her voice two octaves. "My pussy didn't approve," she whispered.

Priya laughed. "You mean Lady Whiskerbottom didn't get along with him?"

"Nothing happens without Her Meowjesty's blessing, you know."

Mumma resurfaced from the kitchen and waved everyone to the table. "Everyone, please come. Food is ready."

Priya's mother had gone into a fritter frenzy. Every vegetable in the kitchen had been sliced, diced, battered, and fried. Potato bhajiyas, onion bhajiyas, spinach bhajiyas, different kinds of chutneys, *sev puri*, and dhokla. As the pièce de résistance, she unveiled a generous bowl of chevda, a crunchy mix of flattened rice flakes, daal, nuts and curry leaves seasoned with salt, sugar, chili powder, and other spices.

"I have to confess, Mrs. Solanki," Brooke said with a grin, spooning chutney onto her plate next to a pile of bhajiyas. "I only became friends with Priya because her lunch game was so strong. While the rest of us were stuck with sandwiches and cafeteria food, Priya's tiffin was a feast for the senses."

"Not everyone was a fan," Priya quipped dryly. She hated carrying her three-tiered stainless steel lunch container to school and wished for lunch money instead, so she could escape the teasing about the overpowering smells from her tiffin.

"Not everyone had a sophisticated international palate like me," Brooke teased.

"Hey, I've always been up for trying new flavors," Ethan said.

"We know all about your diverse tastes," Priya chimed in, a faint smile masking the sting behind her words. She'd never been a dish he cared to sample. "The gossip columns keep us well informed."

Ethan raised an eyebrow. "Glad to know you're keeping tabs on me, Priya."

Priya immediately wished she could rewind and say something else—*anything* else. "Everybody here stalks you," she blurted out instead. "You're this area's claim to fame. A homegrown superstar. My sister Deepa has a shrine dedicated to you." A celebrity collage, actually, but he didn't need to know the details. "We light a *diya* and do *aarti* for you every morning." She smirked as she sat down at the table.

"Priya." Puppa gave her a withering look. "Mr. Ethan, please have a seat." He made a sweeping gesture toward the table. "Have, have."

"Mrs. Solanki, your fritters might just be my greatest weakness," Ethan declared, stacking his plate high.

Mumma blushed fiercely, her cheeks turning a deep pink. "How is Harry?" she asked.

"Dad's doing well," Brooke replied, taking a bit of a dhokla.

"He must be thinking of retiring soon," Puppa remarked.

"I wouldn't count on it," Brooke said.

"It's not easy to step away when you've built something that big," Puppa added.

Brooke and Ethan exchanged a look but said nothing.

"And how is Lady Whiskerbottom?" Mumma asked.

Brooke beamed. "Getting older and fussier by the day. Still as feisty as ever."

As she pulled out her phone to show Mumma a photo of her cat, the lights flickered once again. The hum of the refrigerator cut out, and then, just as quickly, everything blinked back to life.

"Did we just have a power outage?" Ethan asked.

"Not for the whole block," Puppa replied. "Just here. Our electrical system is falling apart. Moksha is an old building."

"It's a money pit," Priya said bluntly. "If it's not the wiring, it's the roof. Or the plumbing. Or the windows. The list never ends."

"Priya is right," Puppa agreed, with a resigned nod. "We've done our best to keep Moksha going, but if we don't come up with the funds to renovate, we may have to shut down."

Wait . . . did he just say that? Priya blinked, unsure if she'd heard him right. Her father, the man who had stubbornly clung to Moksha through debt, exhaustion, and countless setbacks seemed to be facing reality at last. Was he finally accepting the inevitable? That no matter how hard he tried, Moksha was heading toward closure, and this time, there was no stopping it.

A spark of hope flared within Priya, not just at the thought of being free of Moksha but the possibility that it might come even sooner than she'd expected. The offer to buy Moksha was still on the table—and the best part? She didn't have to lift a finger, just let things unfold on their own.

"I would hate to see that happen," Ethan said. "You've been a part of this neighborhood for as long as I can remember."

"It's the last thing we want," Puppa replied, his sadness evident.

"Well, then today's your lucky day!" Brooke announced, flashing a bright smile. "Ethan has a proposal you might want to hear."

Priya shot her a sharp look. *Excuse me?*

"Brooke is right," Ethan said, his eyes shifting between Priya and her parents. "I'm here because I need your help."

"*Our* help?" Puppa repeated, exchanging a baffled look with Mumma.

Ethan nodded before continuing. "Actors get typecast all the time, and I don't want to fall into that trap," he explained. "My next role is a complete departure from action movies. It's about a man who comes alive in a funeral home and has to outsmart death before sundown."

Priya blinked. "You're joking, right?"

"I'm not," Ethan said with a small grin. "And that's why I was hoping I could spend some time at Moksha. Get a feel for the setting. If you're open to it."

"Mr. Ethan," Puppa said, practically beaming, "we would be honored to help in any way we can. You are free to come and go as you please."

"That's just the thing, Mr. Solanki. I tend to attract attention wherever I go. So, I was thinking—what if I rent out the funeral home and move in temporarily? I could immerse myself in the role, and you'd make some extra cash for your renovations. It's a win-win for everyone."

Priya's head jerked back. *What in the actual world is happening right now? No, no, no. This can't be real.* Ethan Knight, of all people, was not sitting at their table, offering her parents a lifeline to keep Moksha going.

Puppa's voice echoed in her mind: *Moksha has a way of calling those it needs.*

"Is that . . . normal?" Priya asked. "I mean, actors don't usually go *that* far to prepare, right?" She forced a laugh, hoping it would sound casual. Meanwhile, her thoughts spun in one direction: *There is no way I'm letting this happen.*

"It's called method acting," Ethan explained. "A lot of actors use it to make their performances as realistic as possible. Robert De Niro, Al Pacino, Daniel Day-Lewis, Hilary Swank . . ."

Priya watched in horror as her parents nodded along, completely hypnotized by him. At this rate, they'd be offering him the deed to the entire grounds. *Nope. Absolutely not.*

"Sorry, Ethan. You can't rent out the funeral home for that," she said firmly, crossing her arms. "It's not like we have a bedroom or live-in space downstairs, and we certainly can't host you here." She gestured around the apartment. Even her parents would agree it was a terrible idea—Ethan Knight brushing his teeth at the kitchen sink because the bathroom was perpetually occupied was *not* happening.

Ethan leaned back, unfazed. "That's fine. My character has to find his way out before sundown, so I can work with daytime access."

Puppa frowned. "Regardless of the hours, we would still have to shut down if you're here."

Priya felt a rush of triumph. Puppa was not going to go for it.

"We have never closed the funeral home," he continued, "but . . ."

No. No buts, Puppa. Priya mentally willed her father to hold his ground.

"We would have to close for the renovations anyway. If another funeral home agrees to accommodate our clients during that time, we can manage."

"But we're the only ones in this area that perform Hindu funerals." Priya's voice sharpened. "We can't just outsource something so important."

"You're very passionate about this all of a sudden." Mumma raised an eyebrow.

"There's a funeral home a bit farther that also serves our community." Puppa rubbed his chin, thoughtful. "We've helped them out a few times in the past. I'm sure they'll be willing to step in while we bring everything up to code. If we don't do this, we risk losing Moksha altogether."

"So, do we have a deal?" Ethan's lips curled into a smile.

"I think we can work something out," Puppa replied.

Priya swallowed back a hysterical laugh—the kind that bubbles up when you're about to lose your mind. Her family was finally on the verge of walking away from Moksha's crumbling legacy, but now Ethan had appeared with his million-dollar smile, derailing a clean, inevitable ending. If there were an Oscar for

Most Meddlesome Actor, he'd be giving his acceptance speech right now.

"Excellent," he declared, clapping his hands together. "How much notice do you need to give your clients?"

"About a week to wrap things up, and there may be a brief overlap for any commitments I need to see through myself." Puppa's voice held a quiet pride, the kind that came from years of shouldering a responsibility he considered both a privilege and a calling.

"A week is perfect. It will give me time to tie up some loose ends on my side too."

"Wonderful. I will stop by your father's estate to let you know when we're all set."

Ethan paused for a moment before replying. "I'm not staying with my father. Just message me when you're ready."

"Of course." Puppa bobbed his head in agreement. "I'll ask Priya to get in touch." He looked at Ethan as if he was turning something over in his mind. "Why aren't you staying with your father, Mr. Ethan?" he finally asked, unable to hold back. The idea of lodging elsewhere when family was close by was downright bizarre.

"Dad!" Priya jumped in, part scolding, part pleading. She turned to Ethan, her expression apologetic. "Sorry, you don't have to answer."

"It's okay," Ethan said tightly. "My father and I haven't spoken in years," he continued, glancing at her parents.

Brooke shifted uncomfortably in her seat as Mumma's eyes widened in pure disbelief. "You are not speaking to Harry?" she asked. Cutting ties with a parent was a path that led straight to the murkiest levels of Narak, the very definition of hell.

"Unfortunately, my father stopped talking to me when I walked away from the family business to pursue acting," Ethan explained.

Priya knew this part of his story from Brooke, but hearing him say it hit differently. She felt a quiet sadness for the boy who had walked away, and for the man still carrying the cost.

Mumma clucked her tongue. "Oh, but surely he must be proud of you! You've accomplished so much."

"He's successful too," Ethan said with a small shrug. "And not easily impressed."

"They're both stubborn as hell," Brooke cut in, rolling her eyes. "I've tried everything—dinners, casual run-ins, fake emergencies. You name it. I even tried convincing Ethan to stay with us this time, but nope. Not happening."

"If you are not next door, then where *are* you staying, Mr. Ethan?" Puppa asked.

"Downtown. At the Hazelton," he replied.

Priya blinked, her mind connecting the dots. The chaos on the highway was because of *him*. Ethan Knight was the kind of star who could bring an entire city to its knees. *I'd stop to gawk too*, she admitted to herself.

"The paparazzi are camped out there around the clock," Brooke said. "It's a nightmare trying to shake them off. I'm not sure how you're going to give them the slip every day to get here." She looked over at her brother.

"I have a solution," Puppa said.

Priya pinched the bridge of her nose. This day wasn't just a lost cause—it was actively conspiring against her.

"You can stay in the coach house, Mr. Ethan. It's not as fancy as your current accommodations, but it's right on our property, and you'll have all the privacy you need."

"You told me the coach house wasn't an option," Priya pointed out, trying to keep the frustration out of her voice. She'd brought up the coach house when she started planning her move back, hoping for some privacy and space, but her parents had shot her down right away. And now they were rolling out the welcome mat for Ethan?

"The coach house hasn't been used in years, and we have a perfectly fine three-bedroom apartment," Puppa replied, before turning back to Ethan. "It *does* need a little work, but once that's sorted, it's a wonderful little space. Bright, cozy, and self-contained. I think you'll really like it."

"Sounds perfect," Ethan said. "But only if you let me pay my share."

"Mr. Ethan, it would be a privilege to have you as our guest while you're here."

"Privilege won't pay for a new electrical system, Mr. Solanki," Ethan joked lightly. "And since I plan on staying for a month, I suggest we arrive at a figure that's mutually beneficial."

Puppa's eyes lit up. Bargaining and negotiation coursed through his Gujarati veins. "If you don't mind me asking, how much are you paying for the hotel?" His tone carried a polite innocence that Priya instantly recognized as the opening act to a full-on haggling session.

After learning the amount, Puppa reached for a pen and paper and started crunching numbers. The final figure seemed to please him, but as he shared it with Ethan, his lips pursed in contemplation.

"Something wrong?" Ethan asked.

Puppa scratched his chin.

Priya cringed, recognizing her father's telltale gesture. He was gearing up to play hardball with Hollywood's resident heartthrob.

"Let's make it U.S. dollars. Cash," he declared, raising both hands in the air as if sealing the deal.

"But I'm paying Canadian at the hotel," Ethan countered.

"But I am charging you half their rate, *and* I will include your meals."

"You're throwing in the fritters?"

"*Arey*, forget the fritters. All-inclusive. Breakfast, lunch, and dinner. Theplas, muthiyas, samosas, fafdas, pendas, ganthias . . . You name it."

"Now we're talking!" Brooke grinned. "I might cancel my flight and move in too."

"Perfect," Priya muttered. "I've been back for five minutes, and suddenly we're running a boardinghouse."

"Priya!" Mumma shot her a warning look.

Ethan chuckled. "So, what's the going rate for renting a funeral home?"

Puppa froze, realizing he had forgotten the larger number. Laxmi, the goddess of wealth, was showering him with money in crisp green U.S. bills.

"I will have to look at the books and let you know," he replied.

"You're not going to overcharge me, are you, Mr. Solanki?" A glimmer danced in Ethan's eyes.

"Overcharge? Never. There is no overcharging at Moksha. Only creative pricing. You'll get the finest deal, I promise."

"In that case . . ." Ethan lifted his glass. "Here's to Moksha."

"And to your next movie." Puppa raised his glass too.

"Cheers." Mumma and Brooke joined in.

Priya had no doubt that Ethan's offer felt like divine intervention to her parents, a miracle sent to save Moksha at its darkest hour. But accepting Ethan's offer was nothing more than a Band-Aid on a gaping wound. Her parents would spend the money on renovations, leaving them in the same difficult position next time something else needed fixing. The cycle of debt and struggle would never end. Selling Moksha wasn't just the smarter option; it was the only real solution. If her father wouldn't see reason, she would have to take matters into her own hands.

Priya's gaze settled on Ethan. Beneath the infuriatingly perfect jawline and dreamy eyes was the root of all their troubles. Priya had to get rid of him before the offer for Moksha expired.

As the lights buzzed overhead again, a plan began to form in her mind. She lifted her glass in a private toast to her mission—to remove Ethan Knight from their lives and send him packing to Tinseltown as quickly as possible.

Three

PRIYA UNLEASHED a karate chop on the couch cushion, leaving a satisfying dent. She had been tasked with transforming Moksha's abandoned coach house into a retreat fit for Hollywood royalty. And so, armed with a stepladder, a mop, and cleaning products, she hauled out the trash, scoured the surfaces, and polished the floor. It took her a full week to get rid of the dust and grime, but the space sparkled when she was done. Now, it was all about the finishing touches.

Priya's eyes drifted across the honey-colored floors, the cozy furnishings, and the rays of sunlight spilling in through the windows. The coach house was compact, with just one bedroom, one bathroom, and a living area that flowed into a small kitchen, but its open layout made it feel far larger. Big windows framed views of the open field beyond, and the privacy of being tucked away at the back of the property made it feel like a world of its own.

For Priya and her sisters, it had always been an elusive treasure, a cozy retreat away from their parents' watchful eyes. They'd begged for weekend sleepovers, promising to clean up and keep things tidy, but her parents had always refused.

"Pay for extra utilities?" Puppa had scoffed once. "*Tara baap ni electricity company chhe?* You think your father owns the power grid?"

Mumma and Puppa tried to rent it out, but nobody was interested in sharing the grounds with a funeral home. And so, it collected dust, until King Ethan descended and unbolted the castle. But all the work spent getting it ready would amount to nothing, because once she sent Ethan packing, her parents would have no option but to sell Moksha.

With that in mind, Priya set up a smart lighting system inside. She tucked the hub away in a hidden spot and installed smart bulbs in the light fixtures. Though she couldn't test the setup because there was still no internet, the system would allow her to remotely control the lights through an app on her phone.

She plucked an apple from the basket of treats her mother had put together, took a satisfying bite, and headed to the bedroom for a final check. Setting the apple on the nightstand, she started smoothing out the sheets, but her elbow knocked it off and sent it rolling under the bed.

Priya crouched on the floor, stretching her arm as far as she could underneath the bed. She craned her neck, peering into the shadows, but the apple remained just out of reach. Shifting her weight, she tried to wedge herself lower for a better angle.

"Well now," a rich, unmistakable voice drawled from the doorway, "that's one hell of a welcome."

Priya froze, booty sky-high, her entire body tensing. That voice. Familiar, dangerous, dripping with confidence. It wasn't just a voice; it was a weapon. And it swept over her like a velvet snare, stealing her breath.

Scrambling to recover, she shot up, only to slam her head directly into the underside of the bed frame.

"Ow!" she yelped, pressing a hand to her scalp.

A low chuckle sounded behind her. "Need some help?" Ethan asked, sounding far too entertained.

"No, thanks." Priya reversed from under the bed on all fours with as much grace as she could muster. She'd get the apple later. Acutely aware of how the fabric of her yoga pants clung to her curves, her nerves fired like sparks under his gaze. Composing herself, she flashed him a casual smile. "Just a few final touches, and I'll get out of your hair."

And what gorgeous hair it is, she noted, her fingers tingling at the thought of running through it. Giving herself a mental shake, she brushed past Ethan and headed to the kitchen.

"The place looks great," Ethan said, taking in the space as he wandered behind her.

"I'm glad you approve." Priya grabbed a bowl and filled it with salt. *Enjoy it while you can*, she thought, trying to contain the wicked glee bubbling beneath. *Because in a few minutes, you'll be running for the hills.*

As Priya swiveled to head back into the bedroom, she slammed straight into Ethan's chest, solid and unyielding.

"Easy there, hotshot," he said, steadying her.

The heat of his touch made her skin prickle.

Ohhh. He smells so good. Woodsy, intoxicating, distractingly good.

"Sorry." She brushed the salt from Ethan's slate-gray hoodie that managed to look expensive despite its simplicity. His sweatpants hung just as perfectly, the kind of look that screamed *celebrity on a coffee run.*

"What's with the bowl?" Ethan prowled after her into the bedroom.

Walking around the bed, Priya sprinkled a circle of salt on the floor, reciting what sounded like ancient incantations.

"It's for warding off evil spirits," she replied. "The circle creates a barrier they can't cross. It will protect you from Bhooa."

"From whom?"

"From Bhooa, the resident ghost. But don't worry. She might stir up a little mischief during the day, but she doesn't usually appear until after you fall asleep. Her breathing's a little raspy, but I doubt it'll be loud enough to wake you. She likes to sit in the rocking chair and watch. Her face remains shrouded, so if you do wake up, all you'll see are her bony fingers curled around the armrests. She doesn't move from the spot unless there's a full moon. Then you may feel something touch your cheek. But that's what the salt is for." Priya handed Ethan the bowl and smiled. "Just keep the circle of salt closed at all times, and you'll be fine."

"You're kidding me, right?"

"I'm dead serious," Priya said, her expression somber. "You remember how the kids used to dare each other to sneak into the funeral home at night, right?"

Ethan looked at her skeptically. "You mean to tell me this place is really haunted?"

"Only the coach house." It was time to take advantage of Moksha's peculiarities. Priya mustered all her skills to convince Ethan of her made-up ghost story. "We think it's the original groundskeeper's wife, but it could be someone from next door."

"Next door?" Ethan set the bowl down on the bedside table.

"Oh, did Puppa forget to tell you? We keep unclaimed human remains in the storage room next door." This part was true, and Ethan's expression was a delightful mix of shock and confusion. Priya mentally high-fived herself as she strolled out of the bedroom.

"Human remains?" Ethan repeated, following her out.

"Just the ashes," she said over her shoulder. "And don't worry. There's a solid brick wall between you and the dead." She tapped her knuckles against the partition. "But some ashes do sneak in through the ventilation. Occasionally." She tilted her hand back and forth as if weighing the likelihood. "If you notice a thin layer of dust on the counter, just wish it well. Oh, and keep your food covered and your mouth closed at night."

"Let me get this straight." Ethan crossed his arms over his chest. "There's a ghost in my room and, possibly, the ashes of the departed floating around?"

"I wouldn't refer to her as a ghost." Priya lowered her voice. "She takes offense to that. We call her Bhooa masi."

"Bhooa . . . *masi*?" Ethan attempted to pronounce the word.

"It means aunt. Auntie Bhooa. We call her Bhooa masi out of respect."

"Bhooa masi," Ethan repeated.

"Very good. None of this is a deal-breaker, right?" Priya stowed a bucket of cleaning supplies under the kitchen sink and gave him an innocent look.

"No. Not at all," Ethan said, his words charged with excitement. "I'm playing a dead guy who wakes up alive, and now there's a ghost involved? This turned out to be even better than I hoped for."

Priya's plan burst in her face like a balloon at a cactus convention. Instead of spooking Ethan into a quick exit, her fake ghost story had only fueled his enthusiasm.

"Does nothing ever scare you?" Priya asked, frustration creeping into her voice. And yet, beneath the irritation, that same fearless energy of his pulled at her like it always had.

"Oh, I've been spooked. And I've run. Plenty of times."

"You?" Priya scoffed. "The mighty Ethan Knight?"

"Don't." His voice dropped, edged with something that wasn't quite anger but carried the weight of something raw. "Don't pretend you see me the same as everyone else does. You know the real me. You *saw* the real me. Way before anyone ever did."

Priya's heart stilled.

Because it was true.

She had known Ethan before the cameras and screaming fans, when he was just Brooke's older brother—the boy she had caught staring up at the night sky, as if trying to untangle something bigger than himself. The boy who had scooted over silently to make room for her, who had shrugged off his busted lip even though his eyes told a different story, who had walked her home even though she insisted she was fine. The boy who had made her feel seen long before she had realized how much that mattered.

Back then, she had spun stories about him, even though he had no place in her dreams—stories as beautiful and impossible as the stars reflected in his eyes. But dreams were just that. There was no universe in which she and Ethan Knight ended up together.

Priya sucked in a sharp breath. This wasn't a walk down memory lane. She was here to get rid of Ethan Knight, not fall back under his spell.

"Excuse me, Mr. Knight," a man interrupted from the door. "Shall I bring in your luggage?"

Ethan glanced at the man in the dark suit—clearly his driver, Priya assumed. "Yes, of course," he said, as if just remembering he was waiting. Turning to Priya, he flashed a grin that left her stomach in knots. "Time really does fly when you're having fun."

"Well, I must fly too," she declared. "Puppa will be here soon to help you get settled in." She had barely taken a step before Ethan reached out, his fingers closing around her arm.

"Hold on," he said, slipping off his jacket and placing it over her shoulders. "It's colder than it looks."

His fingers grazed the back of her neck as he reached out automatically to free her hair. As it tumbled down her back, catching the light, he stilled.

"Ethan?" Priya tilted her head, catching the distant look in his eyes.

"Sorry." He blinked. "I just had a flashback . . . to the first time we met." His voice had softened, as if the memory had pulled him under. "I remember opening my eyes, completely out of it, and seeing you crouched beside me. The sun was so bright I couldn't see your face. All I saw was your hair . . . floating around you like a halo."

A strange tightness coiled in Priya's chest. *He remembers.*

"I thought you were some kind of dream," he said, lifting a strand of her hair. "Funny how memories work. I blocked out so much when I left—but this one just came rushing back."

Priya felt something shift inside her, the carefully placed bricks of her defenses crumbling, one by one. The past felt close enough to touch, when her whole world had revolved around him—every fleeting glance, every casual smile analyzed and stored away like something precious.

But that was a lifetime ago.

She had moved on, or at least tried to. She had built a life, watched it unravel, and now, somehow, she had ended up right back where she started. The bittersweet weight of it all settled in her chest, tugging her back to reality.

Priya slipped the jacket off her shoulders with a casual shrug. "Thanks, but I don't do leather," she said, forcing lightness into her tone. "And honestly? You probably shouldn't wear it around Puppa either. We're big on nonviolence toward animals."

"My apologies." Ethan snatched the jacket back and balled it up behind his back. "I didn't mean any disrespect."

Priya suppressed a twinge of guilt. Sure, her family was all about the vegetarian lifestyle, but they never, *ever* forced their views on anyone else. Still, desperate times called for desperate measures. And if ghost stories weren't going to shake Ethan up, she needed to kick things up a notch, make his stay as uncomfortable as possible. She needed him out of here, and fast. Every day Ethan stuck around meant more money trickling into the renovation fund. The sooner she got rid of him, the better the chances of Moksha closing for good.

"No worries," Priya tossed over her shoulder as she started to walk away, a sly grin curling on her lips. "It's just your first day."

But as her steps carried her toward the door, a strange shift in the air caught her attention. It was subtle but undeniable. She could feel Ethan's gaze on her, making her skin prickle. Without thinking, she turned toward the window, catching his reflection just in time. There he was, his eyes on her, watching her every move.

A thrill shot through Priya's veins. She wasn't the awkward teenager he'd left behind, stumbling over her words and hiding in baggy clothes. She was all grown up, and judging by the way Ethan was looking at her, there was no question he had noticed.

Priya turned her head away, biting back the grin that threatened to break free. Ethan was right—the early May breeze still carried a chill despite the sunlight—but she barely felt it. A rush of elation flooded her, and she let herself bask in its glow. But Ethan's presence wasn't just complicating her plan to shut down Moksha. It also put her at risk of falling for him again—his soulful eyes, his heart-melting smile, his rock-solid shoulders . . .

Lost in a lust-induced stupor, Priya didn't see the low-hanging branch until it smacked her square in the face. The stinging sensation felt like a swift slap, reminding her of her place.

Don't reach too high.

Don't think too big.

Don't dream beyond your station.

Rubbing her cheek, she let herself into the apartment and checked the time. The evening loomed before her like a heavy cloud. She had to accompany her parents to an event she desperately wanted to avoid. But now that she was back home, the net of familial obligations tightened around her, leaving no room for escape.

Priya slipped into the flowing skirt of her chaniya, adjusting the waistband until it fell gracefully around her ankles. Easing her arms through the sleeves of her choli, she fastened the hooks in the front, taking care not to snag the fabric. Reaching for the dupatta, she draped it around her shoulders and looked at herself in the mirror.

Her outfit gleamed with jeweled tones of blue and magenta, the sheer dupatta glittering with beadwork. Priya debated whether to leave her midriff exposed. The style complemented her figure, but the Solanki Modesty Meter wailed like a police siren in her head. Her family's measure of acceptable attire distinguished "good girls" from "bad girls." The strange thing was that no one had actually sat her down and laid out these rules. She just *knew*. And somehow, her divorce had raised the bar even more. Cover up your skin. Cover up your flaws. Cover up your failure.

"Priya, beta?" Mumma knocked on her door. "Ready to go?"

"Do I have to?" Priya groaned as she let her mother in.

Mumma looked at her disapprovingly. "It's not up for debate. You know how much we owe Anandji. We wouldn't even be here if it wasn't for him. Now come on, *fastum fass*."

When it came to Anand Sharma, not only did Mumma add *ji*, but she also resorted to language curry—English words sprinkled with Gujarati spice. Regular speed wasn't fast enough for Anandji. It had to be "fastum fass."

"But Mumma, we don't belong in Anandji's circle." Priya raised her arms as her mother rearranged the dupatta, tucking it into the waistband of her skirt to cover her stomach.

"That may be so, but when Anandji calls, we go. End of story. I know this isn't something you want to do, but it's not easy for us either. Everyone knows you're divorced and back home. We can't avoid them forever, so we might as well face it and be done with it." She stepped back, giving Priya a once-over.

"Don't you have something less flashy?" She started toward Priya's closet but changed her mind. "There's no time to fuss now. I need you to drop off Mr. Ethan's dinner tray before we leave."

Priya's pulse quickened. She could still feel Ethan's eyes lingering on her hours later, as if they had been burned into her skin. Shaking off the thought, she reached for a set of bangles and slid them over her wrists, one by one. Placing a golden bindi on her forehead, she brushed a lock of hair away from her face, her tresses cascading in inky waves down her back.

As Priya finished up, she noticed her mother watching her with a hint of sadness in her eyes. "What's wrong, Mumma?" she asked.

"I can't believe how fast time has gone by," Mumma said. "I remember watching you get ready for school like it was yesterday. But four years at university, five with Manoj, and another just passed . . ." She paused, her expression dimming with a quiet sadness. "Priya, you're far too young to be divorced."

Priya adjusted her earrings, glancing at her mother. "Are you giving me the green light to start dating?" she teased.

"Don't twist my words, Priya. I'm just saying that life moves fast. Puppa and I don't want to see you growing old alone."

Priya had tried to follow the road map her parents had laid out—education, marriage, career, kids—a life painted in steady, predictable strokes. She had wanted it for herself, too, but her plans had crumbled beneath her feet. And now they were nudging her toward that life again. As much as she knew they meant well, living under their roof meant getting their opinions on everything.

"I'm twenty-eight, Mumma, not eighty-eight. It's a little soon to be mourning my youth," Priya quipped, checking her reflection one last time before following her mother out.

"Where's Puppa?" she asked as they entered the kitchen.

"He's downstairs with Mr. Ethan, but he's already showered and shaved. He'll be ready by the time you return."

Mumma handed Priya a beautifully prepared dinner tray for Ethan: flaky samosas filled with potato and peas, crispy pakoras fried to perfection, steaming bowls of daal and rice, and a stack of fresh rotlis glistening with ghee. A jug of chilled mango lassi completed the meal.

Covering the tray with a kitchen towel, Priya set off for the coach house. She knocked gently on the door before stepping inside. Her gaze swept across the room, and she let out a quiet breath. It was thankfully empty. Ethan was still with her father.

As Priya set the tray on the table, she noticed Ethan's jacket balled up on the couch. He'd also left behind his leather sneakers. *So, Ethan Knight isn't unshakable after all. He might laugh in the face of ghost stories but he's treading carefully around my father.* She smiled as she picked up the jacket and hung it in the closet. As her fingers lingered on the buttery leather, her smile faded into a sigh. Ethan had no idea what he'd walked into, no clue he'd turned into a Hollywood-sized roadblock standing in the way of her plan to get her family out of the funeral business.

Priya shut the closet door with a decisive click. She wasn't going to feel bad anymore. No more guilt, no more sympathy. She had to do whatever it took to get rid of Ethan Knight before he unraveled everything she was fighting for.

Four

BY THE TIME PRIYA and her parents arrived at the banquet hall, the party was already in full swing. Outside, a mix of Gujarati and Bollywood tunes spilled from the speakers. A colorful sign welcomed guests to the *sangeet*, a pre-wedding ceremony that promised an evening of music, dancing, and celebration.

"Welcome, Rakesh." Anandji greeted Puppa with a hug. "We're so happy you could join us."

"It's an honor to be a part of your daughter's sangeet," Puppa replied, then offered Anandji's wife a slight bow. "Thank you, Meeraji, for inviting us."

"The pleasure is ours," she said warmly before turning to Mumma and Priya. "It's so lovely to see you both again." She smiled at Priya. "It's been a while, Priya. Are you settling in okay, beta?"

The older woman knew about her divorce, and Priya was thankful for the way she handled it, without fuss or awkwardness.

"I'm well," Priya replied, glancing at the brightly lit hall behind Meeraji. "Looks like it's going to be a fun evening."

Meeraji's smile turned brighter. "I hope you enjoy it. Come, Anand and I will show you to your table."

She led them into the hall, past tables dressed in crisp linens. The walls were draped in bright saris, and fairy lights twinkled above like a sky full of stars. When they reached table 6, Meeraji and Anandji introduced them to the three women already seated, then excused themselves to greet more guests.

The Solankis took their seats, and after a few polite comments about the decor, one of the women smiled and gestured to the vertical strings of marigolds that hung like curtains behind the stage.

"They always remind me of back home," she said. The others nodded, and the conversation shifted to where everyone was from in India.

"What about you?" they asked Mumma and Puppa.

Puppa hesitated for a split second. Priya sensed his discomfort as he steered through the conversation, aware of the subtle cues hinting at the women's upper-caste backgrounds. While Solanki wasn't a common Dalit surname, the little bits Puppa shared about her family's origins and occupation were enough for the women to figure out their caste.

"For us, marigolds have always been tied to funerals," he continued. "We still use them when we can—woven into garlands or just the loose petals. I guess you could say they are our flower."

Priya glanced at the golden strands. Marigolds threaded through every rite in their culture—birth, prayer, celebration, mourning. Always present, from first to last, sacred and enduring.

The conversation moved on, light and pleasant, as if nothing had been revealed. But Priya saw how her father seemed to shrink inward, as if the unspoken had chipped away at something inside him. Her parents did their best to wear a mask of ease, but Priya knew that if they had the choice, they would keep their Dalit identity tucked away, even around people who didn't seem to care.

"Hello, hello!" A woman in a beautiful sari approached the table, gold necklaces glimmering at her neck. Her earrings sparkled as she paused, a younger man trailing behind her.

"*Kem chho?* How's everyone doing?" she asked, her voice lively as she glanced around the table.

"Shruti," one of the women greeted. "You look absolutely beautiful. Just as the mother of the groom should."

"So lovely!" Mumma said, as everyone rose to congratulate Shrutiji on her son's wedding to Anandji's daughter.

"Thank you." She beamed. "Have you met my other son, Ravi?" She motioned toward the man beside her. "MIT graduate. Top class. Already a senior software engineer in Silicon Valley."

Priya froze, her gaze snapping to the man beside Shrutiji. Though his features had changed, there was no mistaking Ravi Tiwari. She remembered him from the computer camp they'd attended together as kids. He looked every bit the dashing, successful man his mother was painting him out to be.

"*Haveh taaro vaaro chhe*," the ladies said to him, almost in unison. Your turn next.

Ravi laughed politely, and Priya felt a bit sorry for him. No Indian wedding was complete without a swarm of matchmaking aunties descending upon unmarried guests.

"Indeed." Shrutiji smiled, pleased they had caught on to the true purpose behind her bragging—to find a suitable match for her son. "Ravi is a catch. Only the best will do."

Ravi's eyes drifted to Priya, a flicker of recognition passing over his face.

"Priya?" he asked, his face breaking into a smile. "Priya Solanki?"

"Hello, Ravi." Priya grinned back at him. "How are you? It's been a while."

"Hello, beta," Puppa cut in, stepping forward with an outstretched hand. "Congratulations on your brother's wedding."

"Thank you," Ravi replied, shaking hands with Puppa and Mumma. He then turned to Priya, reaching for her hand, his fingers holding on a moment longer than necessary.

"I haven't seen you in ages. How have you been?" he asked.

Before Priya could answer, Shrutiji stepped in. "Come, Ravi," she said, placing her hand on his arm. "You must meet Joshiji's daughter. She's just completed her studies in London. It's time you met someone more your match. You don't mind, do you?" She gave Priya a brief, dismissive glance before escorting Ravi away.

Priya wasn't interested in Ravi romantically, but the slight from Shrutiji still stung. Being a divorced woman from a less prestigious background, she knew she didn't fit Shrutiji's vision of a suitable partner for her son. She told herself it didn't really matter, but it still left a bad taste in her mouth.

"I'm going to get something to eat," she announced and began making her way to the buffet line, which was quickly growing.

"Priya." Mumma's hand shot out, pulling her back into her seat. "We have to wait our turn."

Priya let out a sigh, familiar with the routine. There were no rules about who could head to the buffet, but her parents would wait until all the other guests had gone first.

"Fine," she muttered. "I'll go get mehndi on my hands." She spun around and walked off, not bothering to look back.

Standing in line at the henna station, her annoyance only deepened—first at Shrutiji's snub, then at the way her mother still treated her like a reckless teenager who needed managing. The lively strains of garba music enveloped her, pulsing and thrumming all around. She glanced at the dancers, spinning and clapping in perfect unison. They moved in a blur of color and light, their laughter blending with the vibrant beat.

The music was contagious, pulling her in, urging her to move. Priya's feet tapped along, her body swaying to the rhythm. Then the music shifted, and a playful, familiar tune filled the air. Her heart gave a small jolt. A song she used to love. She could see herself as a carefree girl, her bangles jingling in time with the beat, twirling and smiling so hard that her cheeks ached.

Priya found herself stepping out of the henna line and joining the garba. Her first few steps were small and cautious, but soon she was spinning and clapping, her laughter spilling out with each turn. The more she danced, the more her spirits lifted, her earlier frustrations slowly fading away.

Then she noticed Ravi watching her from the sidelines. He smiled and mimed a dance step, asking if he could join the fast-moving circle. Priya made room for him, and he quickly fell into step beside her.

"Think you can keep up?" Priya challenged, raising her voice to be heard.

"As long as you don't step on my feet!" Ravi shouted back, grinning as their movements aligned—small steps, then large, in sync with the rest of the dancers. As the tempo of the music quickened, Ravi's eyes lit up.

"Let's see if *you* can keep up!" He grabbed Priya's hand and drew her to the center of the circle.

Priya felt a pang of awkwardness, dancing in the middle of the garba circle with Ravi as her only companion. But as the music picked up, her hesitation dissolved.

"Bet you can't do this one!" Ravi shouted over the song, switching to a complicated step.

"Oh yeah? Watch this!" Priya shot back, adding a playful twist.

As they danced together, laughing and clapping to the beat, the colors of the crowd blended into a vibrant whirl. Priya's dupatta came undone, leaving her stomach exposed, but she was too wrapped up in the moment to care. There was something freeing about just dancing and forgetting everything else. She felt light and unchained, as if casting away the burden of her divorce, her failures, and the unseen restraints that held her back. Her movements turned bolder, and she added her own flair to the traditional steps, moving with wild, untamed energy.

When the track ended, Priya slowed to a halt, her breath ragged and her cheeks warm from the rush of *really* dancing. She turned to Ravi, a breathless smile on her lips.

"Don't tell me you're done already?" Ravi said, wiping a sheen of sweat from his own brow. "Guess I win this round."

"Win?" Priya scoffed, trying to catch her breath. "You were two beats behind the whole time."

"Strategy," Ravi replied. "I was pacing myself. It's called endurance."

"Fine." Priya laughed. "Let's call it a tie, just like old times." She gave him a quick nod before leaving the garba. But as she moved toward her table, she was suddenly aware of the weight of countless eyes following her. The hum of murmured conversation seemed louder, and Priya could feel the buzz of attention her dance with Ravi had stirred.

Shrutiji stood at the edge of the crowd, every inch of her composed, except for the sharp look in her eyes. It was clear she hadn't expected Priya—of all people—to be the one dancing with her son, and she was not happy about it. Priya's steps slowed as their eyes met. She couldn't resist the flicker of defiance that crept into her own.

You don't mind, do you? Priya glided by, her head held high, pulse still humming with exhilaration.

When she got back to the table, Mumma and Puppa were nowhere to be found. Priya scanned the crowd at the buffet table, but there was no sign of them there either.

"If you're looking for your parents, they stepped outside," one of the women at their table informed her.

"Thanks." Priya made her way out of the banquet room and spotted them in the lobby. The smile on her face vanished instantly as their eyes connected. Puppa stood rigidly, his body tense, while Mumma crossed her arms across her chest. Priya didn't need to guess what this was about. She had drawn too much attention to herself. Their disapproval hung heavily in the air as Priya approached.

Aware of being watched, Priya's parents held their tongues. But that didn't stop Mumma from yanking her dupatta back into place and tucking it tightly into her waistband.

"Mumma," Priya hissed through her teeth. "Can you not? I'm not a kid."

"Then act like it," Mumma replied, her lips tight.

As they walked back to the car, the vibrant notes of the sangeet dissolved into the night. A sense of emptiness washed over Priya as she slid into the driver's seat. She didn't regret dancing, but the guilt that followed hit her hard, making her feel like she'd let her parents down all over again. Their judgment still had the power to make her feel small, as if she was a child again. And it stung, realizing that after all this time, she still wanted their approval.

Priya pulled into Moksha, the drive silent and strained the whole way. Even after she turned off the engine, Mumma and Puppa remained motionless in their seats.

Finally, Puppa spoke, his voice sharp and cutting. "Is this how we raised you?" he asked. "You might not care about what you did, Priya. You and your sisters come and go, but your mother and I live here. We're the ones who have to face the consequences."

Priya's heart thudded in her chest, just like it did back when she was a kid, and her father was angry with her. But she *wasn't* a kid anymore.

"I was just enjoying myself," she snapped back. "Since when is that a crime?"

"Enjoying yourself?" Puppa's voice was tight. "Do you know what people are saying right now? That Rakesh Solanki's daughter is a disgrace. That she has no respect for herself or anyone else because her parents didn't raise her right." His tone rose with each word.

Priya stared at the steering wheel, her jaw tightening. She could feel the unspoken expectation. This was her moment to apologize. But something inside her rebelled. She'd always tried to be the good daughter; tonight, she refused to shrink back into that role.

"We're not saying don't take part in garba," Mumma said. "But flailing around like you are possessed? Such *jungli vera*? How will we ever show our faces to Anandji and Meeraji? Or all those people who saw you dance so recklessly?"

"There will always be people who whisper and judge, but this isn't about what anyone else thinks. It's about what *you* think," Priya shot back. "So, go ahead and say it. Tell me how humiliating it is that your divorced daughter had the guts to dance with someone from a higher caste. And not just dance, but dance like she didn't give a damn—"

"Priya!" Puppa's tone rang out sharply. "You will apologize at once."

"Why should I?" Priya replied, her pitch rising. "Do you think Ravi is apologizing for dancing with me? Why do I always have to be the one apologizing? You probably don't even remember that I know Ravi from computer camp. The first year you enrolled me, I spent the whole summer working on the final project and tied with him for first place. I was so proud and excited, but do you know what I remember most about that day?"

She paused, the memory sharp in her mind. "You walked straight past me to congratulate Ravi and his parents, while I stood there, waiting to show you my medal. That was the first time you explained caste to me, and where we stood in relation to him. It made me feel like Ravi was more worthy even though we both tied for the top spot. That voice inside me is still there, but tonight, for a few moments, I broke free and danced with Ravi as an equal. And I'm *not* going to apologize for that."

Priya exhaled, trying to steady herself. "I grew up in a different world from yours, yet somehow your rules are the only ones that matter. There's no room for me to spread my wings or make my own choices."

Puppa's expression hardened. "You've had more than enough room to make your own choices. And look where that's gotten you. No job, no husband. Nothing to show for it. But sure, go ahead and blame us. Because we took a moment to show our respect to Ravi and his family instead of gushing over you." He unbuckled his seat belt and got out of the car. Then, with a harsh slam, he shut the door and stalked off.

Mumma flinched, her face twisting as she stared after him. "I hate all this fighting." She looked at Priya, her eyes sharp with frustration. "Why do you have to argue? Why can't you just say sorry?"

"Why is it always on me to keep the peace?" Priya replied. "Why can't he ever admit he may be wrong too?"

Mumma's expression tightened like the strings of a sitar pulled taut. "Maybe you should just have stayed in Calgary."

"Maybe I should have," Priya replied. "Maybe I needed a reminder of why I left in the first place."

Mumma released her seat belt with a sharp motion and climbed out of the car.

A wave of sadness washed over Priya as she watched her mother fade into the shadow of the funeral home. Everything was unraveling—her dreams, her relationships, even the pieces of herself she thought she'd finally started to put together. Her parents' idea of what her life should look like, of the daughter they wanted her to be, was driving a wedge between them. And Priya feared that she would end up yielding just to avoid conflict.

The longer she stayed at Moksha, the more it felt like a battleground—one determined to wear her down until she gave in.

Five

PRIYA SWUNG THE CAR DOOR OPEN and stepped out. She reached for the back door, grabbed Mumma's shawl, and draped it around her shoulders. Moonlight bathed the ground, casting a silver glow over the trees and flower beds. The scent of lilacs hung in the air as Priya gathered her heavy beaded skirt and walked past the edge of the property. She followed the abandoned train tracks until she reached an old freight car, its wheels buried in a sea of withered grass. The doors, long stuck open on either side, let the darkness sweep through its hollow shell, weathered by years of rain and wind.

Priya kicked off her shoes and scaled the side of the car, gripping the familiar rungs like she'd done a hundred times before. Rusty flakes of metal crumbled under her fingers as she pulled herself up. Hoisting herself onto the roof, she took a moment to catch her breath. From her vantage point, the estate nearby was veiled by trees, but its lights still pierced through the darkness. With a weary sigh, she stretched out on the roof, drained by the emotional toll of the night.

The sky unfolded above her, deep and endless, though Priya

found no comfort in its beauty. Her parents believed the stars shaped destiny. Tonight they felt like a cruel joke.

"Fuck you," Priya flung her words at them. "Fuck you all." Her voice echoed across the fields, shattering the silence.

"Rough night?" a voice drawled from the shadows.

"Ethan?" Priya jolted upright so fast that she almost tumbled off the roof. "What are you doing here?" He sat a few feet away, barely visible in the dark, his face hidden beneath the shadow of a hoodie.

"Old habits." He exhaled a cloud of smoke, watching it dissolve into the dark sky. The familiar, pungent smell of weed hit her instantly. "Feels like nothing's changed, huh?" His eyes flickered from the glowing tip of his joint as he turned to look at her. "You and me meeting by this same beat-up old freight car."

"Hardly." She tried to mask the all-too-familiar fluttering of her heart. "You've done something with your life, Ethan. Everyone knows your name. I'm still sitting here, exactly where I've always been."

"Right here's not so bad." He took a deep drag, gesturing around them—the glow of the moonlit field, the rustle of leaves, the calm hush of the night. "Sure, I've chased big dreams, and don't get me wrong, it's incredible, but it's fleeting. Just smoke in the wind."

"Please, you're practically a bonfire."

"A bonfire, huh?" Ethan laughed. "Is that your way of finally admitting you think I'm hot?"

Priya tilted her head, pretending to think it over. "You're more like a fire hazard, really. Too much heat for anyone's good."

"How about a *little* heat then? Safe and contained?" He offered her his joint with a playful grin.

"Heathen Knight," Priya teased. "Still tempting everyone to the dark side."

Ethan let out a low chuckle. "Heathen Knight . . . Wow, I haven't heard that in ages. You're the only one who ever called me that. And look at you. Still the same good girl, huh?"

Priya didn't say anything. Instead, she snatched the joint from his hand and took a bold drag, the smoke burning her throat but making her laugh.

"Okay, who are you, and what did you do with Priya?" Ethan grinned.

Blowing the smoke out with a small chuckle, Priya leaned back. "Oh, this is Priya 2.0. Divorced, unemployed, and fresh off a night where I pretty much set the family name on fire."

"I have to admit, I did not see that coming." He let out a short laugh. "I mean, when Brooke told me . . . Priya Solanki, divorced? No way."

"Here." Priya passed him the joint. "Might help you process. Deep breaths, Ethan."

He smiled and took a slow drag, shaking his head.

As they sat together, the night felt strangely nostalgic, like slipping into an old sweater. For a moment, Priya didn't feel like she was sitting next to someone the entire world seemed to know. She was sitting with Ethan, the boy she'd met right here on these train tracks, in the no-man's-land between their two homes. She could still see the dust caked on his jeans, the way he held his arm stiffly even as he insisted it was fine, the beautifully messy way he'd burst into her life. The memories hit her all at once, sharp and alive, pulling her back to that day.

✦

Priya stretched out on the roof of the freight car, reading her book. The sun dipped low, casting a golden hue over the field. At nearly twelve, she was starting to realize she was different from other girls her age, girls who didn't grow up surrounded by death and loss. She loved this time of the day. It was the perfect escape from the funeral home. The roof held the heat of the day but was cool enough to be comfortable.

As the warmth seeped through her bones, a distant roar reached her ears, growing louder as it approached. Priya sat upright and pushed her glasses up her nose. Squinting into the distance, she caught a flash of chrome—a motorcycle barreling toward the freight car at full speed. Priya's stomach churned with rising panic.

It's not slowing down.

She wanted to move, to scramble to safety, but her legs felt like lead, frozen in place as she braced herself for the inevitable impact.

No way, no way . . .

In the split second before disaster struck, the rider yanked the bike into a bone-rattling stop. The tires screeched against the ground, sending a cloud of dust billowing up into the air. As the haze settled, he slowly emerged, streaked with dirt, his hair wild from the wind. When he finally lifted his face, Priya's breath hitched.

Ethan Knight.

She recognized Brooke's older brother right away. In the few months since their mother passed away, Ethan had earned a reputation as a troublemaker. At fifteen, he was only three years older, but in a league of his own. He skipped school, ignored homework, and was always in the principal's office. Brooke spent more time at Priya's place than her own to escape the explosive arguments between her father and brother.

Hidden from view, Priya watched as Ethan brushed the dust from his eyes, unfazed by the close call. He gunned his engine, sped back across the field, and made a sharp turn. Pausing for a second, he gripped the throttle, then shot straight back toward the freight car. The wind tore at his clothes as he drew nearer.

Priya stared in disbelief, her entire world narrowing to one terrifying image: Ethan Knight hurtling toward the freight car, reckless and unstoppable. She saw the scene flash before her—the motorcycle smashing to pieces, Ethan flying through the air, the metallic smell of blood and oil. The engine roared like a death knell, and Priya's hands flew to her ears as Ethan slammed into the car.

But then, as if by magic, Ethan appeared on the other side of the freight car. For a moment, he seemed to hang in the air, his motorcycle frozen in perfect balance. Then gravity reclaimed him, and his tires struck the ground, smooth and sure, as he nailed a flawless landing.

Priya's brain scrambled to catch up. Then it hit her—Ethan had pulled off some insane stunt, zipping through the open doors of the freight car and coming out the other side in one piece.

But then it all went horribly wrong.

"Oh, shit!" Priya gasped, as the impact sent the bike skidding sideways. With a sickening screech, it dragged Ethan's body along with it. They tumbled across the field in a blur of flesh and steel.

"Please be okay," Priya whispered, scrambling down from the roof. She bolted toward Ethan, barely noticing the shattered mirror and jagged shards littering the field. The bike was sprawled on its side, its wheels still spinning. Ethan lay trapped beneath, motionless and frighteningly still.

"Come on, come on." Priya wedged her fingers beneath the bike's frame. Her muscles screamed in protest, but the bike barely budged. "Don't you dare die on me," she grunted through clenched teeth. Planting her feet and digging deep, she shoved with everything she had. With a strained cry, she heaved the bike off Ethan and managed to free him.

Her heart hammered as her eyes darted over his body—the gash on his forehead, the blood seeping from his ankle, the torn jacket, the missing shoe. Ethan let out a low groan and cracked his eyes open, shielding his face from the sun as he squinted at her. Relief flooded through Priya, so sharp and sudden it made her lightheaded. She felt a fluttery sensation, like a thousand tiny wings beating inside her. She didn't know why her pulse quickened or why her thoughts scattered, but she couldn't tear herself away from him.

Ethan tried to move but flinched and sank back to the ground. His eyes drifted to Priya's hair, swaying in the breeze. The motion seemed to soothe him.

"Are you okay?" Priya asked.

"I'll survive," Ethan murmured, cradling his shoulder as he tried to get up again. Priya reached out to help, but he waved her off. "I can manage," he said, dragging himself onto all fours before rising to his feet.

Priya felt a flush creep across her face as he studied her.

"I know you," he said, tilting his head. "You're friends with my sister, right?"

"Priya," she introduced herself. "Priya Solanki."

Ethan winced as they shook hands.

"That was a pretty wild stunt you pulled," she said.

Ethan huffed out a laugh. "Didn't think anyone was watching."

"I was on the roof." Priya gestured toward the freight car. "My parents run the funeral home next door. I come here to get away sometimes." Her words tumbled out in a nervous rush. A strange sensation that had taken hold of her. Being around Ethan made her feel jittery and flustered.

"Cool hideaway." Ethan retrieved his shoe and slipped it on with a grimace.

"Want me to call Brooke?" Priya asked.

"No," he said quickly, picking up the broken pieces of the mirror. His jaw tightened as he hobbled back to his bike. "If she helps me, she'll just get herself in hot water."

Priya nodded. "Sorry about your bike."

He circled the bike, scanning the damage. "It's not too bad. As long as I can get it to start."

"Are you sure you're okay?" Priya's eyes lingered on Ethan. His arm hung awkwardly, and blood dripped from his ankle, staining his jeans. "You should get checked out."

Ethan shook his head. "If my dad finds out I've been on his bike again, he'll lose it. He already yelled at me earlier. I just need to go home, clean up, and stash the bike before he gets back."

Ethan tried to haul the bike off the ground, but the weight was too much for his injured arm to handle. Gritting his teeth, he tried again. Priya rushed to his side, and together they set it upright.

Ethan swung a leg over the bike, wincing as he settled into the seat. Leaning forward, he turned on the ignition. The engine coughed weakly, then died.

"Come on, now. Work with me here," he growled, giving it another shot.

Nothing but a weak sputter.

Swearing under his breath, Ethan tried yet again. This time, the bike roared to life. "Fuck yeah!" Relief washed over his face.

As the engine settled into a steady, throaty rumble, Ethan glanced at Priya, streaks of dirt smeared across his face.

"Thanks," he said, his voice rough but sincere. Twisting the throttle, he jerked forward with a sharp wince. "Until next time, Priya Solanki."

Priya had heard her name spoken countless times, but the way Ethan Knight said it made her senses sizzle, like a jalebi hitting hot oil. A sweet, dizzying rush spiraled through her as she watched him take off.

It wasn't until Ethan faded into the distance that Priya realized what she was feeling. Her first crush had just barreled into her life, and she was utterly and completely captivated.

Six

NOW, SIXTEEN YEARS LATER, as Priya sat with Ethan on the roof of the same freight car, she felt the familiar old flutter return, soft but undeniable, like an old song she hadn't heard in years. Ethan always had a way of pulling people in, his presence magnetic and impossible to ignore. Even now, she could feel that raw energy beneath the surface, tugging at her. Like the ebb of the tide, he had a power that made her feel both at ease and on edge.

Ethan stared at the lights of his father's estate flickering through the trees. The joint burned forgotten between his fingers, until the heat from the ember reached his skin. He blinked and stubbed it out, the motion almost mechanical. Priya could feel the underlying sadness in him, the silent ache for a relationship with his father that felt beyond repair.

"Your dad must have lost it when he saw that bike all those years ago," she said.

"He never did." Ethan's lips quirked into a bittersweet smile. "He took one look at me and assumed I'd been in a fight. Grounded me for a month. Which—as it turns out—was just enough time to fix the bike without him noticing." He turned to look at Priya. "The last time I saw him was at my going-away party.

"He was so happy I'd agreed to go to college," he continued. "He wanted me to take over the family business after I graduated. But I had zero interest in following in his footsteps. I begged, pleaded, screwed up my grades, but when your father is rich and powerful, doors open, so I was accepted into the same college that he went to. We had some epic fights over it, but he wouldn't budge. So, I let him think he'd won."

A hint of determination crept into Ethan's words. "But the day I was supposed to leave for college, I left for New York instead. It may have been a selfish move, but I felt trapped. And he never forgave me. Hasn't spoken to me since." The hurt lingered in Ethan's voice.

Priya reached out and put her hand on his arm. "I get why he was disappointed," she said, "but it was a long time ago. Maybe it's time you reconnected."

"It's not like I haven't tried, Priya. When I moved to Los Angeles and started doing stunt work, he told Brooke I was a no-good risk-taker. Then I caught my big break and thought he'd change his mind. I invited him to every premiere, but he never came. I think he'll always see me as a disappointment."

Priya could see the weight on his shoulders, so she changed the subject. "Hey, how come I never got an invite to any of those premieres?" she teased.

"You weren't even allowed out of the house for a date." Ethan chuckled.

"It's true." Priya laughed. "My parents were super paranoid. Anything outside of school was a big no-no. I think it's because they were adjusting to a new culture here, away from India, and terrified my sisters and I would go off the rails. Get mixed up with the wrong crowd, lose our way, forget where we came from. Little did they know, the parties I snuck off to were nothing more than a bunch of awkward kids trying to play it cool."

"Is that what you thought of my going-away party? A bunch of kids trying to impress each other?"

Priya remembered the biting pain of trying—and failing—to get Ethan's attention that night. Determined to make him see her as more than his sister's friend, she had ditched her glasses and spent the entire week adjusting to contact lenses. She'd also saved up for a new sweater that accentuated her curves.

"You barely spoke to me that night," Priya said, her voice tinged with the hurt of old memories.

"I barely spoke to anyone that night," Ethan replied. "I was trying to keep my plans for New York under wraps. If I'd said anything to you, it would have gotten back to Brooke, and she'd have either tried to stop me or, worse, dragged our father into it."

"Did you tell Chloe Thompson you were leaving for New York?" Priya asked pointedly.

"Chloe who?" Ethan looked confused.

"The girl you brought back here after the party. I saw the two of you making out."

A wry smile tugged at the corners of Ethan's mouth. "Is that why you've been so cold since my arrival? Because you caught me making out with Chloe Thompson that night?"

"I couldn't care less who you make out with."

"And yet you remember her name all these years later." Ethan fixed an amused stare at her.

"I just thought it was rude that you brought her to our spot," Priya said, her voice tight with exasperation she couldn't quite hide.

"*Our* spot, huh?" Ethan's grin got wider.

"Shut up," Priya mumbled, her face burning.

"Why don't you just admit it?"

"Admit what?"

"That I get under your skin."

"Oh, fuck off, Heathen." Priya kept her tone playful, but his comment hit too close to home. She wrapped her shawl tighter, trying to brush it off, but Ethan noticed the shift in her mood.

"I'm sorry I bailed without saying goodbye," he said, cutting straight to the reason for Priya's hurt. "I was young and stupid, and that night was a lot harder than I let on."

Ethan's words made Priya realize something she'd never thought of before. While she'd been drowning in her own sadness that night, Ethan had been dealing with the weight of leaving behind his whole life—his home, his family, everything he knew.

His apology touched a part of her that had never healed. It wasn't just the sting of being overlooked or seeing him with someone else in a place she'd always thought was theirs. It was the way he'd disappeared, as if she'd meant nothing to him. Meanwhile, he'd been more than her first crush. He'd also been her friend. At least that's what she'd believed—but then he was gone. Without any warning. Taking that spark with him, leaving her to deal with the quiet emptiness left in his wake.

"Don't sweat it," she said. "I've been swearing at everything and everyone tonight."

"What's got you so fired up?"

Priya sighed and hugged her knees. "Let's just say I stirred the pot at this party my parents dragged me to."

"Ah, Priya 2.0 strikes again." Ethan grinned. "Go on."

"I danced with Ravi Tiwari."

Ethan raised an eyebrow.

"He's the local catch, the most eligible man around, and I'm a divorced woman from a different caste."

"Caste?" Ethan asked. "You mean like a different religion?"

"Same religion, but like a different group, once separated by occupation and status," Priya explained. "Those divisions don't officially exist anymore. We're all supposed to be equals now, but when it comes to things like marriage, they creep back in. My parents wanted me to marry within our caste too."

"So, your ex was the same caste as you?"

"Yes, Manoj is Dalit too. We were called 'untouchables' back in the day and assigned jobs considered impure for others. A lot has changed, though the echoes of that past still remain. There was a time when my great-grandparents were denied entry to schools and temples. By the time my grandparents were born, they could go to school but had to sit in the back of the classroom and couldn't drink from the same well as the other kids."

"Wow, that's crazy," Ethan said, his expression tightening. "I didn't even know something like that existed. I'm sorry your family had to go through that. Sounds like it's left a mark, even if things are different now."

"It was abolished before my parents were born, although most people from our community can still identify their caste." Priya sighed. "My parents believe that caste is tied to past-life karma. If they don't fulfill their duties in this life, they won't move up the scale in their next one."

"That's . . . wild," Ethan said, letting out a slow breath.

"Right?" Priya nodded. "But not everyone sees it the way my parents do. My dad's friend, Anandji—the one whose daughter's sangeet we attended tonight—is from a higher caste, and he's always encouraging my father to think beyond the Dalit label."

"So, what kinds of jobs were Dalits traditionally expected to do?" Ethan asked.

"Things like cleaning sewers, collecting garbage, looking after the dead," Priya replied. "My dad's family used to take care of last rites in their village in Gujarat. They'd wash and wrap the body, place it on the pyre, and watch over it until the fire burned out. After Anandji lost his grandmother, my dad helped him through a rough patch, and they've been friends ever since. When Anandji moved to Canada, he helped my father get a work permit and start a new life. My father stuck to what he knew, so here we are, still in the funeral business. It's funny how some things never change." Priya grew quiet, then let out a soft laugh. "You should have seen Shrutiji's face when I danced with her son."

"Shrutiji?" Ethan asked.

"Ravi's mom," Priya explained. "Honestly? I didn't mean to cause a scene, but yeah, not my finest moment."

"Well, serves you right for abandoning your station in life," Ethan declared.

"My station in life?" Priya blinked. *Did Ethan just take a page out of my parents' playbook?*

"This station." Ethan grinned, tapping the roof. "This old freight car. These forgotten train tracks. This patch of land that feels like it's been frozen in time. If our destiny is truly cast in the stars, then the only way to break free is to become one. Take all that messy, angry, frustrated stuff inside you and push yourself higher."

"So *that's* your secret, huh?" Priya teased. "You used all that teenage rage to make it big?"

"I wouldn't be where I am if my father hadn't been so hard on me," Ethan said, his voice quiet with reflection. "I had to prove something, not just to him but to myself. It's funny how our toughest challenges can unlock what we're really capable of." His gaze wandered toward the distant lights of his father's estate.

Priya could still feel the deep sorrow in him, as if the memories of the past were wrapped around him like a heavy cloak. She had to try again. "Ethan, why don't you reach out to him while you're here? Maybe just try one more time?"

Ethan shook his head, his expression resigned. "It's on him now."

"Maybe he thinks you have it all, so you don't need him."

"I *do* have it all." Ethan let out a hollow laugh. "I don't need him."

"So that's it? Fame, fortune, and fans. Nothing else matters?"

"It should be enough," he replied with a weary sigh. "But life doesn't work like that. You work so hard chasing after your dreams, but the second you reach them, there's another one waiting. And then another. It's an endless loop, and you never get to fully enjoy where you're at because there's always more to chase. Eventually, it wears you down, and all you want is to sit in silence, under a dark sky away from all the lights."

He fell silent, letting the stillness wrap around him. "You know, I've always longed to return here," he said, stretching out to look at the stars.

A lump rose in Priya's throat. The way he spoke, like this place was still home, gnawed at her. And yet here she was, intent on sending him away. Swallowing hard, she stretched out beside him, lying flat on her back. Together, they lay beneath the sky, letting the night air fill their lungs.

"Everyone loves to watch the stars shine, but no one sees how they're really burning from the inside," Priya said so suddenly, she even surprised herself.

Ethan turned to her slowly. There was a quiet ache in his eyes that made her want to reach for his hand. But she didn't. Because Ethan would leave, just as he had before, and nothing would change for her or her family if she gave in to his pull.

How had she ended up here—caught between wanting him to stay and knowing that she had no option but to send him packing?

Seven

THE NEXT DAY, Priya unpacked the Wi-Fi router and scanned the coach house for the best place to install it. Settling on a bookshelf, she plugged it in and connected it to the modem. As she waited for the lights on the front panel to change, Priya's attention wandered to Ethan. He was deep in his workout, muscles flexing as he powered through his routine.

Priya turned her attention to the router, pretending not to be affected by the sight of him. But her eyes drifted back to his abs.

So ridiculously toned I could play a full-on xylophone melody on them.

Ethan looked up and caught her staring, his grin mischievous and knowing.

"If you flex any harder, you'll pop a vein," Priya said. "But hey, don't let it stop you from trying to impress me. I'm thoroughly entertained."

"Oh, I can tell. And judging by how long it's taking you to hook me up to the internet, it might be a bit *too* entertaining. Want me to ease up, or are you planning to camp out here all day?" Ethan transitioned into his next move, his eyes locking with hers in a playful challenge.

Resisting the urge to react, Priya turned away from him and opened the Wi-Fi settings on her phone. She connected to the new network, entered the password, and felt a sense of satisfaction when she saw full bars of connection.

Ha! Priya, one. Xylophone abs, zero.

As she set her phone aside, it buzzed with an incoming video call from her sister.

"Hey, Pri," Deepa greeted when she answered. "I'm almost done with my exams, and I was thinking—" She froze mid-sentence and leaned forward. "Wait . . . is that . . . ? Holy shit, it's Ethan Knight! Oh my god! I didn't know he was there already."

"Well, if you'd answered my call yesterday, you'd be up-to-date," Priya replied.

Deepa, however, had lost all interest in their conversation.

"Oh lord, he's shirtless," she whispered, practically pressing her face to the screen. "Pri, how are you so calm? Move your phone! Right, right!"

"I'm not your personal cameraman, Dee."

"Almost there, Pri," Deepa said, ignoring her older sister. "A little lower."

"Cut it out," Priya hissed under her breath. Being the youngest, Deepa had always gotten away with more, which explained why she had zero filters. "He'll hear us."

Deepa's expression suddenly froze, her eyes going wide. Priya didn't even have to turn around. She knew Ethan was standing behind her, glowing from his workout.

"He'll hear what?" Ethan asked, peering over Priya's shoulder.

Accepting the inevitable, Priya sighed and introduced him to her starstruck sibling. "Ethan, this is my sister Deepa, who currently looks like she's forgotten how to function. She's in her final year in college."

"Deepa? No way! You were this tall when I last saw you," Ethan said, using his hand to show her height.

"You remember me?" Deepa squealed. "I've loved you in literally *everything*!"

"Good to know I have *some* supporters in the family." Ethan tilted his head toward Priya.

"Don't let her fool you. I've been on Priya's hit list for interrupting one of your movies, and let me tell you, she was ready to shred me to pieces," Deepa revealed with a cheeky grin.

"Well, well." Ethan aimed a teasing glance at Priya. "Seems I have the power to rile you up even when I'm not around."

"Could you kindly cover up?" Priya replied, with a pointed look toward his chest. "Parading around in front of my baby sister. And you . . ." She turned her attention to Deepa. "Shouldn't you be studying for finals?"

"I'm going, I'm going," Deepa replied, rolling her eyes. She extended her hand to give Ethan a virtual high five, which he returned.

"Remember, you can't tell anyone he's here," Priya reminded.

"Bucket list moment, and I have to keep it under wraps," Deepa grumbled. "But my lips are sealed. Bye, Pri. Bye, Ethan. Keep those abs in top form until we speak again!"

Priya shook her head as her sister hung up. *Only Deepa could get away with telling a movie star to keep his abs tight for her.* Thinking Ethan had wandered off, Priya swiveled around, only to find her nose inches from his torso. The heat radiating from his skin made her feel like flames were licking at her senses. Her eyes traced his contours, down to the V that disappeared beneath the waistband of his shorts.

"Enjoying the view?" Ethan asked.

Priya pulled back and looked up at him. "While I can. It won't be long before my mother's fritters turn your abs into *khichdi*."

"What's khichdi?"

"A soft, mushy mess." Priya grinned. "Now, if you don't mind, I need to finish configuring your internet settings."

"Configure away. I'm going to hop in the shower while you work your magic."

Left alone in the living room, Priya waited until she heard the shower running, then accessed the app she had installed earlier to control the lights in the coach house. Connecting it to the Wi-Fi network, she grouped the smart bulbs into patterns and sequences. Casting a quick glance at the bathroom door, she tested the system, turning the lights on and off from her phone. Satisfied with the trial run, she put her phone away and prepared to leave.

As she jotted down the Wi-Fi password for Ethan, he stepped out of the bathroom, towel barely hanging on, hair damp and slicked back. His jawline looked even more defined, and the droplets of water trailing down his chest didn't help.

Priya froze, her pen hovering over the notepad.

"You're all set," she blurted, thrusting the paper toward him without daring to meet his eyes. "Here's . . . uh . . . the password." As their fingers grazed, Priya caught the fresh scent of soap on his skin.

"Thanks, Pri," he said, grabbing his phone and entering the password.

The way he slipped into using her nickname felt effortless, like falling into step with each other again. An unexpected flush bloomed across Priya's cheeks, the casual familiarity affecting her as if he had said something far more intimate.

"I'll be on my way," she said, gathering her things. Reaching for the door, she congratulated herself for successfully laying the groundwork for what was to come. Before she could leave, however, Ethan's voice stopped her in her tracks.

"Wait a minute," he said, glued to his phone.

Priya's heart sank, her mind racing with the possibility of being discovered.

"Looks like I've got a delivery arriving today," Ethan continued. "I put it in your name, so you'll need to sign for it."

"Of course." Priya released her grip on her phone, the incriminating app burning like embers in her palm.

A flutter of nervous excitement buzzed through her veins as she left the coach house. Her plan to drive Ethan away was now in motion. She accessed the remote-control app and set off one of the sequences she had programmed. Then backtracking to the coach house, she knocked lightly on the door and stepped back inside.

"Forgot to ask," she said, leaning casually against the door. "How was your first night?"

"Funny you should ask," Ethan replied, his brow creasing. "I slept well enough last night. No sign of Bhooa masi, but the strangest thing just happened. The light by the entrance came on by itself. Then the lights across the room began to turn on one by one. And just as quickly, they all went out. Except for this one." He motioned toward the floor lamp.

"Ah, yes." Priya nodded. "Sometimes Bhooa masi resorts to other ways of making her presence known during the day. Lights going on and off, static on the TV, strange noises . . . You know, the usual paranormal activities."

"Interesting." Ethan walked around the lamp, his eyes searching for a more logical explanation.

Priya wished Ethan would just embrace his inner scaredy-cat and run for the hills. But she wasn't worried; this was just the tip of the iceberg. The stage was set, and the game had just begun. If that meant facing off against the devil, even one as tempting as a Hollywood star, then so be it.

Back in her room, Priya unleashed another sequence of supernatural lights on Ethan. It would be even more fun at night, but knowing she had the power to make Ethan jump with a flick of her fingers filled her with naughty delight.

As she settled back in her chair, an unexpected message from her ex popped up on her screen. She hadn't heard from him since arriving back home.

Sorry to bug you, but I'm having a hard time integrating a new payment gateway into a client's site. Any chance you could lend a hand?

Intrigued, Priya opened her laptop and analyzed the code until she caught the stumbling block. She rewrote the code and tested it before replying to Manoj.

Done, she messaged, attaching the solution.

Manoj's reply appeared almost instantly. *Miss you.*

Priya stared at her screen. She knew he wasn't just referring to their professional partnership, but that didn't matter. She had no intention of revisiting the past with him.

A moment later, Manoj sent another message: *I'm working on cashing out your share of the company. I'll be in touch. Thanks.*

Priya exhaled and opened a file on her laptop, scrolling through the list of freelance contracts she'd managed to pick up since parting ways with Manoj. She quickly did the math and bit her lip. She was grateful for the work, but it wasn't enough to rebuild her life. What she needed was a fresh start, and that wasn't happening until Manoj handed over her share of the company. Being broke had backed her into a corner, forcing her into a series of compromises, including moving back in with her parents. As much as she appreciated being able to stay with them, doing so also bound her to their wishes and expectations. To reclaim her independence, she had to get back on her feet as soon as possible.

Priya's thoughts were derailed by the doorbell. Normally, Mumma would yell for her to answer it, but ever since last night's sangeet, her parents hadn't been speaking much to her. Silence had always been their favorite form of control—cold, heavy, and impossible to ignore. Growing up, Priya and her sisters had learned that their parents wielded it both as a weapon and a shield. All she could do was wait it out until their anger had cooled.

With a weary sigh, Priya made her way downstairs and answered the door.

"Priya Solanki?" a man in a delivery uniform asked, glancing at the screen of his handheld device.

"Yes, that's me."

"Special delivery. I'm going to need some ID."

"Sure, I'll be right back," Priya said, heading back upstairs. *Crazy that Ethan can't even use his name for something as simple as a delivery. What other compromises does he have to make?*

The delivery man checked Priya's ID and then motioned for her to follow him outside. As soon as she saw the brand-new motorcycle parked beside a transport truck, her jaw dropped. It was a dead ringer for Ethan's old bike, complete with a matching helmet.

She scribbled her signature on the paperwork, her mind still spinning. As the truck rumbled away, Mumma descended on

Priya. Still angry from their argument the night before, her voice escalated to a new level.

"*Aa su?*" Her hands flew to her hips. "You bought a *motorcycle*?"

"Actually, Mrs. Solanki, I did," Ethan's smooth voice interjected.

Mumma and Priya whirled around.

"Oh, how lovely it is!" Mumma's hands quickly relocated to her chest, her change of tune about as subtle as a Bollywood dance number at a funeral.

"Glad you approve," Ethan replied, his lips curling into a grin. "Let's see how she sounds, shall we?"

Mounting the motorcycle, he revved the engine, unleashing a deep rumble that vibrated through Priya's shoes. She barely had time to wince before the funeral home door swung open and Puppa stepped out.

Uh-oh, she thought.

"My apologies, Mr. Solanki." Ethan killed the engine and climbed off the motorcycle with a sheepish smile. "It seems I've once again disturbed the peace with my bike."

"Not at all," Puppa said. "Moksha is officially closed. I was just meeting with the contractors." He gestured toward the van parked nearby. "They'll be tearing out the old wiring, then moving on with the rest of the renovations."

"More noise," Ethan remarked.

"Well, not for another two weeks. That's the earliest they can get to it. Some areas may be off-limits while the crew is here, but I'll make sure it doesn't interfere with your plans."

"I have plenty of commitments I can handle off-site on those days. As long as my privacy isn't compromised, it's all good."

"Of course," Puppa replied, but then his expression changed. "Should I have them sign something? A confidentiality agreement?"

"That's probably a good idea," Ethan said, slowly nodding his head. "I'll have my assistant look after it." Shifting his attention back to his new motorcycle, Ethan caught Mumma checking out the saddle. "I apologize, Mrs. Solanki, if the leather offends you."

Priya winced, knowing her made-up story claiming her parents hated leather was about to fall apart.

Mumma waved off his concern. "I was just admiring how neat the stitching is. Our car's seats are leather too. Secondhand car, so we didn't have much of a choice. But thank you for being so considerate."

Ethan tilted his head toward Priya, and when their eyes met, he raised an eyebrow. He'd caught on to her lie, and she could already sense payback brewing. She glanced at her parents, but they were too busy admiring the bike to notice. Had it actually belonged to Priya, frugality would rear its penny-pinching head, and both parents would probably have passed out on the spot.

"I've never been on a motorcycle before," Mumma confessed.

"Is that so?" Ethan replied. "How would you like to join me for a ride?"

"Oh, no!" Mumma declared, shaking her head. "Motorcycle riding at my age? *Baap re.* Maybe in another life."

"Ah, Mrs. Solanki." Ethan grinned. "You've ruined my winning streak. It's been a while since someone turned me down."

Priya watched in amazement as Mumma's cheeks bloomed with a full-on blush.

"What an idea." She laughed self-consciously. "Me refusing you."

"I can tell there's an adventurer in you, Mrs. Solanki, and now's her chance to shine. What do you say?"

Priya snorted quietly. *Adventurer? Please. Mumma got nervous switching brands of atta.*

"Without a helmet?" Puppa cut in. The Solankis weren't exactly thrill-seekers—they approached new things with plenty of hesitation and a whole lot of caution.

"She can wear mine," Ethan offered. "It won't fit perfectly, but we'll just go for a quick spin around the grounds."

Puppa gave a hesitant nod, and Priya waited for her mother to dismiss the idea—a predictable *No, thank you*. Instead, Mumma's face lit up like a sunflower turning toward the light.

Priya blinked in surprise, watching as Ethan secured the helmet under Mumma's chin and helped her onto the bike.

"Don't be shy. Hold on tight," he said, glancing over his shoulder. "Ready?"

"Ready." Mumma's voice was a blend of fright and delight. She wore a cardigan over her salwar khameez, her dupatta tucked securely to keep it from fluttering in the wind.

With a reassuring nod, Ethan turned the engine on. Mumma let out a gasp. Her hands, perched like timid sparrows on his shoulders, suddenly bear-hugged the life out of him.

Taking off slowly, Ethan guided the bike along the winding paths of the property, weaving around flower beds bursting with the orange and yellow marigolds her parents planted each year. Mumma squealed as they veered left, then right.

"She's having fun," Puppa said, the frosty tension between him and Priya thawing as they watched.

"Yeah . . ." Priya shook her head with a smile. "Would you look at that?"

Mumma's nerves melted, and her grip relaxed. She wasn't just tolerating the ride. She was loving it! Eventually, Ethan steered the motorcycle back to its starting point. Glowing with excitement, Mumma thanked Ethan and dismounted.

"Rakesh, that was incredible!" she said excitedly to Puppa. Priya glimpsed a completely different side of her mother—a woman with a spark for life, not just the strict parent she'd always known. It made Mumma feel far more relatable than Priya had ever imagined.

"Priya, did you see me?" Mumma nudged her daughter with her elbow, a sign that she'd moved past their argument.

"I did, Mumma. You looked like you were having a blast." Priya looked over at Ethan and gave him a grin, part gratitude and part surprise.

Mumma turned to Ethan, her eyes shining. "I will have Priya bring you a special lunch tray," she said, eager to spoil him the only way she knew—with food.

Ethan smiled but shook his head. "Thanks, Mrs. Solanki, but I think I'll just stick with dinner. You've filled up my fridge so well, I'm good to handle breakfast and lunch on my own." Then, noticing Mumma's disappointed expression, Ethan quickly said, "But I'd love to join you for dinner."

Mumma and Puppa shared a brief, uncertain look—they both had assumed Ethan's meals would be delivered to the coach house.

"We'd be honored to host you," Puppa said hesitantly, "but our home is far more modest than the kind of places you're probably used to. If you don't mind, we'll dine in Moksha's hospitality room."

"Your home is more genuine and inviting than many places I've been to," Ethan said. "Dinner at your table would be a real treat."

Priya was caught off guard by the softness in Ethan's tone. He didn't sound like he was just being polite. He sounded . . . grateful. As if he really meant it. Her chest felt strangely tight, and when her eyes met his, her heart stumbled all over again.

Puppa and Mumma glowed with quiet pride. "Then it's settled," Puppa said. "We'll see you upstairs this evening."

"Excellent," Ethan replied. "Now, if you'll excuse me, I'm off to test my new wheels. Want to hop on, Priya?"

Before Priya could respond, Puppa intervened. "I think my family has already taken up enough of your time."

Ethan looked at Priya with a hint of surprise. He hadn't expected her father to speak for her. Still, he waited until Priya gave him a tiny shake of her head. Hosting Ethan came with a to-do list a mile long, and she knew her parents needed her help to pull off dinner tonight.

Looking slightly disappointed, Ethan fastened his helmet and pulled the visor over his face. Its glossy surface hid his face and mirrored the scene around him—the gray building, the tulips bordering the driveway, the three figures looking on. Gravel crunched under his tires as he guided the bike toward the driveway. Then, revving the engine, he let the motor growl before taking off in a blur of motion. The hum of his motorcycle faded as he sped away. Mumma, Puppa, and Priya remained rooted, as if enchanted by a lingering cloud of stardust.

Standing beside her parents, Priya couldn't help but notice the smiles on their faces. Ethan had brought new energy into their lives and to Moksha, a spark of excitement they hadn't felt in a long time. She wondered what her parents would say if they knew how she felt about him, how she'd always felt. To them, the idea of something romantic between her and Ethan wasn't just far-fetched, it was absurd. He wasn't simply an outsider. He existed in an entirely different world.

Yet in his presence, Priya's world transformed into a kaleidoscope of sensations. When their eyes met, goose bumps swept over her. His voice electrified her. Her pulse raced whenever he was around. The years had only intensified her attraction to him. But even as she felt it all so deeply, Priya knew their time together right now was nothing more than a brief intersection. Once Ethan left Moksha, their worlds would drift apart again. All Priya had to do was hold herself together until then. She had already lost her marriage and her career. Her heart was all she had left, and if she wasn't careful, it would be the next casualty.

Eight

THE SOLANKIS WENT ALL OUT to get their house ready for Ethan's visit that evening. Mumma shifted into makeover mode, cleaning and decluttering, while Puppa polished the floors and wiped down every surface to a gleaming shine. Priya bounced between rooms—chopping vegetables, folding napkins into neat triangles, and scrubbing the bathroom until it sparkled. Not a single dust bunny survived. By the time they sat down for dinner, the energy felt different than it had during Ethan's first visit. Her parents were more prepared, though Puppa's excitement was bubbling over.

"That car chase in your second movie? Unbelievable," he gushed. "The way you raced through those alleyways, intercepted the kidnapper, and nailed that drift? Smooth as ghee sliding off a hot dosa. *Eni ma ne!*"

Priya cringed, not just because he'd just switched languages but because he had used a phrase that loosely translated to "Motherfucker!"

"Rakesh," Mumma whispered, nudging him to reel it in. "We love your films, Ethan. You remind me of a Bollywood hero from my childhood—Amitabh Bachchan. He was always going *dishoom-dishoom*, fighting off villains, just like you." She threw some playful punches in the air. "Good thing you're not accident porn."

Ethan's eyebrows shot up, and Priya quickly jumped in. "She means accident *prone*."

Ethan's laughter filled the room. "Well, I've played many roles, but I can't say I've ever accidentally dropped my pants."

Mumma's and Puppa's faces turned vermilion. They cleared the table and disappeared into the kitchen in record time.

Ethan turned to Priya. "Did I just step on a cultural land mine?"

"They get awkward around anything remotely sexual. Puppa dives for the remote whenever there's a kissing scene, and Mumma rushes off to the bathroom. When we were kids, the second there was any intimacy on-screen, it was automatic bedtime for me and my sisters. So, when you mentioned dropping your pants—"

"Mr. Ethan," Mumma called from the kitchen. "Would you like some dessert or tea?"

"Thank you, Mrs. Solanki, but I'm completely stuffed," Ethan replied. "The food was absolutely incredible."

"You must at least try some shrikhand." Mumma's voice bubbled with delight.

"Here." Puppa placed a bowl before Ethan. "It's like Greek yogurt but with saffron, sugar, and a hint of cardamom."

Priya went into the kitchen where her mother was filling teacups with chai. She took one and went back to the table where Puppa and Ethan were digging into their shrikhand.

"Here's your chai, Puppa." Setting the cup in front of him, she returned to her seat. Mumma joined them at the table, carrying her own bowl of shrikhand and a cup of tea for Priya. As she sat down, the lights flickered overhead. Puppa gave Mumma a quick look. When she gave a small nod—as if granting permission—Priya frowned. *What's going on?* Her father straightened and cleared his throat.

"Since we're all here, there's something I'd like to ask you, Mr. Ethan," he said.

"Please, call me Ethan," Ethan said, putting down his spoon and smiling at Priya's parents.

"Mr. Ethan," Puppa continued, unwilling to equalize his standing with Ethan, "given that this is the first time we're closing Moksha, Seema and I thought it would be the perfect opportunity to go on a holiday. We want to visit our youngest daughter, Deepa, who is studying in Windsor. And after that, we'd like to spend some time with my brother, Vinod, and his family. Our other daughter, Meghna, is in India right now, so we won't get to see her. But Priya will stay back to make sure everything runs smoothly while you're here." He glanced at Priya who sat frozen, stunned into silence. *They're taking off and leaving* me *here to look after Ethan?*

"We just want to make sure you're okay with us going away before we finalize anything," her father continued. "We'll be back in two weeks before the renovations begin."

A wave of anger welled up inside Priya before she could stop it. It wasn't that she minded her parents taking a holiday. They absolutely deserved it. The issue was that they just assumed she'd step in, like she had nothing better to do than play bed-and-breakfast manager to Ethan.

"Hang on a second," she cut in. "You never talked to me about this."

"We didn't think it would be an issue," Puppa replied, surprised. "It's only two weeks. Mumma is going to freeze all the meals, so you don't even have to worry about cooking."

"We've stocked up on all the essentials, Priya," Mumma chimed in. "I'll prepare plenty of snacks and make sure you have a fresh supply of linens and towels for Mr. Ethan."

"And I've already notified everyone that the funeral home is closed. You won't have to handle a single thing," Puppa added.

It was a well-oiled plan that left Priya with no excuses. She glanced at Ethan, who was quietly watching the exchange. She was certain that Puppa and Mumma hadn't just sprung this on her randomly. They had planned it, counting on Ethan's presence to defuse any tension. How could she object with him sitting there?

Her temper threatened to boil over, but then a realization hit her. She could turn this to her advantage. With her parents out of the way, she could get rid of Ethan without their interference. By the time they found out, it would already be done. *Two could play that game.*

"Great," Priya said with a bright smile. "I'm all in. As long as it's okay with you?" She looked at Ethan.

Ethan glanced between her and her parents. "Of course it's okay with me," he replied. "I'll certainly miss the pleasure of your company"—he nodded toward Puppa and Mumma—"but I'm sure Priya will cater to my every whim."

Priya felt heat rise in her chest, but before she could reply, her father clapped his hands together.

"Then it's settled," he said. "We'll leave the day after tomorrow."

Priya felt Ethan's eyes on her, and the moment their gazes locked, it was as if the entire room vanished, leaving only the two of them. She quickly lowered her eyes to her teacup, her heart hammering in her chest. *Two weeks alone with Ethan.* Priya wasn't sure exactly what her parents had just set into motion, but even with her determination to get rid of Ethan, she knew she'd be walking a tightrope.

The lights flickered, as if echoing the tension in the air.

"I can't wait for this to get sorted out," Mumma said, looking up at the ceiling. "Every time the lights go out, I have to reset everything."

"The lights in the coach house have been acting up too," Ethan noted.

Priya's foot tapped a soundless confession of guilt under the table. Her plan to convince Ethan that something spooky was going on was starting to work.

"That's strange," Puppa said, his brow furrowing. "The coach house is on its own grid, separate from the main building. You shouldn't be having any issues."

"It doesn't seem random. Not the way it's happening here," Ethan replied. "There's a definite pattern to the way the lights turn on and off. I can't help but think it may have something to do with Bhooa masi."

"You have a masi too?" Mumma's face lit up. "I have six masis, of which only Manjula masi and Kokila masi remain. When they get on the phone, there is no end to the gossip. But tell me about your masi. Where does she—"

"Oh, look!" Priya interrupted, pointing to the sideboard. "The lottery ticket you bought last week is still sitting there, Puppa."

"Ah. I completely forgot." Puppa's eyes gleamed as he reached for it. "You know, Mr. Ethan, this is the best five dollars I spend every Friday. It buys me an entire week of dreams."

Ethan chose that moment to excuse himself and rose from his seat. "I'll leave you to it, Mr. Solanki," he said. "Thank you for a wonderful evening, Mrs. Solanki."

"Leaving so soon?" Mumma asked.

Priya rolled her eyes. Had Ethan stayed until sunrise, she would've asked the same question. In true Gujarati style, no guest could leave without a token protest, even if the host was secretly rooting for them to leave. It was an intricate dance of goodbyes where lingering was expected and every departure was met with ceremonial resistance.

"I'll be back to celebrate if your numbers win," Ethan said with a playful grin.

Puppa chuckled, rising to walk him to the door. "You are our lucky charm, Mr. Ethan. You've already saved us from having to close down."

"Oh, wait!" Mumma exclaimed, her voice bright with excitement. She hurried to her room and returned a few moments later with something gripped in her hand.

"I have a little gift for you. A token of good luck and protection. And a small thank-you for the ride today." She held out a key chain with a miniature figure of an elephant-headed Hindu deity. "This is Lord Ganesh. We pray to him to bless new beginnings and remove obstacles. He'll keep you safe on your new motorcycle."

Ethan took the key chain with a slight bow of his head. "Thank you, Mrs. Solanki. That's very thoughtful."

Mumma's eyes sparkled as she clasped her hands together.

"Good night, Mr. Ethan," Puppa said. "Priya will see you out. She might as well begin her hosting duties before we leave." Priya shot him a withering look, but he just shrugged innocently.

"Good night," Ethan replied, before following Priya down the stairs. She felt his gaze like a weight on her back. "Looks like I've become your official responsibility, Pri," he said under his breath so only she could hear. "Just so you know, I fully intend to take advantage of the situation."

A shiver rippled down Priya's spine and her skin tingled, including parts of her that had no business joining the party.

As they reached the door, she spun to face him. "We'll see who ends up taking advantage of who," she said with a sly grin.

"Are you flirting with me, Priya Solanki?" Ethan asked, his voice dipping into a playful drawl.

Priya's fingers clenched the doorknob a little tighter, her eyes flashing with the mischief she had planned for him. "Keep dreaming, Heathen Knight," she said. But there was no mistaking the smug glint in Ethan's expression—he definitely thought she was flirting.

And maybe she was. Just a teensy-weensy bit.

He stepped closer, his breath stirring the loose tendrils of hair around her face. "Oh, I will," he murmured, his lips grazing her ear. "Good night, Pri."

Heat rose in her cheeks, her heart thudding so loudly, she wondered if he could hear it. This wasn't just playful teasing anymore. This was unmistakable. Ethan Knight was showing interest in her. How was this even happening? Priya pressed her hand against the doorframe.

Inhale. Exhale.

As Ethan stepped outside, she couldn't resist stealing a quick glance at him. *If that booty were a movie, it would totally kick ass at the box office.* Catching herself, Priya gave her head a small shake. *Nope. Not going there. Stick to the plan. Project Bye-Bye Knight isn't going to execute itself.*

"There's a full moon tonight," Priya called out after him. "All the ghosts and goblins are out to play. You might want to watch your back."

Ethan paused, half turning to look at her. "I don't have to." He grinned. "Not when you're already doing it for me." He turned and walked away, his shadow stretching across the path to the coach house.

Priya locked the door and sagged against it, taking a moment to collect herself before facing her parents again. But the ridiculous smile on her face refused to fade. Reluctantly, she pushed herself off the door and headed back upstairs.

As she helped Mumma and Puppa tidy up, Priya's attention shifted to the envelope containing the offer to purchase Moksha. With her parents leaving, she could clear the path and stall the renovations. Starting with Ethan. He was dreamy and captivating but a complication she didn't need.

Or did she?

The warmth of his breath on her skin came rushing back, the low timbre of his voice, the cheeky grin that stirred something entirely inconvenient in her.

Priya glanced at her parents. They had no idea how they had turned her world upside down, first by accepting Ethan Knight's offer and now by leaving her alone with him. She should have been annoyed—and she *was*—but beneath that, a new thought bloomed. Why shouldn't she make the most of it? Why couldn't she stick to her plan *and* have a little fun while she was at it?

This wasn't just any man. This was Ethan Knight—a walking, talking adrenaline shot. The kind of thrill you'd never find in the everyday slog of life. She was at rock bottom, freshly divorced, trying to piece her life together. And now life had dropped Ethan, of all people, straight into her lap. He was her first crush, her teenage obsession—and by some miracle, he seemed into her too. It was too perfect to pass up. What better way to bounce back from her divorce than by turning her fantasy into reality?

Nine

PRIYA WAITED UNTIL the apartment fell silent and her parents were fast asleep. Then, flashlight in hand, she eased open the door and stepped out into the cool night. Moonlight filtered through the trees, creating soft patches of light as she made her way to the coach house.

The stone building stood still and dark, its walls blending into the shadows. Riffling through the keys she had nabbed earlier, Priya let herself in through the side entrance that led to the storage area. The door opened with a mournful creak.

Inside, the air hit her like a wave, thick with the solemn scent of ashes and aged wood. A pang of familiarity swept over her, stirring childhood memories. She recalled the smell that clung to Puppa when he returned from the crematorium, covered in a fine layer of dust. It was a scent rooted in her family's traditions, hanging in the air like a phantom that refused to fade.

Priya's flashlight cut through the darkness, over rows of unclaimed cremated remains. Scanning the area, she spotted the exposed pipe she was looking for. Clenching the flashlight between her teeth, she stepped onto a shelf and climbed higher until she could reach it. Steadying herself with one hand, she struck the flashlight's metal body against the pipe again and again. Each clang reverberated through the coach house, hollow and eerie, like the tread of a shackled soul.

A sly grin tugged at Priya's lips as she pictured Ethan bolting out of bed, his unflappable confidence shattered by the ghostly racket. Just as she was hitting her stride, the door flung open. Startled, she lost her footing, arms flailing for balance. Her hand shot out, grabbing an urn on the shelf, but it slipped from her fingers as she toppled backward. Priya landed hard on her backside, and the urn bounced off her head, its lid popping open.

A cloud of ashes burst into the air, covering Priya from head to toe with the remnants of someone long gone. Fine powder clung to her eyelashes, and she could taste the dust in her mouth.

Ethan stood in the doorway, momentarily frozen.

"Hello?" he called, his voice cutting through the ash hanging in the air.

Priya managed a hoarse reply before giving in to a sharp burst of coughing.

"Priya?" Ethan felt his way along the wall, searching for the light switch before turning it on. Seeing her, he asked, "What on earth are you doing here?"

"I . . . uh . . ." Priya sputtered as he helped her to her feet. Her eyes darted around, finally landing on the empty urn. "I came for this," she said, snatching it up.

"At this time of the night?"

"It's an emergency," Priya blurted.

"An emergency ash retrieval?"

"Yes, actually." Her eyes dropped to the label on the urn. "This person's brother contacted us to claim the remains. He's coming to pick them up first thing in the morning."

Ethan took the container from her hands. "Babulal Gupta," he read. "It says he passed away thirty years ago, aged eighty-nine. You're telling me his brother is still alive?"

"Did I say brother?" Priya backtracked. "I meant his brother's family. Specifically, his brother's son. So, Babulal's nephew. His younger brother's eldest—"

"Priya." Ethan pressed his finger against her lips. "Let's get Babulal off you. And me," he muttered, noticing the ash on his finger.

Equally eager to rid herself of Babulal, Priya followed Ethan out.

"That was quite the tumble," Ethan said, glancing at her. "Are you okay? Why didn't you just turn the light on?"

"I didn't want to disturb you," she lied.

"Oh, and all that noise didn't disturb me?"

"What noise?"

"The banging and clanging. Christ, Pri, I thought an army of the undead was coming alive."

"I didn't hear anything," she said innocently.

"How could you not? It was practically shaking the walls."

"Maybe it's something *in* the walls?" Priya offered with a shrug. "I did warn you, didn't I?"

"Well, I'm still waiting to meet this Bhooa masi of yours," Ethan replied, letting her into the coach house.

As the door clicked shut behind them, Priya's thoughts spun in a hundred directions. *What now?* Her attempt to spook Ethan had gone sideways. He didn't look the least bit rattled. In fact, he seemed as calm and collected as ever. And then it hit her. This didn't have to be a total loss. She was alone with Ethan Knight in the middle of the night. It was the perfect setup for her *other* plan—a fun, thrilling, casual fling to hit the reset button in her life. This was her chance to be bold, spontaneous, and a little reckless.

"Do you mind if I hop in the shower?" Priya asked, her heart thudding in her chest. If she was going to take advantage of this moment, she needed to act fast.

"Oh, I insist," Ethan replied, gesturing toward the trail of powdery prints her shoes had left behind.

Priya offered a small, sheepish smile, slipped off her shoes, and headed to the bathroom. Once inside, she shut the door and leaned against it, taking a deep breath.

Okay, step one complete, she thought, peeling off her dusty clothes. She'd found an excuse to hang around.

As Priya scrubbed her skin and worked shampoo through her hair, a pool of grime collected around her feet. *Gross.* She shuddered and rinsed out her mouth. If there was even the tiniest chance of a kiss, she wasn't about to let Ethan taste Babulal on her lips. A mix of nerves and excitement coursed through her as she plotted her next move. She didn't want to be obvious, but she couldn't play it too safe either. The balance had to be perfect. Flirty but not desperate, confident but not over the top.

Turning off the water, Priya reached for the towel and froze. The rack was empty. A soft laugh escaped her as she realized that fate had already handed her the next move.

Poking her head around the edge of the stall, she called, "Ethan? Can you grab me a towel?"

"Sure thing."

Priya's heart raced as she waited. The steam from the shower clung to her skin, but it wasn't the heat that made her feel lightheaded. *Why does this feel so huge?*

When the knock came, it jolted her like a shock wave.

Aaand action, her inner director announced.

"Just, um, leave it on the counter?" she found herself saying. Suddenly, the idea of stepping out of the shower, wet and naked, sent her stomach into a wild tumble. She needed a second to pull herself together, to shake off the heat prickling at the back of her neck.

Ethan's silhouette appeared through the misty glass as he stepped into the bathroom, the weight of his presence filling the room. Priya expected him to leave after setting the towel down, but he didn't. He paused, close enough for the space between them to feel electric.

Priya swallowed, her mind racing.

What is he doing?

Is he waiting for me to invite him in?

What if he slides the shower door open and steps inside?

Am I ready for Ethan Knight to see me naked?

I haven't shaved.

Oh lord.

The silence stretched, charged and heavy, making her cheeks burn.

And then Ethan's shadow retreated, and the door clicked softly behind him.

Priya let out a shaky breath, her hand flying to her chest as if to keep her heart from bursting through her ribs.

What is wrong with me? she thought, half laughing at herself, half wishing she'd done something, *anything*, different.

She finished drying off and looked for her clothes, but they were nowhere to be found. Spotting Ethan's T-shirt on the hook, she put it on. As she twisted her wet hair into a towel on top of her head, his scent wrapped around her—a spicy, clean mix of cologne and something that was undeniably him.

Stepping out of the bathroom, Priya's eyes searched for Ethan. The faint hum of the washing machine caught her ear, and she stopped in her tracks.

Oh. He'd been collecting her clothes in the bathroom. While she'd been gearing up for a swoon-worthy Hollywood moment, Ethan had been doing something thoughtful. The gesture left her warm and fuzzy, a soft glow blooming in her chest.

The sound of running water led Priya to the kitchen, where Ethan stood by the stove, leaning over a saucepan. It wasn't until she got closer that she noticed how little he had on. In his rush to check on the earlier commotion, he'd only managed to throw on a loose shirt over his boxers.

Priya's gaze swept over him. The way his sleeves were pushed up to reveal his forearms. The set of his shoulders. The solid lines of his legs. She swallowed, her thoughts drifting to how his skin might feel under her fingers, or how warm his neck might be if she leaned in to kiss it.

As if sensing her presence, Ethan turned around.

"Hot chocolate?" he asked, but the words faltered as his eyes landed on her, and he did a quick double take.

He took in her oversized T-shirt—*his* T-shirt—the neckline slipping slightly to reveal one shoulder. The hem grazed the tops of her thighs, leaving her legs bare and exposed. Her hair was twisted into a towel, but the strands framing her face caught the light with shimmering beads of water. The fabric did little to hide her nipples, leaving no doubt that Priya wasn't wearing anything underneath.

"Is this a secret strategy to get guys to do more laundry? Because it's working." Ethan's voice had a teasing edge, but Priya caught the subtle flicker of his throat as he swallowed.

It's working, she thought. *I have his attention.* She felt both powerful and on edge. Could she truly handle a fling with *him*?

"Well, if it works, who am I to argue?" she said, lifting her chin, enjoying the way he was looking at her. Inside, she was practically vibrating, her skin buzzing under his gaze. "Thanks for looking after my clothes," she said, taking the mug he held out. Spinning on her heel, she made her way to the couch.

Enjoy the rear view, Ethan Knight.

She curled up in the corner and took a sip from her cup, her pulse spiking as Ethan wandered over and settled beside her on the cushions, propping his legs up on the ottoman.

"Don't thank me just yet." Ethan leaned back, regarding her. "I haven't done laundry in years. There was no option for human remains, so I picked the steam cycle. Let's hope your delicates don't disintegrate."

Priya opened her mouth but forgot how words worked the moment his shirt shifted. The fabric slid open, baring his chest. Her fingers clenched around the mug. *Easy girl, easy. Let it build. Let it simmer.*

Except her thoughts were racing faster than a Bollywood hero chasing a runaway train. Her eyes flicked to Ethan's bare skin.

"Have you talked to Brooke lately?" she asked, shifting to safer ground.

"Not in the last few days," Ethan replied. "Have you?"

"We talked yesterday. She mentioned Lady Whiskerbottom isn't doing too well."

Ethan chuckled. "My sister's cat is older than dirt. She's been around since Pluto was a planet."

Priya gasped. "Don't be mean! You know how much Brooke loves that cat."

"Truth be told, I'm not a fan, and she can't stand me either. I'm pretty sure she deliberately creates chaos every time Brooke visits. It's like she wants all the attention for herself."

"Sounds like a classic case of jealousy," Priya teased.

Ethan opened his mouth to respond, but his phone suddenly rang on the couch between him. The screen flashed *Babydoll calling*. He dismissed it with a quick swipe, but Priya's brow furrowed. *Babydoll?*

"Who was that?" she asked, trying to keep her tone light. If Ethan had a girlfriend, her whole fling idea was out the window.

"Sienna Deville," he replied. "My costar in the last film I worked on, which hasn't been released yet."

"Do all your costars call you in the middle of the night?" The words tumbled out before Priya could stop herself.

"Don't tell me you're jealous." Ethan's lips curled into an amused smile.

"Just curious," she replied, keeping her face neutral. But deep down, Priya wasn't feeling so neutral. If there was even the smallest possibility that Ethan was involved with someone else, she had to know.

"Just curious, huh?" he repeated. "We worked together on the movie, that's all."

"Then why does her name come up as 'Babydoll' on your phone?" Priya asked.

"Because that's her character's name in the film."

"Oh." It sounded innocent enough, but something still nagged at her. "And she couldn't wait until normal business hours to call you?"

"Am I seeing a little green-eyed monster over there?" He reached out, swiped his thumb across Priya's cheek, and held it up. "Yep. Green as fuck," he announced. "We're settling this right now. Heads up!" He grabbed a cushion and flung it at her.

Priya caught it instinctively, but before she could respond, another one came flying, knocking the towel off her head.

"Seriously?" she shouted, her hair whipping loose. "You did *not* just start a pillow fight!" She picked up the cushion that had just hit her and took aim. Her strike landed squarely on Ethan's face, leaving him momentarily stunned. He turned to her with deliberate slowness.

"Oh, now you've done it," he declared, lunging at her.

Priya shrieked, leaping to her knees to block his attack. Their cushions smacked together with loud, satisfying thuds. Priya grinned as she landed a solid hit.

"Gotcha!" she shouted, earning an exaggerated groan from Ethan before he launched another round of rapid-fire swings that nearly knocked her over.

They were laughing so hard they could barely breathe when Ethan suddenly stopped. The cushion slipped from his hands, and he froze.

"What is it?" Priya blinked. Then she followed his gaze and realized her T-shirt had slipped completely off her shoulder, baring the top of her breast. For a moment, neither of them moved. The air charged between them, their playfulness giving way to something volatile and dangerously close to breaking loose.

"Admit it, Priya," Ethan said, his voice rougher now. "You've always wanted me."

"You wish," she shot back, but the words came out unsteady.

"If you're really indifferent, then you'll feel absolutely nothing when I do this." His hand lifted, and with deliberate slowness, he traced a line down the side of her throat.

Priya felt the shiver but refused to give him the satisfaction of a reaction.

"Huh," he said, pretending not to notice the goose bumps that betrayed her. "Let's try this then?" He leaned in, his hand moving to her hair. His fingers ran through her damp hair, gliding from the roots down to the tips.

Priya's scalp tingled. She clenched her fists, trying to keep it together. *This is really happening*. Ethan was touching her like he couldn't get enough. This was what she had wanted, what she had planned, but it didn't feel like she was in control at all.

Priya tried to say something snarky, but the words stuck in her throat. Ethan's fingers slowly left her hair, and for a second she thought he might pull back. Instead, his hand found her cheek, brushing her skin with surprising tenderness.

"Still no reaction?" he murmured, his eyes holding hers like he knew exactly what he was doing to her.

"This isn't fair," she blurted, sinking back onto the couch.

Ethan leaned in, one hand braced beside her as he loomed overhead. "What's not fair?" he asked, one brow lifting.

"You're playing dirty," she whispered hoarsely.

"Dirty? Oh, Priya, I haven't even started playing with you yet." His thumb glided over her wrist, sending a spark of sensation up her arm.

Priya's eyelids fluttered, her body rising to meet his touch like the tide under the moon. He hovered above her, infuriatingly composed, as if he had all the time in the world to watch her come undone.

"Say it, Priya," he whispered. "Say you want me."

Priya reached out, her fingers grazing his shirt, but he pulled away before she could close the gap.

"You have to say it." His expression softened as he cradled her face in his hands. "I need clear verbal consent."

It hit Priya all at once. Of course he needed to protect himself. He wasn't just Ethan. He was *Ethan Knight*, and all that fame came at a price. In his world, even a kiss wasn't just a kiss. It could escalate into rumors and controversy.

Priya felt the weight of his caution, but beneath it, she felt the edges of his restraint fraying. This was her moment, her chance to take exactly what she wanted.

"I want you," she said.

Ethan stilled, his eyes searching her expression. "And what exactly are you saying yes to, Priya? Because I remember a girl who believed that one kiss meant picking out a wedding dress."

Priya let out a soft laugh. "Been there, done that. And look how it turned out. I'm not that girl anymore, Ethan. Remember—you're dealing with Priya 2.0 now. No strings, no expectations. I'm saying yes to a good time, not a lifetime. Think you can handle that?"

Ethan tilted his head, studying her like he was trying to make sure she really meant it. "You really are full of surprises," he murmured, his gaze dropping to her lips.

When he kissed her, it was like nothing Priya had prepared herself for. His lips were soft and unhurried, like he was giving her the chance to pull back. But Priya didn't pull back. She kissed him harder, her fingers tangling into his shirt, holding on like she might float away.

The world faded into a distant haze. All Priya could feel was the heat of Ethan's mouth, the weight of his body on hers, the way her heart thundered like it had been waiting for this moment her entire life. Ethan's hands moved down her back, pulling her flush against him. The quiet, raspy sound he let out made her knees go weak. No daydream could have ever prepared her for this moment. It was alive, vivid, electric, like being caught in the swirling colors of Holi. When Ethan's hand slid up her thigh, her breath hitched, heat curling deep inside her.

The phone rang again. Ethan didn't seem to notice, his lips moving along her jaw, his stubble grazing her skin. But the name *Babydoll* flashed in Priya's mind, and this time, she couldn't push it aside. What if Ethan was lying to her?

Her hands pressed against his chest, pushing him back. "Ethan, stop."

He froze, his lips lingering on her skin for just a beat before he pulled back. "What's wrong?" he asked, his breath uneven.

"I changed my mind." She tugged the T-shirt down over her thighs.

His brows furrowed, hands falling to his sides. "What's going on?"

The phone buzzed again, loud and persistent.

"You should probably get that," she said, glancing at it before getting up.

The phone kept buzzing, but Ethan remained silent, too stunned to react as he watched her walk to the door.

Priya put on her shoes, her fingers gripping the doorknob as she steadied herself. Without looking back, she stepped outside, shutting the door behind her. The night air hit her bare skin, and she shivered, pulling Ethan's T-shirt tighter around her as she walked briskly back to the apartment.

A wave of relief swept through her as she walked through the door and locked it behind her. Her parents were still asleep, blissfully unaware that she'd come home wearing nothing but Ethan's T-shirt. No awkward questions, no disapproving stares, and no fumbling explanations. Thank god.

Climbing into bed, Priya stared at the ceiling, her heart still pounding. Her grand plan to have a fling with the biggest movie star in the world had fizzled before it even had a chance to take off. But maybe that was for the best. She'd gotten what she always wanted: She'd kissed Ethan Knight, living out the fantasy that had lived quietly in the back of her mind since she was a teenager. Now that it was out of her system, she could put all her energy into getting rid of him and Moksha.

But Ethan's kiss played on a loop in her mind—the way his lips felt against hers, the warmth of his hands, the way his body fit so perfectly with hers.

Priya groaned, throwing an arm over her face.

If it feels like this after one kiss, how would it feel if I was still on that couch, tangled in his arms?

The thought sent a shiver through her. And that was the problem. Ethan was too good at slipping past her defenses. A fling with him wasn't an option anymore, so she'd have to make damn sure it didn't happen again.

Ten

PRIYA DECIDED THAT avoiding Ethan was an entirely valid strategy. Over the next two days, while her parents prepared for their trip, she stayed in her room, pretending to be busy with her work. But concentrating was impossible when his voice kept sneaking into her mind.

Admit it, Priya. Say you want me.

Priya rubbed her temples, muttering under her breath, "Get out of my head, Heathen." But he didn't.

You have to say it.

Her fingers froze on the keyboard as she recalled his thumb tracing slow circles on her wrist. When she tucked her hair behind her ear, she could practically feel his fingers threading through it.

Priya typed *Sienna Deville Ethan Knight* into the search bar, her curiosity dragging her down an internet rabbit hole. *It isn't irrational. It's just research.* She had to figure out if there was truth behind her suspicions. Why else would Sienna be calling him late at night, long after their movie had finished filming?

Every article she found only added fuel to her theory. Sienna's upcoming debut alongside Ethan had already catapulted her into the spotlight. Lines like "poised for stardom" and "breakthrough performance" were everywhere. But what caught Priya's attention was the repeated mention of her "remarkable chemistry with Ethan Knight." Priya scoffed at the phrase, scowling at her screen. There wasn't any solid proof of a relationship, but there wasn't anything to put her mind at ease either. She closed yet another tab and forced herself to turn back to her work.

The sound of a suitcase rolling down the hallway snapped Priya out of her thoughts. Her parents were almost ready to leave. She rushed out of her room, only to trip over a collection of bags in the hallway. There were shopping bags worn out from countless grocery runs, two dusty suitcases with zipper-pulls long gone and replaced by safety pins, and in classic Solanki style, three potlas—makeshift bundles made from knotted bedsheets, bulging with snacks Mumma had prepared.

A tiffin peeked from a wicker basket that was filled with enough food to feed her sister for the whole week. Next to it was the inevitable thermos of chai for the journey. Judging by the mountain of luggage, you'd think her parents were setting out on a trek to the Himalayas, not a four-hour drive to Windsor to visit Deepa.

"Priya?" Mumma called from the kitchen. When Priya stepped into view, she swung the freezer door open, revealing rows of neatly packed containers. "These are all the dinners I've prepared for Mr. Ethan. Don't get so carried away on your computer that you forget to keep up with his schedule. Be attentive, okay?" She waited for Priya's nod before adding, "Now hurry and start taking the bags downstairs or we won't make it to Deepa's on time. Your father hates driving at night."

Priya grabbed two suitcases and the car keys from the table, then made her way down the stairs. She rolled the suitcases across the driveway and set them by the car. As she turned to go back inside for the remaining bags, she froze, seeing Puppa and Ethan step out of Moksha.

Warmth flooded her from the inside out as soon as she saw Ethan. Even in jeans, a T-shirt, and a baseball cap, he was impossible to ignore. The cap cast a shadow over his face, making his expression harder to read. Priya's gaze dropped to his lips, the memory of his kisses rushing back.

"Priya, I've given Mr. Ethan the entry code for the funeral home, so he can come and go as he likes," Puppa informed her. Her father had spent the whole day giving Ethan a tour of every corner of the place, including the prep room where Ethan's character was set to "wake up" for a key scene.

"Got it," Priya said, avoiding Ethan's gaze.

"Just make sure you stay on top of the phone messages in case anyone needs to get a hold of me," Puppa continued. Noticing the bags by Priya's side, he asked, "Is your mother ready to leave?"

"Almost," Priya replied. "There are a few more bags still."

"I'll go check on her." With a quick nod at Ethan, Puppa excused himself, leaving Priya alone with him.

The air immediately felt heavier. Priya fumbled with the car keys.

"You've been avoiding me." Ethan cut straight to the point.

"I've been busy," Priya said, her eyes darting everywhere but to him.

"Busy avoiding me."

"Not at all," Priya replied. "I've just had a lot to do. How about you? Hope your phone hasn't been ringing off the hook at all hours of the night." Her overly cheerful tone had a hint of snark, but she couldn't help herself.

Ethan's brow furrowed. "Hold on . . . Is *that* why you bolted? Because you thought Sienna was calling me again?"

Priya's cheeks burned, but she didn't answer. She busied herself with opening the trunk. Ethan's hand shot out, gripping her wrist.

"Why would you think something's going on with me and Sienna after I told you we're not romantically involved?"

"Because . . . Sienna's stunning and talented. Everyone's talking about your chemistry," Priya admitted with a shaky breath. "But it's not just that," she added before he could respond. "I've been there before. My ex-husband cheated on me with a client. I thought I'd moved on, but I guess I'm still carrying it around." She shrugged, finally meeting Ethan's eyes.

He let her wrist go, his expression softening. "I'm sorry you went through that. But I'm not your ex, Pri." He let out a deep breath, collecting his thoughts. "Look. I'm not in the habit of explaining myself, but that's exactly what I'm going to do. Because you're not just anyone to me, Pri. You remind me of who I was before everything changed, and that history? It's something I've only ever shared with you."

Priya nodded, swallowing hard as his words sank in.

"That call before you bolted?" He paused. "It wasn't Sienna. It was Brooke. Sienna's on location halfway across the world, in another time zone. Same as Brooke. That's just how my life works. People call at odd hours. But here's the thing," he said, holding her gaze. "I can explain myself until I'm blue in the face, but it won't matter if you're going to take off whenever something triggers you. I can't silence the doubts in your head, Priya. That's something only you can do."

Any response Priya could've offered was cut off by Puppa's return. He dropped two potlas at her feet and grinned at her and Ethan, oblivious to the tension between them.

"We're hauling more on this trip than we did when we moved from India to Canada. I've added a little extra baggage myself."

He chuckled, patting his belly, and headed back inside for the rest of the luggage.

Priya opened the trunk and reached for a suitcase, her fingers curling around the handle. Before she could lift it, Ethan took it from her hands. He loaded it into the car, then stacked the rest of the luggage to make sure everything fit.

"I'll see if your parents have more to bring," he said, disappearing into the house.

Priya stood rooted by the car, wondering how on earth she was going to drive him away when every word he said pulled her closer. Lost in thought, she was brought back to the moment by the sound of an approaching car.

A sleek black sedan, glossy as a crow's wing, pulled into the driveway, its tinted windows giving no hint of who was inside. Priya blinked in surprise when the door opened, and Ravi Tiwari stepped out. Dressed to impress, Ravi's sherwani shimmered with gold embroidery, his fitted pants giving the traditional outfit a stylish, modern edge.

"Hey." Ravi's face broke into a smile as he walked over, holding a bright red cardboard box.

"Hi, Ravi." Priya wondered if his mother was watching from the car. "What are you doing here? Shouldn't you be at your brother's wedding?"

"I'm on my way. Anand Uncle said you and your parents won't be attending?"

"That's right," Priya confirmed, gesturing toward the open trunk. "My parents are just about to leave town."

"Well, I thought I'd drop off some sweets," Ravi explained, holding out the box.

"That's very kind of you." Priya reached for the sweets, a

familiar cultural tradition for celebrating special events. "Thanks for coming by."

But Ravi held on to the box as if it were a bargaining chip. "Actually, I was . . . uh . . . wondering if I could get your phone number."

Ah, so that's what this is about, Priya mused. *Ravi found out we're not going to the wedding and used the sweets as an excuse to swing by. No way does he have time for random visits on his brother's big day.*

As she tried to come up with a response, Ethan appeared by her side. He dropped the luggage he was carrying and leveled a pointed glare at Ravi, whose gaze bounced nervously between them.

Well, this is awkward, Priya thought, clearing her throat. *Did Ethan catch Ravi asking for my number?*

"As I was saying . . ." Ravi began, but as he spoke, Ethan took off his baseball cap, adjusted it, and placed it back on his head. Ravi's jaw went slack in surprise.

"Wait. You're Ethan Knight. Oh my god," he blurted, his face a mix of shock and awe. Caught in a starstruck moment, Ravi redirected the sweets to Ethan. The box hovered awkwardly between the two men before Ethan accepted it.

"I'm Ravi Tiwari," Ravi added. "Please enjoy the sweets in honor of my brother's wedding today."

"Ravi Tiwari? As in Priya's dance partner from the other night?" Ethan asked, his eyes shifting to Priya.

"Yes, that's me." Ravi lit up, delighted that Ethan knew his name. "What brings you to Moksha?" he asked. "Is everything okay with your father?"

Ethan's brow lifted. "My father is very much alive and well."

Ravi's face turned red. "Oh no, I didn't mean . . . I wasn't implying . . ." He stumbled over his words, trying to fix the gaffe.

"No offense taken." Ethan waved it off. "I'm staying at the coach house. Keeping a low profile for a bit." He gave Ravi a look that made it clear he expected discretion.

"Absolutely, say no more!" Ravi said, his head bobbing. But Priya knew that Ravi was going to spill the beans, not only to his immediate family but to every branch, twig, and leaf of the family tree.

"Well, Ravi, thanks for these." Ethan nodded toward the sweets in his hands. His tone was polite, but the message was obvious. Ravi's exit was overdue.

"Yes, yes, of course." Ravi nodded, the reality of his brother's wedding cutting through his starstruck daze. "I should get going. It was such an honor meeting you."

After offering Priya a quick goodbye, Ravi headed to his car, his mind clearly spinning from his celebrity encounter. As his car disappeared down the driveway, Priya's parents emerged from the house, lugging the last of their luggage.

"Who was that?" Mumma asked, her eyes following the luxury car as it drove out of sight.

"Ravi Tiwari," Priya replied.

Puppa's eyes narrowed. "What did he want?"

"He brought sweets for his brother's wedding." Priya motioned toward the box Ethan held.

"Is that all?" Puppa asked, as if sensing there was more to the story.

"That and . . . well, he wanted my phone number," Priya confessed.

Puppa's gaze hardened. "You're asking for trouble, Priya. Ravi's family will never approve of you. You'll be nothing more than a passing amusement."

"Listen to your father," Mumma said. "You're already divorced. Do you really want to make another mistake?"

Their words hit Priya like a punch to the gut. And to have them say this in front of Ethan? She felt utterly humiliated. She stole a glance at Ethan and found him watching with a furrowed brow.

"Maybe we should cancel the trip, Rakesh," Mumma said. "What if something happens while we're gone?"

"What if *what* happens, Mumma?" Priya asked sharply, her temper flaring.

"Priya, if you're really ready to meet someone, you just have to say," her mother replied. "We'll be happy to introduce you to someone more suitable. Maybe even someone who lives closer."

Yeah, so you can keep an eye on me, right? Priya thought, but she held her tongue, mortified that this was playing out in front of Ethan.

Puppa cleared his throat and stepped in. "Maybe we should save this for another time, Seema," he said, before turning to Ethan. "Mr. Ethan, please keep an eye on our Priya while we're away."

Priya's jaw nearly hit the floor. *Keep an eye on me?* She whipped her head around to look at Ethan, who seemed at a loss for words.

Priya couldn't believe it herself. Her parents were terrified she'd get tangled up with Ravi but thought nothing of leaving her alone with Ethan Knight. In their minds, he was perched so high above her that they couldn't fathom he'd even glance at her. The idea that he could have any interest in Priya was absurd. Laughable, even. And *that* was the only reason they were okay with leaving. Because, as far as they were concerned, she wasn't even remotely in his league.

Ethan's eyes briefly flicked toward Priya. The glance was quick, almost imperceptible, but Priya caught something in his eyes. Irony? Understanding? Amusement?

"I don't believe Priya needs looking after, Mr. Solanki," he said. "But I appreciate your trust in me."

"You're a good man, Mr. Ethan." Puppa gave Ethan a nod of approval and finished loading the rest of the luggage.

Mumma opened the car door and set the wicker basket on the floor of the front passenger seat, making sure that tea and snacks were within easy reach. She turned to Ethan with a warm smile. "Goodbye, Mr. Ethan. In case Priya forgets, I've prepared all your dinners and extra snacks too. We are just a call away, so please ring if you need anything. Anything at all." Shifting her attention to Priya, she rattled off a laundry list of instructions. "Don't forget to call. Lock the door. And don't stay up late. Oh, and remember to water the plants." She kissed Priya on both cheeks before climbing into the car, shutting the door, and waving at her through the window.

Puppa made one last sweep around the car, checking the tires and mirrors with his usual care, then slid into the driver's seat.

"We'll call when we get there," he said to Priya. "Look after Mr. Ethan."

Priya nodded as he backed out, her gaze trailing the car until her parents disappeared.

"Well, that was an interesting turn of events," Ethan commented.

"What do you mean?" Priya turned to face him.

"Let's see," he began. "Not only am I responsible for keeping you out of trouble, but I've also learned that your parents' standards are so high that even someone from an upper caste doesn't qualify."

"Not that I'm interested, but yeah, if I ever did consider someone, he would have to tick all my parents' boxes. Same caste, same background." Priya rolled her eyes.

"So, I won't cut it?" Ethan teased.

"You check all *my* boxes," Priya shot back with a grin.

"We're back to that, are we? Hot and cold, Priya. It's like you can't decide what you want."

He wasn't wrong. Priya *had* been all over the place. Her heart sank. Had she blown her chances with him?

"Fine," she said. "I admit I overreacted the other night. I shouldn't have jumped to conclusions about you and Sienna." Taking a deep breath, she continued, "The truth is I've had a crush on you for as long as I can remember. Even Brooke doesn't know that. But you figured it out, didn't you? So here's the deal. No more pretending." She looked him straight in the eye. "A fling with you is exactly what I need to bounce back. So . . ." She leaned in closer, her heart racing. "What do you say, Heathen Knight?"

Ethan arched an eyebrow, his lips twitching as if he were fighting a smile. "Your dad practically made me your guardian just two minutes ago, and you're tempting me to cross the line? Shame on you, Priya Solanki."

He reached out, brushing a strand of hair from her face, his fingers sending a spark straight through her. Then, with an exaggerated sigh, he stepped back, raising his hands in mock surrender.

"Alright, Pri. You've got me," he said. "But I'm not breaking your father's trust, so here's how it works. If you want me, you'll have to make the first move. I need to know you're all in. No more back and forth. If it's a fling you want, you'd better be damn sure you can handle it, Pri. Because when I'm done, you'll remember it for the rest of your life."

Priya's pulse stumbled over itself and her legs felt shaky.

"Take your time. Think it over," Ethan said with a provocative smile. "Fair warning, though—resisting me will take more willpower than you have, so if that's what you choose to do, I suggest shackling yourself to the nearest permanent fixture until your parents get back."

With a wink that could melt anyone's resolve, he turned and walked back toward the coach house. Priya's skin flushed as she watched him go, the electric charge of his words still crackling in the air.

How the hell am I supposed to think straight after that?

Ethan Knight wasn't just a star. He was the kind of man who could unravel you with a single glance—make you forget the rules, forget the consequences. Priya was in trouble. But damn, she couldn't wait to fall deeper into it.

If she was going to let herself have this, have *him*, she had to act fast—before her parents got back. No overthinking, no attachments, and no regrets. She'd survived Ethan leaving before, and now she was better prepared. Older, wiser, and hungry for what he offered—something wild, fleeting, and entirely hers. The thought sent a rush of molten heat through her veins, her heart pounding with anticipation for what was about to unfold.

Eleven

PRIYA'S PHONE STARTED BUZZING with calls from her parents the very next morning. She balanced it on her shoulder as she watered the plants inside the funeral home.

"The jasmine needs a good drenching," Mumma said. "And don't forget to sweep away the wilted blooms."

Puppa's voice came through the speaker, adding his own instructions. "Make sure you turn off all the lights. Except the ones in the reception area, and the two outside."

"I know, Puppa," Priya said. "You left me three copies of instructions."

"What's happening with Ravi?" Mumma asked. "Has he called? Have you called him?"

"Nothing is happening with Ravi," Priya replied with a weary sigh as she tipped water into a potted fern. "No calls. No messages. Nothing. I swear."

"And Mr. Ethan?" Puppa said. "You're looking after him, right?"

Priya's stomach did a little flip. "He's fine. Everything's under control. Enjoy your time with Dee and don't worry."

"Is the sprinkler system turning on at the right time? I set it for—"

"Sorry, Puppa, I have another call coming through." Priya hung up before he could add to her growing list of tasks. Setting her phone down, she took a deep breath. Sometimes, you just had to fake being busy to stay sane.

Putting the empty jug back in its place, Priya strolled through the funeral home, making sure everything was in order. With no background music playing, silence pressed into every corner. As she passed the casket showroom, Priya noticed the light glowing under the door.

Strange, she thought, certain she'd turned off all the lights last night.

Pushing the door open, she was struck by the solemn atmosphere. Windowless and hushed, the room displayed rows of caskets, arranged not only by their materials and designs but also by price points and cultural traditions. Shelves showcased rows of urns from simple clay vessels to elaborately designed options.

As Priya moved toward the switch, the lights flickered erratically, throwing shadows across the room. Priya shivered despite herself. The electrical glitches made Moksha feel even creepier. She flipped the switch, throwing the room into darkness with only a faint glow spilling from the hallway.

"Ah, that's much better," a voice cut through the silence.

Priya's head snapped toward the sound, her eyes adjusting to the dim light. There in the middle of the room was Ethan, stretched out in a satin-lined casket, hands folded across his chest. Priya had seen countless bodies in caskets but seeing a very alive Ethan Knight in one hit differently.

"Would you mind shutting the lid before you leave?" he asked.

"Seriously?" Priya stared, rattled by his request.

"It's called research, and it's why I'm here." He cracked an eye open. "Now come on, give me a hand."

Priya stepped closer until she was right above him. Ethan shut his eyes, his lashes resting like dark crescents on his face. She placed her hands on the lid, slowly starting to lower it. As Ethan slipped out of view, a tightness gripped her chest. Watching him fade into the shadows hit her harder than she expected. The idea of a world without him was almost too much to bear. She had convinced herself that he was a part of her past, but the truth welled up in her, as timeless and sacred as the Ganges. She loved him—more deeply than she had ever allowed herself to believe.

"That's enough," Priya said, yanking the lid back open.

Ethan's eyes fluttered open. "That was strangely . . . therapeutic," he said. "Peaceful. But it also makes you wonder . . . If there's nothing after this, what does it all matter?"

"Is that what you think? That there's nothing on the other side?"

Ethan sat up and considered her question. "When I was a kid, I bought into everything my mother told me. She used to say living a good Christian life guaranteed a spot in heaven. I still respect that. And when the time comes, I'll be buried in the family plot, just like her. But I'm more skeptical about some of the other stuff. I'd *like* to think there's peace and happiness waiting for us on the other side."

"No lakes of fire? No punishment for the wicked?"

"Lakes of fire?" Ethan laughed. "That's quite a take on the afterlife, hotshot."

Priya shrugged. "I grew up in a funeral home." Though her tone was casual, her mind was racing. If there was ever a time to spook Ethan, this was it. She couldn't be distracted by feelings of *love*. "You see things, hear things. Not all souls go to heaven, you know. Some get stuck. Here. Or in hellfire."

Ethan's brow lifted. "Do tell."

"Are you sure you want to have this conversation while you're lying in a casket?"

"Why not? It's the perfect setting, don't you think? You should try it."

Priya hesitated, glancing at the casket beside him. It felt a bit morbid, but anything to get Ethan to leave was fair game. Taking a deep breath, she slipped off her shoes and climbed in. The satin was unexpectedly cool, sending a shiver down her back. Viewing the world from inside the confined space was unsettling, but oddly fascinating too.

"Comfortable?" Ethan teased, settling back in his casket.

"Yeah, but this isn't entirely relevant to me," she replied, closing her eyes and arranging herself as she had seen her father arrange countless bodies in their final repose. "I'm going to be cremated, not buried."

"So, fire for you, earth for me," Ethan said.

Priya let out a soft laugh. Their worlds were already so different, and even in death, their paths diverged.

"Opposites, even in the afterlife," she joked.

"Maybe we should try out the cremation chamber next, just to make sure you're all set."

"Why stop there? Let's get embalmed too. Go big or go home, right?"

Ethan's laughter filled the room. "Honestly? I've always loved the idea of a Viking send-off. A burning ship sailing out to the horizon? Majestic as hell."

"You would totally rock the Viking warlord look. All fur and brooding stares."

"Brooding, huh?" Ethan replied, his voice tinged with amusement. "So, tell me—of all the people your family's encountered over the years, who do you think has it right?"

Priya paused, considering the question. "Everyone. And at the same time, no one. Because the moment you say your way is the only way, you're limiting something boundless—God, a higher power, call it what you will—to a box that only fits your perspective. It's like saying you own the sun. It shines on everyone. That's what divinity is to me, a light that's inside all of us."

As she spoke, Priya realized that the conversation had slipped out of her hands. Somehow, they'd gone from ghost stories to something deeper.

"Interesting," Ethan said. "So, if God—or this universal light—resides within all of us, then a murderer is just as divine as a saint?"

"Wow. Going straight to the deep end, huh?"

Ethan laughed, but when he spoke again, his tone had shifted. "I've missed this, Pri. Talking to you. Hanging out together. I didn't realize how much until just now."

Priya's breath caught. There was no teasing in his voice, no playful edge. Just honesty. She wanted to brush it off, make a joke, anything to deflect the way it tugged at her. But she couldn't. She'd missed him too.

"I'm sorry for taking Zoe Clompson to our spot," he said.

"Chloe Thompson," Priya reminded yet again. "She had you in her sights forever. All the girls did. You had this presence, like you were already heading for something bigger. You didn't just leave, Ethan. You took a leap. I wish I had that kind of courage. To change the template like you did."

"What template?"

"The template we're born into. Like the landing page of a website. It's the layout we start off with—family, religion, ethnicity, circumstances, birthplace. All the bits and pieces that make up the default design of our life."

"Only you would compare life to a website." Ethan chuckled softly. "Go on."

"Well," Priya continued, "you didn't just change your landing page when you left. You rewrote the entire code. Most of us stick to the default settings. If we want something to change, we submit a ticket: 'Dear Webmaster, please activate the "more money" option on my page.' Or 'Dear Webmaster, please clear my cache so I can start over.' We keep submitting request after request, hoping they'll get approved. Sometimes we even try to bargain. 'I'll quit drinking if you enable this feature,' or 'I'll do one good deed a day if you approve my request faster.' But here's the thing—every webmaster is connected to the same universal server."

"So, you're saying religions and beliefs are like different webmasters, but they all plug into the same source?"

"Exactly." Priya couldn't help but smile. She could dive into the geekiest corners of her mind with Ethan, say things she wouldn't dream of sharing with anyone else, and still feel completely understood. No judgments. No sneering. Even after all this time.

"And the template we're born into is sort of a predestined path, but we have the free will to change it if we are brave enough to change the code," Ethan continued.

"Right, except there's one thing that's hard coded into all our pages. And that's death," Priya said. "I don't know how your character is going to outsmart that one, Ethan."

"Neither do I," Ethan said with a quiet laugh. "I can't wait to get my hands on the final script."

"Well, my final script is already written, and guess what?" Priya said. "I turn to ashes."

"And I turn to dust," Ethan said.

"Please," Priya groaned. "More like stardust, Mr. Hollywood."

"Ashes to ashes, and dust to dust."

"Landing pages and ending pages," Priya quipped.

Ethan let out a slow breath, his voice softening. "I couldn't have picked a better place for character research than right here with you, Pri."

The ghost stories on the tip of Priya's tongue evaporated, replaced by an ache she didn't expect. The need to flee rose fast, so she climbed out of the casket.

"Well," she said, "I'll let you get back to your role."

"Leaving me so soon, Ashes?" Ethan propped himself up with a smile.

Priya stopped in the doorway and cast a parting glance over her shoulder. The light from the corridor traced the angles of Ethan's face, giving him a glow that was both haunting and beautiful.

"Enjoy your solitude, Stardust," Priya replied, before slipping out.

Twelve

HEADING TO THE RECEPTION DESK, Priya checked Moksha's voicemail. One message. She listened and then hit Replay.

"Hello, Mr. Solanki," the caller said. "Jeremy Foster here. I'm following up on the proposal I left with you. My client is eager to close the deal on Moksha. Please call me back at your earliest convenience."

Jotting down the number, Priya sank back into the chair, tapping her pen against a notepad. She had to get her father on board with selling Moksha, which meant speeding up Ethan's departure before the deal disappeared. She closed her eyes, then sat up sharply. *That's it!* There was an easy way to do this. One call to the press, tipping them off to Ethan's whereabouts, and the paparazzi would descend like vultures. Ethan would have no choice but to leave. It was simple. Foolproof.

But she couldn't bring herself to do it. It was too much of a personal betrayal. And deep down, she *wanted* him to stay. There was no guarantee she'd ever see him again after he left. At the same time, she had to think about what this sale would mean for her parents, and not just in terms of financial security. It was a chance to break free of a cycle that had trapped her family for generations.

As Priya wrestled with her thoughts, her phone buzzed with a call from Brooke. Before she could even say hello, Brooke asked, "Is everything okay with Ethan?"

Priya frowned. "Why?"

"Because he just called me. From inside a *casket.* To tell me he loves me."

"That's sweet." Priya laughed.

"Sweet? Try bizarre. He sounds like he's spiraling into some kind of existential crisis. He acts like he doesn't care, but he's clearly wrestling some demons, so close to home yet cut off from our father. Do me a favor. Keep an eye on him?"

Priya chuckled to herself. *First my parents tell Ethan to keep an eye on me, and now Brooke is asking me to keep tabs on Ethan? Life sure knows how to set up a plot twist.*

"I will," Priya replied. *I couldn't keep my eyes off your brother if I tried, Brooke.* "Now tell me what's going on at your end."

Brooke launched into stories about her oddball experiences and a potential new romance.

"He's really into sound baths," she said. "Always making me lie down while he plays gongs. And don't even get me started on the sage. He insists we smudge everything with it, including *down there*, every time we're together."

Priya couldn't stop laughing. "What, like a whole ceremony?"

"Oh yeah. There's incense, chanting, and enough smoke to get us flagged by Environment Canada."

They giggled, the conversation light and fun, until Brooke announced, "Oh, crap, I have to go! I'm late for my Paw-lates session with Lady Whiskerbottom."

"Paw-lates? I'm almost afraid to ask."

"It's like Pilates but designed to align your core *and* your cat's energy."

"Ah, the ancient art of holding a plank while your cat silently judges you."

"Please, Lady Whiskerbottom doesn't judge. She supervises. Anyway, gotta run. Miss you, Pri!"

"Have fun! Tell your supervisor not to knock over your water bottle," Priya called out before hanging up.

As she set her phone down, Ethan came out of the showroom, his face wearing a look that said he was on a mission.

"Everything okay?" Priya asked, watching him head straight for the door.

"That remains to be seen."

"Ethan?" Priya rushed out of the funeral home after him. "What's going on?

"It's now or never." He tugged his hood over his head and began charging down the road toward his father's home.

Priya jogged to keep up, her breath catching as they approached the entrance to Knight Estates—a pair of imposing gates set into a high brick wall, the family crest gleaming on the ironwork. A sprawling driveway stretched ahead, framed by sugar maples that guarded the property like ancient sentinels.

A glimpse of the manor, half hidden by trees, stirred a tide of memories for Priya. She could still see herself wandering its long hallways, sneaking quick looks into Ethan's room before she got to Brooke's. Every detail she'd noticed back then—books on his desk, posters on the wall—had felt like a clue, pieces of a puzzle that fed her infatuation with him.

Standing outside the grounds now, she glanced at Ethan. The boy she'd once obsessed over had returned a man admired by millions. But fame had only widened the gap between him and his father, and the iron gate before them was a stark reminder of just how deep the divide ran. Ethan was about to revisit a home where he was no longer welcome. Still, he stood, tall and unflinching, giving it yet another shot.

He reached for the brass box mounted on the wall and pressed the call button. Above the intercom, partially hidden by a tangle of ivy, a security camera gleamed in the sunlight. Ethan pulled back his hood and met the camera's gaze, shoulders squared as he waited.

A faint static crackled from the speaker before a voice came through. "Welcome home, Master Knight."

"Sebastian." Ethan recognized the voice immediately and smiled hopefully at Priya. "Still holding things together, I see."

"Still standing, Master Knight, tall as a spruce," Sebastian replied with a touch of humor.

"I'm here to see my father," Ethan stated.

"Of course, sir. One moment while I check if he's available."

A long silence followed. Ethan rubbed the back of his neck and stared at his feet as they waited. Priya picked at a loose thread on her sleeve, her eyes flicking between Ethan and the speaker. When Sebastian finally returned, there was a faint hesitation in his tone. "I'm afraid Mr. Knight is not home."

Ethan's jaw tensed, his eyes snapping toward the camera. "I see," he said. "Please let my father know I'd like permission to visit my mother's grave."

Another pause, shorter this time, before Sebastian replied, "By all means, sir."

The gates opened with a low groan. Ethan glanced at Priya. "You coming?"

Without a word, she fell into step beside him, matching his pace as they walked up the driveway. Halfway to the manor,

Ethan turned onto the path leading to his family's burial plot. After a few minutes, the path sloped gently to a clearing, where polished headstones lined carefully tended paths.

Ethan's pace slowed as they approached his mother's grave. He sank to his knees when they reached the tombstone, his fingers tracing the letters with a tenderness that stirred an ache in Priya's chest. She stood silently, feeling the storm of emotions he was struggling to hold back. Once again, she caught a glimpse of the boy beneath the man. A boy who had endured the kind of heartbreak no one should ever have to bear.

"It wasn't your fault, Ethan," she said softly, resting her hand on his shoulder.

"If I'd just come home when I was supposed to, she wouldn't have been out picking me up," he said. "She wouldn't have been in that truck's path."

Priya's heart sank. He was still holding himself responsible for the accident that killed his mother. She could hear the ache in his voice, see it carved into his face.

"My dad blames me too," Ethan said after a moment, his voice quieter. "He's never come out and said it, but I can feel his anger, his resentment. I didn't just lose my mom because of the accident. I lost my dad too. Every meal, every moment in that house was unbearable. I was in so much pain, I gave him more reasons to hate me and fled the first chance I got. He may have forgiven me for turning my back on the plans he had for me, but he's never going to forgive me for my mother's death. That's why he refuses to see me."

"You don't know that, Ethan," Priya said, a wave of sadness washing over her. "I'm sure he would have seen you if he was home."

"He *is* home, Pri," Ethan murmured, his voice strained. "Brooke said he's here. I thought if I showed up, he would . . ." The words caught in his throat. "But nothing's changed. And I don't blame him for shutting me out. I'll never forgive myself either."

Priya squeezed Ethan's shoulder. Until he found a way to reconcile with his father, Ethan would keep carrying this burden. Nothing could ease the pain of his mother's death, especially when he believed his father held him responsible too. Priya stepped back, allowing him some privacy. Her gaze drifted across the sprawling grounds around her. The manor stood a short distance away, its walls softened by ivy curling up toward the second-story windows.

Ethan knelt by the grave, head bowed as his fingers brushed the soil. After a while, he wandered into the meadow around the cemetery and picked a handful of wildflowers. When he returned, he placed them gently on his mother's grave. Against the carefully curated surroundings, his small offering stood out—simple and raw.

As Ethan turned to head back toward Priya, she caught movement in one of the windows. A curtain shifted and Priya spotted Harry Knight—Brooke and Ethan's father—before it fell back into place. Ethan had been right all along. His father *was* home, watching from the shadows.

Priya thought about her own parents. They sometimes drove her crazy, but she'd rather deal with their constant interference than ever endure this kind of cold rejection.

As she walked with Ethan toward the exit, the iron gates swung open. Ethan paused at the threshold, turning for one last look at the manor. In that quiet moment, Priya knew: He wasn't coming back here.

When they reached the sidewalk, Ethan tugged his hood around his face and stuffed his hands into his jacket. The irony wasn't lost on Priya. Ethan had to hide from strangers who adored him but was shunned by his own father. He had the world at his feet, while the one thing he needed the most remained beyond his grasp.

Matching his stride, Priya threaded her arm through Ethan's. He glanced at her, then pulled her hand into his pocket, his fingers lacing with hers. Together they walked back to Moksha. As cars zoomed by, Priya had a fleeting taste of an alternate reality—one where Ethan wasn't the larger-than-life celebrity, and she wasn't the ordinary girl next door. They were simply two people walking hand in hand down the street.

Priya held on tightly to the moment, squeezing Ethan's hand as though her grip could freeze time—stop it from slipping away like sand through her fingers.

Thirteen

THAT AFTERNOON, from their vantage point on top of the freight car, Priya and Ethan had a panoramic view of the field that separated Moksha from Knight Estates. The sky was overcast, but shafts of sunlight broke through. As Priya soaked it all in, her phone buzzed with a call from her parents.

"Hello again," she answered.

"I forgot to ask," her mother said. "How's Mr. Ethan enjoying the food? Everything okay?"

Priya glanced at Ethan as he dipped a samosa into tamarind chutney. He took a bite and closed his eyes, a look of pure satisfaction on his face.

"Everything is perfect," Priya replied, scanning the rooftop spread.

There was paneer tikka, marinated in spiced yogurt and charred to perfection, a fragrant pulao sprinkled with cashews and raisins, a vegetable curry, and, of course, the samosas that Ethan was enjoying.

"How are things going with you and Puppa?" Priya asked.

"Pri!" Deepa cut in, snatching the phone from Mumma. "How's Ethan?"

"How about a 'Hey, hello, how are you?' for your sister?"

"I know exactly how *you* are. Hanging out with Ethan Knight while I'm stuck here with Mumma and Puppa."

"Life's unfair, Dee," Priya shot back with a grin.

"Oh, you have no idea," Deepa said, her voice softening. "I need to fill you in. You're not going to believe what's going on."

"Tell me."

"You know Mumma and Puppa are visiting Vinod Uncle next week, right? Well, they're going to—"

Before she could finish, Puppa grabbed the phone from her. "Priya, beta. How are you?"

From the background, Deepa shouted, "Pri! They're checking out some guy that Vinod Uncle has in mind for you!"

A flicker of unease passed through Priya. "Puppa, what is she talking about?"

"Beta, I've misplaced my address book," Puppa said. "Can you check if it's in my office?"

"Don't change the subject," Priya insisted. "What's going on with Vinod Uncle?"

"It's no big deal." Puppa sighed. "He just wants us to meet someone while we're there. It would be rude to say no, Priya, since we're already visiting. So, we'll just have tea with this fellow. That's all."

"That's all?" Priya huffed. "Well, have fun at your *matchmaking* tea, but leave me out of it. I'm not interested, and I don't need you and Mumma sizing someone up on my behalf."

"Relax, it's not like we're planning your wedding behind your back. Now, about that address book. Can you look for it and let me know if you find it? I need to let Mr. Foster know I'm turning down the offer to sell Moksha."

Priya's heart sank. "So that's it? You've made up your mind?"

Her father's silence stretched long enough for Priya to realize that further discussion was pointless. "Fine," she said stiffly. "I'll look for your address book and call you back." Ending the call, she tucked her phone back inside her bag.

"Everything okay?" Ethan asked, setting his plate aside.

"Just family stuff." Priya averted her gaze, adding more failures to her list. She had not been able to convince her father to sell Moksha *or* send Ethan away.

Forcing herself to shift gears, she glanced at Ethan's plate. "Mumma wanted to know if you're enjoying the food. I didn't tell her you've been ordering delivery on the side."

"Listen, I love your mum's cooking, but I'm not cut out for the vegetarian lifestyle. Man can't live on potato samosas alone." Ethan grinned and speared a piece of steak with his fork.

Priya raised a hand to her heart in mock offense. "Really, Heathen? Eating steak right in front of me? You know how sacred cows are to us!"

"Listen, you. I'm not falling for that again. 'Don't wear leather, Ethan, you'll offend my father. Don't eat steak, Ethan, you're disrespecting me.' You're worse than my entire PR team."

"Keep that up, and Bollywood won't touch you with a ten-foot pole," Priya teased. "And you *need* Indian fans, Ethan. We're taking over one samosa at a time. Doctors, CEOs, tech billionaires. Throw a stone and you'll probably hit one of us."

Ethan's smile was entirely too smug. "I don't know about the stones, Pri, but I definitely know someone who's ready to hit it with me."

"You did *not* just slide that into our conversation like that." Priya tossed a cashew at him. "You've grown way too comfortable,

Ethan. Sitting back, letting women chase you while you barely lift a finger. 'Make the first move, Priya. I need to be sure, Priya.'" She rolled her eyes.

Ethan chuckled, the sound low and deep. "I get my fair share of no-strings-attached offers. But this is *you*, Pri. And I'm willing to bet it's the first time you've ever thought about doing something like this. So, if you're going for it, then it can't be with just anyone. That Ravi guy?" Ethan let out a soft laugh, shaking his head. "He doesn't have a clue. It has to be me. I know exactly what you need."

"And what exactly do I need?" Priya's pulse raced as his eyes held hers, unflinching and full of quiet intensity.

"You need someone who won't rush you but won't hold back when it counts." Ethan's voice turned huskier. "Someone who can turn off your thoughts with a touch. Someone who will leave you breathless, who'll show you what it feels like to lose control—completely—and love every second of it."

A tightness gripped Priya's throat, tension crackling through her like the air right before a storm breaks.

"You need someone," Ethan said, his voice dipping into a smoky murmur that wrapped around her like a velvet ribbon, "who will make you so unapologetically sure of yourself, so completely alive, that when you walk into a room, people can't help but stop and take notice. *That's* how you bounce back. But you have to trust me, Pri. Trust that I'm not out to hurt you. Or cheat. Or lie. And more than that? You have to trust yourself enough to know that this is exactly what you want."

"Ethan?" Priya said, every inch of her lit up, alive, pulling toward him like gravity.

He stilled, as if he knew exactly what was coming—and he was waiting for it.

Because this part was hers.

"Stop talking," she whispered. She didn't want to wait another second to make her move, not with him looking at her like that, not with him talking to her with *that* voice.

Closing the gap, she cradled his face between her hands. Her kiss was awkward and fierce, all edges and emotion, years of longing rushing to the surface all at once. Priya almost pulled back in embarrassment, but before she could, Ethan's hands moved to her waist, drawing her into him with a heat that made her knees weak.

The feel of his hands through the fabric of her clothes, the scrape of his stubble, the soft noise he made low in his throat—it all tangled together and sent her reeling. She leaned back, drawing Ethan down with her.

Priya's world condensed to the sensation of lying beneath Ethan, his breath mingling with hers, the weight of his limbs, the liquid fire of his kisses.

A sudden drop of rain hit Priya's forehead, pulling her out of the moment. Opening her eyes, she spotted dark clouds looming overhead.

A passing shower, she told herself.

But nature had other plans. Within seconds, rain started to patter softly on the metal roof.

Ethan froze as it hit the back of his neck. He pulled back just enough to look at her, his lips inches from hers. His hair was already starting to dampen, dark strands falling into his eyes. "Are we seriously getting rained on right now?"

Priya let out a breathless laugh, her fingers still clutching the fabric of his shirt. "Of course it's raining. The heavens have impeccable timing."

Ethan laughed, then leaned down to kiss her again. His lips were warm and soft, and she forgot the rain entirely. Each drop on her skin felt like the sizzling hiss of water hitting a scalding hot tawa. But soon, her clothes clung to her, the rain coming down harder and faster.

Ethan pulled back, his forehead pressing lightly against hers. "As much as I'd love to stay right here, we need to leave."

He stood and helped her up, his other hand steading her as she wobbled on the wet roof. "Got you," he said.

"My Knight in soaking armor," Priya teased, brushing the rain from her face.

As they turned to their ruined picnic, Ethan picked up his plate. "Well, there goes my steak," he declared, tipping it into the tiffin.

"Everything's turned to mush," Priya cried, scraping the rest of their food away. She slammed the tiffin shut and stood, feeling the rain running down her back.

"It went better than expected." Ethan stepped behind her, pulling her against him.

"How do you figure?" Priya turned in his arms, staring at him like he'd lost his mind. "You're soaked, I'm shivering, and you're over here acting like we're in the middle of a romantic Bollywood rain song."

Ethan, however, just pulled her closer. "You kissed me, Pri." His lips trailed down the curve of her neck.

Drenched to the bone, Priya melted into Ethan's embrace. She was lost in his arms, oblivious to the world until a sudden clap of thunder broke the spell.

"Would you look at that?" Ethan chuckled. "Even the gods are applauding."

"Or telling us to get a move on." Priya grabbed her bag and started descending the ladder. Halfway down, she tossed a grin at him. "Race you back, Heathen!"

"Hey, that's cheating! You got a head start," Ethan called out as she peered at him over the edge of the roof. Sweeping their things onto the picnic blanket, he knotted the ends and chased after her.

Priya hopped off the ladder, her laughter echoing in the rain as she sprinted toward Moksha. She didn't make it far before Ethan closed the distance. He caught her hand and spun her around, drawing a surprised squeal from her.

"Easy, hotshot," he said. "We're never going to make it that way unless you want a mud bath."

Priya's eyes dropped to the waterlogged patch of ground ahead, slick with mud.

"I have a better idea." Ethan grabbed her by the waist and hoisted her up in one swift motion.

Priya's legs instinctively locked around his hips, her arms circling his neck as he carried her back to the freight car through the rain. His warmth sank into her, igniting a slow burn that made her forget the chill of the rain. She gripped him tighter, the storm around them nothing compared to the storm building within her.

When they reached the abandoned carriage, Ethan lowered her inside and Priya instantly missed the heat of his body against hers. She watched as he set their drenched picnic bundle on the floor and climbed in after her, the rain clinging to his clothes, emphasizing every curve and line of muscle. A shiver raced through Priya, but it wasn't from the cold.

The inside of the boxcar was like a different world altogether. Rain hammered on the roof. A moody, muted light spilled in through the open doors. Priya felt cocooned with Ethan in a space that seemed impossibly small with him in it. He was like a storm of his own, his energy crackling between them. Her skin tingled, her pulse racing as his gaze settled on her.

"You're awfully quiet," Ethan said, scanning her face. "Having second thoughts about making that first move?"

"Not a chance." Priya's hands were clammy and her stomach a riot of nerves, but there wasn't a single doubt in her mind. Sitting here with Ethan, in the space that had once been their hideout, felt like a homecoming—like something long overdue was finally happening.

Leaning forward, she slid her hands into his hair, her fingers tangling in the wet strands as she brought his face to hers. Their lips met, and the world tilted on its axis. The rain, the chill, the world outside—all of it fell away.

Ethan responded slowly at first. His hands found the curve of her back, drawing her closer until there was no space left between them. As the kiss deepened, so did the ache low in her belly, setting off a chain reaction she felt everywhere.

Breaking away, Ethan shrugged out of his jacket and spread it beneath her. "Can't have you lying on cold metal," he said.

Priya's laugh came out breathless, cut short as Ethan dipped his head. His kiss was hungrier, the feel of his body making her head spin. She gasped as his lips moved from her mouth to her jawline, then lower, brushing against the hollow of her neck. Every inch of her hummed, every nerve sparking to life under his touch.

"Still with me?" he whispered, the words muffled against her skin.

Priya knew he was giving her an out, a chance to pull back if she wasn't sure. But she didn't want out. She wanted *him*.

"Yes," she breathed, her fingers moving to unbutton his shirt.

Her pulse quickened as the fabric parted, revealing his skin inch by inch. Just as she reached the last button, Ethan grabbed the hem and yanked the shirt over his head. His skin gleamed in the dim light, as if he were part of a rain-kissed dream.

Priya's eyes roamed over him, mapping the breadth of his shoulders, the length of his arms, the contours of his chest. This was Ethan—her first crush, and also the man whose face graced countless magazine covers. And now, here he was, like a masterpiece before her, waiting to be explored.

Priya fumbled with the hem of her top, trying to pull it off. Ethan took hold of the sides as she raised her arms. As the top slid upward, exposing her stomach, a sudden wave of self-consciousness hit her.

What if I don't measure up? Her mind flashed to Ethan's star-studded dating history. She couldn't help but wonder how she compared to the women who belonged in his world. To make matters worse, Priya's top caught around her neck. The rain had shrunk the fabric, making it cling to her.

"Let's try this again." Ethan gave another pull, but instead of slipping loose, the fabric stretched, wrapping more tightly around Priya. Ethan stood, braced one foot in front of the other, and gave a firmer tug.

That's when he spotted Priya's face through the opening—eyes wide, arms raised in an almost comical cry for help. Their gazes met and held for a moment. Then the absurdity of the situation hit, and they cracked up.

"Okay, okay." Ethan dropped down beside Priya, still laughing. "Clearly, this is not how it's supposed to go. We need to do this properly, somewhere less . . . rustic." He gestured around the metal container. "You, me, a proper bed, and zero wardrobe malfunctions."

Priya chuckled, shaking her head as her pulse settled. The air buzzed with unspoken energy, but slowly the intensity between them started to ease. With a quiet sigh, she tugged her top back into place, her gaze drifting outside.

"Hey, look," she said. "It stopped raining."

Ethan turned toward the open doors and the rain-drenched field. The storm clouds had broken apart, leaving streaks of soft light on the horizon. The scent of rain-soaked earth filled the air, tugging at Priya's memories.

Ethan tilted his head. "You've got that faraway look, Pri. What's going on in that head of yours?"

"Well, if you must know . . ." Priya leaned forward with a wistful smile. "I was thinking of *you*. Something about this rainy air always takes me back to that motorcycle ride. You know, when you crashed my school trip and practically kidnapped me?"

"Kidnapped?" Ethan scoffed. "Please. That was a textbook rescue mission. You should've seen yourself, sitting by the water. Sad as fuck. Looking even droopier than your top right now."

"Wow, thanks," Priya shot back, grabbing his jacket and tossing it at him. "I wasn't miserable. You just happened to catch me while I was . . . deep in thought."

But even as she joked, Priya knew the truth. She *had* been miserable that day—sitting on the pier, counting down the hours until the trip was over. But then Ethan had arrived. And just like that, the shadows lifted—the roar of his bike and the grin on his face shaking her out of her gloom. The memory swept over her, drawing her back into the past.

Fourteen

PRIYA SAT AT THE EDGE of the pier, her boots grazing the lake's surface. The storm had passed, and raindrops shimmered on the trees along the shoreline. The setting sun cast a muted glow over the water, but the soft hum of laughter from the camp's common area only made her chest ache even more.

For years, she had begged her parents to let her come on this week-long school trip. Brooke went every year, and all Priya wanted was to be part of it. She'd imagined them huddled around the campfire, giggling over silly jokes, and whispering late into the night. She'd even managed to convince the camp coordinator to let them share a room, along with a girl named Rachel from another school.

But the trip hadn't turned out the way Priya had thought. Turning fifteen had changed the entire dynamic. Brooke and Rachel seemed more interested in boys than anything else—who had kissed whom, what it felt like, and which guys at camp were the cutest. Brooke had found her own distraction, a boy who played the guitar and had all the girls swooning with his laid-back charm.

One evening, she flopped down on Priya's bunk with a dramatic sigh. "You know," she said, "this is kinda the perfect time for you."

"Perfect time for what?" Priya glanced up from her book.

"Your first kiss!" Brooke declared. "I mean, think about it. You're away from home, no parents watching your every move, and no one's gonna rat you out. You can actually have a little fun for once!"

"I'm not just going to kiss someone because I'm away from home." Priya let out a small laugh.

Brooke's smile turned mischievous. "Ryan's been asking about you."

"Who's Ryan?" Priya ventured cautiously.

"Caleb's friend. He's super cute and totally into you. I may have suggested that you're interested in him too."

"Brooke!" Priya exclaimed, swatting her with a pillow.

"Relax! It's no big deal." She paused, her grin widening. "Actually . . . I kinda invited Caleb, Ryan, and one of their friends to hang out with us tomorrow. Rachel's in. She thinks it'll be fun."

Priya stared at her. "Seriously?"

"It's not like a date or anything, Pri. If you're not into him, just make up an excuse and bail. Easy peasy."

But it wasn't easy for Priya. Not at all. The only guy she was into was Ethan. Every time she closed her eyes and imagined kissing someone, it was his *face that appeared—his messy hair, his lopsided grin, his eyes crinkling when he teased her.*

The secret felt heavy in her chest, like a stone she couldn't shake. Brooke was her best friend. They told each other everything. Keeping it from her felt wrong, but what was she supposed to say? Hey, by the way, I've been quietly crushing on your brother this whole time. *What if Brooke laughed and didn't take her seriously? Worse—what if she* did *and told Ethan?*

The weight of it all pressed down on Priya, and she felt trapped—too scared to tell Brooke but hating herself for keeping it in.

The next day, the rain drove everyone indoors, so Brooke claimed the covered porch outside the arts and crafts cabin—a cozy little space with wooden benches and a couple of small tables tucked beneath the overhang. Priya sat stiffly on the edge of her bench, her fingers twisting in her hoodie's drawstring when the boys arrived.

"Hey!" Caleb gave Brooke a mock salute before plopping down beside her. "We bring gifts." He dropped two crushed bags of Skittles and a handful of granola bars on the table.

"Wow," Brooke replied. "Such gentlemen."

"It's the best we could do," Caleb said with a grin, his gaze flicking to Priya and Rachel. "You guys met my friends, Ryan and Tyler?"

Priya watched as Tyler tossed his hoodie over Rachel's bench like he was claiming the spot. "Hope you don't mind some company," he said.

Ryan grinned at Priya before settling down beside her. He cleared his throat and shuffled closer, his sleeve brushing her arm. "So . . . Brooke said you, uh . . . might be interested in hanging out some time," he said.

Priya's smile faltered. "Oh!" she said, scrambling to her feet. "I totally forgot. I told Mrs. Harper I'd tidy up the boathouse."

"Seriously?" Rachel threw her an incredulous glance. "You're ditching us to go untangle fishing lines?"

"I promised," Priya replied, her gaze moving apologetically around the group.

"I'll go with you," Ryan offered, already starting to stand.

"Oh, no!" Priya said quickly, raising a hand. "It's honestly just going to be me mopping up puddles and hanging life vests up to dry. Pretty boring stuff." She forced a smile. "But hey, if I'm done soon, I'll swing back after."

"Sure you will." Brooke shot her a knowing grin.

Priya waved a vague goodbye and bolted toward the boathouse, her face hot. This was what happened when you kept secrets from your best friend. And the longer she stayed silent, the harder it would be to tell the truth.

As she walked briskly past the main lodge, ignoring the warm glow of the fire crackling inside, a light mist settled on her glasses. When she reached the boathouse, she headed to the pier, far enough so the others couldn't see her. The planks creaked under her feet, and she sat at the edge, her legs dangling over the side. The world was covered with a shimmering translucence, and everything was quiet. The lake stretched before her, raindrops falling from the leaves with a hushed pitter-patter.

Priya drew her knees up to her chest and wrapped her arms around them. She stared at the ripples in the lake, willing her mind to go blank, but her thoughts kept circling back to one thing: I just want to go home.

She could *be having fun like Brooke and Rachel, but here she was instead—cold, miserable, and stuck in an endless loop—always comparing every guy to Ethan. She couldn't be with anyone else, not when her heart was already so full of him, even if he never realized it or returned her feelings.*

The sound of heavy footsteps broke through her thoughts, the vibrations carrying through the wood. Priya turned and froze, her heart leaping when she saw Ethan walking toward her. He looked like he'd ridden straight through the storm, rain streaking his leather jacket, his dark hair plastered to his forehead. Yet somehow, he still looked impossibly handsome. As their eyes locked, a slow smile tugged at the corners of his lips. A tingling sensation stirred in the pit of Priya's stomach.

"What are you doing here?" she asked.

"Brooke forgot her phone charger, so I offered to drop it off. I was headed to the office when I saw you sitting here, all by your lonesome. Everything okay?" He dropped down beside her, his legs swinging over the edge.

"Yeah." Priya put on a casual smile even as her heart thudded painfully. How was she supposed to tell him that she was sad because she was hung up on him? "I guess I'm just not vibing with this place. It's tough when you want to do one thing, but your squad is into something totally different."

Ethan let out a dry laugh. "I hated this place when I was here. I'm not exactly the team spirit type."

"And yet, somehow, it just makes you more popular."

"Apparently girls like the whole loner-rebel vibe."

His words were playful, but Priya wasn't blind to how everyone practically melted when he passed by in the school hallway. Ethan had always been a head-turner, but now, closing in on eighteen, he'd become undeniably hotter. The scruff along his jaw gave him a rugged edge. His build had filled out—shoulders wider, chest defined—making it hard not to notice every move he made. His moody, smoldering energy only intensified how impossible he was to ignore. It was no wonder everyone was drawn to him. Including her.

As Ethan leaned back and propped himself up on his wrist, Priya averted her gaze and peered at her own reflection in the water. There was something about being around Ethan that mended the frayed edges of her heart. Her emotions settled like the lake's surface after a storm. Around them, everything felt vividly alive—the quiet drip of water from the trees, the heavy scent of rain, the shimmer of the sun's reflection as it slipped beneath the water.

Priya glanced back at Ethan with a smile. "Your jeans are completely soaked, you know."

"It probably wasn't the best time to come out, but hey, here I am." He gave her a lopsided grin.

"Let's go inside so you can dry off." Priya motioned toward the glow spilling out of the lodge.

"Good call." Ethan rose to his feet and extended his hand toward Priya. "It'll save me from riding back with a soggy ass."

Priya laughed as they strolled off the pier. Their boots sank into the ground, squelching with each step. At the lodge's entrance, Ethan spotted a tap and turned it on, washing the mud off Priya's boots.

"Go on in," he said, cleaning his own. "I won't be long."

Priya stepped inside, greeted by the cozy scent of pine and hot chocolate. The common area was buzzing with kids—laughing, chatting, and playing board games. Some stretched out on sofas, scrolling through their phones. Priya spotted an empty couch near the hearth and began making her way toward it. She was halfway there when a familiar voice stopped her.

"Priya! Over here!" Rachel's voice carried through the noise of the crowd.

"Rachel?" Priya blinked. "What are you doing here?"

Rachel's grin turned sheepish. "Well, Ryan bailed right after you left and Tyler turned out to be super annoying, so I took off too."

Priya scanned the room. "Brooke's still with Caleb?"

Rachel leaned closer, lowering her voice to a whisper. "Actually, they snuck off together. Pretty sure they headed back to our cabin."

"Oh shit!" Priya said. "We have to give Brooke a heads-up. Her brother just showed up . . ." She trailed off as Rachel's eyes flicked past her and settled on something behind her.

The chatter around them slowed, then stopped entirely, like a record scratching to a halt. Priya didn't need to turn around to know that Ethan had made his entrance. The silence seemed to grow louder, broken only by the sound of his footsteps. His presence shifted the atmosphere, curiosity rippling through the room.

She watched as he strolled into view and headed for the couch, unbothered by the attention trailing him. He shrugged off his jacket, draped it over the armrest, and sank onto the cushions. After tugging his boots off and stretching his legs toward the fire, he locked eyes with Priya and flashed her a grin.

"You coming?" he drawled, patting the seat beside him.

Heat rushed into Priya's cheeks. Beside her, Rachel's mouth fell open. She shot Priya a stunned glance. Priya swallowed and forced a smile before crossing the room. She lowered herself next to him, keenly aware of how every set of eyes was glued to them.

"You've officially silenced the room," Priya whispered, trying to ignore the flush crawling up her neck.

"Good." Ethan grinned. "I wasn't in the mood for small talk."

Before Priya could respond, Rachel interrupted.

"Are you going to introduce me to your friend, Priya?" she asked, her eyes sparkling with curiosity.

"Oh sorry, Rachel," Priya said. "This is Brooke's brother, Ethan."

Rachel gave Ethan an appreciative smile. "Brooke's been holding out on me."

A sudden, possessive warmth flooded Priya's chest. Without thinking, she moved closer to Ethan, letting their shoulders touch. Rachel's gaze flicked between them, eyebrows lifting.

"So . . . are you two an item?" she asked.

"No," Priya mumbled.

"Not yet," Ethan added smoothly, a grin playing on his lips. "I keep asking, but Priya keeps shooting me down."

Priya's jaw nearly dropped, but Rachel cut in before she could say anything. "Priya, you and Brooke are officially the worst at sharing." She shook her head with exaggerated offense. Then she flashed a mischievous smile and wandered off to deliver the juicy gossip to the rest of the room.

"Why did you say that?" Priya hissed at Ethan as soon as she left.

"It's easier this way." He stretched his arms out along the back of the couch. "If she thinks I'm interested in you, she'll leave me alone. No small talk. No flirting. Nobody's feelings get hurt. It's a win-win."

"And what about me?" Priya shot back.

Ethan leaned closer, his voice dipping. "You don't like the idea of everyone thinking you've got me wrapped around your finger?"

Priya's pulse quickened. She wasn't mad that he'd lied. She was mad because, for a second, she'd let herself believe that Ethan really was into her. Her heart had felt like a shaken-up can of soda, ready to burst.

"Never mind," she muttered under her breath.

Ethan slid his boots back on and gave his jacket a shake before putting it on. "Come on, Pri. Let's get out of here," he said, rising to his feet.

Priya squared her shoulders and followed him out, pretending not to feel the weight of stares. As soon as the door clicked shut behind them, she exhaled sharply. "You're such a troublemaker, Heathen Knight."

"Troublemaker?" Ethan chuckled, his face soft and indistinct under the night sky. "Pretty sure everyone in there thinks you're *the troublemaker. Turning me down left, right, and center."*

"Yeah. No doubt you're real torn up about it," Priya said dryly, shoving her hands into her pockets. "Just wait till Brooke hears about tonight. She'll be so mad you didn't tell her about your big fat crush on me."

"Why don't we go tell her right now?" Ethan said with a grin. "Where's your room? I can drop off her phone charger while we're at it."

Alarm bells rang in Priya's head. There was no way she could risk Ethan walking in on Brooke and Caleb.

"Uh, that's okay!" She waved her hand dismissively. "Brooke's probably asleep already. She had a headache earlier. Just give it to me and I'll pass it on. You don't want to deal with Grumpy Brooke."

"Better you than me." Ethan handed her the charger. "It's too nice a night to risk my sister's wrath."

Relieved that Ethan hadn't pressed to see Brooke, Priya slipped the charger into her pocket. "It really is pretty out here," she said, glancing around. The air carried a freshness from the earlier rain, and the moon cast silver shadows across the gravel as they walked to the parking lot.

"How about a ride before I head out?"

"You want me to hop on with you?" Priya had never gotten on the bike with him before.

"Unless you'd prefer to ride solo," Ethan teased.

"Sure. Let me just pull out my top-secret motorcycle license," Priya said, mock-patting her sweatpants.

"See? I knew it—Priya Solanki, undercover biker."

"Busted." She grinned, throwing her hands up.

"Here, put this on." He shrugged off his jacket and handed it to her.

"What about you?" Priya asked, eyeing his thin T-shirt.

"I'm used to it." He guided her arms through the sleeves. When the jacket settled over her shoulders, he zipped it up snugly to her chin.

Even through her sweatshirt, Priya could feel Ethan's body heat radiating from the jacket. It caught her off guard, and she glanced away, toying with the sleeves and feeling uncharacteristically shy around him.

Ethan pulled her hood around her face. "Ready to roll?" he asked, nudging her glasses back into place.

Blinking at him from behind her round lenses, Priya nodded. Ethan paused, glanced at her with a chuckle, then swung his leg over the bike and gripped the handlebars. The engine came alive with a growl, its echo rippling across the night.

Priya mounted the bike and shifted her weight, her feet finding the pegs, as she looped her arms around Ethan. If she could, she would have happily suction-cupped herself to him.

"Whoa, take it easy, hotshot," Ethan said.

"Sorry." She let out a nervous laugh and loosened her hold.

"Not that *loose." Ethan guided her hands back around his waist, gave the engine a quick rev, and pulled out of the parking lot.*

As they sped away, Priya's heart picked up. Headlights pierced the darkness, casting an arc of light before them. The road stretched out ahead, a rain-slicked ribbon weaving through open fields. In the aftermath of the storm, the stars seemed to shimmer even more brightly. Bathed in moonlight, away from any lights, it felt as if they were the only two people on earth.

Priya had never felt this kind of freedom before, unrestrained and electrifying, coasting toward an endless horizon. As the wind yanked her hood away, something stirred within her—a craving she didn't fully understand. It wasn't the gentle adolescent longing of a fifteen-year-old. It was fierce and electric.

With each curve they rounded, Priya became acutely aware of the way Ethan's muscles moved under his T-shirt, the rush of clinging to him, and the steady, powerful vibration of the engine beneath her.

The night air nipped at her face. Shadowy grass swayed in their wake, and the world whizzed by in a mosaic of moonlit fields. Priya snuggled closer, her arms gliding up Ethan's torso to his chest. For a fleeting moment, he tensed, looking over his shoulder as she nestled her cheek between his shoulder blades.

Then he grinned and turned back to the road. "Please, make yourself right at home," he said, over the roar of the engine.

Priya smiled and closed her eyes. The smell of his jacket and fresh wet earth wrapped around her senses, embedding itself in her mind.

In the years that followed, whenever the earthy fusion of leather and damp soil hit her, it took her straight back to this moment—the feeling of holding Ethan tight, of dancing on the edge of a dream, of never wanting the road to end.

Fifteen

"THAT WAS THE ONLY TIME you rode with me," Ethan said, running a hand through his hair.

"You left soon after," Priya replied, fiddling with a dried twig on the floor of the freight car. "Brooke was on my case after that night at camp. Everyone thought there was something going on between us."

"Imagine if they could see you now, practically ripping my shirt to shreds," Ethan teased as he slipped it back over his shoulders.

"At least your shirt is still a shirt. You *murdered* my top."

"A heroic sacrifice on the altar of passion," Ethan said. "We should perform the last rites right away. Bury it in the field before we head back."

Priya squealed as he tried to pry it off her again.

Ethan laughed, then pulled her close, their playful energy dissolving into something softer as they lay side by side. Sliding his fingers between hers, Ethan lifted their intertwined hands and gazed at them.

"What are you looking at?" Priya asked, acutely aware of the way her hand rested within his, the sheen of his watch, the contrast between their skin tones.

"Just enjoying the way your hand feels in mine."

The moment was cut short by the intrusive ring of his phone. Ethan sighed and sat up.

"Yes, Zach?" He paused before glancing at his watch. "Damn. Is that today? No, it's fine. Tell them I'm running a little late."

"Everything okay?" Priya asked when he hung up.

"That was my assistant reminding me that Sienna and I have a conference call with the PR team. I'm afraid I have to run." Rising to his feet, he helped Priya up.

The light had shifted, casting long shadows across the field. "Can't believe how quickly the afternoon slipped away," Priya said, not quite ready to leave.

"I know." Ethan smiled, brushing a leaf off her shoulder. "But I'll be quick—I promise."

As they grabbed their things, a shaft of hazy sunlight broke through the clouds. Hopping off the freight car, they trudged through the field toward Moksha, the ground still giving a little squelch here and there. Ethan carried the picnic bundle up the stairs and walked her to the door of the apartment.

"You, me, and no interruptions. As soon as I'm done," he said, his voice low and full of intent. "Be at the coach house in two hours." He leaned in to nuzzle her neck, but his phone buzzed again.

"Hey, Sienna," he answered. "Yeah, go ahead and start without me. I'll join you in a minute." He chuckled at something she said. "Well, they did warn us we'd be doing plenty of those together."

As he continued chatting, Priya waved him off and shut the door. She pressed her forehead against the cool wood, listening to Ethan's voice fade as he descended the stairs. After a moment, Priya heard the muffled thud of the door downstairs. She took a deep breath, letting herself get used to the silence. She was rehearsing for a day she knew was coming.

Priya stepped into the shower and let the water wash over her. This was no ordinary shower. It was the prelude to getting naked with someone. And not just anyone—Ethan Knight. That made it, arguably, the most important shower she'd ever taken.

She squeezed a ridiculous amount of body wash onto her loofah. This wasn't your standard-issue Solanki family soap. None of that bargain-basement stuff for her today. This was the fancy kind that had come as a freebie with another purchase because no one in their right mind would pay full price for it. Working the loofah into a creamy lather, she took her time, letting the suds glide over her skin. If she was going all out, she might as well enjoy it.

By the time her hair was washed and conditioned, Priya was ready for the big leagues. Her bikini line. It had been way too long since she'd gone to this much effort. Even before she and Manoj split, their bedroom had been a snooze-fest. They were perfect on paper, and they worked well together, but the spark? Nonexistent. Priya had known that from the start, so she had no one to blame but herself. Manoj had been the safe choice, and back then, safe was exactly what she'd needed. But Ethan? Ethan was dangerous in a way that stole the air from her lungs. When he looked at her, it was like gravity shifted, and she had to fight to keep her balance. And that's exactly what she needed *now.*

Priya did a quick armpit check before proceeding.

Still good, thank god.

Picking up her razor, she cursed her genes for her dark, stubborn hair. Meanwhile, Sienna Deville probably had a hairless bikini line, or at the very least, a team of professionals on speed dial. Armed with a mirror, Priya twisted herself into Olympic-level contortions as she groomed herself. The result was a landing strip that veered off with a noticeable slant. Priya decided it would have to do, as long as Ethan landed somewhere in the vicinity.

Just as Priya shut off the shower, the lights gave an ominous flicker and went out.

"You have got to be kidding me!" Priya groaned out loud.

Luckily, the blackout was short-lived, and the power came back on a moment later. Still, it felt like Moksha was messing with her—as if it *knew* she had a hot date with Ethan and was doing its best to sabotage her plans. She stepped out of the shower, a towel wrapped snugly around her. *Time to hustle, Priya. No telling how long these lights will hold.*

After drying off, she secured her damp locks in a towel. With Act One of the Most Important Shower of Her Life completed, it was time for Act Two.

Lotion.

Lots and lots of lotion.

As she smoothed it over her legs, she felt a little buzz of excitement, imagining Ethan's hands running over her skin. Priya spritzed her favorite perfume into the air and walked through it. She wanted Ethan to catch a few teasing notes, as if she naturally smelled that way. Then it was time for the all-important decision.

Underwear.

Priya stared at her drawer and sighed. She wanted something bold and sexy, but nothing matched up to the electric potential of the night. She slid the drawer shut with a sly smile. Nope, no underwear tonight—she was going commando.

She slipped into a slouchy sweater and a pair of wide-legged trousers that fell gracefully around her legs. Setting her hair in rollers, she leaned into the mirror and layered on the mascara.

Bring on the eye contact, she thought, adding a touch of blush and lip gloss. There was something undeniably hot about meeting someone's eyes in *those* moments.

Stepping back, she took in her reflection. She was glowing in a way that had nothing to do with her makeup—it was from the spark Ethan lit inside her.

As she started to shake out her hair, her phone rang. Her sister's name flashed on the screen, and Priya answered instantly.

"Megs!" she exclaimed, thrilled to finally connect with her middle sister. "I can never get through to you."

"Sorry, Pri," Meghna replied. "There's no network where I am. I have to trek to the nearest town to get in touch."

"Did you call Mumma and Puppa?" Priya asked. "They've been worried." Ever since Meghna had accepted a job in a remote part of India, their parents' anxiety had reached new levels.

"I just spoke with them. I'm making all the calls while I can." Meghna let out a short laugh.

"What's it like teaching so far from home?"

"Let's just say I'll never take the internet for granted again. And having no phone service is way more isolating than I imagined. It's been one thing after another, but I'm managing." Meghna paused, then her tone brightened. "Hey, Dee just told me that *Ethan Knight* is at Moksha . . ." Meghna let her words hang in the air. "Pri, that is wild!"

"I know. And Dee wants nothing more than to be here," Priya said, not wanting to say too much. She wasn't about to spill her steamy plans with Ethan. This was her decision, her moment, and she didn't want anyone else weighing in.

"And you?" Meghna pressed. "The divorce, moving back home, hosting Ethan Knight at Moksha—how are you dealing with all of it?"

"I'm . . . uh . . . I'm hanging in there." Priya's mind flashed back to her top hanging inside out around her neck while Ethan tried to pry it off. "But enough about me. I'm dying to hear how things are going with you."

Meghna launched into an update about her new life in rural India—about how things hadn't gone quite as planned, and she was in a new spot now. "Oh, and one more thing," she said before hanging up. "When I spoke to Puppa, he asked me to remind you to find his address book."

"Oh, right!" In all the excitement, Priya had nearly forgotten. "I'll look after it right away." *There's no way I'm letting my parents' knack for ill-timed calls derail my evening with Ethan.*

Priya slipped into a pair of flats and put on a necklace. As she reached for the door, she paused, then went back to her room to remove it. The last thing she wanted was for Ethan to think she was trying too hard. Ironically, looking effortlessly casual took a lot of effort.

Locking the door behind her, Priya skipped down the stairs, excitement buzzing through her. She had a hot date with Ethan and could barely think straight. Letting herself into Moksha, she headed straight for the basement and stepped into her father's office. The familiar hum of the dehumidifier filled the space, droning on like it always did to keep the records safe from mold and mildew. Priya searched Puppa's desk for his address book, riffling through the drawers. She finally spotted it under a ledger just as the lights gave a flicker. Snatching it up, she shut the drawer and headed for the door—but before she could reach it, the lights went out entirely, plunging the basement into darkness.

"Damn it!" Priya said out loud. She was still trying to remember where Puppa kept the flashlight when the power surged back on.

Priya sighed. The blackouts were becoming more and more frequent. Even without the required upgrade, Moksha's wiring was due for a complete overhaul. It would cost a small fortune, and she wasn't convinced it was the right move.

Priya looked at the address book in her hands, and wondered if she should just say she couldn't find it. It would buy her some time, but it also meant she'd need to move faster with her plan to get Ethan out of here.

A sudden sharp, sizzling buzz jolted her from her thoughts. Priya froze, her eyes zeroing in on the old outlet powering the dehumidifier. A wisp of smoke curled into the air, followed by the acrid smell of burning wires. Within a second, a shower of sparks erupted from the socket, raining down on a cardboard box. The embers caught, flickering for a moment before exploding into flames.

Priya's pulse slammed into overdrive. Grabbing the trash can, she braced herself to smother the flames. But then a thought crept in, insidious and undeniable. *What if I just . . . let it burn? What if this accidental fire is a blessing in disguise?* If Moksha went up in flames, her parents would have no choice but to walk away. The developer didn't want the building anyway, just the land. This fire could solve everything.

As the flames climbed higher, Priya's gaze darted around the room. Framed on the wall was the first Canadian two-dollar bill her father had earned, a relic from a time when two-dollar bills were still in circulation. Beside it hung a photo from Moksha's opening day, a garland of dried marigolds draped around it. Priya's gaze snapped to the shelf where a worn album held the only photos her parents had carried from India. A studio portrait from her childhood sat on Puppa's desk—Mumma, Puppa, her sisters, and a much younger version of herself, all lined up in stiff formality.

The smoke alarm shrieked to life as the room filled with a thick haze. Heat pressed against Priya's skin, but she hesitated, staring at the flames. This wasn't just a building. It was a house of stories, of lives, of history. Every box, every file contained records of people who had been mourned, celebrated, and remembered here. It was also a place of incredible hardship and restriction for her family. Priya's heart pounded as she stood rooted to the spot, caught in the push and pull between past and future, duty and freedom.

As the blaze intensified, something shifted within Priya. The sense of responsibility her parents had tried so hard to impress upon her turned into gut-deep instinct—something sacred, something worth protecting. Priya slammed the trash can down over the fire, but the flames shot out from beneath the edges, crawling along the baseboard like a living thing.

Priya staggered back, her nostrils stinging from the smoke. *The curtain! Use the curtain!* She seized a corner of the panel and yanked it hard. But before she could free it, a sudden sting flared up her leg.

"Fuck!" she gasped, glancing down in horror. Flames were creeping up the hem of her pants. She yelped and pulled them off, using the fabric to beat down the blaze.

But the smoke was winning. Hot, heavy, and pungent. Panic surged through Priya's chest. *I'm going to die trying to save the very place I want to escape.*

Her breath came in short, frantic gasps. Her head spun, the room swimming in a hazy blur. *Get down*, her brain screamed, something she vaguely remembered from old fire drills.

Priya dropped to her knees, pressing herself to the floor. *Where's the door?* She couldn't tell, but she dragged herself forward, praying she was crawling in the right direction.

Somewhere behind her, wood crackled and split with a sharp pop. The fire was growing, its heat prickling against her skin. Beads of sweat slid down her neck. Priya coughed violently, her throat raw, her eyes burning so badly she could barely keep them open.

Then a sudden hiss. A cold mist exploded into the air, forcing back the flames around her. Priya blinked, tears rolling down her face. Through the haze, she saw Ethan, gripping a fire extinguisher as he fought the flames. Relief swept over her, and she collapsed onto the floor, limp and exhausted.

Ethan worked methodically, driving the fire back with each sweep. The flames sputtered and shrank until only small pockets of smoke remained. Tossing the extinguisher aside, he dropped to his knees beside Priya, his hands gripping her shoulders.

"Pri," he called, his voice tight with worry. "Are you okay?" The alarm blaring around them couldn't drown out the urgency in his tone.

Priya nodded, her breath coming in shallow bursts. Ethan let out a sharp exhale, relief flickering across his face. He shot to his feet and cranked the basement window open. Cool air rushed in, soothing Priya's throat. Ethan's gaze remained sharp, his body tense and on high alert.

"Damn it, Pri," his voice cracked as he ran a hand down his face. "You scared the living hell out of me." Sliding an arm under her, he helped her to her feet. "What the hell happened?"

Before Priya could answer, a loud snap echoed through the room and sparks leaped from another outlet.

"Don't move! And don't touch anything!" Ethan barked, grabbing the extinguisher and rushing toward the flare.

Priya's head throbbed from the shriek of the alarm, the sound rattling her skull. Her limbs felt heavy, her balance wobbly as she climbed onto the desk. The room seemed to tilt, but she managed to wave a folder beneath the smoke detector. Relief washed over her as the piercing noise finally stopped.

Ethan's gaze snapped to her, his eyes narrowing. "Can you *not* do the opposite of what I just told you?" He rushed toward her, ready to help her down, and suddenly stopped in his tracks.

"What?" Priya frowned.

Ethan rubbed his eyes, blinked, and looked again. "Priya Solanki, are you standing bare-assed on your father's desk?"

Priya quickly used the folder to shield her lady parts. "No," she said. "I'm wearing nude underwear."

Ethan bent down, plucked her scorched pants off the floor, and held them up between his fingers. "Liar, liar, pants on fire."

"Ethan," Priya groaned.

"Relax, I've got you." He ripped down the curtain that was now hanging askew and approached her.

"Don't even think about coming any closer," Priya snapped, pointing at him like a scolding teacher. His current trajectory would bring him face-to-face with her nether regions.

"Fine," he conceded, holding the curtain out for her. "Not that I haven't seen my fair share of 'nude underwear.'"

"Turn around," Priya instructed.

"Really?" Ethan raised an eyebrow, but he did as she asked.

Priya hopped off the desk, yanked her sweater down as far as it would go, and tied the curtain around her waist.

Ethan turned around, taking in her makeshift skirt, and his attention quickly turned to her ankle. "Is that a burn?"

"Just a sting." Priya brushed it off. "It could've been much worse if you hadn't shown up." She felt like she'd been choking on the smoke forever, though she knew it couldn't have been more than a few minutes. The fire had spread fast, but Ethan had acted faster.

"I heard the smoke alarm and bolted over," Ethan explained. "I remembered seeing a fire extinguisher by the stairs when your father was showing me around, so I grabbed it on the way in."

"It started with that outlet." Priya nodded toward the fried socket.

Ethan nudged the charred box with his boot, making sure no embers remained. "It's under control, but we need to report it."

"Let's wait until I talk to Puppa," Priya said. "Moksha's already on thin ice. If they find out, Puppa might lose his license before the reno's even started."

"Fine. But we're cutting the power until the contractors get here."

"But that will shut down the power in the apartment too."

"You're staying with me." Ethan left no room for debate. "There's no way you're entering this place until it's safe again. Now let's go turn the power off."

He followed Priya to the electrical panel, an old box that looked one spark away from falling apart. Inside was a tangled mess of wires. Priya located the main switch and flipped it off. The metallic clack reverberated through the space before everything plunged into darkness.

"Come on." Ethan took Priya's hand and led her upstairs. As the light from his phone lit the way, Priya realized if she had succeeded in pushing him away, tonight would've been a disaster for both her and Moksha. She owed him her life.

Outside, Priya took a deep breath, welcoming the rush of cool air. As she stood before Moksha with Ethan, it felt less menacing than before. The windows that glowed like ever-watchful eyes were now extinguished. But the shift wasn't just in Moksha. Something inside her had changed too. The fire had reframed the way she saw things, and no one was more stunned about it than she was.

"Come on. Let's get you back to the coach house," Ethan said, his arm wrapping securely around her.

Priya didn't resist. She was too drained to argue, but there was something different in the way he held her now—steadier, more protective. His body curved instinctively around hers, like he meant to shield her from everything outside this moment. And his eyes, darker than usual and unreadably intense, made her pulse falter.

Had something changed in him too? Or was it just the fog of exhaustion playing tricks on her? Maybe. But as they walked together toward the coach house, Priya knew one thing for sure—she didn't want to push Ethan away anymore.

Sixteen

STEAM SWIRLED AROUND PRIYA as she stood under the shower, letting the water pour over her. This was not how she'd pictured the night going at all. And now, for the second time, she found herself washing ashes away in Ethan's bathroom. Except this time, when the door swung open and Ethan stepped inside the shower stall with her, it felt completely natural. He took the loofah from her hands and began to wash her back in slow circles.

As Priya's muscles relaxed and the buzz from the fire faded, her thoughts finally slowed. And that's when it hit her. *God, I've been such a hypocrite.*

She'd always wanted her parents to trust her choices, to believe she knew what was best for herself. But now she realized she hadn't offered them that same trust. Going behind their backs to sell Moksha wasn't some bold, heroic move. It was her deciding *for* them, as if she knew better. She'd told herself it was for their own good, that they'd thank her later. Because deep down, she hadn't trusted them to know what was best for themselves.

I thought I was fixing everything, but I was actually pushing my idea of what their future should be, the same way they've always tried to shape my life. The truth hit hard, knocking the breath from her chest and leaving her hollow.

Ethan noticed the shift in her. He set the loofah down and wrapped his arms around her, but it only made her feel worse. She'd been lying to him too.

"I'm a horrible person, Ethan." Priya buried her face in his chest, her words barely audible over the water pounding down on them.

"No, you're not," he murmured, rubbing her back. "You just went through something terrifying. And it's shaken you up. It's okay, baby. I've got you."

Priya clung to him, sobbing harder.

"Shhh." Ethan stroked her hair, and it reminded Priya of how perfect her curls had been earlier. Now she was a wreck.

"This wasn't how it was supposed to play out," she cried.

"Oh, yeah?" Ethan tilted her chin so he could look into her eyes. "How exactly was it supposed to play out?"

As he wiped her tears, Priya caught the smudge of mascara on his finger. Between her limp hair and smeared makeup, she knew she must look like a drowned raccoon. Meanwhile, each droplet of water on Ethan looked like it was strategically placed by a team of stylists.

Catching her defeated gaze, Ethan shut the water off. "Let's get you out of here. You're exhausted."

"Wait," Priya said, her heart pounding. "There's something I need to tell you." She couldn't keep the lies hanging between them anymore, her secret attempts to get him to leave. He deserved the truth, even if it meant he might walk away from her.

"Pri." Ethan's eyes swept over her, slow and hungry, before locking on hers again. "If we stand here another second, I'll have you pinned against this wall. And I won't stop until I've had all of you."

Priya's lips opened with a silent "Oh." A deep flush crept through her, making her hyperaware of everything—their bare bodies radiating heat, water sliding down their skin in glistening trails.

"Ethan . . ." she whispered.

He let out a slow breath and put some distance between them. "You've had one hell of a night. Let's just get you in bed, okay?" He handed her a towel before stepping out of the stall.

They dried off, the steam curling between them, before he slung a towel around his hips and led her to the bedroom. Pulling the covers back, he waited until she slipped into bed. Her eyes fluttered shut, the weight of the day pressing on her. When she opened them again, Ethan had returned with a first aid kit. He knelt at the foot of the bed, cradling her ankle in his hands.

"Does that hurt?" he asked, glancing up at her.

"No." She flinched slightly as he smoothed a cool layer of gel over her skin.

"You got off easy." He inspected the burn again and wrapped it with gauze. "It'll heal."

The bed shifted under his weight as he slid in next to her. "Come here," he said, opening his arm to her.

Priya let out a long sigh and moved into his warmth, resting her head against his chest. The steady beat of his heart soothed her, quieting her mind and making everything else melt away. She was glad she hadn't said anything. Missing out on this moment would have been unbearable. Tomorrow, she'd tell him the truth. As she drifted off, another thought crept in. What if Ethan didn't understand? What if everything between them ended up falling apart?

Seventeen

PRIYA AWAKENED TO the soft glow of morning light filtering through the curtains. For a moment, she lay still, piecing together where she was. As the events of the previous night rushed back, she became aware of Ethan's arm resting over her waist, his slow, steady breath against the back of her neck. Her towel had come undone during the night, and she could feel the warmth of Ethan's chest pressed against her back as he spooned her. She closed her eyes, savoring the fit of their bodies, their legs twisted together beneath the covers.

But then, curiosity got the better of her. She wanted to see what he looked like when he slept. Lifting his arm and setting it aside, she untangled their legs, inch by inch. Congratulating herself on her stealthy maneuver, Priya held her breath and rolled over, hoping the bed wouldn't creak.

Only to find Ethan watching her with an amused look.

"Hey," she croaked.

"Morning," he said, his voice husky and low. "Sleep well?" Ethan in the morning was a sight to behold. The contrast of stubble against the soft curve of his mouth was mesmerizing.

"I did," she replied. "You?"

"Not a wink."

"Oh?" *Did I snore? Did I mumble something embarrassing?*

"How could I?" he murmured, leaning in. "When all I wanted was this . . ."

With a swift tug, he pulled her closer, capturing her lips in a slow, heated kiss. Every sensation magnified. The slide of her legs against his, the whisper of the towel falling away from her completely, the seductive play of his tongue.

Priya sucked in a breath as Ethan's mouth found the hollow of her neck. Her toes curled. Her fingers tangled in his hair. The sheets slipped away, leaving her bare beneath the heat of his eyes. They burned as they traced every inch of her.

Priya squirmed, even though he'd already seen her naked in the shower. This felt different—more raw, more intimate. Her hands rose instinctively to cover herself, but Ethan caught her wrist.

"You're stunning," he said, his gaze holding hers. "Let me see." He guided her hands away. "Let me touch you." His lips brushed against her ear. "And taste you." His tongue dragged along the sensitive spot just behind her ear. "And feel you . . ."

A soft sound escaped Priya as she melted into the sensation. Ethan drew in a sharp breath at the way her body pressed against his. His hand slid down, claiming her waist. "I've waited long enough, Pri." His eyes met hers, full of raw, restless hunger. "Tell me you want this just as much."

"I do," Priya whispered, her voice breathy and thick with desire. "I want you, Ethan."

"That's my girl," he said, his lips brushing the hollow of her neck, breath scorching her skin and sending a tremor through her.

"Tell me where you want my tongue," he said, voice gravel and smoke. "Here?"

Her hands twisted in his hair as his mouth found her nipple, teasing in slow, deliberate swirls.

"Here?" His lips wrapped around the other, sucking until it tightened against his tongue.

"God . . . everywhere," she moaned, hips shifting restlessly.

His hand slipped between her thighs, and she tipped her head back, muscles coiling. But Ethan was in no rush to go straight *there*. He teased her with his fingers, circling. Slowly. Softly. Drawing it out. Priya felt herself melting, opening to him in ways that left her raw and exposed.

"Ethan . . ." Her voice was raw, nearly breaking.

"Not yet," he murmured, lips brushing her skin as he moved lower, trailing hot, open-mouthed kisses along her inner thigh. Just when she thought she couldn't take another second, his tongue flicked over her clit.

Priya gasped, her back arching off the bed. Ethan's mouth devoured her with bold, unrelenting heat. Every time she got close, he withdrew just enough to make her whimper, to make her crave more. He controlled every wave of pleasure, building her up piece by piece until she was breathless, aching, and shaking beneath him.

Sliding over her, eyes dark and fixed on hers, he dragged his thumb across her mouth, tugging her lip down to toy with the soft flesh inside. Her lips parted for him, and she drew his thumb into her mouth, slow and deliberate.

"Fuck . . . you're going to make me come right here . . ." Ethan growled, his voice thick with restraint. "All over this beautiful, filthy mouth." He grazed her lip with his teeth before pulling back just far enough to meet her eyes.

"Don't hold back," Priya murmured, her nails trailing down the sculpted lines of his chest.

"Oh, I won't," Ethan rasped. "But you're going to feel all of it first." His hand covered hers, guiding her down until her fingers wrapped around him. A groan rumbled from his chest as she began to stroke him with slow, deliberate movements. Swearing under his breath, he reached for the drawer, his motions swift and smooth as he tore open the condom and rolled it on.

Priya's breath caught as she felt the blunt heat of his tip pressed against her entrance, teasing the edge of everything she craved. She'd never felt so alive, so completely undone by anticipation alone. Ethan shifted, easing into her with slow, deliberate pressure. The stretch was exquisite—sharp, overwhelming—and stole the air from her lungs. She gasped, eyes fluttering shut as he sank deeper. A soft groan left him as he buried his face in the curve of her neck, lips brushing her skin.

For a moment, they remained motionless—bodies locked, nerves alight, drowning in sensation. Then Ethan pulled back and drove into her again, deeper, harder. Priya met him stroke for stroke, lost in the rhythm, the friction, the fire. This was Ethan—*her* Ethan—and he was all over her, his body moving with fierce intent, his lips igniting a melting sweetness inside her. Awkwardness melted, masks disappeared, only want remained.

Priya's fingers slipped between them, circling her clit in time with their rhythm. Ethan groaned, the sound pure heat.

"Eyes on me," he said, voice dark and commanding.

Priya's eyes fluttered open, and the sheer hunger in his gaze made her body quake.

"I want to see you come," he ground out.

That was all it took. Priya surrendered completely, her body pulsing around him, waves of ecstasy crashing over her—raw, endless, shattering.

Ethan followed with a deep, primal growl, his body tensing before shuddering hard against hers. For a moment, he remained on top of her, their bodies fused together in the afterglow. Priya savored the weight of him, grounding her in the quiet storm of what they'd just shared. Then, with a soft breath, he shifted and drew her into his arms.

As the glow of the morning sun brightened, Ethan laced his fingers with hers and lifted their hands toward the light. Rotating his wrist, he watched how the light illuminated their hands. Then he pressed a soft kiss onto the back of her hand.

"I could stay like this forever." Priya curled deeper into the warmth of his body.

"Good." Ethan's hand slipped to her waist, pulling her closer. "Because I'm not letting you get out of bed."

"Lucky for you, it's a comfortable bed." Priya smiled, her cheek pressed to his chest. The steady rhythm of his breath, the rise and fall of his chest . . . everything about this moment felt perfect. "I thought I'd be wired after everything that happened last night, but nope. I barely remember closing my eyes."

"That tired, huh?" Ethan brushed a strand of hair away from her face. His fingers stilled for a moment, and he shifted slightly, like something had just clicked in his mind. "Wait . . . didn't you say you wanted to tell me something last night?"

Priya's heart lurched.

Now? He wants to have this conversation now?

She could barely wrap her head around the fact that she was lying next to him after the most mind-melting experience of her life. She *wanted* to come clean—but seriously, who in their right mind would risk ruining things with Ethan Knight? And for what? It wasn't like he was sticking around forever, so why ruin the time they had left together? The fire had given her the perfect out. She could have let Moksha burn, and she hadn't. Her parents were keeping it, and she'd finally come to terms with it. She didn't have to like it, but she'd made her peace.

So, what was the point in telling him? Why drag them both into a conversation that could tear apart the one perfect thing in her life right now?

"I wanted to tell you that I'm a horrible person because, well . . . I can be sneaky." Priya's hand slipped under the covers, her fingers closing around him.

"Interesting." Ethan's lips curved as if weighing her confession. "I think we need to explore this side of you a little more."

Priya chuckled, then disappeared under the covers. Her mouth opened, warm and inviting, her tongue swirling over him in slow, tantalizing strokes.

Ethan exhaled slowly, his head falling back against the pillows. Everything was momentarily perfect—the soft white sheets, the beams of light playing through the curtains, the distant hum of the world awakening to a new day. Around the bed, Priya's circle of salt marked the fraying edges of their newfound bliss.

Eighteen

IT WAS EARLY AFTERNOON by the time Priya managed to pull herself away from Ethan. After showering and getting herself ready, she sat at the small dining table in the coach house and made the call she had been dreading. As her father's voice came through the line, Priya took a steadying breath.

"Okay . . . don't freak out," she said. "Everything's under control, but . . . there was a fire in the basement last night." She braced herself, instinctively pulling the phone away from her ear just in time to hear her father's startled outburst.

"*Su?*" he exclaimed. "*Aag?*" What? A fire?

Priya winced as the panic on the other end escalated.

"*Aag?*" her mother screeched in the background. "*Kya? Kyare? Kevi ritey?*" Where? When? How?

"*Su?*" Deepa chimed in over the speaker.

Priya took a deep breath and tried again. "There's some damage, but it's just the office. I was getting Puppa's address book when the outlet sparked and—"

"*Suuu?*" A collective gasp echoed.

"You were inside the building when it happened?" her mother cried.

"I tried to stop it, but it spread quickly. If Ethan hadn't shown up in time, neither Moksha nor I would have made it."

There was a brief pause before a barrage of questions hit.

"Mr. Ethan saved you?"

"And Moksha?"

"Are you both okay?"

"How bad is the damage?"

"We're fine," Priya replied, switching her phone to speakerphone. "It was an electrical issue. I've shut off the main power and taken photos. I wanted to check in with you before reporting—"

"We are on our way," her father declared. "We'll be there by this evening."

"There's no need to rush back," Priya said quickly. "The power's out in the apartment, and there's nothing you can do until the reno crew arrives."

"Mr. Ethan is okay?" Puppa asked. "No issues at the coach house, right?"

"He's fine. We—"

"Priya! The food!" Mumma shrieked. "Did you move it to the fridge in the coach house?"

Mumma's priorities were always clear. First, her daughter. Second, her high-profile tenant. And a very enthusiastic third? Her homemade food. Priya's list was, however, a little more streamlined at the moment. She watched as Ethan finished another set of push-ups, his muscles flexing with each slow, controlled movement. A light sheen of sweat clung to his skin, catching the light.

"Beta," her father said, "how did you cope with no power in the apartment last night?"

"I . . . uh . . . I stayed at the coach house."

"*Suuu?*" Mumma, Puppa, and Deepa squawked like a chorus of parrots over the speaker.

Priya recoiled from her phone, mentally face-palming herself. The mere mention of spending the night in the coach house with Ethan was enough to send her parents racing home, tires squealing. What was she thinking? Oh wait. She *wasn't*. No brain cells were firing today.

"I slept on the sofa bed," she improvised.

Ethan paused mid-workout, one eyebrow lifting as he looked over at her.

"At least you had the sense to use the sofa bed," Mumma said. "You know better than to let a guest take the sofa bed. And Mr. Ethan isn't just any guest. You give that man anything he wants."

Priya met Ethan's eyes across the room as he toweled off. He shot her a wide grin, daring her to argue.

"Power or no power, you can't stay at the coach house," Puppa said. "I'll see if I can buy a backup generator on the way home. We'll make do until things get sorted."

Priya heard Mumma say something to Puppa, their voices dropping into a hushed conversation.

"Deepa?" she asked. "You still there? What's going on?"

"Okay, listen." Deepa's voice dipped to a low whisper, the kind that meant drama was incoming. "Remember how I said Vinod Uncle set up a meeting so Mumma and Puppa could meet that guy for you? Well, if they come back early, they'll miss it. That's what they're discussing right now."

"You have *got* to be kidding me." Priya pinched the bridge of her nose. "I told them I'm not interested."

"You know how they are, Pri. They're not giving up that easily."

"Well, they can do what they want," Priya muttered. "But I have no interest in meeting—"

"Dinesh," Deepa filled in with a snort. "Vinod Uncle sent a

full report . . . birth date, height, weight, job . . . honestly, it's like a résumé."

"I don't care who Vinod Uncle's parading in front of them: Dinesh, Ramesh, Nilesh, Paresh . . . it's not happening. But thanks for keeping me posted."

"You know I've got your back," Deepa replied. "Besides, whatever happens to you is just a preview of what Megs and I will have to face too. We're in this together, Pri."

"Priya, beta," Puppa returned to the phone. "Mumma and I are in a bit of a bind. Vinod Uncle and Poonam Auntie have taken time off for us. If you truly don't need us at Moksha right now—"

"It's totally fine," Priya said, cutting him off. "Go to Vinod Uncle's." *Go meet this Dinesh guy. Have chai, have theplas. Just don't come back yet.* "Everything is under control here." Her voice wavered as Ethan closed the gap between. He was all heat and muscle, his nearness clouding her thoughts.

"Are you sure?" Puppa asked, then, with a trace of worry. "And Mr. Ethan? Will he be leaving, since Moksha isn't usable right now?"

Priya froze for a beat. She hadn't even considered that Ethan might go. She turned toward him, a twist of unease in her stomach. He met her eyes and gave a decisive, almost teasing shake of his head.

"He hasn't mentioned leaving," Priya replied, unable to hide the smile in her voice. "But you can call him yourself to confirm." Her breath caught as Ethan's fingers slid under her sweatshirt.

"Okay, then. And send me the photos of the fire. I'll see if our insurance will cover it."

Priya's eyes fluttered shut as Ethan's hands slipped beneath the waistband of her jeans.

"Priya?" Puppa asked. "Are you listening?"

"Uh-huh . . . Photos . . . Fire . . ." Her words trailed off as Ethan picked her up and sat her on the table.

"And I need that number from my address book. Do you still have it?"

"Yes," Priya replied, as Ethan kissed her neck, his hands tracing a slow path down her back. "Yesss."

A saltshaker toppled to the floor as her legs wrapped around him.

"Yes, *what*?" Puppa snapped. "What's going on over there, Priya?"

Priya hopped off the table, giving Ethan the side-eye. He was clearly enjoying distracting her.

"I have the address book right here," she said, flipping to the page with Mr. Foster's number and giving it to Puppa.

"Mumma and I will call Mr. Ethan later," Puppa said. "He is a real-life hero for saving you and Moksha."

Ethan flexed his biceps, then mimed a slam dunk just as she hung up. "Would you look at that?" He grinned. "Your father likes me. I might have to swing by more often. Maybe even stay in the coach house again when I'm back in September for TIFF."

"You'll be back in September?" Priya asked, surprised. *And he'd want to see me?*

"Yeah. My movie with Sienna is premiering at the film festival."

Priya frowned. The timeline she'd built for their fling, ending neatly with Ethan's departure, scattered like leaves in the wind. If he was coming back in a few months' time, that was going to complicate things in a big way.

"Try not to faint from excitement," Ethan said, catching the look on her face. He caught her hand in his, tugging her closer, and gave her hand a gentle squeeze. "Want to come with me to the premiere?"

"To the *movie* premiere?"

"No, darling, my highly classified sock-puppet performance," Ethan said with a laugh. "Yes, the premiere."

"Like on the red carpet?" Priya bit her lip. She couldn't imagine walking *any* red carpet. With or without Ethan. What would she even wear?

"Would that really freak you out that much?" he asked, raising an eyebrow.

"I don't want to be plastered all over the media, Ethan," she said, letting go of his hand. "I thought we agreed this was just a fling."

"I'm not asking for anything serious, Pri. Just a fun night out—get dressed up, hit the town, maybe go out after. You could come with Brooke if you don't want to be seen with me," he offered, the corner of his mouth quirking up in a smile that almost looked sad. He glanced away, and Priya felt awful. Ethan didn't offer himself up for rejection easily, not after the way his father had hurt him. Yet here he was, nudging the boundaries of their arrangement. A part of her soared, buzzing with the possibility that he might want more. But another part was terrified. They were so different, and they lived in entirely opposite worlds. *He* was Hollywood; *she* was . . . Moksha.

"I totally get it if you're not ready," Ethan said. "The press, the limelight, the attention . . . it can be overwhelming. And even though you've upgraded to Priya 2.0, you still like to live life as if it's a program you can code. Neatly. Line by line."

"Yeah, well, the program's malfunctioning," Priya said with a dry laugh. Her divorce, her career, and her bank account flashed through her mind. And now, as Ethan nibbled his way down the side of her neck, she realized her firewall had been breached too. Her whole system was breaking down, byte by byte, and despite how scary it was, she was loving every second of it.

"Okay, okay. Time-out." She caught his hands before they wandered farther. "There's work to be done. Photos to send, a fridge to empty . . ."

"Fine." Ethan drew back in mock disappointment. "You look after the photos, then we'll tackle the fridge together."

"How noble of you. My parents would be mortified if they knew you were moonlighting as a janitor in their absence."

"It's the least I can do. Especially considering what I plan to do with their daughter later." He cradled her chin, brushing his lips over hers in a slow, tantalizing kiss. Just as Priya started to melt, he broke away.

"Chop-chop, Pri." He grinned. "And no slacking off until it's done." With a cheeky swat to her backside, he turned her around and sent her on her way.

Nineteen

"YOU SLACKED OFF," Ethan teased. Lying under the faded quilt in her room, he looked far too content about it.

Priya laughed. "I was dealing with some very important matters."

He tucked her hair behind her ear, lips grazing the sensitive spot just beneath it. Then he paused, his mouth still close. "Huh," he murmured, his voice low and thoughtful.

"What?"

"You've got a little beauty mark here, tucked away behind your ear," he said, fingertips brushing her skin.

"You're cataloguing me now?" Priya replied playfully.

"Every detail."

Stretched out beside Ethan, legs entangled in her small bed, Priya felt as if she were peering over the edge of a dream. No figment of her imagination could have prepared her for the sight before her—Ethan Knight sprawled out on her bed, his presence clashing with the floral pillowcases and lavender walls.

"So, this is your room." Ethan adjusted his pillow and leaned back.

Priya shifted, resting her head on his chest. "Until I get back on my feet."

"And there's your window," he declared.

Priya gave him a puzzled look.

"The morning after my going-away party, right before I left for New York, I stood out there," he said. "I had my backpack on, and my escape route planned, but as I rolled my motorcycle out of Knight Estates, I found myself turning into Moksha." A wistful smile formed on Ethan's lips. "I found a twig and thought I'd tap on your window. But I couldn't figure out which one was yours, and I didn't want to get you into trouble, so I turned around and left."

"Really?" Priya asked, looking up at him. "Why did you want to see me?"

"I wanted to say goodbye."

"So romantic. Except for the part where you gave up and left," she joked. "But now here you are. In my room. I still can't believe it."

"It's a very scholarly room." Ethan gestured at the pile of textbooks on her desk.

"I'm taking some courses online. App development. Stuff like that," Priya explained.

"Don't tell me you're trying to design your dream guy, line by line."

"Why in the world would I do that when I've got the ultimate prototype right here?" she said, giving his bicep an appreciative squeeze. "Premium model . . ." Her hand glided over his chest. "Impressive specs . . ." She traced the contours of his abs. "Just need to run some live performance tests . . ." As her fingers inched lower, Ethan grabbed her wrist.

"Easy now," Ethan said, his voice a dark murmur. "You're about to initiate a full launch sequence."

Before Priya could go any further, Ethan's phone buzzed yet

again. "You should check that." She sighed, propping herself up on her elbow. "Someone's been trying to reach you all afternoon."

"Right." Ethan dragged his attention to his phone. "It's my social media manager asking for a new photo," he said, scrolling through his messages. "Apparently, my absence is starting to fuel rumors."

He began typing, reading his response out loud. "I'll . . . send . . . one . . . soon." Then he set the phone down, his focus shifting fully to Priya. "Now, let's pick up where we left off."

Stretched out on his side, the quilt barely clinging to his hips, Ethan looked like a Renaissance sculpture carved from light and shadow—sun-warmed skin stretched over chiseled muscle, every inch of him gloriously bare. The light from the window skimmed his jaw, poured over his chest and dipped into the valleys of his abs. His hair was a tousled mess, his jaw dusted with stubble, and that lazy, knowing smile? Yeah, she was done for.

"You're ridiculous," Priya murmured with a shaky laugh. "No one should look this good without a filter." She grabbed Ethan's phone, swiped the camera open, and pointed the lens at him.

Ethan's smile curled at the edges, slow and sinful. Then his gaze shifted—darker, hungrier—and Priya forgot to breathe. She felt the heat of his stare straight through the lens, in her chest, in her pulse, curling between her thighs. That look didn't flirt. It claimed. There was no softness, no sweetness. Just a raw, consuming need that promised he'd take her apart with his hands, his mouth, his body, and take his sweet, dirty time doing it.

"Holy hell," Priya whispered, her breath catching as she took the photo. "Do you even know what you're doing to me right now?"

Ethan didn't answer. He grabbed the phone and tossed it aside. Reality slipped away as they kissed, leaving only the electrifying graze of lips and the tangled burn of desire. Ethan's phone buzzed again, but neither of them paid attention. It was only when the notifications came flooding in, one after the other, that they pulled apart.

"What the hell is going on?" Ethan muttered, grabbing his phone and scrolling through the messages. "Fuck," he said, his brow furrowing. "The photo you took auto-synced to my cloud storage. My social media manager saw it, thought it was the photo I said I'd send him, and posted it everywhere."

Priya stared at him, mouth slightly open. "Are you serious? That was a *private* moment between us. And now it's up for everyone to see?" A wave of disbelief rolled through her, followed by the urge to see it with her own eyes.

As Ethan worked through the avalanche of notifications, Priya unlocked her phone and pulled up his Instagram profile. Among the carefully curated posts, there it was—the photo she'd taken, raw and unfiltered, a glimpse of something they hadn't meant to share. There was no caption, but it didn't matter. It was crystal clear that Ethan Knight was enjoying a very personal, intimate afternoon.

Scrolling through the comments, Priya felt like she was witnessing the epicenter of a digital earthquake:

"Too much sauce, Ethan. Too much."
"I've never wanted to be a quilt so badly in my life."
"That's a whole meal right there."
"I feel personally victimized by Ethan Knight's hotness."
"Whoever took this pic, you're doing God's work."
"Ethan Knight breaking the internet yet again."

She hit refresh and saw that the photo was being shared at an equally astonishing pace. Every gossip magazine, fan page, and entertainment account had reposted it. Hell, it was even popping up in her friends' stories. Priya couldn't believe it. The fascination aimed at Ethan was unreal, unlike anything she'd ever seen or experienced herself. A swirl of emotions hit Priya: awe, pride, disbelief . . . and a gnawing sense of invasion. Her private moment with Ethan was splashed all over the internet for the world to analyze. Deleting the photo was not an option. It would only spark more curiosity.

"This is insane," she whispered, looking up at Ethan.

"Welcome to my world." His half smile hinted at the resilience that came with years of living under the microscope. "I'm sorry our afternoon took an unexpected turn. Let me handle this really quick." Switching to his social media accounts, he scrolled through to assess the damage.

Priya turned her attention back to her phone and refreshed the page again. It was then that she noticed a new comment by Sienna Deville: *"Whoa, Ethan, didn't know you were casting for your next love scene. Auditions still open?"*

Priya rolled her eyes so hard she saw the back of her head. Without thinking, she clicked Follow.

"Okay . . . this just got crazy," Ethan said, his voice low with disbelief.

Priya's stomach dropped. "What now?"

"Priya Solanki just followed me," Ethan declared with a grin. "Took her long enough."

A new notification popped up on Priya's phone. Ethan Knight was now following *her*. She looked up, but Ethan was still on his phone. "And now to follow a bunch of random people to throw off the gossip-hunters." He looked up and winked at her.

Despite the crisis, Priya felt giddy.

A moment later, Ethan tossed his phone aside and leaned in. "Enough of that. Remind me. Where were we before we got interrupted?"

"About to clean out the fridge," Priya quipped.

"Oh right, the fridge," Ethan drawled. "I'm going to have to veto that plan for now."

"It's getting dark, Ethan. We have to do it now or we won't be able to see anything."

His lips brushed her earlobe. "Sometimes it's just better to feel your way through things."

As his tongue blazed a trail to her stomach, Priya lost all sense of the world beyond her bedroom. The fridge, the fire, the photo, the fans . . . everything faded into sweet oblivion.

Tucked away in the coach house, Priya let herself play house—setting the table, arranging the plates, lighting a candle. With time still on her side, she stepped outside and returned with a sprig of lilac from the garden for her centerpiece. As she adjusted the flower, her gaze drifted to her phone. Despite her best efforts, the temptation to check in was too strong.

Settling on the couch, Priya opened Ethan's profile and homed in on Sienna's comment like a heat-seeking missile. A happy grin spread across her face when she saw that Ethan hadn't replied. Just as she was about to log out, her phone buzzed with a call from Brooke.

"What the hell are you doing, Priya?" Brooke's voice exploded through the phone, so sharp that Priya whipped around, half expecting to find Brooke peering over her shoulder as she stalked Ethan online.

"Huh?" Priya fumbled.

"Don't you 'huh' me. What's going on with you and Ethan?"

"I . . . uh . . . we . . ."

"That's right. My brother and bestie are playing tonsil hockey, and I had to find out from *Instagram*?"

Priya froze, caught completely off guard. "How did you . . . I was going to . . . Everything happened so quickly—"

"Oh, I bet it did." Brooke let out a sharp breath, her voice tight. "As quickly as the snapshot you took of him in bed?"

Priya opened her mouth, but no words came out. She hated that Brooke had found out like this—through a screen, like a stranger.

"I know your room, Priya," Brooke said. "I've slept in that bed, snacked in that bed, cried in that bed. I knew exactly where Ethan was the moment I laid eyes on that photo. What in the world is going on with you? My brother, Priya? Seriously? I mean, hookups are *my* department, not yours."

"It's not like that, Brooke," Priya said. "We're not *hooking up*."

"So, you guys are together-together?"

"No . . . I just . . ." Priya took a deep breath before going for it. "I used to have a massive crush on him. It was kind of a thing for years."

"Are you kidding me right now?" Brooke said, practically choking on disbelief. "I told you every single detail about my crushes—the good, the bad, the *cringey*—and you were keeping *this* from me? Seriously, Priya!"

"And what would you have done if I had told you?"

"Oh, I would have marched straight up to Ethan and told him about it. Or made up horrible stories about you, just to keep you to myself."

Priya shook her head, laughing. "Yeah, sounds like you had my back, for sure."

"Hey! Nobody takes my best friend away without a fight."

"Nobody's stealing me away from you," Priya said. "It's just . . . I felt like I was at rock bottom after the divorce. Then Ethan showed up, and something just clicked, like I had a shot at feeling alive again."

"So what . . . he's your rebound?"

Priya sighed. "It's complicated."

"Complicated? Oh, Pri, that's dangerous territory. You know how it is with him—you only have to follow the trail of emotionally wrecked exes he's left in his wake. But honestly? I'm not just worried about you. I'm worried about him too. You're nothing like the girls he's dated before. His walls are down, Pri."

"What are you saying?" Priya asked, the pulse quickening in her veins. "That he's into me?"

Brooke let out a quiet breath. "Well, first there was that weird call the other day. He just sounded different, you know? Softer. Distracted. And now this photo. One look at him and I knew. He's not just fooling around. He's letting you in." Brooke paused for a beat. "Where *is* he, by the way? I've been trying to get a hold of him."

"He's out riding," Priya replied, turning Brooke's words over in her mind. Brooke was right. She'd been so caught up in the way Ethan made her feel that she hadn't stopped to think about what he might need from her.

"Hey . . ." Brooke sensed the shift in her energy. "You know I'm rooting for you, right? I just don't want either of you to get hurt. Today, his photo is trending. Tomorrow, it could be yours. I'm not sure if you're ready for that kind of attention."

"I know, I know . . . And really, thank you." Priya meant it more than Brooke probably realized. A lot had surfaced today, including her years-long crush on Ethan, and Brooke had been more understanding than she ever expected.

"Hey, Brooke?" A smile tugged at her lips. "When did you become so wise? Weren't you the one who used to ask me if you should break up over a text or a call?"

"I'm a genius, except when it comes to my own relationships." Brooke giggled.

"Okay, but seriously, enough about me, your brother, and this whole photo situation. What's happening at your end? I can't keep track of where you are anymore."

"I'm in Indonesia with my fur baby, darling. A wonderful little healing sanctuary in Ubud," Brooke replied. "Hang on, I'll send you a pic."

A photo popped up on Priya's screen: Lady Whiskerbottom lounging on a mat, lush greenery spilling through open windows.

"Aww." Priya's heart ached a little at the sight of her. "She still carries herself like a queen, even if time's caught up with her."

"Yeah, she's slowing down, and it's hitting me harder than I expected. But I've found her a brilliant spiritual healer. She's getting a catnip chakra cleanse today."

"Really?" Priya laughed. "And you? What have you been up to?"

"I'm exploring orgasmic enlightenment," Brooke announced.

Priya gave a small nod. "Of course you are. Let me guess. The book deal is next? *Eat, Pray, Meow.*"

"Who has time to write, Pri? Unless it's a memoir for Lady Whiskerbottom."

"She'll sell more copies than you."

"No doubt about that." Brooke snorted. "Okay, I'm being summoned by her royal highness. Say hi to Ethan for me, will ya? And tell him to keep his shirt on. I don't need to be ambushed by fifty shades of my brother every time I check my feed."

"Bye." Priya grinned as she ended the call.

A second later, her phone buzzed again.

"Priiiii!" Deepa's voice sang out when Priya answered.

"Hey. What's up?"

"Oh, nothing much," Deepa drawled. "Except my oldest sister getting her groove on—with Ethan frickin' Knight."

Rubbing her temples, Priya cursed her lack of foresight. Of course Deepa would put two and two together, too, just like Brooke. "Oh god," she moaned, as another thought hit her. "Please tell me Mumma and Puppa haven't caught on."

"Don't worry, they're not exactly screen-obsessed, so you're in the clear. But now I get why you wanted them to visit Vinod Uncle. Such a dutiful daughter. 'Please go. Don't worry about the fire. Everything is under control.' Everything except the fire in your pants, Pri. There's a five-alarm blaze going on in their absence."

"It's a long story, Dee," Priya explained. "We kind of had a connection back in the day."

Deepa gasped. "Oh my god, what? And you're only just telling me now? I have posters of him in my room." She paused. "Wait, is he going to be my *jiju*?"

"Calm down. He's never going to be your brother-in-law. And for the record, I never saw this coming."

Deepa tried to muffle her laughter, but a snicker escaped.

"What's so funny?" Priya asked.

"'Coming attractions' just got a whole new meaning."

"Oh, for heaven's sake, Dee."

"Okay, okay." Deepa's tone shifted. "We have to make sure Mumma and Puppa don't find out. This is actual visual proof of Ethan in your bed for the whole world to see."

"God, you're right." A wave of dread washed over Priya. "And it's out there forever."

"Look, I only figured it out because I know your room."

"You and Brooke."

"Okay, that's just two people. And we've got your back. Mumma and Puppa aren't on social media, so chances are they'll never see that photo."

"You're right," Priya replied. "That makes me feel a lot better."

"I still don't believe it. You and Ethan Knight," Deepa marveled. "Oh shit. Mumma's coming! Gotta run. Bye!"

Priya hung up and leaned back with a sigh. As she set her phone down, it rang again.

"Seriously?" she groaned.

An unknown number flashed on the screen. She ignored it, but the caller rang again. Priya's heart sank. Had someone tracked her down? A gossip columnist? A tabloid writer? The ringing resumed, sounding even more insistent.

Priya stood and switched her phone off. As she walked away from it, a series of sharp knocks rattled the front door. Creeping to the window, she slowly pulled the curtain aside and was greeted by a face pressed up against the glass. Priya screamed and leaped back. The man held up a package with a courier logo. Letting out a shaky breath, Priya opened the door.

"Sorry, didn't mean to scare you," the man said as Priya signed for the package. "I called the number on the slip several times because nobody was answering at the funeral home, so I thought I'd try my luck here."

"Thanks for going the extra mile." Priya took the package and closed the door behind her. *Get a grip*, she scolded herself. *Like* you *would suddenly be the latest tabloid sensation.*

As the delivery van rumbled away, Priya examined the package. It was wrapped in iridescent paper with her name embossed on a sapphire-blue tag. Curious, she peeled back the paper to reveal a small velvet box. Inside was a gossamer-thin chain with a star-shaped pendant made from tiny diamonds that looked like they had been plucked straight from the sky.

The accompanying note read: *This star burns for you.*

Priya smiled softly, remembering the conversation she and Ethan had shared. Walking to the bathroom, she turned on the light and fastened the necklace. The star nestled perfectly in the dip between her collarbones. Gazing at her reflection, Priya realized that the sparkle in her eyes had nothing to do with the diamonds—it was something Ethan had ignited in her. All the distractions and worries of the day faded like cosmic dust trailing a supernova.

The front door opened, interrupting her thoughts. Ethan was back. Priya's heart leaped as she raced to greet him.

"Miss me?" he teased, tossing his helmet aside just in time to catch her in his arms. He twirled her around like they'd been apart for years instead of hours. He brought her down slowly, his hands resting at her waist.

"Someone's in a good mood," he said.

"Someone's happy to see you." She slipped her arms around him. He smelled of the wind and woods and earth and leather. "How was your ride?"

"Pure torture." His kiss was slow and deep. "I couldn't wait to get back."

Before she could reply, he scooped her up and carried her toward the bedroom.

"What about dinner?" she asked, as he strode past the table.

"What's that?" He tossed her onto the bed and stripped off his jacket. Crawling over her, he nibbled on her ear, kissing a path down her neck.

His attention dropped to the star pendant resting between her collarbones. "It couldn't have found a more perfect spot." His fingertips brushed over it.

Priya caught his hand, holding his gaze. "I adore it, but no more gifts, okay?"

"I don't make promises I can't keep," he murmured, lowering his head to lick the sensitive skin just below the pendant.

Priya melted beneath the possessive heat of Ethan's touch, her hands gliding over his shoulders as the rising tide of desire swept her away.

Twenty

DAYS MELDED INTO NIGHTS, weaving together like chapters of a story that Priya never wanted to end. Although spring brought warmer days, mornings and evenings retained a chill. It was as if the universe, too, was urging Priya and Ethan closer. They cuddled under the blankets at dawn, and in the evenings, they lit a bonfire in the field and watched the embers float to the sky.

Sitting in the open doorway of the forgotten freight car, with her shoulder leaning against its metal frame, Priya's legs dangled over the edge. Ethan lay on her lap, reading a screenplay. His expression transformed with each page, the storyline pulling him into its world. A carpet of grass and wildflowers surrounded them, swaying under the afternoon sun.

As she scrolled lazily through her phone, Priya suddenly perked up. "Ooh. This looks cool."

"What is it?" Ethan put his script aside and sat up.

"An app-building contest." Priya tilted her screen toward him. "Hosted by a nonprofit that supports tech start-ups. You come up with an original idea; build a prototype across Android, iOS, and the web; and submit it."

"Winner gets fifty thousand dollars and help launching a real app." Ethan skimmed through the description. "Not bad."

"I know, right? I've been playing around with a bunch of ideas, but this gives me a reason to commit and actually start building an app."

Ethan gave her a thoughtful look. "How much would you need to launch something like this on your own? I mean, if you bypass the contest? I do a bit of angel investing if you're interested."

"I appreciate the offer, but after what went down with Manoj, I've learned my lesson. I'm never mixing business and personal stuff again."

"Pri, I'm not Manoj. We could—"

She pressed a finger to his lips. "Just having you here, listening to me ramble on is more than enough. I need to do this on my own, to prove to myself and my parents that I've got what it takes. Funding is only one part of the puzzle. Winning could open doors to mentorship, collaborations, and sponsorships too."

"You can do anything you set your mind to, Pri," Ethan said, his eyes scanning her face. "You've always had a quiet courage inside you. When life knocks me down, I raise hell, spewing smoke and exhaust fumes everywhere. But you? You just rise, dust yourself off, and push forward."

"I liked the hell-raising biker." Priya smiled. "But I always saw beyond the rebel to the guy with a soft, gentle heart. Fame hasn't changed you one bit."

As their gazes caught, the moment stretched—charged, weighty, and peaceful all at once. Priya's heart hammered in her chest. Something was shifting between them.

For a second, it felt like their younger selves were right there, giving them a push to own this connection. They had come full circle—from kids escaping to this hidden spot to adults who had made it back to each other through all of life's twists and turns.

The rusty walls around them, the train tracks swallowed by wild plants, the pages of Ethan's screenplay, all seemed to dissolve. But then Priya's phone went off, shattering the moment.

"It's Manoj." She sighed, silencing the call. "Probably work stuff."

She tried to move past the interruption, but the phone buzzed again.

"Persistent little fucker," Ethan muttered, glaring at the screen.

Priya frowned. "Actually, it's Ravi now. How the hell did he get my number?"

"What's with all these guys making cameo appearances?" Ethan grabbed Priya's phone and sent Ravi to voicemail. "The lead role's been cast, and spoiler alert—it's me."

He was about to mute the phone when it chimed with a new notification. "Oh, for fuck's sake," he growled. Then he paused, his brow furrowing. "It's a message from your sister Deepa," he said, handing the phone back to Priya.

Priya glanced at the message preview: *This is Dinesh.* Curious, she tapped it open and read the rest: *Mumma and Puppa met with him and his family today. Heads up—they asked for your number.*

The image took a second to load, then filled the screen. Dinesh stood in the center, looking as wholesome as a matrimonial ad—tidy hair, friendly smile, very "good boy" energy. On his right were, presumably, his parents, and on his left, her own. Mumma clutched his arm like he was already family, and her father was grinning, eyes crinkled at the corners. As Priya stared at the photo, a wave of déjà vu washed over her. Her parents had given Manoj the same stamp of approval, praised his ambition, his charm, and how he would "secure her future."

"You okay?" Ethan asked, grazing her arm with his fingers.

"Meet Dinesh." Priya angled her screen so he could see the photo. "My parents' latest attempt to fix my life. They think being with the right man will magically solve everything."

Ethan looked at her phone for half a second, his expression tightening. Then he pried it from her hand and turned it face down. "Enough interruptions, Priya. We need to talk. I know we both agreed this was just a fling, but let's be honest . . . there's something more happening here." His eyes searched hers, his voice rough around the edges.

Priya's throat tightened as the words hung between them. "I know," she said softly. "But do you actually *want* something more? With me?"

Ethan held her gaze, steady and unwavering. "More than I've wanted anything in a long time. Being with you feels solid. It feels *real*, Pri. And I'm not ready to walk away from that. Question is, do *you* want to take this further?"

"I do," Priya admitted, drawing in a shaky breath. "But I don't know how to handle this—my family, your fame . . ." Her gaze dropped as she continued. "I mean, even if I say yes to us, I can't handle the attention that follows you. The press would be all over me. If we don't work out . . . that's another failure I'll have to carry. My divorce already feels like a black mark against me, and this would be so much more public. So much harder to escape."

"I get it." Ethan reached for her hand, his grip warm and grounding. "I know how scary this feels, but I think we deserve a chance. A *real* one. I'm not saying it's going to be easy, but I'll be right here with you for all of it. The messy parts too. You don't have to go through it alone, Pri. I may not understand everything you're facing, but I know what it's like to choose between what you want and what's expected of you. I'm paying for that choice myself." His gaze drifted toward his father's home. Then he turned back to her. "We can figure it out together—you and me. Whatever happens, I can promise you that."

Priya rested her head on his shoulder and let out a soft sigh. She wasn't used to leaning on anyone else. As the eldest daughter of immigrant parents, she carried more than just her own dreams. She was their firstborn, the one meant to pave the way for her sisters and justify the sacrifices her parents had made. Their hopes and struggles were all tied to her choices.

But here, in this quiet little pocket of time with Ethan, she could just *be*—be seen, held, and understood. She had three whole days with him before her parents came back. Enough time to figure things out. She closed her eyes, soothed by the soft murmur of pages as Ethan flipped through his script again. Every detail—the hum of insects weaving through sun-dried stalks, the sun-heated metal of the freight car under her legs, the distant call of birds—etched itself into her mind.

"Do you think we're happy when we get what we want because we finally have it, or because the wanting is over?" she mused.

Ethan glanced at her from the corner of his eye. "A bit of both, I'd say. Why?"

"Because right now, I don't want anything else."

"Oh, just wait," he said with a grin. "I've got a whole list of things that'll have you begging for more before the night's over."

Priya let out a soft laugh. "Being proven wrong has never sounded so good. How did I get so lucky?" She whispered the last part to herself, as if speaking the words any louder would jinx things.

Ethan flipped the final page, pausing for a long moment before setting the screenplay down.

"Any good?" Priya asked.

"It's better than good. It's absolutely brilliant. But the real question is . . ." He brushed a strand of hair from her face. "Are *you* done?"

"Done with what?" she asked.

"Thinking about your app," he teased, playfully tapping her forehead. "Thinking about your parents. Thinking about us. Thinking. Thinking. Thinking . . ."

"Well, I still haven't figure out how to explain *you* to my parents."

"So, you *are* thinking about coming clean with them?"

"It's a lot. I mean, you're . . . *you*. But if I can somehow sell us to my parents, pitching the app will be a piece of cake," she said, chuckling. "I just need one good idea, but it has to be a game changer."

"You know what's the ultimate game changer?" Ethan picked up his script and waved it at her. "Death."

"Yeah, I doubt I'll be solving *that* with an app." Priya laughed. "How does your script handle it?"

"Well, my character has seven days to cheat death. For six days, he wakes up in a casket and spends every moment planning ways to escape. But Death always gets him by sunset. On the last day, he stops fighting and leaves the funeral home. He goes home, walks his dog, makes his wife breakfast, flies a kite with his son, listens to his favorite album, has a drink with his friends."

"And then?"

"The final scene shows him on a park bench, watching the sun set. Children are playing. His son's feeding pigeons, his wife's taking photos, and their dog's pulling on the leash. He just sits there, totally at peace."

"No more running?"

"Exactly. He stops looking over his shoulder and just enjoys his last day."

"And the movie ends with him on that bench?"

"Not quite. As the sun dips below the horizon, a single leaf drifts down from the sky. It brushes past him and lands quietly at his feet, like a kiss from Death. His family's voices, children shouting, the distant sound of a siren—all of it keeps going. It's like he fades quietly into the moment, dissolving slowly into the night."

"That's haunting and beautiful," Priya whispered.

"There's a real emotional weight to this. It's unlike anything I've done before. Could be a major turning point in my career."

"Sounds like the perfect excuse for a movie night at the coach house," Priya declared. "Pillows, blankets, wine, cheese, and popcorn!"

"Tomorrow," Ethan said. "Tonight, I'm taking you out for a night on the town."

"You know you can't go anywhere without getting mobbed, right?"

"I've got ways to stay under the radar," he teased. "I'm thinking dinner, music, dancing, and cocktails under the city lights."

"Do you always plan dates like they're pulled from a movie?" Priya laughed.

"When I'm with you, every moment feels screen-worthy." He cupped her face and kissed her softly. "So just relax and let me take care of everything."

Twenty-One

JUST BEFORE SUNSET, an unassuming van dropped Ethan and Priya off at a quiet pier. The lake stretched out before them, glittering like a jewel under the soft colors of the setting sun. Birds skimmed across the water, their wings leaving ripples in their wake. Moored at the end of the pier was a sleek, two-tiered yacht.

Priya gasped as Ethan led her toward it. "I thought you said dinner, not a cruise!"

Ethan grinned, clearly loving her reaction. "Why pick one when you can have both?"

At the dock, the crew waited with a mix of excitement and professionalism.

"Welcome aboard, Mr. Knight," the captain said with a warm smile. "It's a pleasure to host you and your guest tonight."

"Thank you." Ethan extended his hand to Priya, helping her step onto the deck.

"Refreshments?" A crew member approached with a tray holding two champagne flutes. "I'm Yara," she said, guiding them toward the lounge. "I'll be looking after you this evening. Please let me know if there's anything I can do to make your evening more enjoyable." Though there was a starry look in her eyes, she remained composed. "I'll return shortly with an update on our departure." With a graceful nod, she excused herself.

"Here's to making a dream come true," Ethan declared, raising his glass.

"What dream?" Priya asked, still feeling a little overwhelmed. Just hours ago, in the freight car, she'd thought she was as happy as she could ever be. Now, her heart stretched in ways she hadn't expected.

"Remember that school camping trip? When I saw you sitting alone by the water, I wanted nothing more than to whisk you away and make you smile. And now . . . there it is. That smile."

"You did whisk me away," Priya said. "On your motorcycle."

"I haven't forgotten. Especially the way you clung to me." Ethan grinned. "But that was reckless. We didn't even have helmets on. Tonight's different. I can offer you more now, the kind of magic you deserve."

The yacht's lounge glowed with soft light, and the lake shimmered around them. Curled up next to Ethan on a couch, Priya felt like she was floating, as if gravity had lost its grip on her. The distant chatter of the crew and the sound of equipment faded as the engine hummed to life. Yara reappeared at the door with a gentle knock.

"The captain says we're ready to depart. Would you like to enjoy the view from the deck?"

Priya and Ethan followed her to an open-air section. Though May was inching toward its second half, the evening was still cooler than expected. Heat lamps bathed the loungers in warmth, keeping the chill at bay. As the yacht began to glide away from the dock, Priya leaned over the railing, smiling as Ethan's arms slid around her from behind. They stood like figureheads at the front of the yacht, the lake's surface rippling endlessly toward the edge of the horizon. The sun cast long shadows on the deck and the sky erupted in a kaleidoscope of pink and lavender hues.

"It's like something out of a movie," Priya said, awe coloring her voice.

"Well, as long it's not *Titanic*."

Priya grinned. "If this were *Titanic*, we'd be standing like this . . ." She spread her arms wide.

Ethan joined her, grinning as he mimicked the iconic pose. The yacht surged forward, and for a fleeting moment, Priya felt like she was flying. She closed her eyes, the wind brushing over her skin, cool and clean with the touch of spring's chill. She felt Ethan's warmth at her back, solid and sure. Distant laughter floated up from the crew's quarters, and somewhere, a cork popped.

When Priya opened her eyes, the sky had transformed. A burnished blaze of apricot and deep violet stretched across the horizon. The lake mirrored the colors, every ripple catching fire with the molten light.

"So beautiful," Priya breathed, her voice thick with wonder. She lowered her arms and turned to Ethan. His arms slipped around her again, as if he *knew* she needed anchoring, as if it was second nature to him now. He smelled warm and citrusy, like sun-warmed orange peel and sea salt. Priya closed her eyes, her forehead brushing his chest. *This. This is what being cherished feels like.* Her heart felt as boundless as the lake itself.

"I don't think I've ever had a moment like this," she said softly.

Ethan kissed the top of her head, his hand slipping down to lace their fingers together. "Then let's make it the first of many."

They stood in silence as the sun dipped lower, the colors deepening as the sky surrendered to twilight.

"Promise me if we hit an iceberg, you'll share the door." Ethan's voice held a grin as he referenced another scene in *Titanic*, but underneath it was something more—a question, quiet and careful.

Priya turned her face to him, her eyes shining. "You think I'm letting go of the one person who makes me feel like this?"

She leaned in until their foreheads touched. The world quieted around them—just the rhythm of the water, the whisper of the wind, and unspoken promises hanging between them like stars waiting to appear. As the yacht glided across the lake, soft lights flicked on around the deck. Ethan pulled back the slightest bit, just enough to look at Priya. His gaze dropped to her mouth, the moment stretching—silent and shimmering. Priya didn't dare move, didn't dare break the spell that had wrapped around them.

When Ethan kissed her, the rest of the world disappeared. There was only the heat of his mouth, the way his hand cupped her jaw, the slow, possessive slide of his other hand down her back, pulling her flush against him. Her knees went soft, her breath forgotten, every thought knocked clean out of her head. She kissed him back as if loving him had always been written under her skin, as if she finally understood what all the poems were about.

When they finally pulled apart, Priya's eyes fluttered open, her breath unsteady. "Is it weird that I feel like we just said something? Without actually saying anything?"

Ethan's mouth quirked. "No. I heard it too."

The faint click of polished shoes on the deck made them turn. Yara stepped into view, hands clasped in front of her.

"Gorgeous sunset tonight," she said. "Are you ready to head back inside, or would you like a few more moments?"

Ethan glanced at Priya, who nodded. "We're ready," he said.

"Right this way," Yara replied.

They followed her into the softly lit interior, warm and glowing like an old movie set. "Where's the restroom?" Priya asked as they passed through the hallway.

"Down the corridor to your right," Yara answered.

"I'll join you in a sec," Priya said to Ethan. "I just need to freshen up."

The restroom was stunning, like everything else on the yacht. Cool marble counters. Warm, flattering light. A crystal dish of rose petals by the sink that felt absurdly extra and somehow perfect.

Priya stood at the mirror, her lips still tingling from Ethan's kiss. She shook her head, a mix of disbelief and giddiness rising in her chest. *Is this real life?*

She touched up her lip gloss and smoothed her windblown hair, but there was no fixing the look in her eyes—unguarded and undone in the best way. She caught herself smiling. No. More than smiling. Glowing.

With one last breath, she stepped out of the restroom and made her way to the dining area. Outside, the lake was cloaked in darkness, with golden pinpricks of light on the horizon. A lone candelabra bathed the room in moody candlelight, dim enough to make everything feel like a dream. Shadows pooled in corners, and the scent of something warm and savory drifted from the galley.

Priya's gaze swept past the flickering candlelight, searching for Ethan. Then she spotted him—standing by the door, half swallowed by shadow. His jacket was gone, and his white shirt caught the dim light, glowing faintly in the corner. He held a glass in one hand as he gazed out at the lake, his silhouette framed against the dark water.

Priya's chest tightened with something tender and full. Swept up in the dreamy haze of the evening, she crossed the room and wrapped her arms around him from behind, resting her head on his back.

He went as still as stone beneath her touch.

Priya stiffened in horror. *Wait a second . . . Ethan had been wearing a blue shirt under his jacket!*

Her heart dropped as she realized she was hugging another man. Her arms, hyperaware of their blunder, remained locked in place, paralyzed by embarrassment.

"Pri?" Ethan's voice floated in from the deck.

Awkwardly, she craned her neck and saw Ethan stepping inside.

"Ethan," she stammered, still clinging to Not-Ethan.

"Your drink, Mr. Knight," the man said smoothly, nodding slightly toward the glass he held.

Priya's arms fell limply to her sides as mortification washed over her. She had just been snuggling the yacht's cocktail steward.

"Would you like a beverage, miss?" he asked.

"Sorry," Priya mumbled. "I thought you were Ethan."

"No worries," the man replied with a polite smile. Priya knew her faux pas would be a part of the evening's entertainment for the crew.

"Handing out complimentary hugs tonight?" Ethan asked, his voice warm with amusement as the steward made his exit.

Priya covered her face with one hand. "Everything looks shadowy and attractive in this moody lighting."

"That's on me." Ethan chuckled. "I asked for romantic, and they went for a vampire's love nest." He tugged her closer, guiding her hands around his waist. "We better get your bearings straight, so there are no more mistakes. Take your time. There are many important landmarks for you to map out." He nudged her hand to his butt. "Vital region. May require multiple passes." Guiding it away, he moved it to his chest. "This here? Prime real estate. Make sure you can navigate it properly, whatever the lighting situation."

Priya laughed and looked up at him. "What happens if I get lost here?"

"Then I hope you stay," he said softly, suddenly serious.

Priya hung on the edge of the moment, her heart hammering against her chest.

Yara's bright voice cut through the stillness. "Ready for dinner?"

Ethan glanced over, then back at Priya. "Yes, we are."

"Perfect. I'll inform the chef right away," Yara replied, beaming as she retreated.

"Shall we?" Ethan offered his arm.

Looping her arm through his, Priya let him guide her to the table. As he pulled out her chair, he leaned in close, his lips grazing her neck in a kiss that sent heat rippling down her spine.

"Whatever's on tonight's menu," he said, his voice dropping just enough to make her stomach flip, "I'm already looking forward to what comes after." Heat threaded through each syllable, his eyes on her like he was already unwrapping every inch of her in his mind.

Priya's brain short-circuited. Her mouth went dry, her pulse unhinged. She somehow managed to lay her napkin in her lap, as if it might save her from combusting.

Taking his seat, Ethan noticed the candles on the table and quickly stood to move the candelabra farther away. "I think we've had enough fires for one lifetime," he said. "From now on, I'm only interested in the slow-burning kind. With you."

"Careful." Priya's lips curled in a smile. "You keep talking like that, and we might start another one right here."

"Promises, promises." He chuckled, taking his seat across from her.

Priya caught herself full-on staring. The candlelight carved shadows along Ethan's jawline, his shirt collar open just enough to hint at the strength beneath. The night felt unreal, like something spun from stardust and magic.

This is my life right now. I'm on a date with Ethan freaking Knight.

Every half-formed daydream, every secret wish she'd ever had about him had somehow crystallized into this evening. Reality had turned out to be sweeter, more vivid, and more beautiful than anything she could have imagined.

As dinner progressed, each dish outshining the previous, an aching fullness stirred within Priya. She knew the world wasn't really shimmering, that it wasn't the food or the setting making her feel this way. It was something more profound. Her heart strained as she tried to contain her emotions, but they coursed through her veins and her bones, spilling from her fingertips to reach for Ethan across the table.

Priya had always loved Ethan, but it felt different now, like a living, breathing thing that expanded and contracted with each moment. She understood now why love sparked wars, why it brought kings and queens to their knees, why the end of a relationship could feel like death—and why, no matter what anyone said or how much they tried to convince themselves, the broken simply could not carry on.

Like anyone who dared to love, Priya clung to the hope that she would never have to face that kind of pain. Yet, even as she allowed herself to open up to the possibility of a future with Ethan, the quiet echo of generations past stirred within her, making her question whether she was truly worthy of such grace.

Twenty-Two

AS PRIYA AND ETHAN wrapped up their meal, the yacht cruised toward the city harbor, leaving the darkness of the lake behind. The skyline slowly took shape, gleaming skyscrapers coming into view. Yara and Not-Ethan whisked away the last of the dishes.

"Dessert on the upper deck, or would you prefer it served here?" Yara asked.

"Upper deck sounds great," Ethan said, standing and offering his hand to Priya.

They stepped into the elevator, and when the doors opened on the next deck, Priya stopped in her tracks. The city stretched before them like a titan rising from the water—the CN Tower standing tall against the night, high-rises glittering on either side, and the steady stream of traffic painting light trails along the highway.

As the yacht glided into the harbor, the buildings shimmered like pillars of light. Hazy outlines of other boats appeared around them, and waves lapped at the shore, blending with the distant hum of the city.

"Wow," Priya whispered, leaning over the railing. Her night out with Ethan was far from the frenzied spectacle she had feared.

"See?" Ethan teased, wrapping his arms around her from behind. "Hanging out with me isn't so bad."

They stood quietly admiring the view, soft music streaming through the speakers. Ethan gave Priya a spin, drawing her arms around his shoulders as they slipped into a slow dance.

"Sorry to interrupt," someone said behind them. They turned to see a man approach. "I'm Chef Marco. I trust the meal was to your liking?"

"Dinner was amazing," Ethan replied. "We enjoyed every dish."

"Thank you! It's truly an honor to have you here, Mr. Knight," Chef Marco replied. "I've prepared something special for dessert. May I present it to you both?"

"Of course," Ethan agreed.

Chef Marco guided them to a glass-enclosed area with a stunning view of the city. The space was warm and inviting, the table draped in dark linens with a sparkling star motif. A telescope stood aimed at the skies, ready for stargazing. With a practiced hand, he lifted the silver dome on the table, revealing an array of beautifully crafted desserts. Priya let out a soft gasp, which made him beam with pride.

"First, we have a dark chocolate mousse, topped with edible gold leaf and a delicate spun-sugar star," he explained, pouring warm raspberry coulis over it for a dramatic finish.

"Next, a white chocolate sphere filled with caramel gelato and passion fruit sorbet, designed to mimic the beauty of a star-lit pearl," he said, cracking it open gently with a silver mallet.

"And finally, a raspberry and rosewater panna cotta, hand-crafted to resemble the star of my garden this time of the year—a tea rose in full bloom—on a bed of edible flowers." He sprinkled candied violets on top and stepped back, enjoying their expressions.

"I'm sensing a bit of a star theme," Ethan said.

"Your presence inspired me," Chef Marco replied.

"Well, you've truly outdone yourself. These desserts are works of art."

"Almost too beautiful to eat," Priya added.

The chef smiled and gave a small bow. "Would it be too much to ask for an autograph?" He handed over a napkin and pen.

"Who should I make it out to?" Ethan asked, taking the pen.

"To me, please," the man replied. "I'm a huge fan."

"Thank you, Chef Marco, for an unforgettable night." Ethan penned the message and signed his name with bold strokes.

"I appreciate it." Chef Marco beamed. "Would you like some tea or coffee to go with dessert?"

"We'll help ourselves," Ethan replied. "Please thank the rest of the crew for their exceptional service. We'd appreciate having the rest of the night to ourselves."

"Of course. I'll let the crew know you're not to be disturbed. If you need anything, just use the intercom. Enjoy the rest of your evening." He gave a final nod and left.

With the dessert platter and a couple of spoons in hand, Ethan led Priya over to the couch. Setting the platter on a stool, he pulled Priya onto his lap. She curled into him, spreading a soft throw over their legs. As they sank into the cushions, the yacht began its return journey, away from the dazzling lights of the waterfront.

Ethan's hand settled on Priya's knee and trailed down her leg to her foot. He slipped off her shoe and let it fall to the floor, then did the same with her other one. Priya let out a contented sigh. As enchanting as the entire evening had been, being alone with Ethan was the most perfect part.

"Hang on a minute . . ." Ethan moved her off his lap and stood.

Priya's heart went into overdrive when he dropped to one knee, something small and shiny glinting between his fingers. She gawked, her mouth opening and closing like a fish gasping for air.

Oh my god! Is Ethan about to propose?!

Her brain spun in circles—part exhilaration, part panic.

"It's not yours?" Ethan asked.

"Huh?" Priya croaked.

"The earring." He placed it gently in her hand. "It must have slipped off when I pulled you onto my lap." .

Priya's hand flew to her ear, and she let out an awkward laugh. "Oh. Right. Thanks." She slipped it back on.

"You okay?" Ethan asked, settling back beside her.

Priya's face burned as she nodded. *Yeah, sure, just embarrassed as hell for thinking you were about to propose.*

Ethan tilted his head, eyes narrowing as he studied her face. Slowly, a knowing grin tugged at the corners of his mouth.

"I think I just pulled off the impossible—I made Priya Solanki swoon. You looked like you were about to pass out."

"Please. Don't flatter yourself." Priya scrambled to explain herself. "You plan this super romantic evening. Fancy yacht, fancy dinner, then you get down on one knee with something sparkling in your hands. What's a girl supposed to think?"

"You realize we're having our first fight because I *didn't* propose on our first date?"

"We're not arguing because you didn't propose. We're arguing because—" Priya broke off and threw him an accusing glare. "You're enjoying this."

"Damn right I am." Ethan grinned. "I love seeing you all fired up. You get that spark in your eyes, like lightning in a bottle. Do you know what happens when lightning meets chocolate?"

Before she could continue, Ethan slipped a spoonful of mousse into her mouth. It melted on her tongue, and she let out a soft, satisfied hum.

"Apparently, lightning purrs with delight," Ethan concluded.

"You think you're so smooth, huh?" Priya snatched the spoon. "Okay, smart guy. My turn." She dipped a piece of chocolate into the sorbet and slowly guided it to his lips.

Ethan's eyes stayed on hers as he took a bite, his mouth grazing the spoon. His tongue flicked briefly over the corner of his mouth, and Priya felt heat rush to her cheeks.

"Good?" she asked.

"Delicious. I think you should feed me everything from now on."

"Oh, really?" Priya teased. "Should I hand-feed you these berries next?"

"Go for it. You make everything taste better."

Priya rolled her eyes. "Flattery will get you . . . one more bite." She scooped up another spoonful and offered it to him.

They took turns feeding each other until the platter was empty. Ethan gathered Priya in his arms, and they stretched out on the couch, watching the city lights recede from view. Overhead, the stars began to reveal themselves, one by one, in the dark expanse of the sky.

Ethan laced his fingers with Priya's, tracing his thumb along her knuckles. "Our hands fit like they were made for each other," he said.

As her gaze dropped to their hands, Priya's heart stilled, a wave of clarity breaking over her. She was holding back for so many reasons. Ethan's fame terrified her. She hated the idea of being judged and scrutinized. And even if she got past that, there was practical stuff to consider. He lived thousands of miles away. Dating him didn't come with a trial run. Everything was out in the open, on the world stage. If things fell apart, she wouldn't just be heartbroken: She'd be humiliated, forever branded as the girl who got left behind by Ethan Knight.

Yet somehow, at that moment, all her fears faded into the background. The warmth of Ethan's hand in hers and the way he looked at her, made her feel like she had finally come home. Something clicked into place, like a lost star finding its path in the cosmos.

The idea of walking away from him seemed impossible. She had to at least *try*. Ethan didn't just see her. He made her feel valued and understood in ways she had never experienced before. For the first time, Priya felt powerful enough to claim the life and the love she wanted.

"Let's do it!" she declared.

"Here?" Ethan raised a playful brow. "I'm totally game if you are."

Priya giggled. "No, not *that*! I'm saying . . . let's go to the premiere together."

Ethan paused, his grin softening as he studied her. "Really? You sure?"

Priya swallowed and nodded. "Yes . . . I mean, it's still months away. I have lots of time to prepare for it."

Ethan tilted his head, his eyes narrowing. "Okay, but which Priya am I bringing along—Priya 1.0 or 2.0?"

"What difference does that make?" Priya laughed.

"Well, Priya 1.0 will probably panic and vanish the second the cameras come out. Priya 2.0, on the other hand? She told me straight up she wanted a fling. Hell, she was practically ready to throw me overboard tonight because I didn't propose."

"Do you want to go to the premiere with me or not, Heathen Knight?"

"You bet I do! And I'll take both Priyas," Ethan replied with a grin. "I probably should've asked while I was down on one knee . . . but what do you say to officially being my girlfriend?"

Priya's heart flipped nervously. Ethan wasn't leaving any wiggle room. If she said yes to the premiere, she'd be going as his date, on full display for the world to see. There would be no hiding, no pretending it was casual. This was Ethan asking her to be *his*.

"That terrifies me." Her laugh barely covered the tremble in her voice. "And yet saying yes to you feels like the safest thing I've ever done," she declared, her heart pounding harder. "Yes, Ethan Knight. Yes!"

Ethan grinned, that signature smile lighting up his whole face. "Wow. Full name and all. That felt official." He pulled her into him, forehead to forehead, voice rough at the edges. "I know how hard that was for you, and I'll make damn sure you never regret it." And then his lips were on hers, fierce and breath-stealing.

Priya melted into his kiss, her fingertips curling into the fabric of his shirt. When they finally broke apart, her hands lingered on his chest. "You realize this means we'll have to talk to my parents, right?"

"I think it's the right call." Ethan gave her hand a squeeze. "We'll keep things low-key after that. It'll give us time to adjust and figure things out. By the time the premiere rolls around, you'll be ready to own it. And I'll be right there, showing you off on my arm."

Priya's breath shuddered out of her, anxiety tightening in her stomach.

"Nervous?" Ethan pulled her gently into his arms.

"Uh, just a *tiny* bit. Like on every level imaginable."

Ethan brushed a strand of hair from her face and smiled. "Lucky for you, I'm an expert at dealing with nerves. Let's see . . . maybe one's hiding right here." His lips grazed the curve of her neck, soft and teasing.

"Hmm . . ." Priya's eyes slipped shut. "It's hard to tell . . . You might need to check again."

Ethan kissed her again, slower this time, until Priya was lost in the warmth of his touch. Time seemed to stall as they gave in to the moment, the yacht gliding quietly across the lake, leaving a silver trail in its wake.

Twenty-Three

PRIYA HAD GROWN USED TO the warmth of Ethan's arm draped around her waist as she slept. Stirred by a faint sound, her eyes fluttered open. The room took shape in hazy shadows, the soft glow from the hallway casting a dim light across the floor. Seeing nothing out of place, she closed her eyes. But the noise came again. A creaking sound from near the window.

Priya grabbed her glasses and squinted into the shadows. As her sight adjusted, she made out a faint movement. The rocking chair in the corner moved, back and forth. Priya's pulse quickened as a figure began to materialize on the chair.

No way . . . A chill prickled her skin. *Did I actually summon Bhooa masi with my fake ghost story?*

The woman rocked slowly, her face shifting in and out of the hallway's dim light. Priya's gaze climbed to her face, and she froze in horror. It wasn't Bhooa masi at all. It was her own face staring back at her.

Trapped in a bizarre situation where she was both the observer and the observed, Priya was hit by a sudden jolt of dread. She snapped awake, gasping sharply as the terrifying dream faded away.

"Pri, you okay?" Ethan's voice was groggy as his hand found hers.

She glanced at the chair, her heart slowing when she saw it was empty.

"I had a bad dream," she whispered, her voice shaky.

Ethan gathered her in his arms. "It's just your brain playing tricks. Right before we went to bed, you pointed out that the circle of salt around the bed is broken. That's probably what triggered it. Christ, your heart is pounding like crazy."

"It felt so real."

"I know, but you're safe," Ethan murmured, rocking her gently. "Everything's all right."

But everything was not all right. Priya had come face-to-face with her own guilt for spinning lies to scare Ethan away. He might not know the truth, but she couldn't hide it from herself. Her conscience was right there, watching, judging, keeping her awake the rest of the night. Yet there was no point in confessing now. By the time dawn broke, Priya was desperate for distraction.

"Let's go for a bike ride today," she suggested as soon as Ethan was up. "A long drive through the back roads."

"Sounds perfect," Ethan said, resting a hand on her hip. "But you need the right gear. The helmet we ordered online is too loose."

"And how exactly are we going to manage that without you being recognized every five steps?"

Ethan grinned, a knowing glint in his eyes. "Oh, let's just say I know a place where no one will bother us."

The parking lot was empty when Ethan and Priya arrived, the shops yet to open. Morning light spilled over the plaza, casting long shadows across the pavement. Nestled in a quiet neighborhood away from the main roads, it had a peaceful, almost nostalgic vibe.

"It hasn't changed one bit," Ethan said, taking in the motorcycle shop before them.

Flanked by a car repair garage on one side and a convenience store on the other, the store's sign was faded from years of exposure to the sun.

"This is where I got my first helmet." Ethan's eyes softened. "The owner runs the garage too. He helped me fix my dad's bike after I crashed it. Wonder if he's still around."

Just then, the shop's Closed sign flipped to Open.

Priya hopped off the bike and walked inside, the bell above the door announcing her presence. Scanning the inside, she sent Ethan a quick text that all was clear.

"Good morning." A man with silver-streaked hair emerged from behind the counter. His gaze shifted to the entrance as Ethan entered, setting the bell off again.

"Hello, Mr. Khan," Ethan greeted, removing his helmet. "It's been a while."

Mr. Khan's expression transformed to astonishment. "Ethan? Is it really you?"

"You thought you'd seen the last of me, huh?"

"Not at all! My whole family's glued to the TV whenever you're on. This is . . . Wow. I can't believe it—you're really standing here! What brings you to my shop today?"

"We're actually here for Priya," Ethan replied, gesturing to the helmet she held. "She needs something that fits better, plus some extra gear."

"Of course! Right this way." Mr. Khan led them to the helmet display.

As they browsed the selection, Mr. Khan's phone rang. "My son," he said, silencing it with an apologetic smile.

"Please don't ignore him on our behalf," Priya said with a smile. "We'll look around."

Grateful, Mr. Khan stepped away to return the call. At first, his conversation was hushed, but his tone soon became sharp and agitated.

"Sorry about that," he said when he returned. "My son won't believe you're here." Then a spark of excitement lit his face. "Would it be too much to ask for a photo together?"

"After everything you've done for me? It's the least I can do," Ethan replied.

Mr. Khan handed his phone to Priya, beaming as he stood beside Ethan.

Priya snapped a photo of the two men standing by the counter with the store's logo in the background. She took a few more shots from different angles before handing the phone back.

"Thank you so much," Mr. Khan said, scrolling through the images. "Let's see him doubt his old man now . . . Bet he's kicking himself for sleeping in." He tapped out a quick message, then slipped his phone into his pocket and returned to help Priya.

Priya chose a helmet to match Ethan's bike. It had an anti-fog visor and comfortable padding inside. Ethan added a jacket, a pair of gloves, and boots. Priya mentally calculated the damage, debating how to scale back, but before she could say anything, Ethan insisted on paying for all of it.

"Payment? Out of the question." Mr. Khan declared as they debated back and forth. "Having you as my first customer of the day is a blessing, a sign of good luck. It means a lot that you thought of me, Ethan. Please, let me cover this. It's on the house."

Priya blinked, surprised by his generosity. She opened her

mouth to protest, but Mr. Khan was already slipping the jacket over her shoulders. She shot Ethan a look. He just shook his head, smiling. Arguing with Mr. Khan was useless.

"Thank you, Mr. Khan," Ethan said, his tone appreciative. "Can we leave the packaging and Priya's other helmet with you? Feel free to pass it on to someone who needs it."

"Of course." Mr. Khan removed the gloves and boots from their boxes and arranged them neatly on the counter.

"Thank you," Priya said as she slipped them on. She glanced at Ethan, still adjusting to the unexpected kindness.

"Don't worry," he whispered, leaning in. "I'll make sure he gets a proper thank-you gift later."

As they headed out, Ethan opened the door for her and glanced over his shoulder. "It was good seeing you again, Mr. Khan," he said.

The door shut with a jingling echo, and Mr. Khan stood frozen on the other side, as if he was trying to wrap his head around what had just happened.

"Damn, Priya 2.0." Ethan's eyes swept over her as they walked to the bike. "You've got troublemaker written all over you."

"I've finally crossed over to your side of the tracks," Priya shot back with a grin.

Ethan laughed and hooked their helmets on the bike. He tugged on her sleeve, pulling her closer. "Forget the ride," he murmured, his voice husky as his gaze dropped to her lips. "Let's go back to the coach house."

In an instant, Priya's entire world narrowed to the heat radiating between them. The warmth of Ethan's breath brushed her skin as their lips hovered, inches apart. His voice, his body, everything about him made Priya's senses spin. She leaned in, eyelids fluttering shut.

But before their lips could meet, a sharp staccato of camera clicks pierced the stillness. Startled, they pulled back and spotted a man leaning out of an SUV. Across the lot, another photographer dashed from a parked sedan, positioning himself for a clearer angle. A third crouched behind the convenience store, snapping away.

"Fuck." Ethan's entire demeanor shifted, his expression turning ice-cold. "Here. Helmet on." He secured Priya's helmet, pulling the visor down to shield her face.

"Come on, buddy. Don't be like that," one of the paparazzi yelled.

"Who's the mystery woman, Ethan?" another shouted.

"Show us some love, Ethan!"

Ethan ignored them, putting on his own helmet. He turned to Priya, his voice sharp but steady. "Hold on tight and don't let go. No matter what."

Priya nodded, her grip tightening around him. Ethan fired up the engine, its roar drowning out the chorus of shouts. Tires squealed as they tore out of the parking lot, speeding toward the road. They barely had time to merge before three cars closed in, cameras flashing. Ethan gunned the engine, swerving to avoid them as they tried to box him in. Priya clung to him as he zigzagged between vehicles, trying to shake them off. The world melted into a chaotic blur of headlights and buildings.

Out of nowhere, a paparazzi van cut across their path, forcing Ethan to steer up onto the sidewalk. He quickly hopped back onto the road, making a sharp turn at the next intersection. The van overshot, but the other cars stayed hot on their trail. One of them nudged dangerously close, its bumper brushing the rear of the bike. A photographer leaned out of the window, snapping photo after photo.

Ethan sped up, his eyes scanning for an opening. Priya clung tighter, her pulse pounding as they hurtled down the road. As they approached an intersection, the light turned red. Ethan slammed on the brakes, bringing them to a skidding halt. The air filled with the acrid smell of scorched rubber.

The car tailing them screeched to a halt beside them. The photographer jumped out, his camera trained on them. Priya turned her head, only to see a swarm of paparazzi sprinting toward them, closing in from every direction.

"Over here!" someone shouted, camera flashing in her face.

"Back off," Ethan said, his voice menacing even through the helmet. He turned to Priya and asked, "You okay?"

Panic prickled Priya's skin like a thousand tiny needles. Chaos pressed in from all sides. She couldn't see Ethan's face behind his visor, but the moment she turned toward him, something in her stilled. She gave him a quick nod even though her hands were shaking inside her gloves.

The simple act drew another wave of rapid flashes from the paparazzi, each frame capturing the moment like a trophy. Ethan's entire posture radiated protectiveness. He revved the engine, frustration simmering as the light refused to change.

"Hey, sweetheart," a man called, stepping closer and tapping Priya's shoulder. "Why don't you show us that pretty face?"

In an instant, Ethan swung off the bike, kickstand down with a sharp snap. The other photographers backed off as he advanced on the man. Priya's heart surged into her throat. She wanted to call out, to call him back—but she sat paralyzed, caught between fear and the electric thrill of watching him charge into the crowd for *her*.

"Touch her again," he growled, his voice low and menacing, "and it'll be the last thing you do. You want a face?" Tearing off his helmet, he grabbed the man's camera and shoved the lens up to his own face. "Here it is. Take your best shot, but leave her the hell out of it. I'm the one who signed up for this, not her. Clear?"

The man stumbled back, his camera still caught in Ethan's grip. The strap around his neck snapped taut, pulling the camera free and sending it crashing into his chest with a loud thump. Cameras flashed nonstop as the other photographers seized the opportunity. Ethan's fiery reaction made the situation even spicier.

"Anybody else want a shot?" Ethan's eyes swept over the crowd. "No? Well then, we'll be on our way."

Ethan got back on the bike and turned to Priya. "It's not over," he said. "They'll keep tailing us. If we head back to Moksha, they'll turn the place into a circus. We have to lose them. You ready for this?"

Priya nodded, though her chest tightened. Even with her helmet on, she felt exposed and defenseless. Traffic had come to a halt. People gathered at the edges of the road, drawn by the commotion.

"Look, it's Ethan Knight!" someone shouted before Ethan slipped his helmet back on.

Phones rose high in the air as the crowd burst into cheers. Ethan revved the engine, warning everyone to move out of the way. The paparazzi scrambled to get back to their vehicles.

"Brace yourself," Ethan said, over the roar of the engine.

Priya's arms tightened around him as they shot forward. Looking back, she saw a convoy of cars chasing them. Ahead, the traffic light turned amber, but Ethan didn't slow. He pushed through the intersection as three cars barreled after them, narrowly missing a pedestrian. Horns blared and chaos erupted behind them.

Priya's eyes widened as they passed familiar landmarks. They were nearing Knight Estates, Ethan's old stomping ground, an area he knew like the back of his hand. He took a sharp turn down a dead-end street, spinning the bike around to face their pursuers. As the paparazzi scrambled to reverse, Ethan and Priya gained a fleeting lead. But more cars converged on them, closing the gap.

Ethan raced past the funeral home and his father's property, veering into the parking lot of a local hiking trail. The paparazzi followed, kicking up clouds of dust in the unpaved lot. Priya's heart raced as she scanned her surroundings. The path ahead led straight into a steep embankment. Behind them, photographers sealed off the only exit. They were cornered with nowhere left to run.

Ethan swiveled the bike around to face the reporters. "Hey, Pri," he said, scanning the line of cars blocking them. "Remember when we first met? That crazy stunt I pulled?"

"This isn't a stunt, Ethan. You can't jump over those cars!"

"Trust me?" he asked softly, his voice steady over the engine's hum.

Priya swallowed hard and nodded. "Completely."

"Then hold on to me, tight as you can." He revved the engine as photographers advanced toward them on foot.

Priya braced herself, ready for Ethan to charge toward the exit. Instead, he whipped the bike toward a grassy slope beside the lot. They tore up the incline, tires clawing the earth beneath them. For a heartbeat, they lifted off the ground at the top. Priya tensed, her mind flashing back to a younger Ethan crashing the bike. This time, he landed with controlled precision. The bike hit the ground with a thud, jostling Priya out of her seat before she settled back.

They thundered down a narrow, rugged trail. Tree roots and rocks jolted the tires beneath them. The trees merged in a blur of shifting greens as Ethan dodged and twisted to avoid the branches. Priya's senses went into overdrive, her body moving instinctively with his, every reflex tested as they made their escape.

It wasn't until they reached a clearing deep in the woods that Ethan finally slowed. He killed the engine and removed his helmet, listening to their surroundings. The only sounds Priya could hear were the gentle flow of a nearby stream and the call of birds in the trees.

"I think we lost them," he said.

Priya let out her breath and released her hold, feeling a surge of blood flow back into her arms. She flexed her fingers to shake off the numbness, then removed her helmet. As soon as it was off, she began to shiver uncontrollably.

"Hey." Ethan hopped off the bike and eased the helmet from her hands.

Priya tried to stand, but her legs felt weak, muscles quivering as if she was still running for her life. With the adrenaline subsiding, the full weight of the ordeal pressed down on her. Ethan helped her dismount and sat her down on a tree stump. Crouching before her, he peeled off her gloves.

"It's over, Pri," he said, rubbing her hands between his palms. "You're safe now."

Priya knew they'd shaken off the paparazzi. She knew the immediate threat was gone, but her body hadn't caught up. She couldn't stop trembling. Her hands and feet were like ice, her heart racing so fast that she couldn't take a full breath.

"Shhh," Ethan murmured, squeezing her hands. "It's okay."

He slid onto the stump beside her and wrapped her in his arms. Slowly, the woods worked their magic: the smell of pine and wildflowers, the soft rustle of leaves, sunlight filtering through the canopy of trees. Like a storm quieting, Priya's body slowly unwound.

Ethan, however, wasn't calm, his gaze stormy with emotions he couldn't quite hide.

"Feeling any better?" he asked.

Priya nodded. "I think I'm good now."

"I put you in danger today. Just like I did with my mother."

"Ethan, no." Priya reached for his hand. "Your mom's accident wasn't your fault. And today wasn't your fault either. I knew what could happen the moment we stepped outside together. The world is obsessed with you—where you go, what you do. Anyone you're with is a fair target, and that's something I have to learn to deal with. You can't shield me from everything. But that jump you pulled?" She chuckled. "My heart practically left my chest."

Ethan's lips lifted in a small, bittersweet smile. "Catch your breath, Pri," he said. "We need to head out soon."

Priya turned her face up to the sun, relieved to have survived the chaos of being spotted with Ethan. She had no idea, however, that this was only the beginning—the calm before a much greater storm.

Twenty-Four

ETHAN STUCK TO the back roads on the way to Moksha, following the hidden route along the deserted railway tracks. As they skirted past Knight Estates, Priya spotted photographers staked out near the entrance, expecting him to show up there. When they reached Moksha, Ethan stashed the bike behind the coach house, so no one driving by the front gate could spot it. Inside, they pulled off their helmets, relieved to have made it back in one piece.

Priya sank into Ethan's arms, wishing she could freeze time right there. The stillness felt fragile, and sure enough, it dissolved as Ethan's phone began to ring.

"Talk to me, Zach," Ethan answered, stepping away to speak to his assistant.

Priya went to the window and pulled the curtains shut.

Ethan returned with a grim look. "That picture with Mr. Khan is what started this. His son posted it on the shop's page, and it spread like wildfire. That's how the press tracked us down."

Before Priya could react, his phone buzzed again. He gave her an apologetic glance. "I need to handle this. My whole team's trying to get a hold of me."

"Don't worry about it," Priya said, taking a seat at the dining table and unlocking her phone to reply to a backlog of work-related messages. Her thumbs hovered uselessly above the screen, her mind stuck on Ethan's voice.

"What do you mean, damage control?" he asked, his steps slow as he crossed to the window and back. "I want to be proactive about this. We do whatever needs to be done. Across the board."

Curiosity got better of Priya, and she opened her social media app. It was flooded with images of her and Ethan—initial shots where her face was visible, followed by flashes of chaos. The pursuit. Ethan's confrontation with the paparazzi. Their daring escape into the woods. But the one photo that had taken over the internet was still. Quiet. Just the two of them by his bike on the verge of a kiss, unaware of anyone around them including the figure stalking them silently in the background.

There was something haunting about the image. Something beautiful. Like a frame pulled straight from a movie. Priya's throat tightened, tears welling before she could blink them away. It felt like someone had reached inside her, dragged out something sacred, and turned it into a spectacle.

The possibility that Ethan could be in love was the hot topic stirring up reactions across his fan base. Opinions flew in from every corner. Priya's emotions swung wildly as she read through the stream of comments.

"@Allycat Now we know who took that photo on his feed."
"Damn, I want someone to look at me like that 💔"
"Bruh, y'all really think this girl's in it for love? She's after that fame bag."
"Guess he's dating regular people now?"
"Really? A brown girl??"

"They look so in love!"
"Someone tag me with her name."

Priya scrolled through the threads, struck by how deeply people were invested in their celebrity crush. It was as if buying into Ethan's stardom gave them a stakeholder claim to his life, allowing them a vote in his personal choices. She was about to sign off when a notification popped up on her screen. Before she could check it, another one pinged. Then another, and another. She was gaining followers by the second—ten, thirty, two hundred.

Priya's pulse quickened as her phone buzzed nonstop. Something was wrong. People were not only following and messaging her but also tagging her. She clicked on the first tagged post. Sure enough, there it was—the viral photo of her and Ethan. Underneath, the caption read "Meet Priya Solanki."

Priya's heart began pounding wildly. Her anonymity was crumbling in real time. Another post popped up, the user hitting a dead end while trying to trace the bike's license plate, but disclosing an interesting discovery: "Ethan Knight's bike was signed for by Priya Solanki at Moksha Funeral Home."

Her personal information was making the rounds: age, religion, cultural background, the schools she'd attended, the company she founded. Even her ex, Manoj, was dragged into the fray. Every piece of her life was suddenly fair game for public examination. Her friendship with Brooke, too, was twisted into a calculated scheme to cozy up to Ethan. One comment in particular caught Priya off guard in a way she hadn't expected: *She's bad luck, Ethan. Run while you can.*

The words of this stranger triggered something in her, memories of her parents' stories, of a time when even the shadow of a Dalit was thought to be unlucky, a harbinger of misfortune. She'd dismissed those tales as distant history, something that could never touch her life. Now the weight of history didn't feel quite so abstract. It felt real and alive, breathing down her neck.

As past and present collided, with comments rolling in faster than she could process, Priya's mind raced with comebacks. She wanted to push back, to shout, *You don't know me!* But another part whispered, *What's the point?* Her parents had always warned her.

Don't reach too high.

Don't think too big.

Don't dream beyond your station.

She hadn't listened. Being with Ethan had made her feel unstoppable, as if she could take on anything. Now she wasn't so sure. She shrank into herself, wishing she could vanish completely, fade into a shadow where no one could see or judge her. Had she been too reckless, too naïve?

Priya looked up from her screen to Ethan. His face was tight with frustration as he argued on the phone.

"I don't care if it jeopardizes the release," he said. "I *know* they want to spin a romance with Sienna to boost the marketing campaign, but I'm not postponing the announcement. If anyone's got a problem with it, they know where to reach me." He hung up, pacing the floor like a caged lion.

His screen lit up again before he'd even caught his breath. "What now?" he snapped, his tone all steel. "Sure, I confronted the guy, but assault? Seriously?" Ethan dragged a hand through his hair. "The bruise is probably from his own camera hitting him . . . Yeah, I grabbed his camera . . . I don't remember the exact words. Maybe I *did* make a threat. You know what? Have my lawyer handle it."

Priya's stomach twisted. Ethan was catching heat all because of her. Maybe her parents were right—maybe some things were like a cosmic loop she couldn't break. And she'd tried. God, she'd tried. She'd thrown herself into escape after escape, desperate for something that felt like freedom. Somehow, all roads circled right back to Moksha. Every move she made to step away from it had ended in disappointment and failure.

Calgary.

My marriage.

The company.

The last ten years of my life.

And now Ethan was being dragged into her mess, forced to deal with the fallout of her choices. Everything pointed to the same truth: *She* was the common denominator. There was no denying it anymore. She really was bad luck.

Her phone buzzed without stopping. Deepa. Brooke. Manoj. Dozens of unknown numbers stacking on top of one another in a rising tide. Someone had leaked her number. Priya's chest felt tight, her hands weirdly cold, and for a moment, she felt like she might crawl out of her skin.

Make it stop. Make it stop. Make it—

And then . . . nothing.

Instead of going over the edge, Priya shut down. Everything around her dulled and blurred. It was as if her brain had pulled an emergency lever. She sat there, physically present, while the rest of her backed into a corner somewhere inside herself and curled up. And in that weird, numb stillness, only one thought remained: *I have to walk away from Ethan before I cause him any more harm.*

"Pri." Ethan's voice sliced through the fog in her mind. She blinked, trying to focus as he muted his phone and sat across from her. "We have to go public earlier than anticipated."

Priya sat perfectly still, feeling like she was watching someone else in her place.

"There's a gala tomorrow," Ethan continued. "We'll go together, but we need to talk to your parents so they're not blindsided. I'll forward you a draft of my statement. We'll also have to prep for press questions. I've lined up some interviews to take control of the story."

She nodded slowly, almost automatically, her numbness starting to splinter. A slow ache bloomed in her chest. Galas, press statements, interviews—all things and places where she didn't belong. For a brief moment, she'd thought she'd finally found her place—right there, beside Ethan—but in only a few hours, the world had bulldozed its way between them, stripping her of all illusions. Ethan belonged among the stars—and she couldn't risk doing anything that would taint his future.

"Are you listening, Pri?" Ethan asked.

She was, but it felt like the words were landing on a version of her that was already slipping out of reach.

"I can't do this," she whispered, her throat tight.

Ethan stilled, then reached for her hand, threading his fingers through hers. "I know it's a lot," he said, his voice softer now. "It's fast, and unfair, and overwhelming. But we don't have a choice." He lifted her chin until their eyes locked. "My team's already in motion. Hair, makeup, wardrobe. Whatever you need. You just need to show up. I'll handle everything else, including the gala stuff."

"It's not just the gala," Priya said, her voice full with emotion. "It's the whole thing. I'm not made for this, Ethan. I can't be in this . . . with you." The words tasted bitter on her tongue, and she felt her heart crumbling piece by piece.

Ethan froze as he absorbed her words. "Pri . . . You're scared. I get it. But you're also incredibly strong. You can do this. *We* can do this. You just need time to adjust."

"It's not that simple." She shook her head, her vision blurring as she looked at their clasped hands. "I'm no good for you, Ethan. I'm only going to bring you down. Everything I touch falls apart. This is already affecting your movie's release. And you're facing a potential lawsuit from that photographer. Meanwhile, everyone out there is picking apart my entire life." Tears slipped down her cheeks. "I'll never be good enough for you in their eyes. Not now, not ever. No matter how long we hold on. The spotlight isn't for me, Ethan. I'm already cracking under all the attention. And you, you'll get tired of constantly reassuring me. Eventually, you'll start resenting me. And I couldn't bear that, Ethan. I never want to see that day," she choked out. "This is the hardest thing I've ever done, but it's better for me to walk away."

As Priya began to withdraw her hand, Ethan's grip tightened. "Don't," he said. "Don't do this, Pri."

Priya's heart ached as she met his gaze. She could already see the endless cycle they would fall into—breakups and makeups, their souls refusing to untangle. Their connection defied a clean break. Ethan wasn't going to give up without a fight, and her own resolve would waver time and again. But the same issues would keep emerging, pulling them apart. Priya preferred to endure the pain of separation over the unbearable agony of losing Ethan over and over.

Taking a deep breath, she gently pulled her hand free. It was more than just an unclasping of hands—it was an unscripting of a future, an unsparking of dreams, an unmerging of lives.

Ethan's eyes dropped to his hand as if he could still feel Priya's warmth slipping away. "This isn't over." He lifted his head and looked at her. "You told me you wanted this, Pri. We agreed we'd face it together. You're spooked, Priya, and I'm not letting you give up at the first sign of trouble. We'll—"

"I never wanted you here to begin with," Priya said, cutting him off.

Ethan's laugh was sharp and incredulous. "What the hell are you talking about?"

Moving almost mechanically, Priya picked up her phone and launched the app she had installed to control the lights in the coach house. She chose a sequence, and almost immediately, the kitchen lights began to flicker. Ethan's eyes narrowed, his gaze shifting between her and the bulbs. Tilting the screen toward Ethan, Priya selected another sequence. This time, the lights at the entrance began to turn on and off.

Confusion crept into Ethan's expression as he realized Priya was remotely controlling the lights. "You rigged the lights?"

She lowered her eyes, her hands trembling slightly as she placed the phone down. "I made up the rest, too—the circle of salt, the stories about Bhooa masi, the haunting. None of it was real."

"Why?" He shook his head in disbelief. "Why would you do all that?"

"Because I wanted you gone." The words tore out of her like a jagged blade.

"I don't get it." Ethan's eyes searched hers as he tried to make sense of what she was saying. "If you really wanted me gone, why get involved with me in the first place?"

"It was just supposed to be a fling," Priya said. "I told myself I could handle it, that I'd walk away when the time came. But somewhere along the way, I got lost in this . . . in *us*. I thought we could actually make it work. But we were living in a bubble, Ethan, and now that bubble's burst. The truth is we'll never be equals."

"And what exactly would make us equals, Priya?" Ethan's voice was thick with frustration. "The same fame? The same paycheck? The same social standing? That sounds a lot like what your parents believe. What about the things that *really* matter? Like how you melt when I touch you? Or how my whole world shifts when you smile? What happened to all the talk about breaking free of the template you're born into? Of rewriting your code and changing your story?"

Priya flinched as his words hit home. *Maybe I am more like my parents than I realized. How do I escape something so deeply embedded in me?*

"Break free with me, Pri." Ethan reached across the table, offering his hand. His words hung in the air, an invitation to change the scripts that had been running her life for too long.

The sudden glow from Priya's phone caught their attention—an incoming call from her parents' cell phone. Their eyes locked, both understanding the weight of the moment. They either stood together or fell apart, depending on how they handled the conversation ahead.

Slowly, Priya put the phone on speaker. "Hello?"

"Priya," her father's voice came through. The way he said her name sent a sinking feeling straight to her heart.

Twenty-Five

"YES, PUPPA."

"Don't 'yes, Puppa' me. I just got off the phone with Suraj Verma."

"With who?"

"Dinesh's father. We met him and his family just this week," Puppa said, sounding impatient. "He's seen the photos of you and Mr. Ethan. He says you're romantically involved. Is this true, Priya?"

Priya felt her throat tighten. Answering her father while Ethan watched was like being caught between two fires.

"Answer us, Priya!" Her mother joined the call, her voice crackling through the speaker. "We are here trying to find you a decent guy, and you are fooling around with Mr. Ethan there?"

Across from her, Ethan's expression shuttered. *Now he knows exactly what they think, that he's a wrong turn I should never have taken.* Face burning, Priya took the call off speaker. "It's not like that, Mumma."

"No? Then let me ask you one thing," her father cut in. "Has Mr. Ethan proposed?"

"No, but—"

"Then it's just as we thought," Puppa muttered. "I am reading these headlines as we speak."

"*Hai Ram!*" Mumma wailed, her voice spiraling into despair. "What are we supposed to do now?"

Her parents' voices merged with the calls of the paparazzi, the endless comments, the relentless shutter of cameras. Priya's heart raced as though she was reliving everything all over again—the chase through the streets, the posts, strangers digging through her life.

"You have gone too far this time, Priya," Puppa said. "Now the whole world is going after you. And not just you. Moksha has been dragged into this too. Do you know what this will do to our reputation, Priya?" His voice turned cold. "This is what happens when you don't stay within your limits. Mr. Ethan is used to this. Every day, a new story, a new sensation. But you, Priya. You are out of your league. You think we are being strict, but we are just trying to protect you."

"*Amari vaat maan*," her mother said. Listen to us. "Whatever is going on between you and Mr. Ethan is make-believe, Priya. It may be fun, but it's just fantasy."

Mumma's words hit hard, not because they were harsh but because she was probably right. Priya looked across the table at Ethan—he was unwavering, testing her without a word. It was up to her. Her response could either solidify their future or unravel everything between them. And no matter what she chose to say, someone she loved would pay the price.

Priya gripped the phone tight. "Those photos have been taken out of context and blown way out of proportion," she said, her voice flat and brittle, so distant it barely sounded like her own. "Ethan and I are just friends."

For an intense, excruciating moment, Ethan's gaze burned into hers. Pain and betrayal flashed across his face before he shut down, a wall sliding into place. Priya knew that look well. It was the look he wore outside Knight Estates when his father pretended he wasn't home. And now she'd put the same anguish in his eyes.

His hand retreated slowly from where it rested on the table. Every part of Priya wanted to reach out and undo the damage, but it was too late. She had finally driven him away, not just out of Moksha but out of her life too.

Ethan turned away as if he could no longer bear to look at her. Her parents' voices blurred into the background. She mumbled something in reply, wanting only to end the call. The moment she disconnected, a heavy, suffocating silence filled the room. Ethan sat like a statue, his jaw clenched, face unreadable.

"Ethan—"

With a flicker of resolve, he reached for his phone. "Mr. Solanki," he said, when Priya's father answered the call. "This is Ethan. I'm afraid word has gotten out about me being at Moksha. It's also creating problems for you and your family. Given the circumstances, I've decided to leave sooner than expected."

A deep, immovable sadness settled in Priya's chest. He was closing the door, sealing all possibilities.

"No, please keep the payment," he added. "I apologize for any problems my presence created. I'll be leaving tonight, as soon as I arrange a pickup. The sooner I leave, the faster you and your family can move past the media spotlight. Thank you for the kindness you've shown me. Please give my regards to Mrs. Solanki."

As soon as the call ended, Ethan dialed out again. "Zach, I need a ride out of Moksha. Right away." He listened for a moment, then nodded. "Yeah, I know they're camped outside. Let's throw them off like we did in Vegas. Let me know when we're good to go."

He shoved his chair back and stood, moving quickly as he gathered his things with quiet, deliberate efficiency. Priya flinched at the swiftness of it, at how completely he shut her out, as if she no longer existed. Grabbing his toiletries from the bathroom, he retreated to the bedroom. When he returned, he had his luggage in tow and headed straight for the door. As he put on his jacket, Priya felt their connection slipping through her fingers.

A hollow ache spread through her as she replayed the moments they had shared. His stubble grazing her cheek at dawn. Nights spent stargazing on the roof of the freight car. Sharing quiet cups of coffee. His laughter filling the silent spaces around her.

"Ethan," she said, her voice catching.

But Ethan did not once look at her. Not when four identical sedans with tinted windows rolled into Moksha. Not when his bags were loaded into one of the cars, and not when the vehicles sped away in a storm of camera flashes, leading the paparazzi on a wild-goose chase. He did not look at her as she followed him to his motorcycle, nor when he tugged on his gloves and fastened his helmet.

"Ethan," she tried again. She didn't know what to say next, only that they could be the last words she ever said to him. But Ethan ignored her. Instead, he clutched the handlebars and began pushing his motorcycle silently toward the open field beyond the train tracks.

"Ethan!" she cried out, her voice cracking with desperation.

He still did not turn around. He moved steadily past the freight car, disappearing gradually into the dusk. Priya stared after his silhouette until darkness consumed it entirely. Only when he was safely out of range of any remaining press did his engine come alive. The sound echoed briefly through the air, then receded, until there was nothing left but silence.

Priya stood motionless, her mind flashing back to the first time she had watched him disappear into that field. Eventually, she forced herself to move, retracing her steps to the coach house. She grabbed a flashlight and walked to the funeral home, her footsteps echoing through the empty corridors. Shadows twisted and bent as the beam of light cut through the gloom. Her breath faltered when she entered the casket showroom. The casket Ethan had rested in seemed to call her.

Priya climbed inside and turned off her flashlight. Darkness settled around her. Whoever said it was better to have loved and lost had never lived through this kind of grief—raw, searing, and inescapable. She wasn't just mourning the end of her relationship with Ethan. She was mourning herself, too—the version of her who had dared to dream of more. That part of her was now buried under the weight of failure. And here she was, laying down her arms, finding comfort in the very place that had been waiting to claim her.

Twenty-Six

THE MEDIA ATTENTION didn't die down just because Ethan left. Two days later, when Mumma and Puppa returned from their trip, the press greeted them with flashing lenses. They continued to hover even as the renovation crew began work on the funeral home.

With the main building undergoing repairs and the power still out at the apartment, the coach house turned into a temporary home for the Solanki family. Priya shut herself inside, keeping the curtains tightly drawn. From dawn until dusk, she buried herself in her freelance work and online classes, as though the steady tap of the keyboard could drown out thoughts of Ethan. But once night came, and she settled on the couch, the hollow ache beneath her ribs stretched wide and raw. It was there on that very couch that Ethan had first kissed her. The memory was like a blade twisting sharper with every breath.

Priya reminded herself that she had lived through heartbreak before. Her divorce from Manoj had been tough, but she'd managed to pick up the pieces and move on. Losing Ethan, though, cut far more painfully. It wasn't simply that her feelings for him were stronger. It was the fact that with Ethan, she'd felt like she was on the verge of something extraordinary, something beyond the boundaries she'd always known. But the part she could hardly bear was knowing she'd deeply hurt him. That guilt gnawed at her more than the loss itself. Whenever her mind wandered back to Ethan, she saw the wounded look in his eyes. The memory alone stole her breath.

And unlike her divorce from Manoj, Priya had no space to grieve in private. She had to maintain a facade of normalcy for her parents. She nodded in all the right places, forced a hollow smile, and went through the motions even though she felt numb inside. Her parents welcomed this subdued, agreeable version of their daughter. They seemed to readily accept that her involvement with Ethan had been exaggerated by the media. Priya sensed that even if they had their doubts, they were relieved the experience had served as a sobering reminder to stay within her limits.

As summer approached and the calendar edged toward mid-June, the renovation crew wrapped up their work at Moksha. Priya trailed her parents as they moved from room to room, inspecting the newly renovated space. The acrid smell from the fire had been replaced by the scent of fresh paint.

"It's so nice to finally have the lights working properly," Mumma said, flipping a switch. The basement lit up, shadows scattering in the wake of clean, bright light.

Moksha wore a mask of rebirth, like a phoenix rising from the ashes. Priya, on the other hand, doubted she would ever be able to rebuild herself.

"Rakesh!" Mumma called Priya's father, who had wandered into his office. "We are about to begin the *pooja*."

The prayer ritual was intended to bless the new electrical panel and mark a new beginning for Moksha. Priya carried the pooja tray, neatly arranged with a small oil lamp, incense sticks, a brass handbell, fresh flowers, and a small container of kumkum powder.

Puppa joined them as Mumma lit the oil lamp, a symbol of light triumphing over darkness. She then lit the incense, the fragrant smoke curling gently as it filled the room. Together, the three of them recited prayers and offered flowers. Mumma added the finishing touch—a *tilak* of kumkum powder on the electrical panel for divine protection—before handing out *prasad* to share the blessings and celebrate a new beginning.

Puppa returned to his office and came back waving a document. "The inspector signed off on everything," he announced. "Moksha is back in business!"

"Priya, inform everyone on the family group. *Badha ne kaide!* We're celebrating tonight!" Mumma beamed.

Celebrating for the Solankis usually meant a nice dinner at home. Spending money on dining out was as rare as snow in the Kutch desert. The best gatherings were ones where wallets remained firmly zipped. Maximum joy, minimal expense. Now *that* was true cause for celebration. Priya smiled as she followed her parents out of Moksha, the sun catching on the freshly cleaned windows.

"I'm so glad the power is back on in the apartment," Mumma said, pausing to take in the uncluttered lot. No more contractor trucks, tangled extension cords, and dust-covered tarps.

"Now if only the reporters would take off too," Puppa muttered, nodding toward the cars still parked on the gravel patch outside the property.

Mumma sighed, started for the apartment door, then turned back. "Priya, can you bring my blue suitcase from the coach house? I need the spice mix I brought from Vinod Uncle's."

Priya nodded and headed toward the coach house. Just as she stepped inside, her phone buzzed. She glanced at the screen—then exhaled with relief. Finally, a familiar name.

"Brooke!" she answered. "Where have you been? I've been trying to get a hold of you for days."

"I'm still in Ubud," Brooke replied, her voice heavy and cracking.

"Are you okay?" Priya froze, concerned for her best friend.

"I'm never going to recover, Pri. Ever."

Priya's stomach dropped. "What's wrong? Talk to me, Brooke."

"It's Lady Whiskerbottom," Brooke wailed. "She's gone, Pri. And it's my fault she's dead."

"Oh, Brooke. I'm so sorry. What happened?"

Brooke sniffed loudly. "You know how she hated all my boyfriends, right? Well, I hooked up with her healer. He's so yummy, Pri, I couldn't help it. I didn't want it to interfere with her therapy, so I made sure she never saw us together, but last night . . ." Her sobs intensified. "I thought she was out after her session, so I told him to stay. I'm pretty sure she woke up and saw us. She can't jump on the bed anymore, so she probably just watched."

Brooke's voice cracked as she continued, barely able to get the words out. "I just keep imagining her little eyes peeking over the edge, completely devastated, Pri! It must have broken her heart then and there. I'm such a shithead. My cat died while I was having the best orgasm of my life."

"You don't know that for sure, Brooke," Priya said, biting her lip.

"I do! She made sure I knew. She peed all over the guy's pants, then she crawled into my favorite bag and died."

"The Birkin?"

"Yes, it's ruined forever, Pri. Whenever I see it now, I'll think of how I failed her in her final moments."

"Oh Brooke, you gave Lady Whiskerbottom the life of royalty. She knew she was loved, and that's what counts." Priya paused, then said solemnly, "She lived a long and full life, and she couldn't have asked for a better mom."

"I have to announce her death on social media," Brooke moaned, blowing her nose again. "A final picture of her on her favorite throw with her monogrammed collar."

"I'm so sorry, Brooke. Is there anything I can do to help?"

"I'm flying back with her body. I want her buried at Knight Estates, and I'd like her to have a proper send-off. Could you arrange a funeral for her at Moksha?"

"A pet funeral?" Priya asked, taken aback. "We've never done one, but I'll talk to Puppa and see what he says."

"Thanks, Pri. I'll check in with you when I land." Brooke hung up with a quiet sniff.

Priya stared at her phone for a second. Only Brooke could turn a story about a spiritual healer and a ruined handbag into something both tragic and absurd. But loss was loss, and Priya knew the pain of it all too well. Brooke was hurting, and if there was any way to help her, she'd find it.

Priya tucked her phone away and grabbed her mother's suitcase, her mind already running through how to pitch the idea of a pet funeral to Puppa. As she wheeled the clattering luggage into the apartment, her parents snapped their heads around from the couch.

"Shh!" they said, turning back to the television.

Priya froze in the hallway. On the screen was Ethan—*her* Ethan—seated across from a well-known talk show host. It was the first time she'd seen him since the night he left . . . and he looked incredible. Dressed in a tailored gray suit and open-collared shirt, he was both handsome and painfully distant. His hair, slightly tousled, was perfectly imperfect. Priya's eyes traced the familiar line of his jaw, lingering on his smile. Her heart swelled at the smooth and rich sound of his voice.

The host grinned at Ethan. "We're thrilled about your movie, but here's what everyone's really dying to know . . ." He pointed to a screen where the now-infamous picture of Ethan and Priya flickered, their faces close enough to kiss.

"What's the deal?" the host teased, prompting cheers and applause from the audience.

"You're all a bunch of pot stirrers, you know that?" Ethan joked, though his smile didn't quite reach his eyes.

Priya's stomach tightened as the camera panned to reveal Sienna Deville seated beside him. Effortlessly glamorous with high cheekbones and long legs, she radiated pure Hollywood allure. Priya's eyes stung at the sight.

"Well?" the host continued, tapping his desk for dramatic effect. "Is Ethan Knight single or spoken for?"

The camera zoomed in on Ethan. He lowered his lids briefly, almost imperceptibly, before he spoke. "Priya Solanki and I are just friends. Those photos have been taken out of context and blown way out of proportion."

Even though they were the very words she had used over the phone with her parents while he had silently watched, hearing Ethan repeat them on TV broke Priya's heart. It was like he was saying them directly to her. A public, undeniable farewell. She knew she had no right to feel hurt; after all, she'd been the one to push him away. But the pain came anyway, raw and overwhelming. The word *just* nullified everything that had transpired between them, downgrading their embraces to just kisses, their conversations to just talks, their intimate moments to just sex. It stripped their bond, diminishing it into something unremarkable and ordinary.

Priya's parents exchanged a look of relief. Ethan's words had given them exactly what they needed—a clean dismissal of any romantic link between him and their daughter.

"Maybe now the reporters will leave us alone," Puppa said. "The calls are nonstop!"

"Shh." Mumma pointed toward the TV as the interview went on.

"I don't know . . ." The host raised an eyebrow, looking at the photo, then back to the audience. "Sure doesn't look like 'just friends' to me."

Laughter echoed in the studio.

Ethan leaned back with an easy grace, showing no interest in being lured into a discussion about his personal life.

"So how did you end up in this plaza with reporters hot on your trail?" the host asked, trying to draw out a new perspective.

"I was staying with an incredibly kind family while preparing for my next role," Ethan explained. "I needed some new riding gear, and their daughter—who's known me and my sister for many years—came along to help. We had no clue things would spiral out of control the way they did."

"That's right." The host nodded. "You ended up in a pretty intense situation. Let's look at what went down."

The screen showed a clip of Ethan confronting the photographer. "Touch her again and it'll be the last thing you do," Ethan's voice snarled through the speakers.

"Yikes. Wouldn't want to be *that* guy," the host quipped, mock-wiping his brow.

"Ah, but every woman wants to be the girl on that bike," Sienna Deville chimed in, throwing Ethan a sultry look.

The host perked up. "Now, *this* is interesting," he said, gesturing between them. "Rumor has it there's major chemistry between you two in your new movie. Care to share?"

"Details about the chemistry or the movie?" Sienna arched an eyebrow playfully.

"Both, of course." The host grinned.

Priya watched as Sienna and Ethan bantered with the host. *They look so natural together, like two stars perfectly aligned.*

"Alright, let's have a sneak peek," the host said. "Roll the clip!"

The trailer played, full of high-octane scenes and insane stunts, closing with an electrifying moment between Ethan and Sienna that left the audience buzzing.

"Is it just me, or did things suddenly heat up in here?" the host joked, fanning himself. "I think we need a reenactment of that scene. Who's with me?"

The crowd erupted in cheers as Sienna gave a thumbs-up.

"I don't know. I'm not feeling it." Ethan raised his hand to his ear, playfully tuning in to the crowd's energy. The cheering grew louder.

"Come on, Ethan. The people have spoken." Sienna stood and pulled Ethan to his feet. They stood back to back, getting into character.

"And action!" the host declared.

The studio dimmed, leaving only Ethan and Sienna in the spotlight. Priya's grip on the suitcase tightened as they pivoted to face each other. Ethan's expression sharpened, a fire in his eyes that Priya knew all too well. Sienna met him head-on, her stance full of defiance. Their voices clashed in a heated exchange, each line igniting the next. Priya could almost feel the intensity emanating from the screen, as if she were right there in the studio.

In the middle of their argument, Ethan's gaze dropped to Sienna's mouth, shifting the entire dynamic. A tightness gripped Priya's chest as the space between them charged. And yet she couldn't look away. The audience held its breath, expecting the moment to end where it had in the trailer.

Instead, Sienna closed the space between them, her mouth claiming Ethan's in a kiss that stunned both him and the audience. He recovered quickly, his hand finding her waist as the kiss intensified. The spotlight bathed them in golden light, illuminating every angle of their faces. It was breathtaking, a moment of flawless Hollywood magic—two beautiful people lost in a kiss that seemed to hold the promise of every great romance.

Priya's heart splintered into pieces. *This is just a scene . . . Just acting.*

She had seen Ethan kiss on-screen before, but it was entirely different now. She knew exactly how his lips felt, how those kisses tasted. In the morning, they were warm and minty, edged with his first cup of coffee. At night, they tasted like wine and magic, leaving her breathless and raw.

Now, watching Ethan and Sienna kiss, Priya felt her composure crack. The sight of them was too perfect, too convincing. When Ethan finally pulled back and they returned to the couch, the audience shot to their feet, roaring with applause.

Priya felt an overwhelming urge to flee to her room, but the pull of curiosity held her in place. She remained frozen, drawn to Ethan's every word, every glance.

"Well, well," the host teased. "You two sure know how to make sparks fly. Is there a little off-screen chemistry at play here?"

Sienna leaned back, letting the suspense build with a playful pause. "Sometimes it's hard to tell where the acting stops"—she gave Ethan a sly look—"and where real life begins." Her smile was as captivating as it was calculated.

Priya told herself this was exactly what she needed to fade back into peaceful anonymity—a new rumored love interest for Ethan. Her parents could relax, and life would slip back to normal. No more intrusions, no more chaos.

So why did she feel like her soul had just been scraped raw? The numbness she'd been clinging to cracked open, and the flood of pain that followed stole the air from her lungs.

Twenty-Seven

THE CLIP OF SIENNA and Ethan's kiss skyrocketed to the top of trending topics. As they made appearances for the new movie, their vagueness—neither confirming nor denying the rumors—kept everyone guessing. Was their connection genuine or a promotional tactic? Their silence only added to the intrigue, drumming up enthusiasm for the movie.

As for Priya, her brief moment in the spotlight faded just as quickly as it had arrived. The flood of messages, calls, and social media alerts slowed to a trickle. The reporters camped outside Moksha moved on, on the hunt for the next big scoop.

"How are you holding up?" Deepa asked one day over their video chat. She was the only one in the family who knew the truth about Ethan.

"I'm fine," Priya replied. It was easier than trying to explain how empty she felt. Deep down, she wondered if she would ever be okay again. Being with Ethan had lifted her to an exhilarating high. But now that feeling was gone. In its place was a deep, gnawing ache. Each moment blurred into the next—tasteless, colorless, formless.

"How's your app going?" Deepa asked.

"It's stalled. Mumma doesn't get the whole work-from-home thing. She thinks being at home means I'm available all the time. And Puppa's having a hard time arranging Lady Whiskerbottom's funeral. Brooke's asking for live streaming and other things we've never done before, so I'm handling all the tech-related stuff."

"Live streaming? At Moksha? For a cat?" Deepa made a face.

"Lady Whiskerbottom had a massive fan base," Priya replied, smiling. "We're planning the biggest funeral Moksha's ever seen, Dee. It's turning out to be quite a financial win."

"No wonder Puppa agreed!"

Just then, Mumma stormed into Priya's room.

"Hey, Mumma," Deepa greeted. "Bye, Mumma! Bye, Pri!" She hastily ended the call.

"What do you want to eat today?" Mumma asked.

"I'm good with anything. Whatever's easiest," Priya replied.

"There must be something you want," Mumma insisted. "*Sev tameta nu shaak?*"

"That's perfect."

"But that has onions. You know I don't eat onions on Thursdays."

"Khichdi-kadhi?" Priya suggested.

"We just had that last week."

"Potato curry with rotli, then?"

"I don't have time to make rotli, Priya. It's not like I'm running a restaurant here," Mumma huffed. "We're having green beans curry with *bajra no rotlo*. Eat it or go hungry."

Priya pinched the bridge of her nose as Mumma exited the room. Every day, she asked Priya for suggestions only to reject them because she already had the menu planned. Living with her parents felt like being stuck in a sitcom full of absurd routines and quirky challenges. But that didn't make it any less frustrating. She tried to focus on her work again, only to be interrupted by a phone call from her ex.

"Finally!" Manoj said when she answered. "You've been dodging my calls."

"Things have been a bit crazy around here. What's up?"

"Well . . ." Manoj paused for effect. "I've finally got the funds to buy you out . . ."

"Why do I feel like there's a *but*?" Priya leaned back in her chair and waited for her ex-husband to respond.

"See, you still get me," Manoj replied with a small, nervous laugh.

"Go on. I'm listening."

"It's just that . . . I miss you, Priya. I know I screwed up. Big time. And I've regretted it every day since you left. Those photos of you with Ethan Knight really hit me hard. When I heard there was nothing between you, it felt like I'd been given a second chance." He took a deep breath before barreling on. "I'm wondering if you'd like to meet up—"

"Let's not, Manoj," Priya cut in. "Whatever was between us, it's done now." What she didn't say was that even if she could ever trust Manoj again, there was no returning to a life that felt comfortably dull. Ethan had changed everything for her.

"I'm not asking you to make any decisions right now," Manoj insisted. "Let's meet up and talk it over."

"Priya!" Mumma called from the doorway. "Puppa needs your help."

Priya sighed. "Sorry, Manoj. I have to go. Just transfer the funds like we agreed."

As she hung up and hit Save on her work, an invisible weight settled on Priya's chest. The endless interruptions—her parents, the phone calls, Lady Whiskerbottom's funeral—were derailing her ability to meet deadlines and build her business. She couldn't keep helping her parents while managing her own projects.

Priya headed downstairs to Moksha, where Puppa greeted her with a sigh of relief. "The technicians are here to set up the live streaming equipment, but they have a ton of questions," he said. "Microphones, camera angles, internet stuff. Could you take care of it?"

"Sure, Puppa." Priya went into the setup room and was greeted by a mess of cables and cameras. She stepped in, coordinating the arrangement of equipment and suggesting placements. Just as things started to fall into place, her father approached.

"Can you handle the reception desk for a while?" he asked. "Franzi is sick, and there's a service starting, so I'm stepping in until Meera gets here."

Priya glanced toward the setup crew that was waiting for her. She swallowed the frustration rising in her chest and forced a smile. "Sure, Puppa."

"Thanks, beta." He started walking away, then paused and turned around. "Oh, and can you help me book that violinist tonight?"

"Brooke is coming over tonight so we can work on Lady Whiskerbottom's slideshow. Can we do it in the morning?"

Puppa gave a wave of agreement before disappearing down the hallway. Priya took his place at the reception, her mind too full of all the things she had to do. Just as she settled in, her phone rang again. She debated ignoring it until she saw it was her sister Meghna calling from India.

"Megs!" she said, her voice softening with warmth. "It's so good to hear from you."

"I've missed you too!" Meghna replied. "If I get cut off, I'll call you back. The signal is still spotty at my end."

Before Priya could reply, a crew member tapped her shoulder. "Miss, where do you want us to set up the projector?"

"I'll be there in a sec," Priya answered, suppressing a sigh.

"Everything okay?" Meghna asked.

"It's a bit of a madhouse here at the moment."

"I bet. Moksha is back in business, and you're right in the thick of it. I'm sure Mumma and Puppa are glad to have you around, but how are *you* doing?"

Priya opened her mouth to say, "I'm fine" again, but the words caught in her throat. She wasn't fine. Far from it. She was exhausted and overwhelmed from pretending to be fine. And now, as her sister's voice echoed through the phone, the dam of her emotions broke, and with it came a torrent of tears—not the silent ones that spilled onto her pillow at night, but deep, racking sobs that she could no longer contain.

"Hey, hey . . ." Meghna's voice sharpened with concern. "What's going on, Pri?"

Priya took a shaky breath, her sobs slowing to a tremble. "I don't know how to explain it," she said. "It's like Moksha is taking over my life, Megs. You know how Mumma and Puppa say it's our destiny, right? Well, I feel like I'm slowly sliding into its belly, being swallowed alive. I'm trying so hard to get back on track, but there's no escape. I'm trapped, Megs, and I don't know how to get out."

"Oh Pri." Meghna sighed. "You've never backed down from anything, especially not with Mumma and Puppa. But you sound . . . done. I've never heard you like this, not even after things ended with Manoj. What's really going on?"

Priya stayed silent, unable to find the words.

"You sounded happy when we spoke last month," Meghna said slowly. "Mumma and Puppa were away, and you were holding things down at Moksha with—" She gasped in realization. "It's Ethan Knight, isn't it? Ever since he came to Moksha, you haven't been the same . . . Oh my god, Pri. You're heartbroken. I can hear it in your voice." She lowered her voice. "Did something happen between you two?"

"Yes, we had a thing. And I foolishly let myself believe we stood a chance," Priya said, her voice cracking. "But I can't escape Moksha, Megs. No matter what I do or how far I run, it's always going to pull me back in."

Meghna was quiet for a moment. "I know it feels like you've hit rock bottom, but this isn't some fate you must accept. Losing Ethan might've been the tipping point, but that doesn't mean Moksha is your only option. Everything that's happened—all the setbacks, the challenges, the heartache—that's just life, Pri. Sometimes it leads and you follow. Sometimes you lead and it follows. And right now, you need to take charge. If you don't find your footing, you'll keep spinning to everyone else's tunes." Meghna paused, letting her words sink in. "The only power anything or anyone has over you is what you allow. You're the only one who can break free, and that's not going to happen if you give up."

Priya nodded but felt as if she were standing at the bottom of an insurmountable mountain. "I don't even know where to begin, Megs. I don't know what to do."

"You don't have to figure it all out in one go," Meghna said. "Just trust that you're not stuck. You've been knocked down, but you can rise again. One step at a time, Pri. You've got this."

Priya wiped her cheeks, blinking through the tears as guests passed by. It was embarrassing to be caught with her guard down, but they barely noticed. Her tears fit right in, just another ripple in the endless tide of grief that flowed through Moksha. Meghna was right. If Priya didn't pull herself together soon, she would end up disappearing into the shadows of the funeral home like a forgotten statue collecting dust.

Twenty-Eight

PRIYA'S STOMACH WAS IN KNOTS on the day of Lady Whiskerbottom's funeral. She knew Ethan wasn't coming, but that didn't make it any easier. She had stayed out of sight since he'd left, and it was time to face the world again.

The reporters were back, though only a select few, invited specifically to cover the event. Puppa hired extra help and pulled out all the stops to meet Brooke's every request—an ice sculpture of Lady Whiskerbottom, paw-print tapestries, and even a violinist crooning a mournful ditty for her kitty. Pet influencers began arriving in droves, some with their own cats in tow.

Lady Whiskerbottom lay perfectly poised in a silk-lined casket, wearing a tiara and a hot-pink tutu. Even in death, she looked as though the tributes around her weren't quite good enough—not the catnip wreaths, and certainly not the memorial mugs with her face on them. Strategically placed cameras streamed every angle of the service for her fans, who flooded the live feed with reactions and comments. A separate screen showed a mosaic of virtual attendees, Lady Whiskerbottom's exclusive circle of influencer cats.

Madame Clawdia, a poised Siamese, had a handkerchief tucked in her collar. Muffin, the orange tabby, swatted furiously at his human, while Pinot, the playful Bengal, kept presenting his backside to the camera.

Lady Whiskerbottom's veterinarian delivered the eulogy, touching on her social media career and her influence in the feline fashion world. He chuckled as he recalled her bites and scratches, proof that she did not tolerate being handled by just anyone. His voice softened as he spoke about her final days and how she became an advocate for feline health.

Brooke sat beside Priya, tears streaming freely. Priya put an arm around her as the room dimmed for the next part of the service—a slideshow of the cat's most iconic posts, as well as some candid moments. The screen lit up with Lady Whiskerbottom's life from her early days as a kitten to her rise as an influencer. Brooke's tears gave way to soft laughter at some of the photos. As the last slide appeared, a stylishly groomed cat in the audience yawned, sparking a wave of laughter.

The service ended with a reel of Lady Whiskerbottom's brand endorsements. Guests were treated to a commemorative collar and encouraged to donate to a feline charity in her name.

Brooke turned to Priya, eyes red but shining with gratitude. "Thank you. This was everything and more. You and your family arranged the most perfect goodbye for my fur queen. I just wish Ethan and my father were here."

"I know it would have meant a lot." Priya drew her in and gave her a kiss on the cheek. "But Ethan's in the middle of his promo tour, and your father will be joining you at the cemetery."

"You're coming too, right?" Brooke asked.

"Of course. I just have to take care of a few things, so I'll meet you there. Your ride is all set, whenever you're ready to leave."

"You're the best." Brooke gave Priya a grateful hug.

As Priya watched Brooke mingle with the other guests, a small pang tightened in her chest. There was something about the way Brooke tilted her head and smiled at people that brought a sudden, vivid flash of Ethan to mind. Taking a deep breath, she slipped out of the room in search of Mumma and Puppa.

They stood by the reception desk, their "funeral faces" firmly in place—kind but restrained. Too wide a smile and they risked conveying a party vibe. Too solemn and they would appear cold and uncaring. Priya admired how calm and collected they looked, but she also sensed the dual current running beneath. Moksha was getting its first taste of exposure outside the tiny community they'd been serving, and it was both exhilarating and overwhelming.

Puppa caught Priya's eye and beckoned her over. Lowering his voice, he whispered, "Priya, beta, check this out. All the business cards are gone!"

Priya stared at the empty cardholder, then looked at her parents excitedly. She could not remember a single time that they had run out of cards. Catching the pride in Puppa's voice, Mumma adjusted her posture, lifting her chin as though the missing business cards granted her a new level of prestige.

"*Le, joyle,*" Puppa quipped. "One pet funeral and she's acting like royalty."

"Maybe we should get her a tiara from Lady Whiskerbottom's collection." Priya laughed.

It had been a long time since Priya had laughed like that—light and genuine. She quickly slipped on her "funeral face" as a group of guests passed by, but deep inside, something shifted. A moment of joy had found its way through the cracks. As she stood there beside her parents, Priya thought that maybe, just maybe, with enough of these moments, she could emerge into the light again.

Twenty-Nine

BY THE TIME Priya arrived at Knight Estates, a small crowd was already gathered at the family's private cemetery. Brooke stood by a small grave with her father, a hot-pink hat perched perfectly on her head to honor Lady Whiskerbottom's signature color. Her father rested his hand on her shoulder. His hair was neatly combed back, and his dark suit gave him an air of quiet command.

Catching sight of Priya, Brooke motioned her over. As Priya stepped beside her, Harry Knight turned toward her. He had always been a distant figure during her childhood visits; now he seemed to assess her with quiet curiosity—the woman who had not only accompanied his son to the estate but was rumored to have been involved with him. After a beat, he gave her a polite nod.

"Good afternoon, everyone," the officiant began, clearing his throat. "It was my privilege to serve as Lady Whiskerbottom's spiritual counselor." Chuckles rippled through the crowd, and he met them with an easy smile. "You may laugh, but she truly had a gift for tuning out the world and finding peace in any situation."

He painted a picture of feline paradise—eternal sunbeams, catnip fields, and endless napping spots. Around them, a few reporters quietly snapped photos, capturing the ceremony. When it was time to lower the casket, Brooke sobbed openly as she dropped in a final offering: Lady Whiskerbottom's favorite toy.

Harry Knight shifted uncomfortably beside his daughter, uncertain of how to comfort her. Priya stepped in, gently squeezing Brooke's hand and guiding her inside for the wake. The manor greeted them with its familiar grandeur—the sweeping staircase, ornately framed paintings, and marble floors covered with thick, luxurious rugs. Sebastian welcomed them with his signature calm demeanor, while Harry bid Brooke farewell.

"Have a . . . good wake," he said, with a stilted hug. Nodding at Priya, he disappeared down the hall.

Sebastian led everyone into the conservatory—a bright, airy space with sweeping views of the estate's gardens. As guests gathered around Brooke, Priya gave them space and wandered to the refreshment table. She nibbled on a slice of sharp cheddar and had just popped a grape in her mouth when Brooke called for her.

"Do I look okay?" she asked, dabbing her eyes. "I've been asked to do a quick interview for a pet magazine—" Before she could finish, her phone rang.

"Ethan!" Brooke's face lit up as she answered. "It went well. Really? You tuned in?" She paused, listening intently, then glanced at Priya with an apologetic smile.

Priya smiled reassuringly, then motioned that she'd be right back. She stepped into the hallway, her smile fading the moment she was out of sight. It didn't matter that Ethan wasn't there in person. Just hearing his voice, even through Brooke's phone, brought it all back. She leaned back against the wall, her heart racing in a way she still hadn't learned how to control.

"Miss, are you all right?"

Priya turned to see Sebastian regarding her with polite concern. "Hi, Sebastian. Sorry—I mean, yes. I'm fine. I just need some fresh air." Nodding toward the exit, she continued on her way.

As she rounded the corner, her phone pinged with a message from Deepa: *Call me when you're free.*

Priya speed-dialed her sister. "Hey, what's up?"

"Have you been on social media today?" Deepa asked.

"No," Priya replied with a sinking feeling. "Is something wrong?"

"Far from it! Moksha's account has blown up. Lady Whiskerbottom's funeral put us on the map!"

"That's cool, Dee, but let's be real. Most of these new followers are probably pet people. Puppa made an exception for Brooke. We had to meet a lot of regulations—separate rooms, equipment, protocols . . . It wasn't easy."

"But everything's set up now, right?"

"It is. But that doesn't mean Puppa's switching gears. You know he's all about serving the community."

"True," Deepa said. "But you know what else he's all about?"

"Money!" they shouted in unison, dissolving into laughter.

Priya quickly lowered her voice as a guest strolled by, glancing at her. "Listen, Dee, I have to go," she said. "I'm at Lady Whiskerbottom's wake."

As she made her way back to the conservatory, she noticed the library door slightly ajar. Priya paused. It had been strictly off-limits during her visits as a child. Harry Knight's office was in there—and she'd always wondered what it looked like. Driven by curiosity, she stepped inside.

The scent of old books and worn leather filled the room, giving it a sense of history and quiet dignity. Towering shelves surrounded her, filled with books, souvenirs, and personal mementos. Sunlight trickled through tall windows, catching the edges of glass-framed photographs—Ethan's parents, along with Brooke and Ethan, through different phases of life. A row of trophies caught Priya's eye, and she reached for one, reading the inscription engraved on its base.

"Those belonged to Ethan," a voice broke the stillness.

Startled, Priya turned to see Brooke and Ethan's father rising from a leather chair. He approached her slowly, his presence filling the room.

"My wife collected them all," he said, his voice soft. "Rebecca had a sentimental heart, always celebrating the kids' milestones and achievements." He took the trophy from Priya and returned it to its place, exactly where his wife had left it.

"Sorry," Priya said. "I didn't mean to intrude."

"Not at all." Harry offered a faint smile. "You're our guest today."

The emphasis on *today* hit Priya hard. The last time she'd visited Knight Estates, it had been with Ethan, and they hadn't exactly been greeted with open arms.

"It would've meant a lot to Ethan if you had welcomed him that day," Priya blurted out, unable to hold back even though she knew she was treading on dangerous ground.

"It would have meant a lot to *me* if Ethan hadn't left the way he did," Harry said sharply. "If he'd kept his word and gone to college instead of putting himself first."

Priya refused to back down. "Mr. Knight, your son was running from the guilt he carried after your wife's death. He blamed himself for his mother's accident." She drew a slow breath and met his gaze head-on. "He thought you blamed him too, and it nearly destroyed him."

Harry's expression wavered for an instant, an almost imperceptible wince, as though Priya had struck a nerve.

"You were so consumed by your own grief, you didn't stop to see what it was doing to Ethan," she continued. "He followed the path you laid out because he thought he owed it to you. But he got tired of chasing after something you wouldn't give—your approval, your forgiveness—so he set out to prove himself without it."

Harry remained silent, taking in her words.

Priya's voice softened. "Ethan has tried to reach out to you many times, but each time you turned him away. He wasn't here just to visit his mother's grave. He wanted to see you too. But once again, you rejected him. I doubt he'll ever try again. It's up to you now. You can either keep things the way they are . . ." Her finger traced the dusty surface of the trophy. "Or start making changes." She shifted it slightly in a small but deliberate gesture.

Before she left the room, Priya paused and looked over her shoulder. "For what it's worth, I think your wife would have wanted you to mend things with your son. She'd be devastated knowing her death drove this wedge between the two of you. She'd want you to show up—for both your kids."

As Priya walked out, a long, steady breath escaped her lips. She had sown the seeds and could only hope that they took. There was no changing the past, but perhaps there was still a chance for Harry and Ethan. She straightened her shoulders and walked back to the conservatory. Life with all its messiness kept moving forward.

Thirty

WHEN PRIYA RETURNED to Moksha, she spotted a few cars still parked outside.

That's odd, she thought, letting herself in through the side entrance, her mind still replaying the conversation with Ethan's dad.

As she climbed the stairs, a memory surfaced—of leading Ethan up these very stairs when he'd shown up with Brooke. Her hand instinctively sought out the star pendant at her neck, a bittersweet reminder that somehow still grounded her. At the top, she slipped off her shoes and entered the apartment with a soft sigh.

"There you are!" Puppa called, sounding overly cheerful.

Priya stepped into the living room and froze. Her parents sat on the couch with a man who looked vaguely familiar, though she couldn't place him.

"We have guests, beta." Mumma smiled tensely, gesturing toward a chair across from the couch.

Priya followed the direction of her mother's gaze and froze when she saw Ravi Tiwari seated in the corner. Before she could recover, Puppa chimed in.

"Look who else is here." Puppa nodded pointedly at another chair.

Manoj swiveled around in his chair and gave her an awkward wave.

Priya blinked, stunned. *Is this some kind of ambush? A guy from my childhood, who still seems to carry a torch, and my ex-husband sitting together in my parents' living room*? She glanced between Ravi and Manoj, trying to make sense of the moment.

"And this is Dinesh Verma," Puppa explained, motioning toward the stranger. "We met him at Vinod Uncle's."

The name landed, and Priya connected the dots. This was the guy in the photo Deepa had sent—the one her parents were trying to set her up with.

"Um, hi," she said as Dinesh got to his feet.

"Nice to meet you," he replied. "I hope I'm not intruding. I was in the area and thought I'd drop in."

"Not at all!" Mumma interjected cheerfully. "You're always welcome. Priya, you sit here!" She patted her seat as she rose. "I'll go and make some tea."

Priya offered Dinesh a tentative smile and took a seat. Her eyes drifted to Ravi, then Manoj. An awkward silence hung in the air. Dinesh pretended to admire the apartment. Ravi focused on the carpet as though it held the answers to life, and Manoj stared at the small Ganesh figurine on the family's altar. Meanwhile, Puppa kept nodding his head like a bobblehead doll. Priya glanced at her feet. In a congregation of socks, she was the only one with bare feet.

She cleared her throat. "So, um. Ravi, Manoj—what are you doing here?"

Before they could answer, Mumma called her to the kitchen.

"Coming!" Priya leaped to her feet, grateful for the excuse.

"Can you grab that pot for me?" Mumma asked, her voice loud enough for everyone to hear. Then under her breath, she hissed, "Why is Ravi here? And what on earth is Manoj showing up for now?"

"I have no idea," Priya whispered back. There was a time when all her parents wanted was for her to patch things up with her ex-husband, not that they knew what had really happened. But now that they'd met Dinesh, their priorities seemed to have shifted.

"Thank you, beta," Mumma said, continuing the charade. Through clenched teeth, she added, "Get rid of them."

"Okay, okay. I'll try," Priya replied. As she returned to the living room, Mumma swept past her, extending her hand to Dinesh.

"Come, beta. I must show you our balcony," she said. "You can pick some herbs to take home." Leading Dinesh away, she gave Puppa a meaningful look and gestured toward Ravi.

Puppa caught on and cleared his throat. "Ravi," he said. "Have you seen Moksha's new electrical panel? It's quite impressive! Come, let me show you." He got up, put on his shoes, and waited by the door.

Ravi shot a puzzled look at Puppa, then at Priya, and back again. "Alright," he agreed, a little perplexed, before getting up and putting on his own shoes.

"We won't be long," Puppa declared, nodding toward Manoj and winking at Priya as he led Ravi out.

Priya sighed. *Here goes nothing.* Her mission was to politely get rid of Manoj.

"Finally, some privacy," Manoj said, letting out a relieved breath.

Priya sat on the sofa across from her ex-husband and looked at him. "What exactly are you doing here?" she asked.

"I brought you a certified check for your share of the company." Manoj extended an envelope.

"Thank you." Priya glanced at the number on the check before closing the envelope again. "But you didn't have to fly all the way from Calgary to deliver this; you could just have transferred it, like we agreed."

"I know. But I wanted to see you, Priya. I meant what I said on the phone. I'm hoping you can give us another shot. I'm ready to do whatever it takes to make things right."

"Manoj, I need to stop you right there," Priya said. "I know you're sorry. And I'm sorry too. The truth is you weren't the only one to blame for our marriage ending. I wasn't completely present in our relationship, even before you cheated."

His face clouded with confusion. "I thought we were fine. Until I . . . well, until I ruined it."

Priya sighed, searching for the right words. "We were fine on paper, Manoj. We had the same background, the same interests . . . Our families got along. I told myself that would be enough. But deep down, I know now—I didn't marry you for the right reasons."

A puzzled look crossed Manoj's face. "What do you mean?"

"I was looking for something safe. Something uncomplicated. And you gave me that," she admitted gently. "But my heart has always belonged to someone else, and I didn't face that until I returned home."

"Someone else?" Manoj rose from his seat, his voice filled with disbelief. "I don't get it, Priya. I was your first kiss, your first boyfriend . . . The only person you've ever been intimate with . . ." He trailed off and stopped pacing. "This has to do with your parents." He frowned, his gaze sharp and searching. "You told them I had an affair, so now they're setting you up with someone else, right? Is it that guy?" He gestured toward the balcony. "Or the one who left with your father?"

Priya shook her head, but before she could reply, the door swung open.

"We're back," Puppa announced, leading Ravi through the door.

Manoj closed his eyes and swore under his breath. "Well," he said, his lips pressed tightly together. "I guess this is it. I've said what I needed to, but it looks like you've moved on."

Priya's eyes met his in a silent apology, and he looked away. Turning on his heel, he headed for the door where Puppa and Ravi were taking off their shoes. The three men jostled for space in an awkward dance of elbows and apologies. Finally, Manoj put on his shoes, tipped his head in a mock bow, and strode out.

A smug smile spread across Puppa's face. "I think I'll join your mother and Dinesh." He sent Priya a quick glance in Ravi's direction, a silent cue to get rid of him too.

"Please give my regards to your family," he added to Ravi.

Ravi chuckled as Puppa disappeared onto the balcony. "I've had a lot of introductions in my time. Parents, siblings, even a family astrologer once, but never to an electrical panel. That was a first."

Priya smiled. "Yeah, my dad's obsessed with it."

A small pause settled between them, the silence stretching out a little too long.

Priya cleared her throat. "I'm sorry for not getting back to you. It's been a bit crazy around here."

"I bet." Ravi let out a short laugh. "You were hosting *Ethan Knight* of all people, and then the media practically set up camp at your door. Remember when computer camp was the most exciting thing happening around here? Now look at you—front-page gossip, rubbing shoulders with the paparazzi."

"Not by choice, believe me."

"I didn't think so," Ravi said. "Although you've come a long way from the Priya I used to know. I was surprised to hear about your divorce, but not exactly heartbroken over it." His lips quirked into a small smile. "I've always liked you, Priya." He let the words hang in the air for a moment before continuing, his tone more casual. "Anyway, I'm in town for a few days and thought maybe we could grab dinner?"

Priya smiled, shaking her head. "Do you really think your mother would approve of you wining and dining a divorced woman from a lower caste?"

"If I stuck to my mom's approved list, my dating pool would be about this big." He pinched his fingers together.

Priya laughed. "Oh, I'm pretty sure Shrutiji has a whole spreadsheet of approved partners lined up for you. You're her golden boy, Ravi. We both know she has plans for you. And they don't involve someone like me."

"I think you're giving my mom way too much power."

"Am I?" Priya arched an eyebrow. "You and I grew up the same way, Ravi. First-gen kids whose parents uprooted their whole lives so we could have a better one here. But let's be real. We're not as free as we want to believe. We may not care about things like caste or race or religion, but they still do. They may not say it out loud because they know better than to be *that* obvious. Dating is one thing, but actually committing to someone? Bringing them home to meet the family? That's where it all starts to unravel."

"Isn't that where we come in though?" Ravi said. "To push through all that?"

Priya gave him a small smile. "You're right. And maybe you're ready to take on that fight, but I'm not. I feel like all I've done lately is try to prove myself—to my family, to the media, to people who don't even know me. I've been through enough to know exactly what I *don't* want." Her voice softened as she continued. "My life isn't perfect, but it's mine, and right now, the only fight I have left in me is for myself. I'm sorry, Ravi. I hope you find what you're looking for."

Ravi hesitated, a flicker of disappointment crossing his face. Then he nodded, keeping his tone calm. "I hope you do too."

Priya offered him a grateful smile before gently closing the door behind him. She stayed there for a moment, one hand on the doorknob. *That's two down.*

Turning around, she watched Dinesh with her parents on the balcony. *One more to go.*

Before she could gather herself, the balcony door slid open and her mother popped her head inside.

"Has Ravi left?" she asked, her voice laced with an almost too-sweet curiosity.

"Yes, he has," Priya said, nodding.

"Rakesh!" Mumma called. "I could use your help in the kitchen."

The second Puppa reentered the apartment, Mumma nudged Priya onto the balcony. "You keep Dinesh company," she said.

Priya rolled her eyes before stepping out. Her mother slid the balcony door shut behind her and disappeared into the kitchen.

"Quite the view, huh?" Dinesh said, trying to break the ice.

"Mm-hmm." Priya sat on the folding chair beside him. "One of a kind."

They stared at the back lot of Moksha—two industrial dumpsters, a worn-out parking lot, and a fence that had seen better days. The spindly trees lining the perimeter did little to improve the scenery.

After a beat, Dinesh turned to her. "You're very pretty, Priya," he said. "I was hoping to see you at your uncle's, the first time our families met."

Priya sighed. "Yeah . . . The thing is my parents kind of took matters into their own hands with this whole setup."

Dinesh raised an eyebrow. "So, you're *not* interested?"

"No offense, but I really don't want any part of this."

Dinesh studied her in silence, and Priya cringed, realizing how harsh that had sounded. "It's nothing personal," she added. "You seem like a great guy. I'm just not looking to meet anyone right now."

A slow grin spread across Dinesh's face. "You have no idea how happy I am to hear that."

Priya blinked. "Wait. You don't want this either?"

"Nope." Dinesh chuckled, shaking his head. "I've been dodging these setups for years. But lately, my parents have stopped accepting my excuses. So now I'm going along but making sure none of my dates work out."

"What do you mean?"

"Oh, just minor sabotage," Dinesh said, his eyes twinkling. "One time, I took this girl to a high-end restaurant, then made a scene about the prices. Another time, I typed out a list of expectations and read it out loud."

Priya grinned. "Okay, I have to know. What was today's strategy?"

Without missing a beat, Dinesh pulled a magnifying glass from his pocket and peered at her through it. His eye looked absurdly large behind the lens.

"Well, you see, I have a particular fondness for feet. Would you mind if I take a closer look?" He patted his lap.

"Oh, that's priceless!" Priya laughed.

Dinesh placed a hand over his heart. "I do my best."

"So, let me get this straight. Meeting my parents at Vinod Uncle's, asking for my number, showing up today . . . ?"

"Parents. Parents. And, you guessed it, parents!" Dinesh checked off imaginary boxes. "They want me hitched yesterday."

"And you're not interested in getting married?"

"I am. But my parents would never approve."

"She's not Gujarati?"

"She's not a she," Dinesh quipped.

Priya's eyes widened. "You're Gujarati *and* gay? Oh, Dinesh."

"Right? But it's okay." Dinesh smiled. "I'm dancing to the beat of my own *dandiya* stick."

"Well, I, for one, am glad your dandiya stick swings to a different tune." Priya chuckled. "This went much better than I imagined."

"For me too," Dinesh replied, sitting back relaxed. A comfortable silence settled between them.

"So, what are you going to tell your parents once I make my grand exit?" Dinesh asked. "We should get our stories straight."

Priya thought about it for a moment. "The truth," she said. Catching his panicked expression, she quickly added, "Not *your* truth, don't worry. Just mine."

"Oh my god! You're gay too?"

Priya shook her head, laughing. "No, but I've been keeping something from them."

Dinesh nodded in understanding. "Ah. I know the struggle well. So, what is it? Or do I have to sit here and guess?"

"It's not exactly a mystery. My truth is already out there for everyone to see."

Dinesh's brows furrowed, trying to piece together her statement. Then, like a light bulb coming on, it hit him. "Wait . . . hold on . . . Are you telling me that you and Ethan Knight . . . that those headlines were actually true?!"

Priya gave a simple shrug.

"*Baap re!*" Dinesh slapped a hand over his mouth. "*Tu ne* Ethan Knight! Excuse me. *What?!* My parents weren't keen on a divorcee to begin with and immediately crossed you off the list after the rumors broke. But when Ethan shut them down and your parents swore it was a misunderstanding, *boom*—you were back on the matchmaking menu." He let out an incredulous laugh.

Then something else clicked, and his eyes widened all over again. "Wait. Oh my God. You're the girl behind *that* photo." He gasped, pointing at her. "Ethan Knight, looking like he was sculpted by the gods themselves after a night of . . . *well.*" He waggled his eyebrows. "I zoomed in more than once. Honestly? I'm feeling personally betrayed right now."

Priya smiled wistfully. "There's nothing to be jealous of. That chapter of my life is closed."

Dinesh sighed, shaking his head. "Life is wild, isn't it?"

"I have a feeling it's about to get even messier when I tell my parents the truth."

"Yikes. Wishing you *all* the luck with that." Standing up, he gave her a nod. "Maybe one day I'll be brave enough to do the same." He opened his arms. "This was a surprisingly great conversation."

Priya grinned. "Likewise." She hugged him.

Out of the corner of her eye, she caught Puppa approaching the door, only to immediately retreat to the kitchen. *Great,* she thought. *He's definitely reporting the hug to Mumma, and the two of them are high-fiving over their matchmaking plan.*

By the time she walked inside with Dinesh, Mumma was already beaming. "Tea is ready!" she declared, her voice humming with joy.

"Thank you, Seema Auntie, but I really should get going," Dinesh said, offering a polite smile. "Goodbye, Rakesh Uncle."

Puppa's expression faltered, his smile slipping as he watched Dinesh move toward the door.

"But Dinesh, beta, bhajiya . . ." Mumma hurried after him, with a plate of potato fritters.

"I wish I could stay." Dinesh gave her an apologetic smile as he slipped into his shoes.

"Chai?" Puppa lifted a cup of tea.

"I really have to go, but thank you so much for everything. I had a wonderful time." He shot Priya a warm smile before closing the door behind him.

The room fell into a charged silence. Priya didn't need to turn around to feel her parents staring at her, waiting for an explanation.

Thirty-One

AS PRIYA TURNED to face her parents, Mumma wasted no time. "What did you say to Dinesh?"

Puppa set his cup of tea down and crossed his arms, his lips pressed into a thin line.

"Just so you know," Priya began, "I didn't do anything to send Dinesh packing. I just told him the truth. And it's time you know it too."

Mumma's eyes narrowed. "What are you talking about?"

Priya took a deep breath, pulled up a photo on her phone, and held it out. Her parents leaned in, peering at the screen.

"Why are you showing us a photo of Mr. Ethan?" Puppa asked, confused.

"Look closer."

Puppa's expression clouded as the pieces clicked into place. Sensing the shift in his demeanor, Mumma grabbed the phone and studied the details more closely—the room, the quilt, the pillowcase.

Her voice was sharp, almost breathless. "Mr. Ethan was sleeping in your bed? Was there an issue at the coach house?"

Puppa let out a frustrated breath. "Think, Seema. Think."

Mumma studied the image again, this time truly seeing it. The bare chest. The smoldering gaze. The unmistakable intimacy of the moment. And worst of all, the realization that Priya was the one who had taken the photo. She let out a sharp gasp, her hands flying to her mouth.

"*Hai Ram,*" her voice wavered as she sank into a chair, cradling her head. "*Patigya.* We are finished, Rakesh."

The paparazzi photos had been easy to dismiss, a scandal manufactured for headlines. Priya and Ethan had both denied involvement, and that had been enough for Priya's parents to push aside any nagging unease. But this? This crushed every excuse, every attempt to believe it was just a passing rumor. It stripped Priya of any shield she might have had against their judgment.

"Is this how we raised you?" Puppa's voice cut through the silence, low and sharp and shaking with something that almost sounded like heartbreak. "No wonder Dinesh bolted. Who will accept you now?"

Priya's fingers curled into her palms, but she refused to give in to the sting of his words. "What does it matter who accepts me when my own parents can't?" she said, forcing the words past the lump in her throat. "And it's not what you think. I *love* Ethan. I've loved him since the first time I set eyes on him."

For a fraction of a second, Puppa looked thrown, as if he'd never considered a deeper connection. But just as quickly, disappointment settled in, heavier than before. "And what did that love get you?" he said. "A few nights in his bed?"

"In *her* bed," Mumma cried, lifting her face from her hands. Her eyes darted around the apartment—the couch, the kitchen counter, the dining table—as if searching for evidence of where else her daughter had disgraced the family.

Puppa let out a humorless laugh, shaking his head. "I thought Mr. Ethan was a good man. I trusted him. I welcomed him into our home. And this is how he repays me? By taking advantage of my daughter?"

"Ethan didn't take advantage of me," Priya shot back, her cheeks burning. "This was *my* choice. I was the one who wanted a fling, and I was the one who ended it."

Her parents stared at her, shock written all over their faces.

Priya took a shaky breath and went on. "At first, I tried to get him to leave. I wanted you to take the Moksha offer so badly that I . . . I made up a ghost story. I messed with the lights. I faked hauntings. Anything to scare him away. But the more time I spent with him, the harder it was to ignore how I felt.

"After you left, things changed between us. It wasn't just casual anymore. For either of us. Ethan *wanted* me to tell you the truth, and I was going to. But then the press found out, and suddenly everyone was watching, judging, speculating. The spotlight, the scrutiny . . . I couldn't handle it, so I broke it off." She swallowed, her throat tightening. "But even then, he didn't throw me under the bus. He could have let the world rip me apart, but he didn't. He protected me. And he protected *you* by denying everything."

Her parents glanced at each other, their expressions faltering.

"I've been acting like everything's fine, but the truth is I'm not fine." Priya's voice cracked at the edges. "I feel like I'm failing at *everything*, including meeting your expectations. But I'm doing my best." She lifted her chin, even as emotion filled her voice. "Look, I know you're trying to help, but fixing me up with someone isn't the solution. What I really need is some time and space to fix *myself.* To heal, to work, to rest, to recover. So I've decided it's time for me to move out."

Mumma's head snapped up, but before she could say anything, Puppa cut in. "Move out?" he scoffed. "To where? Do you know what rent costs around here these days? How are you even going to afford a place of your own?"

Priya retrieved the envelope Manoj had dropped off, pulled out the check inside, and laid it on the table, nudging it in her parents' direction.

Puppa picked it up and stared at the amount as if trying to make sense of it. "Where did this come from?"

"It's what I was owed from the business," Priya said. "Manoj finally made good on it. I'm not just jumping without a plan. I've got it covered."

"So that's it, huh?" Mumma crossed her arms tight across her chest. "You get a little money and suddenly you're out the door?" She shook her head. "Are we so unbearable to live with? What's wrong with staying here?"

"Nothing is wrong, Mumma. I just—"

"No, there *is* something wrong," Mumma interrupted, her voice rising. "Because suddenly, my daughter, who I carried, who I raised, who I have given everything to, thinks she's too good to live with her parents?"

"That's not fair, Mumma," Priya said hotly.

"No? Then tell me, Priya. Why do you want to leave? Is our love suffocating you? Is having a mother who cooks for you and a father who worries about you such a terrible burden?"

Priya threw up her hands in exasperation. "It's not like I'm cutting off ties with you. I'm just moving to my own apartment, right here in the same city."

"Today, it's the same city. Tomorrow, it's another country."

Puppa cleared his throat. "Seema—"

But Mumma wasn't done. "Do you know how hard it was for me after your divorce? Knowing my daughter was living alone in Calgary? Ask your father. I used to—"

The sharp smack of paper hitting the table cut her off midsentence. Mumma blinked as Puppa slammed the check down in front of her. Her gaze dropped to the paper, confusion furrowing her brow. At first, she barely registered the numbers, her mind still caught up in her argument. But then, as the full amount sank in, her eyes widened.

"This . . ." She looked at Priya in disbelief. "This is *yours*?"

"I know you think I'm just sitting in my room typing away on the keyboard," Priya said. "But my job is *real*, even if I'm not leaving the house every morning. I work hard. And I need a quiet space to do it. I can't focus here with constant interruptions. That's why I need my own place."

Her parents glanced at each other, and in that moment, Priya could feel the weight of what they were processing. Their daughter wasn't just capable of standing on her own. She had been doing so for a while now. Without a husband to lean on. Or parents to hold her hand.

Puppa tapped the check, his expression unreadable. "I have a better solution." His glance shifted from Mumma to Priya. "Why give your money to a stranger when you can just move into the coach house? You can pay us instead and still have your own space."

Priya blinked, caught off guard. She hadn't expected her father to come up with a compromise, let alone such a clever one. Now that she had the means to live wherever she pleased, he wasn't willing to risk her slipping too far away. Allowing her to move into the coach house meant he could keep her close *and* keep the money in the family.

She looked at Mumma, who was still tight and closed off, but not as fired up as before—not exactly on board, not totally against it either.

Priya gave a slow nod. "It might be the best middle ground. We can sort out the details later, but can I start moving my things into the coach house?"

Puppa extended his hand, giving Priya a nod as they shook on it. Mumma, however, turned her face away.

Priya lowered herself beside her mother, wrapping an arm around her in a half hug. "I know you're upset, but I'm not going anywhere. I'll be staying right here in your backyard."

"Go then." Mumma brushed her arm away. "You didn't ask for permission when you were fooling around with Mr. Ethan, so why do you need my permission now?"

Priya rose slowly, telling herself that her mother would come around with time. This compromise wasn't easy for her either. Her father was finally handing over the keys to the coach house, but the space came with its own challenges—it was truly haunted now. With memories of Ethan. The bed, the couch, the spaces where he once stood, laughed, pulled her into his arms.

Priya had fought for her own place and won. Now she just had to learn to live with the ghosts that came with it.

Thirty-Two

MORNINGS WERE THE HARDEST. For a few blissful seconds, between sleep and consciousness, Priya would forget. She would stretch in the soft hush of the morning, and her mind would trick her into thinking Ethan was there. That nothing had changed. That if she rolled over, she'd find him watching her with that lazy smile. Then reality would crash in, the ache stealing her breath away.

Priya stretched her arm toward the ceiling as if she could touch a memory hanging in the air. She remembered the way Ethan used to intertwine their fingers, tracing the lines of her palm, pressing lazy kisses against her knuckles. With a sigh, she swung her legs over the edge of the bed, shaking off the last tendrils of sleep. Work was waiting. And work was survival. Priya was grateful for her long to-do list. It kept her busy and kept her going.

As she hunched over her laptop that afternoon, fingers flying over the keyboard, her phone rang.

"Hey, Pri!" Brooke chirped, her voice lighter than it had been since Lady Whiskerbottom had passed away. "Guess what? I'm going to be a mom!"

Priya nearly choked. "You're pregnant?"

"No, silly." Brooke laughed. "I'm going to be a *fur* mom. I'm getting a kitten! You have to come with me to pick him up."

Priya thought of her never-ending to-do list. Moving into the coach house was supposed to give her more time to focus, but between handling Moksha's sudden popularity, keeping up with her own clients, and preparing her app for submission, she was stretched thinner than ever. On top of that, she was building a pet portal for Moksha's website, so customers could book services, schedule tours, and explore packages online.

"I wish I could," she replied. "But I'm drowning over here."

"I still can't believe Moksha is doing pet funerals now," Brooke said. "I thought Lady Whiskerbottom's service was just a one-off."

"Puppa wasn't keen at first, until he started to see the business side of it," Priya said with a laugh.

"Moksha's modernizing. I never thought I'd see the day." Brooke chuckled. Then her tone softened. "How are *you*? I've been drowning in my grief over Lady Whiskerbottom, but I know what happened with Ethan has been rough on you."

And him? How's he doing? Does he ask about me? Has he moved on? Is he with Sienna now? Priya didn't ask those questions. Instead, she cleared her throat. "I'm managing. Um, how's Ethan?" The question slipped out before she could stop herself.

Brooke didn't miss a beat. "You know he'll be back in a few months for TIFF, right?"

Priya's fingers tightened around the mug next to her laptop. Of course she knew. Ethan had asked her to go with him.

"Yeah," she replied, keeping her voice neutral. "Are you going?"

"I wouldn't miss it for the world! He sent me two tickets, like he always does. And you won't believe who's finally agreed to go with me." Brooke's excitement was palpable as she continued.

"My father! I'm keeping everything crossed that this is the start of them finally mending things."

Priya blinked, surprised. She'd never know for sure if her words had influenced Harry Knight, but the thought that she might have helped, even in the smallest way, sent warmth through her chest. She wanted this for Ethan. So badly.

Still, a quiet sadness lingered beneath the warmth. Because if things had been different, she would have been there beside him, witnessing it unfold. She would have been the one squeezing his hand, whispering, *See? He's here. He showed up for you.*

Priya knew better than to dwell on impossible scenarios. She and Ethan were like oil and water, swirling together to create rainbow moments but always destined to drift apart.

"That's amazing, Brooke," she said sincerely. "I hope it goes well."

"Me too. And if they can fix things, maybe you and Ethan—"

"Brooke," Priya cut in gently.

"I know, I know. If you'd asked me before, I'd never have put the two of you together, but now that I've seen it, I can't unsee it. It drives me crazy that you ended it before it even had the chance to take off. And I hate that you're not even talking anymore. But hey, what do I know? My longest relationship has been with a cat. Speaking of which, I need to roll out the red carpet for Sir Puffington."

"Sir Puffington?" Priya let out a soft laugh. "I can't wait to meet him."

Still smiling, she ended the call and turned back to her laptop. But her conversation with Brooke had shaken loose memories that refused to be contained—Ethan stealing bites of whatever she was cooking, grinning as she swatted him away. His hand trailing absentmindedly across her back as he passed behind her. And the moments when his touch had been anything but casual—his lips pressing urgently against hers, his hands tightening around her waist as he backed her into the bedroom, as if he couldn't stand the space between them for even a second longer.

Priya inhaled sharply and pushed away from her desk. *I have to get out of here.*

Summer was just around the corner, and the air had that in-between feel—mild but not quite warm—as she stepped outside. The field was bursting with wildflowers, and trees rustled softly in the breeze. Priya let her feet lead her, walking until her mind began to slow. Eventually, she drifted toward the freight car and climbed inside, her legs swinging over the edge. As she closed her eyes and tilted her face toward the sun, her phone rang.

"Hey, Puppa," she answered.

"Your mother wants to know if you're coming over for dinner," he said.

A smile touched Priya's lips. Every day, despite the quiet strain between them, Mumma reached out in the only way she knew how—through an invitation to eat together. Although she was still curt with Priya, she made her favorite dishes, silently refilling her plate as they ate.

"I'd love to," Priya replied.

"I got the report you left in my office." There was a brief pause as her father cleared his throat. "Thank you."

Priya's heart lifted at his words. She knew Puppa wasn't only thanking her for the report. For the first time, he wasn't hustling just to get by. Business was booming, and it was because Priya had stepped into a space he wasn't equipped to navigate, taking Moksha into the digital world.

"I'm glad I can help," she said. "See you tonight, Puppa."

As she hung up, a strange but welcome sense of belonging settled over her. Moksha had never been a part of her plan, but as she sat there, she realized that maybe there was a way to continue her family's work *and* carve out her own path at the same time. But first, she had another problem to solve. The deadline for the app competition was closing in, and she was still searching for the perfect idea.

Then, like an echo from the past, she heard Ethan's voice. *You know what's the ultimate game changer? Death.*

Her breath hitched. *Of course.* It was so obvious, she couldn't believe she hadn't seen it before. Buzzing with excitement, she rushed back to the coach house, grabbed the nearest notepad, and began scribbling her thoughts down before they slipped away. The pieces that had once felt scattered fell into place. Magically. Almost effortlessly. She wouldn't just be building an app. She would be creating something bigger, something that tied together her family's legacy with her own passion.

Hours slipped away without her realizing. It wasn't until a notification reminded her about dinner that she finally surfaced from her work. Leaning back, she scanned the table. Papers everywhere, but in their chaos, she saw clarity. A road map of everything she had envisioned.

For the first time in a long while, Priya felt a rush of purpose and excitement. The work ahead was daunting, and she couldn't wait to see where it led. Grabbing her things, she hurried off to dinner, already itching to get back and pick up where she had left off.

✦

As the long summer days passed, Priya poured everything she had into building her app—testing, debugging, and refining every line of code. She put each feature through its paces, making sure it not only met the competition's standards but surpassed them. Every flaw was smoothed out, every feature polished until there was nothing left to fix.

In the hushed quiet of the coach house, her fingers hovered over the Submit button. When she finally clicked it, the sound echoed in the silence, sharper than expected. A slow breath escaped Priya as she leaned back in her chair, stretching out the stiffness in her neck. She had built something she was proud of, and she had made it happen just in time. Yet beneath the sense of accomplishment, another feeling lurked. A quiet, unsettling sense of emptiness.

In the three months since Ethan had left, the app had been more than a project to her. In a way, it had been her last real connection to Ethan. His words had sparked the idea, and through every late night and setback, he had been there in the background, challenging her to think bigger. And now that it was done, so was that connection.

Priya had avoided seeking out news about him, but in this moment she felt herself slipping, the pull of curiosity creeping back in. *Just a quick scroll, just a glimpse into his life without me . . .* She drew in a steadying breath to stop herself. She had fought too hard to get here, to build something for herself, to prove that her happiness didn't begin and end with Ethan Knight.

But god, she missed him. And not just in the quiet moments when she let her guard slip. She missed him at the most random times, like when she passed by a restaurant they had never even gone to but she knew he would love. When she heard a song and knew exactly what face he'd make. When she found herself in a room and it suddenly felt dull because he wasn't in it.

What haunted her the most was how things had ended between them. She had made that call, and she had to live with it. But he deserved more. He deserved *better*. Did he hate her for it?

Priya sucked in a breath and walked to the window, trying to shake off the thought. The scent of summer clung to the air, thick with freshly cut grass. Zinnias and sunflowers dotted the field. August was heavy and golden, and the light had begun to soften; already there was a crispness in the air. A change was coming, and though Priya didn't know what it would bring, she was ready to step into it.

She turned back to her desk, staring at the screen. The confirmation message still glowed, solid and undeniable. *Submission received.*

Somehow, she had pulled it off. She had crammed what should've taken far longer into a fraction of the time, pushing herself harder than she thought possible. There was nothing left to do but wait. In a few weeks, she'd have her answer. Whatever the outcome, she knew she had given it everything she had.

For the first time since moving back home, Priya realized she no longer felt trapped—waiting for life to change, waiting to feel like herself again, waiting for when she'd finally be ready. She wasn't fully healed or entirely at peace, and maybe she never would be. But she had taken control of her own life. Not perfectly. Not easily. And certainly not without missteps. But that, she decided, was enough.

Thirty-Three

THREE WEEKS LATER, Priya sat beside her parents in the auditorium, gripping the event program as she took in the scene around her. The energy in the room was electric—contestants shifting in their seats, judges reviewing their notes, industry insiders scanning the room for the next breakout talent. Large screens displayed the competing apps, rotating through their descriptions and logos. This was the kind of room where careers were made. Where people got noticed. Where everything Priya had been working toward finally had a chance to become real.

And then, from her left—

"Chai, beta?"

Priya turned just in time to see Mumma pulling a thermos and a steel glass out of her bottomless bag.

"Mumma!" Priya shot her a *you cannot be serious* look.

Puppa didn't even bother looking up. "Seema, this is not the time or place for tea."

"It's eleven o'clock," Mumma muttered, stowing the thermos back into her bag. A moment later, she retrieved a container and popped it open to reveal a stack of flatbreads.

"Thepla?" she asked.

"Seema!" Puppa hissed as the pungent smell of fenugreek and spices filled the air, heads turning in their direction. Priya sank into her seat, cringing.

Mumma sealed the container with a sharp click and crossed her arms. "So many people, and not *one* snack in sight! I know, I know." She waved Puppa off before he could respond. "It's not that kind of gathering, but still. Would a few pastries kill them? Instead, we have all these screens. Tech zone, schmeck zone. *Ato* total no-snack zone."

"Shh," Puppa silenced, as the lights dimmed and the event began.

The host stepped up to the podium and introduced the judges, highlighting their contributions to the tech industry. He described the success stories of past winners. Some had turned their prize money into full-fledged businesses, some had secured major funding, and others had partnered with top companies to leave their mark on the virtual world. As the speech wrapped up, a tide of anticipation swept through the crowd. It was time to reveal the winners. All eyes turned to the giant screen onstage to see which app would take the top spot.

Priya held her breath. This was it. The moment she had been working toward.

And then, loud enough to be heard over the stillness, Mumma's stomach let out an unholy growl. She coughed and reached for a water bottle, feigning a dry throat.

A few chuckles rippled through the audience. Priya pressed her lips together, willing herself not to react.

The screen in front of her flickered, names shifting, rankings updating. And then . . . Priya's heart slammed into her ribs. There it was. *Her app.* Lit up among the top three.

Beside her, Puppa's eyes flared with pride, though he quickly smoothed it over with a measured smile. Mumma, on the other hand, gave nothing away. Drawing attention wasn't the Solanki way—and years of running a funeral home had trained them to keep their reactions contained.

The speaker leaned into the mic, his smile wide as the murmurs died down. "Every year, we see brilliant minds walk through these doors, but only one entry can take the top spot. As always, it was a tough decision. I'm thrilled to announce that this year's winner is . . ." He let the silence stretch for just a beat as the screen refreshed.

Her name popped up the exact moment he said it aloud.

Priya's stomach flipped. *Oh my god. He actually said my name!* She blinked at the screen again, almost needing confirmation. *That's me.*

Puppa nearly jumped from his seat, looking like he might actually cheer. Mumma's hand flew to her mouth, her eyes growing wide.

"*Ketla mayla?* How much?" she asked, leaning over Puppa to squeeze Priya's hand. Because for Mumma, the payout was the real headline.

Priya let out a shaky breath, half laughing, half in shock.

"Seema." Puppa pried Mumma's hands from Priya's lap, his eyes twinkling. "The man is still talking." He gestured toward the podium, where the speaker was detailing why Priya's app had caught the judges' attention.

"This app transforms the funeral planning experience," the man said. "It centralizes everything a family needs into one easy-to-navigate platform, eliminating the stress of researching dozens of sites separately."

He clicked the remote, and the app's interface appeared on the screen. "Imagine being able to find exactly what you need based on your location, cultural background, religious beliefs, and personal wishes—from traditional burials and cremations to aquamations and eco-friendly choices. Need live streaming? Multilanguage support? A florist? A grief counselor? Just set your preferences and browse through profiles that include photos and reviews."

The slides kept shifting, each one showcasing another feature. The speaker walked the audience through the customization options, virtual memorial spaces, the calendar tool, and private chat rooms.

Priya heard the words, but they drifted past her, distant and blurred. Suddenly, she was eight years old again, standing under the glare of the school auditorium lights. She hopped off the stage, excitement buzzing through her—eager to show Mumma and Puppa her gold medal. But they gravitated toward Ravi, hands folded, voices full of praise. Priya's steps faltered, confusion twisting inside her.

Afterward, Puppa had explained caste to her. Congratulating Ravi wasn't about ignoring her. It was about acknowledging the place Ravi's family held in the community. Priya had nodded like a good daughter, but something had shifted inside her. There were lines in the world she hadn't seen before that day.

She told herself it didn't matter. That she would work harder, climb higher, push further, until she was no longer standing in anyone's shadow, waiting to be seen. And now here she was, in an auditorium filled with the sharpest minds in the industry, her name glowing on a screen for the world to see.

She had done it. She had arrived.

A lump formed in her throat as she listened to the final words of the presentation: ". . . a solid revenue model . . . strategic advertising . . . scalable for international expansion."

The speaker paused, scanning the audience before continuing. "And now, I would like to invite one of our judges to present the award to this year's winner, Priya Solanki. Priya, please join us onstage."

The room erupted, but Priya could barely move. *Get up. Get up. This is your moment.*

"Priya," her father nudged.

From the corner of her eye, Priya caught her mother's animated gesture, encouraging her to rise.

As Priya stood, the applause grew, rolling through the room like thunder. It sounded like it belonged to someone bigger, someone greater—but it was for her. Each step toward the podium felt surreal, like she was moving through a dream. But the weight in her hands was real when she accepted the award—solid and heavy with meaning. In that moment, Priya felt like she was standing up there not only for herself but for every person who had ever reached for more and refused to let go.

She turned toward the audience, lifting her trophy high. Mumma and Puppa shot to their feet, their cheers cutting through the noise. There were no reserved claps, no subtle nods. They were *beaming*, their excitement spilling out, raw and unfiltered.

As Priya's eyes swept over the crowd, an ache tightened in her chest.

Ethan.

Without him by her side, she felt like a galaxy missing its brightest star. She instinctively reached for the pendant he had given her, and felt a quiet glow burn within her, as if she had a star of her own, shining steadily—hidden yet enduring. It had carried her through the moments when no one was watching, because real growth happened away from the spotlight. In its own time, in its own space.

"Congratulations, Priya," the judge said. "Please tell us about your app in your own words."

Priya's heartbeat was calm now. No hesitation, no second-guessing. She set the trophy down, her fingers lingering over the cool metal for just a second before turning to the audience.

"Thank you," she said. "While it may seem like I created Moksha, the truth is that, in many ways Moksha created me. Moksha isn't just the name of this app. It's also the name of the funeral home that my parents run, the place that shaped my childhood. The word itself comes from the Sanskrit term for liberation or freedom."

Her voice softened as she continued. "My app is a tribute to the work my parents have done every single day, treating every family, every loss, with the same level of dignity, regardless of wealth, background or . . . as of late, species."

Priya waited for the laughter to settle. "Moksha is my way of carrying that legacy forward. It's about making space for every person's story, ensuring they get a farewell that truly reflects them. Because no matter how different our lives are, in the end, we all walk through the same door. Death treats us with the same profound equality. When we cross that threshold, we leave all the labels, all the division behind."

She took a slow breath. "For me, Moksha is more than an app. It's a promise to help people navigate something inevitable with dignity, peace, and choice, all from the privacy of their own homes."

Looking around the auditorium, Priya let herself absorb the moment—the eyes watching her, the energy buzzing around her. "Thank you all for believing in me and making this vision a reality." Lifting her trophy again, she locked eyes with her parents and smiled. "To Moksha!"

"There she is!" Puppa exclaimed when Priya emerged from a whirlwind of cameras and handshakes.

"Our Priya." Mumma took Priya's hands in hers. "A shining bacon."

"Beacon," Puppa corrected.

Mumma only squeezed Priya's hands tighter. "You've filled our hearts today, beta," she said, her voice quavering with pride. "Here, feel." She placed Priya's hand on her chest. "See how round and puffed up it is—like the perfect rotli."

Priya chuckled. Mumma's gesture was more than a moment of pride. It was her way of inviting Priya back into her heart. There was an unspoken rule in the Solanki family. Parents didn't apologize to kids. They simply pulled the threads tighter after every fray—an extra piece of dessert, a softened tone, a hand pressed over the heart.

Priya wrapped her arms around Mumma and gave her a hug.

"Hello?" Puppa piped up, his voice expectant.

Smiling, Priya pulled him in, too, the hug growing into a tangle of arms and hearts.

"All this . . . it's beyond anything we imagined," he said. "Companies offering you jobs, partnerships, opportunities . . ."

He stepped back, his hands resting on her shoulders. "I get it now, Priya. All this time, we couldn't figure out why you kept fighting, why you wouldn't just do as you were told. But you weren't meant for the life we imagined. You were meant for something we never dared to reach for ourselves."

Priya blinked back her tears, the pressure to justify her choices lifting.

Mumma reached for her, squeezing her arm. "We thought we were guiding you, keeping you safe. Even after the divorce, we wanted you to be with someone, so you'd never have to face life alone. But you are strong, Priya. Strong enough to stand on your own."

"Oh, Mumma . . ." A soft sob escaped Priya. "You know what would make this moment absolutely perfect?"

"What, beta?"

"Chai and thepla." Priya tilted her head toward Mumma's tote.

Mumma's eyes lit up. "Really? You think it's okay now?" She glanced around as if they were sneaking food into a theater. The event had nearly wrapped up—booths coming down, banners rolled up, people heading out.

"Come." Priya reached for her mother's hand.

They found a quiet bench nestled behind tall plants, away from the fading chatter of the day. Mumma pulled out the thermos and poured the chai into steel glasses. Priya held it by the rim and breathed in the rich swirl of ginger, cardamom, cinnamon, and cloves. Passing the container of theplas between them, they tore off pieces with their fingers. The combination of spiced tea and soft theplas felt like a quiet kind of healing.

Mumma wiped her hands and turned to Priya. "Give me the key."

"What key?" Priya asked.

"The coach house key," Mumma said, holding out her hand.

Priya's heart sank. Asking for the keys back could only mean one thing. Mumma expected her to move back into the apartment. Had all of this—her independence, her space—been temporary?

She placed the key in Mumma's hand, swallowing back the knot of disappointment. All of her progress had just been dialed back.

Mumma took the key, but instead of putting it away, she dug into her purse. A second later, she pulled out a charm, attached it to the key, and placed it back in Priya's palm.

"Today is a new beginning," she said. "May it be free of obstacles ahead."

Priya's breath caught as she looked at her palm. A tiny Lord Ganesh key chain dangled from the key, just like the one Mumma had given Ethan. It wasn't just a charm. It was a blessing, a silent acknowledgment that Mumma had finally accepted her choice to live in the coach house. Priya had won something greater than her parents' permission. She had earned their trust.

As her thumb glided over the charm, it felt like a thread tying her to Ethan. She wondered if he ever thought about her. Did her name ever drift through his mind in the quiet moments before sleep? Or had he banished her to the corners of his mind, still refusing to look at her? Was she now an untouchable relic, distanced and set apart from the rest of his memories?

Thirty-Four

SEPTEMBER ARRIVED WITH cooler mornings, shorter days, and the first signs of fall. Even though the awards ceremony was just a few days behind her, life started to shift in small, noticeable ways for Priya. She steered her new car into Moksha's driveway and eased into the parking lot. As the engine hushed to a whisper, even Puppa, the Chancellor of Cheapskates, couldn't suppress an appreciative nod.

"This car . . . it glides more than it drives," he said, stroking the dashboard with a touch of awe.

"It's beautiful. Like a wow." Mumma inhaled the rich, heady new-car fragrance before climbing out.

Puppa circled the car, oohing and aahing over its contours. Chrome accents sparkled in the sunlight, and softly tinted windows added just the right touch of mystery.

"We must perform a blessing ceremony," Mumma declared.

"Not right now," Puppa said. "It's time for . . ." His words trailed off as Mumma shot him a warning look.

Pretending not to notice, Priya brushed off an invisible speck from the car. In just a few hours, Ethan's new movie was premiering at TIFF, the Toronto International Film Festival. Puppa remained a die-hard fan of Ethan, even more so now that he knew Ethan had protected his family from a scandal. Her parents were itching to watch the red-carpet moments, but they were playing it cool for Priya's sake.

"I think I'll pass on dinner tonight," Priya said. "I have a ton of work to catch up on."

"*Su?*" Mumma's hands landed on her hips. "Working, working. Always working. You will eat first, then go." Hooking her arm through Priya's, she pulled her back toward the apartment.

As soon as they got upstairs, Puppa sprang into action, reaching for the remote. Caught up in the excitement of the day, he had left the TV running—a rare lapse of his frugal ways. But before he could press the button, the room filled with TIFF footage.

"It's okay, Puppa," Priya said. "You and Mumma watch. I'll set the table."

"Please." Mumma scoffed. "It's the same every year."

"Waste of time." Puppa turned off the TV.

They were pretending not to care, but Priya knew that the second she was gone, they'd be parked in front of the screen, volume up, waiting for a glimpse of Ethan.

As they ate around the table, Mumma and Puppa kept things casual, smiling and chatting about everything except the one thing on their minds. Priya wasn't fooled. Her parents were tiptoeing around the fact that Ethan was in town, and that they were dying to watch his new movie.

"I'll clean up," Priya said, standing and stacking the plates.

"No, no," Mumma said, shooing her away. "We'll handle it. You go, beta. *Ja*, go do your work."

Priya suppressed a knowing smile. It was clear her parents were trying to get rid of her. "I was thinking I could show you how to access Moksha's website in case you ever want to make changes," she said to Puppa.

"It can wait, beta," he replied, herding her toward the door. "I know I keep saying I want to learn, but the truth is I'm too old for all this tech. Your work is more important. Go, beta." With a firm push, he nudged her out of the apartment.

"See you tomorrow!" Mumma waved as the door clicked shut.

Priya stared at it for a second, then let out a chuckle. *This has to be the fastest, most well-coordinated goodbye in Solanki history. No lingering at the door, no warning to mind the stairs, not even an offer to send me off with leftovers.*

Before she even made it down the first step, the TV hummed back to life behind her. Priya smiled and started making her way back to the coach house. No matter how much she tried to avoid it, Ethan's shadow would always stretch over her.

She lay flat on her back, staring at the ceiling for what felt like hours. Sleep was not happening. Not with him so close. Priya's entire body was buzzing, every nerve, every fiber on high alert. She curled onto her side, squeezing her eyes shut, but it didn't stop the ache. She could have been by his side tonight, her fingers tangled in his, their hands locked like they had been made to fit together. Instead, she lay in bed, in an old T-shirt and pajama bottoms, fighting the urge to check her phone. It would be so easy. Just a quick scroll through, a glance at the live stream.

But she wasn't going to give in.

She couldn't.

Priya reached for her phone. Just as she was about to unlock it, it buzzed in her hands. She sat up so fast she nearly dropped it. Could it be Ethan? Had he somehow felt the silent pull of her thoughts? She fumbled for her glasses, a foolish hope rising her chest. Until she saw the name on the screen.

"Brooke?" She glanced at the time. "Everything okay?"

"Oh, Pri," Brooke moaned. "It's a disaster."

Priya's heart dropped. Brooke was supposed to be at TIFF with her father. She had hoped this call meant good news about Harry and Ethan making amends. Instead, the edge in Brooke's voice set off warning bells. "What happened?"

"He's being an absolute nightmare, Pri! I've never seen him like this."

"Oh no." A wave of guilt crashed over Priya. It sounded like Harry had tried to mend things with Ethan, and it had backfired. Had she meddled too much? The thought of their confrontation made her insides clench.

"Can you come get him?" Brooke rushed on. "We booked a car for the night, but I need it to head to the after-party."

"Drive downtown? Right now? Are you serious?" Priya groaned. "TIFF traffic is a nightmare. Just put him in a cab."

"Priya, please. He's traumatized. And I'm trying to avoid a scene." Brooke's exasperation crackled through the phone. "I know you hate driving downtown, but I swear this'll be easy. Just pull up to the side entrance, and we'll pop right out."

"But—"

"Texting you the address now."

"But—"

"You're the best, babe!"

"Damn it, Brooke." Priya exhaled. "What exactly happened?"

"What?" Brooke's voice was muffled under the noise. "Pri, I can't hear a thing! It's insane in here. The screening just wrapped, and everyone's talking at once. Just get here fast, okay? See you soon!"

Pulling a sweatshirt over her head, Priya grabbed her keys and dashed out. The thought of the press getting wind of Harry and Ethan's fallout at a high-profile event made her stomach churn. But as she sped down the highway, another thought crept in. Was Brooke orchestrating a run-in between her and Ethan?

She glanced at herself in the rearview mirror. *Damn it.* Brooke could have at least warned her to swipe on some lipstick. She was totally unprepared to see Ethan. Her hair was a disaster, her glasses smudged, and her eyebrows were in dire need of plucking.

Navigating downtown was worse than she had imagined. What should've taken just under an hour stretched into nearly two. TIFF had turned the streets into a maze of roadblocks, festival-goers, and flashing cameras. Thankfully, Brooke had picked a secluded pickup spot. Priya finally pulled up to the curb, scanning her surroundings.

A figure emerged from the building, stepping into the dim glow of the streetlamp.

Priya's heart jumped—then dropped.

It wasn't Ethan.

It was Harry Knight.

There was no setup after all. Disappointment struck Priya deeper than she'd expected.

Rolling down the window, she forced a polite smile. "Hello, Mr. Knight."

"Hello, Priya," Harry replied. "Thank you for coming on such short notice."

"Of course," Priya said, unsure of what exactly had happened. "I'm sorry it didn't go as expected." She unlocked the door, expecting him to get in, but he spun around and headed back into the building.

"Mr. Knight?" Priya cut the engine, flipped on the hazards, and scrambled out after him.

"I'll just be a minute," he said. "Brooke asked me to give her a heads-up when you got here."

"Of course." Priya's heart kicked up once again. A rendezvous with Ethan was still possible!

But when Brooke emerged, it was only with her father in tow.

"I'm so sorry to drag you out, but he's been driving me up the wall all night," she said.

"Brooke," Priya muttered, her eyes darting to Harry, who stood listening to her every word.

"He's good to go." Brooke handed Priya a tote. "All his stuff is in here, but he's so worked up, he'll probably crash as soon as you get home. I'll swing by to pick him up in the morning."

"You want me . . . to take him to my place?" Priya's voice faltered as she mechanically slung Brooke's bag over her shoulder.

"Of course! He's too tiny to be left alone, right, my little angel?" Brooke cooed, reaching inside to pull out Sir Puffington.

Priya blinked. All this time, she'd thought Brooke had been talking to her father, but she actually meant her kitten. A flush crept up her neck as she sneaked an apologetic glance at Harry Knight, inwardly cringing at her own assumption.

"I'm . . . uh . . ." Priya fumbled over her words. "I didn't know you were bringing Sir Puffington."

"Technically, he's not supposed to be here," Brooke confessed, as she placed the kitten back inside the tote. "I just didn't have the heart to leave him with a sitter." She kissed the top of his fluffy head. "But he's been a menace all evening. You're a lifesaver." Handing over her precious bundle, she gave Priya a quick peck on the cheek.

"Let's go, Dad." She turned to him, ready to head indoors.

"I'll be there in a moment," Harry replied, lingering as Brooke vanished from view. "Thank you for what you said the last time we spoke," he told Priya. "I managed to have a word with Ethan today. We have a long way to go, but it's a step in the right direction."

Priya breathed a sigh of relief, struggling to keep Sir Puffington from jumping out of the tote. "I'm so happy to hear that. I hope you're able to patch things up."

"Me too," Harry replied, eyeing the wriggling kitten. "All the best with that tiny terror." With a final nod, he made his way back inside.

Priya scooped Sir Puffington out of the tote and placed him against her shoulder, using one hand to hold him in place. He settled comfortably into the crook of her neck.

"Okay, fluffball," she murmured, rubbing his back. "Let's get you home before you cause more trouble."

As Priya reached for the car door, the Ganesh key chain slipped from her hand, her keys falling into the narrow gap between the tire and the curb. She knelt, stretching to grab it, and suddenly Sir Puffington leaped from her shoulder and darted away.

"Oh, come on!" Priya groaned, snatching her keys and bolting after him.

The kitten disappeared around the corner, zigzagging through the crowd, slipping between feet, and barely avoiding getting stepped on. Priya chased after him, her heart pounding. The last thing she needed was to explain to Brooke that her prized kitten had disappeared into the chaos of TIFF. She veered into the bicycle lane, crouching to keep track of him through the gaps between people's legs.

"Sir Puffington!" she called, her voice rising, but the kitten didn't even glance her way.

She crashed into a signpost, her foot catching on its base, and nearly nose-dived into the pavement.

"Miss! Excuse me, miss!" a voice rang out.

But Priya had no time to stop. The crowd ahead parted, revealing a path straight to the kitten, who stood momentarily frozen in place.

"Hey," she called, rushing forward. "Over here, little guy."

Spotting her, Sir Puffington bolted in the opposite direction.

It was at that moment that Priya realized he was sprinting down a red carpet toward a set of lofty stairs: The grand entrance to tonight's film festival screenings. Around her, throngs of festival-goers and photographers stood behind the ropes. Priya had unwittingly raced past the barrier and was now standing on the red carpet with her greasy hair and saggy pajama bottoms.

Everything slowed to an unbearable crawl. Priya could hear her heart beating in her ears. *Ba-boom. Ba-boom.* Out of the corner of her eye, she spotted two security guards charging toward her. A few feet away, Sir Puffington was about to hop up the stairs and slip from her grasp.

In a split-second decision, Priya lunged forward, reaching for him, only to be yanked back by the guards.

"Sir Puffington!" she called over her shoulder as they escorted her away. "No, wait! I'm not leaving without that kitten!"

With a bold jerk, Priya tried to free herself. The crowd broke into cheers. Priya's heart leaped. *They're on my side!* She could feel the energy shift, the murmurs rising in her favor. Even the guards stilled.

But then she realized the commotion had nothing to do with her. The real spectacle was unfolding behind her. As she turned, her breath caught.

Ethan stood at the foot of the stairs, bending over Sir Puffington, his hand extended toward him. Sir Puffington hesitated, then melted under Ethan's touch, purring as Ethan scratched behind his ears. In one smooth move, Ethan scooped up the kitten and stood, cradling him in his arms.

The crowd went wild. Toronto's homegrown movie star had just saved a helpless kitten on the red carpet. Cameras flashed. The press clamored for Ethan's attention, yelling his name.

Ethan looked up. His gaze cut through the sea of bodies and locked onto Priya.

Priya's world stopped. Her heart came to a jarring halt. She forgot about the noise, the cameras, and all the people around them. The world shrank to just the two of them. And damn, the man took her breath away. Lit by the glow of the festival, his tux crisp and perfectly tailored, he looked every bit the Hollywood heartthrob the world worshipped.

But to Priya, he was so much more. He was lazy mornings and whispered jokes. He was the warmth of fingertips and the heartbeat beneath her cheek at night. She had seen the version of him no one else had, broken and breathtakingly human. And now, standing at the other end of the red carpet, Priya felt the pull between them tugging at the core of her being.

Then reality came crashing down. Priya's eyes shifted to the top of the stairs as Sienna Deville descended like a queen in a gold-and-nude gown that clung to her like second skin. Reaching Ethan's side, she slipped her arm through his and waved, her smile practiced to perfection. The crowd roared its approval. Together, they were cinematic royalty, his dark intensity complementing her sultry allure.

"Over here!" the photographers shouted. "Over here!"

Sienna obliged with a graceful turn, showcasing her best angles, her gown shimmering under the lights. Her eyes skimmed over Sir Puffington before returning to the real moment, the one where she and Ethan owned the night.

Ethan, however, was a beat behind. Sensing her costar's distraction, Sienna leaned in and whispered something in his ear. Ethan seemed to refocus, as if suddenly remembering his surroundings. He said something, then pulled away and started walking. Straight toward Priya.

Thirty-Five

AS ETHAN CLOSED the space between them, the security guards retreated as if his presence rendered them irrelevant. The noise, the flashes, the electric hum of the crowd became nothing more than a blur at the edges of Priya's awareness. Because, for the first time since he had ridden away that night, Ethan's eyes were on her.

She stood immobilized, her heart pounding as Ethan stopped before her. Priya had feared a million different possibilities for this moment. That he'd be cold. Angry. Hurt. Resentful.

But there was nothing there. Not even a flicker of the Ethan she knew.

And that neutrality? That nothingness? It wrecked her.

She had turned him away when he was willing to fight for her, convinced she was doing the right thing. And now he was showing her what it meant to be on the other side of that choice.

"I'm guessing you're on kitten duty for Brooke?" Ethan said, nodding toward the tote slung over Priya's shoulder, his sister's initials stitched neatly on the side.

It took Priya a second to process his words. She had been so lost in the moment that she had forgotten about Sir Puffington.

"Oh . . . yeah," she managed, clearing her throat. "He got away from me."

Ethan lifted Sir Puffington from the crook of his arm and held him out toward her. As Priya took the kitten from him, their fingers brushed for a second. The contact was featherlight, but it stole the air from her lungs.

"Thanks," she said, her voice tight as she tucked Sir Puffington back inside the tote. She wanted to say more, but the words just wouldn't come, so she adjusted the strap over her shoulder, holding it like it might hold her together.

Ethan gave a small nod and started to walk away, then hesitated and turned back. "I hear you really went to bat for me with my father," he said. "He said you're the reason he showed up today."

"I just wanted the two of you to make things right," Priya said, her throat thick with emotion.

Ethan studied her for a moment, his expression unreadable. "Thank you," he said, his eyes dropping to the pendant around her neck. For a fraction of a second, his expression softened. Just long enough for her to see the man she loved, to see that maybe this wasn't easy for him either.

"Goodbye, Priya Solanki," he said.

Priya's chest tightened. This was where she was supposed to meet his goodbye with her own, to say the words that would bring them closure. But her voice failed her. So, she stood silently, her heart hammering in protest.

As Ethan turned to leave, something snapped inside Priya. This wasn't how their story ended. Not with a hollow goodbye that felt like hammering the last nail in a coffin.

She reached for him without thinking, her fingers curling around his wrist. Ethan looked down at their hands, then back up to her face.

For a moment, neither of them moved.

Then Priya pulled him toward her, heart pounding wildly, not giving herself the chance to hesitate. She saw the flicker of surprise in his eyes, and before he could react, she rose onto her toes, fingers sliding into the collar of his jacket, and kissed him.

The world exploded in a burst of flashing lights.

Ethan went completely still, his hands hovering at her sides. Priya knew that he didn't owe her anything. Not forgiveness. Not love. Not even a reaction.

But that wasn't why she kissed him. She kissed him because she wanted him to know that she was done hiding. Because, for the first time in her life, she was brave enough to love out loud, in vivid, breathtaking Technicolor.

Even if he rejected her. Even if he walked away.

Because loving Ethan Knight had been the truest thing she had ever done. And if she was going to lose him forever, she wanted him to feel it, to know that he had been loved. Recklessly. Entirely. Unconditionally.

She pulled away, breathless. But Ethan still didn't react. Didn't blink. Didn't swallow.

The moment stretched impossibly long.

Priya took a step back. *Now* she could say goodbye.

But then Ethan moved. His hand curled around her waist, the other tilting her chin for a kiss that stole the air from her lungs. It was hungry and desperate and punishing, like he had been waiting for this moment all along. His mouth moved against hers with a heat that chased every rational thought from her mind. It was fire and longing, frustration and surrender all at once.

Priya clung to his jacket, feeling the thud of his heartbeat. He kissed her like he had something to prove, like he needed her to understand just how much she had wrecked him. And god, she did. Because she felt the same.

Around them, shutters clicked in rapid succession, voices murmuring in shock, excitement, disbelief. Someone let out a loud whistle, setting off a ripple of whoops and catcalls. It all blurred into the background. Priya didn't care. Kissing Ethan in front of the whole world felt like a beautiful surrender, like leaping off a cliff and finally remembering how to fly. She was breathless, buzzing, invincible.

Until a sharp sting shot through her.

Startled, she broke away from Ethan, and spotted Sir Puffington halfway out of the tote hanging from her shoulder—tiny teeth clamped onto her sweatshirt as he nipped on her arm.

"Shoot, I forgot all about him!" Priya exclaimed.

Ethan reached over and pried him loose. "Alright, tiny terror," he scolded, lifting the kitten into his arms. "That's my girl you're chomping on."

Priya laughed, rubbing her arm. "At least he's sticking close to me. Brooke would have my head if I lost him again."

"She'd have to go through me first," Ethan said, adjusting his hold on Sir Puffington.

Priya's heart skipped. There it was—that feeling again—that electric, terrifying, thrilling feeling, as if their lives had snapped back into place. She wasn't sure whether to laugh or cry. What mattered was that she'd taken a leap, and instead of walking away, Ethan had caught her. And now, all she wanted was to hold on to this beautiful, unexpected moment.

But the world had other plans. The press clamored for attention, each reporter shouting over the other.

"Ethan, Priya! Just one shot!"

"To your right. Over here!"

The flashes were relentless and blinding.

As the questions flew, Ethan shifted instinctively to shield Priya. For a split second, she felt it all. The scrutiny, the speculation, the razor-sharp assessment.

What the hell is she wearing?

What is she even doing here?

What does he see in her?

She knew what *they* saw. Frizzy hair. No makeup. A sweatshirt two sizes too big. Pajama pants. She looked like she had just rolled out of bed. Which, in fact, was true.

And yet, somehow, she felt like she was exactly where she belonged. Standing beside Ethan. On the red carpet. Just like they had planned. It was as if this moment had been cast in the stars. She was meant to be here. Maybe not in the way the world expected. Maybe not in the way she expected either. But she wasn't about to let anyone—reporters, critics, internet trolls—diminish her. Let them talk. About her clothes, her failures, her background. Let them post photos of her mismatched pajamas. Let them call her undeserving.

Priya nudged her glasses up the bridge of her nose, squared her shoulders, and sent Ethan a sideways glance. *I've got this.*

Ethan's eyes lingered on her, his lips curving into a smile. He gave a small nod, a silent acknowledgment. Then, as if coming to a decision, he tucked Sir Puffington back inside the tote and reached for her hand, their fingers lacing together like they had never forgotten the way.

"Want to get out of here?" he asked.

"Can we?" Priya asked back, blinking in surprise. "I thought you had an after-party."

"Forget the after-party. I'm more interested in an exclusive event starring you and me." Ethan turned toward Sienna and lifted two fingers in a quick, almost lazy salute. Sienna's lips pressed together in the briefest flicker of irritation before she caught herself. Tossing her hair over her shoulder, she turned back to the cameras with a megawatt smile. She wasn't about to let anyone steal her moment.

Priya glanced between them, a pang of doubt hitting her. "I hope I didn't—"

"You didn't." Ethan laughed under his breath. "Sienna's not my date. We were never a thing." He led them off the carpet and then pulled out his phone to send a message. Within seconds, a luxury sedan rolled to the curb.

Priya raised an eyebrow, a smile tugging at her lips. "I'm impressed."

"What can I say? I like to make quick exits." Ethan grinned. "Coming?"

Priya slipped her hand through the crook of his elbow. This was her moment, and more importantly, this was her man. And she was claiming him before the world.

As the driver held the door open, the press surged forward, a whirlwind of questions, cameras, and eager eyes pressing in from all sides.

"Can we get a statement about your relationship?"

"Are we going to see you later tonight?"

"Was there any truth to the two of you being just friends?"

Security closed in, forming a barrier as Ethan helped Priya into the car, setting Sir Puffington's tote beside her. Before slipping in after her, he turned and gave the crowd a final wave, only adding fuel to the frenzy.

The moment the doors shut, muting the deafening noise outside, Priya let out a long breath. Sir Puffington curled into a ball and let out a tiny purr. Ethan turned to Priya, his eyes narrowing. Then, without warning, he swept her hair to one side and looked behind her ear.

"What are you doing?" Priya asked.

"Checking to see if your beauty mark is still there," he said, his thumb brushing over the familiar spot. "Because the Priya I knew couldn't even tell her own parents about us. She would've been halfway across the city before letting herself be caught in a media storm like that." His lips quirked in a teasing smile. "Priya 2.0 seems to have had a major upgrade."

Priya shrugged playfully. "It took a while to rewrite the code, but all the bugs are fixed. Stronger firewall. New security patches. No more crash reports."

"And what about compatibility?" Ethan grinned. "Still runs with Knight OS?"

"Exclusively with Knight OS."

"Good to know," Ethan murmured, leaning in. Before he could kiss her, the driver's voice cut in over the partition.

"Where to, Mr. Knight?"

Ethan's gaze flicked to Priya. "I can only think of one place to keep this party going."

She nodded, her lips curving as he gave the driver the address to the coach house. But just as the words left his mouth, Priya's entire expression changed.

"What is it?" Ethan asked, concern creeping into his tone.

"That's my car!" Priya gestured frantically toward the window behind him.

Ethan turned in his seat, just in time to see a tow truck hauling away a brand-new car down the road, its hazard lights blinking.

"I left it at the curb," Priya groaned. "I was only going to be a minute."

"Change of plans." Ethan knocked on the partition. "Follow that tow truck."

"Understood." The driver pulled out, steering the car seamlessly onto the road.

"Here we go again," Ethan said to Priya, glancing over his shoulder.

Behind them, a convoy of vehicles merged into the traffic, the paparazzi pursuing them as they pursued the tow truck.

Priya let out an exasperated sigh before nestling into the curve of Ethan's arms. "Guess I better get used to it."

"Look at you, rolling with the punches like a pro."

"No matter what happens, there's one thing I know for sure."

"What's that?"

Priya smiled and laced her fingers through his. "Life is never going to be boring with you."

As their lips met, the driver shifted lanes, weaving through traffic to shake off the press. The city blurred in a kaleidoscope of colors. The chase was on, but Ethan and Priya were too wrapped up in each other to care.

Thirty-Six

ETHAN TRACED A featherlight path along Priya's neck, his fingers warm against her skin. "Time to wake up, sleepyhead."

Priya stretched with a contented sigh before rolling over, a grin spreading across her face. This wasn't a dream. Last night had really happened. The red carpet, the kiss, the chaos. The hours they'd spent tangled up in each other afterward. And now, Ethan was sitting beside her, fresh from the shower, a towel wrapped low around his waist, his hair damp and tousled.

"What time is it?" she murmured.

"Three." His lips grazed hers in a light, teasing kiss. "P.M."

Priya's eyes flew open. "Oh shit!"

"I know, I know. I really wore you out."

Priya let out a strangled chuckle. "I forgot to feed Sir Puffington."

"Already handled. Brooke picked him up hours ago." He lounged back against the headboard. "For the record, she's revoked our godparent privileges. Something about us being a little too preoccupied with each other last night to be responsible pet guardians."

"Well . . . she's not *wrong*." Priya grinned and flopped back onto the pillows. But then everything from last night came rushing back, and she slapped a hand over her face.

"How bad is it?" She peeked out from between her fingers. "Am I getting roasted? Are you getting hated on for skipping the after-party?"

"See for yourself." Ethan handed her his phone.

Priya took a deep breath and scrolled through the posts. She paused, glanced at him, then continued in disbelief.

"Movie debut turns into a kitten rescue! Ethan Knight proves he's a hero on- and off-screen. #RealLifeHero"
"Move over, action heroes. Priya Solanki just took on security for a cat. *Absolute legend."*

In the post was a cinematic slow-motion clip of Priya resisting the guards as they tried to contain her. Right before they hauled her away, she turned and delivered a perfectly executed battle cry over her shoulder: "Sir Puffington!"

"The moment Ethan glared at security and they backed off?"
"Sienna missed the memo last night. Ignoring a kitten? I mean, who doesn't melt at the sight of a fluffball?"
"Forget the movie. The real action was on the red carpet."
"Ethan Knight really out there living the dream—first a surprise TV kiss from Sienna, and now a red carpet rendezvous with a kitten crusader."
"Watching Ethan and Priya kiss, suddenly Sienna doesn't seem like the one."
"Ethan Knight: 'We're just friends.' Also Ethan Knight: 'Screw the biggest night of my career. I'm outta here!' when she kisses him. #FriendzoneToFairyTale"

A rough, uneven laugh slipped from Priya. "Wait . . . they're actually rooting for us? I thought I'd face a huge backlash for stealing you away last night."

"That's social media for you," Ethan replied. "You never know which way the tide will turn."

As Priya continued to scroll, she stumbled upon a completely unexpected trend.

"This Halloween, I'm going as Priya Solanki at TIFF. Why?
✔ *Comfy as hell*
✔ *Instantly iconic*
✔ *Comes with a fake kitten and a security escort."*

Her eyes widened when she saw the photo. Someone was wearing the exact same outfit, recreated down to the last detail. The replies were rolling in fast.

"Where do I buy the 'I Accidentally Stole the Spotlight' Pajamas™?"
"Only doing this if my man abandons an A-list party for me too."
"Does it come with the celebrity boyfriend?"
"Can we talk about the fact that she REALLY OWNED IT?"
"Amazon better have this in stock. I need it pronto."

Priya buried her face in her hands. "Oh my god."

"What?" Ethan leaned over to look at the screen. He let out a deep chuckle as he scrolled through the posts. "Priya Solanki, you're a cultural phenomenon. People are dressing up as you for Halloween."

"I looked like a total disaster," she muttered, shaking her head. "But you know what's crazy? My biggest regret from last night isn't the outfit. Or the press. Or any of this."

Ethan gave her a curious look. "Tell me."

She swallowed, feeling a little ridiculous for admitting it out loud. "I regret not sitting beside you last night. Not being at the screening, the way we planned. I was right here on this bed, pretending I didn't care that other people were watching your new movie. It was like desperately wanting to go to the ball but having no way of making it happen."

"Until Sir Puffington turned into your fairy godmother," Ethan said with a grin, his voice dipping as he leaned in and kissed her.

Priya had exactly half a second to enjoy it before her phone rang.

"Oh no, my parents!" She bolted upright.

"Are they going to be a problem?" Ethan's tone shifted.

"I don't know," Priya admitted. "I think they must have already seen the news." She groaned, pressing her palms to her face. "And if the press is lurking outside Moksha again, then they definitely know you're here. Worse, they know exactly what we've been up to all night."

"Well then, you better pick up and reassure them there's absolutely nothing scandalous happening here." Lifting the covers, he began to wiggle his way between her legs.

"Ethan!" Priya smacked his arm, trying to hold back a laugh.

He popped his head back up, his grin downright sinful. "Pick up, Pri. Before your mother bursts in here with a rolling pin."

Priya shot him a warning look, pressing a finger to her lips as she swiped to accept the call. "It's my sisters," she said, feeling only slightly relieved. "A coordinated ambush."

Tucking her hair behind her ear, she tried to sound casual as Deepa and Meghna popped up on-screen. "Hey, guys."

From beneath the covers, Ethan's tongue skimmed her stomach. Before she could stop him, he crawled up beside her, shirtless and disheveled.

"Hello." He grinned into the camera, pulling Priya closer so they were both in the frame.

Deepa made a strangled sound as if she'd just swallowed her gum, while Meghna leaned so far back in her chair she nearly disappeared from frame.

Priya *should* have been embarrassed that her sisters were getting an unfiltered peek into her personal life, but she wasn't. Not after kissing him in front of the whole world. So what if Deepa and Meghna saw them tangled up in bed now?

"Hi, Ethan," Deepa choked out.

"Hey. Hi there." Meghna cleared her throat. "Uh. Hey, Pri. Sorry for interrupting. We'll catch up another time, yeah?"

"Leaving so soon?" Priya asked, fighting a grin.

Priya's sisters nodded in perfect synchronization. Whatever grilling her sisters had prepared vanished the moment Ethan appeared on-screen. They hurried their goodbyes, but not before shooting Priya a look that promised this wasn't over.

"Well, that was fun," Ethan said with a smirk, setting her phone aside.

Before she could respond, he ducked under the covers, his lips ghosting over her skin. As Ethan ventured lower, a shiver ran through Priya. Her fingers curled into the fabric beneath her, tension coiling tight and electric beneath her skin.

Thirty-Seven

AS EVENING APPROACHED, Priya sat at her desk, trying to power through the work she had ignored all day. The creak of the front door sent a jolt through her, her fingers freezing mid-keystroke.

Ethan was back. A moment later, she felt his warmth behind her, his lips brushing her cheek in a soft kiss. "Ready?"

"Almost." Saving her work, she turned slightly, eyeing him. "You're still not going to tell me where we're going?"

"Not a chance." He dangled a blindfold before her.

"You're killing me. You know that, right?" Priya grinned, clicking her laptop shut. She could barely sit still, buzzing with curiosity over whatever surprise Ethan had been out planning. "Are you sure I'm okay wearing this?" She gestured toward her sweatshirt and jeans.

"You *do* realize you just made pajama pants the most sought-after look of the year, right?" He slid her glasses back up her nose before tying the blindfold around her eyes. "No peeking."

Priya expected him to lead her to the car, but instead, he guided her past it. It was warm for September, and although the sun was setting, the air still carried a trace of heat. The familiar crunch of gravel turned into the whisper of grass under her feet. Priya recognized the route they were taking. It led past the tracks to the open field beyond.

"A picnic?" Priya guessed.

"You'll see soon enough," Ethan said.

After a few more steps, they stopped.

"Ready?" His voice was right next to her ear, his breath warm on her neck.

As he untied the blindfold, Priya's eyes adjusted to the soft glow of twilight. The first thing that came into focus was the freight car. A vast sheet of white canvas had been draped over one side, masking the rusted exterior.

"What's going on?" she asked, looking from Ethan to the transformed space around them. It was as if she had wandered onto the dreamiest film set, a private, cozy screening under the stars. A large rug lay on the ground, with pillows and chairs arranged on top. Marigold and rose petals formed a scattered trail around the edges. The smell of buttery popcorn filled the air. Twinkling lights were strung above them, their glow illuminating trays of drinks and snacks.

Ethan's arms circled her from behind. "You said you were disappointed about missing the premiere, so I brought the movie to you." He pressed a kiss against her temple. "Truth is, not having you at TIFF hit me hard. I kept thinking back to when I invited you, and it made me sad that we were in the same city, but so far apart." A soft smile played on his lips as his gaze met hers. "So, this is our do-over."

Priya turned in his arms, eyes wide with wonder. "It's beautiful. Like we've stepped into another world."

As they settled onto the floor pillows, Ethan placed a bowl of popcorn on his lap and fed her a few pieces.

"All set?" he asked, his hand on the remote.

"Couldn't be more excited."

The projector hummed to life, casting a glow on the makeshift screen. But instead of the opening credits, bold white text appeared: "For Priya."

Priya's head snapped toward Ethan. "What's this?"

On the screen, Ethan appeared, standing in the very spot they were now. He looked into the camera and began to speak.

"Pri, tonight isn't about the movie. It's about us," he said. "Out of all the roles I've played, the only one that really matters is the one I get to share with you. Not for a fleeting scene or a single act, but for the full-length feature of our lives. I want you as my costar, my partner, my love—through every take, every plot twist, and every sequel life throws our way."

Priya's fingers curled into the blanket beneath her as her heart threatened to take flight. It fluttered in her chest, wings unfurling—ready to soar straight into the unknown.

On-screen, Ethan let out a breathy chuckle. "I know what you're thinking—this is insane, right? But Pri, this story? *Our* story? It's been in production for years. I felt drawn to you the moment I laid eyes on you. Right here in this field—kneeling over me, your hair catching the wind like something out of a dream. And something shifted in me. Even before I understood what that meant, before I had the words for it—I knew you were special. If I kept my distance, it wasn't because you didn't matter. It was because you did."

Ethan's voice was steady, but there was something raw beneath it that made Priya's chest tighten.

"I always knew you had a crush on me," he said. "I saw it in the way you looked at me when you thought I wasn't paying attention. And even though you never said a word, your silence was the loudest thing I heard. But you weren't just another girl. You were untouchable, Pri. I couldn't think of you *that* way. You were too important to be part of some reckless phase of mine.

"Then I came back." Ethan exhaled. "And there you were, impossible to ignore. And this time, I wasn't some stupid kid with no direction. I knew exactly what I wanted. And it was you. In any way, in any form, on any terms, you'd have me.

"But when the fire happened and I saw you lying there, I thought . . . I thought I'd lost you for good. That was when everything changed. That deal we made—to walk away from each other? It shattered in a heartbeat.

"Because the truth is, Pri, I've never wanted anything more in my life. I don't need any rehearsals. I don't need another take. I know exactly how this ends—with you."

Priya's pulse thundered in her ears, her vision blurring with unshed tears as the Ethan on-screen dropped to one knee. At the same time, the real Ethan reached into the popcorn for a small box and held it open for her.

"Will you marry me?" both Ethans asked in perfect unison.

For a heartbeat, Priya was split into two people. The one who had spent years aching for him in silence. And the one here now, standing on the brink of something extraordinary.

Her breath hitched. This wasn't a dream. It was really happening. On-screen Ethan remained frozen, waiting and hopeful. The one beside her held out more than an engagement ring—he held a future, the promise of forever.

A breathless, giddy laugh escaped her. "Priya 1.0 and Priya 2.0 have only one answer for both Ethans. Yes, yes, a thousand times yes!"

Ethan let out an incredulous laugh as the ring settled perfectly onto her finger. Priya couldn't take her eyes off the design—simple, timeless, and impossibly lovely.

"It was my mother's," he said quietly, watching her reaction.

Her breath caught. "How did you even get it?"

"I told Brooke about the proposal when she picked up Sir Puffington. She came back with the ring not long after."

"But . . . Harry?" Priya's mind flashed to the man who couldn't even bring himself to shift a single photo or trophy his wife had left behind—let alone part with something as precious as her ring.

"Apparently, it was his idea," Ethan murmured, cupping her face in his hands. When he kissed her, it was as if the world had stopped spinning for a beat.

Priya melted into him, her hands tangling in his shirt. They fell back on the pillows, their embrace deepening until a sound pricked the edge of Priya's awareness. She frowned, her body going still. Something . . . or someone . . . was moving nearby. Glancing over Ethan's shoulder, she saw a figure creeping away in the dim light.

"Mumma?" she called, sitting up.

The figure froze mid-step. Just ahead, another guilty shape emerged.

"Puppa?"

Priya's parents turned around slowly, looking like two kids caught snooping.

"Hello, beta. Hello, Mr. Ethan," Mumma greeted. "We thought you were . . . uh . . . inside. We saw all these cars arriving and wanted to see what was going on." She waved at the setup around them before turning to Puppa for backup.

Puppa looked everywhere but at his daughter, currently sprawled out on a pile of pillows with Ethan Knight. "Yes, well.

We will be on our way." His head bobbed, as if trying to shake off the image of what they had just interrupted.

"Please stay." Ethan propped himself up on his elbows and rose. He reached for Priya's hand, helping her up.

"I asked Priya to marry me," he stated, his fingers lacing with hers. "And she said yes."

Mumma let out a soft gasp. Puppa blinked, his expression unreadable.

"You are going to marry our Priya?" he asked.

"With your blessing, I hope." Ethan gave Priya's hand a small squeeze, his shoulder brushing hers in silent support. Priya glanced between her parents, heart caught in her throat as she waited for them to speak.

Mumma's hand flew to her chest, and Puppa blinked as if rebooting his thoughts.

"We saw you two on the red carpet last night," Mumma finally spoke. "But we thought it would end in another public scandal."

"This isn't like before, Mumma," Priya said. "I wouldn't have said yes if I wasn't sure."

"I truly love your daughter," Ethan added. "And I would love to be a part of your family, if you'll have me."

Mumma and Puppa exchanged a long look.

Finally, Puppa cleared his throat and held out his hand. "If that's the case, then you have our blessing, Mr. Ethan."

"Thank you." Ethan shook his hand. "And please—call me Ethan." He looked at Priya and smiled before turning back to her parents. "We'd love for you to join us," he continued. "There's plenty of food, and we haven't even started the movie yet."

Puppa hesitated, glancing at Priya and Ethan's interlocked hands before nodding. "Thank you, son. But you two enjoy."

Priya's smile wobbled, her heart so full it left her breathless. She had hoped Puppa would drop the formality, but he had gone a step further and welcomed Ethan into the family. When she looked at Mumma, she found pride shining in her eyes. A smile bloomed across her mother's face, and the knot in Priya's chest finally began to loosen.

They had accepted her choice. They had accepted *him*.

"I love you both," Priya said, her voice thick with feeling.

Mumma reached over, gently squeezing her hand. "We know, beta. And we love you more."

"Come, Seema," Puppa said, waiting for Mumma to join him.

"We're about to start the new movie," Ethan called after them.

Puppa stopped mid-step. "*Your* new movie?"

"The very same," Priya said, biting back a smile as Puppa's eyes flickered toward the screen.

"Well . . ." Puppa's fingers twitched at his sides. "Maybe just a few minutes then."

Ethan grinned and guided Mumma and Puppa toward the chairs. Priya watched as they sank into the cushions—trying, and completely failing, to contain their excitement.

A private screening.

Under the stars.

Of a Hollywood blockbuster.

Starring their *future son-in-law*.

Any objections about Priya not marrying within their community? Completely obliterated. Because their daughter had found her place. She wasn't living a bare-minimum, acceptable version of happiness. She was glowing, thriving, flourishing.

Priya could see the exact moment they let go and relaxed. As the opening scene lit up the screen, Mumma sighed, settling against Puppa. And Puppa—her stoic, reserved father—draped an arm around his wife and kissed her forehead.

Priya's heart swelled as she settled back on the pillows beside Ethan.

He laced his fingers with hers, pressing a silent question into her palm.

You okay?

She was more than okay. She was the happiest she'd ever been.

Her fingers curled around his, her head finding its perfect place against his shoulder. As the movie played on, Priya felt strong and rooted, like she was finally on solid ground. Somewhere between Moksha and Hollywood, she had found her place—one where she was truly and irrevocably untouchable.

Thirty-Eight

"WHAT A FUN EVENING," Priya said as Ethan unlocked the door to the coach house. "It was so nice of your dad to host a dinner party for us."

The last time Ethan's father threw a party for him, it was a send-off to college. But when Ethan had chosen his own path instead, the door to his father's house had shut behind him. Until now. So, tonight wasn't just an engagement party. It was a homecoming, an invitation back into the place he had once called home.

"What did you and your dad talk about when you disappeared?" Priya asked, as they stepped inside.

Ethan rubbed a hand over his jaw. "Not much. We visited my mom's grave."

Priya stilled. "Oh," she said softly. "Are you okay?" Her hand found his arm, and she searched his face for what he wasn't saying.

"Yeah. It wasn't really planned," he continued. "One second, we were in the house, and the next . . . I just knew where we were going."

Priya's heart ached. "How was it?"

Ethan was quiet for a moment. "We just stood there. Remembering her. And when we turned to leave . . ." His throat bobbed. "My dad put a hand on my shoulder. Just . . . this firm squeeze."

Priya reached for his hand. "I'm glad you went."

"Me too." A small smile touched his lips, weary but lighter than before. Then he tilted his head, studying her. "And what did you get up to while I was gone?"

"I stayed on video chat with my sisters after you left. It was nice having them at the engagement party, even virtually. Then I watched Brooke work her magic. She launched Sir Puffington into superstardom in under five minutes! He has fifteen thousand followers already." Priya pulled out her phone and flashed the screen at him.

"The Puffington Post?" Ethan laughed before scanning the page. "Pri, there's just one photo on his account. *One*. And it's with me."

"Oh, really?" Priya grinned, playing innocent.

"This is a straight-up exploitation," Ethan declared, staring at an image from earlier that night—Sir Puffington lounging on his lap with a digital crown perched on his head. The caption underneath read, "Rescued at TIFF. Crowned at dinner. Living the dream. #BreakingMeows #FromRescueToRoyalty #KnightInFurryArmor #MoveOverEthanKnight."

"I've been played, Pri. Look at all these brand deal pitches. My own sister is monetizing me. And look at this comment about me and my emotional support cat."

Priya bit her lip to keep from laughing. "I mean . . . the internet *is* obsessed with you saving him at TIFF."

"Oh, so the first image that goes viral since we got engaged is of me with . . . some pussy?"

"Ethan!" Priya gasped, smacking his arm as laughter burst out of her. "We've only been engaged for two days."

"That's way too long for my fiancée to be missing from my feed. We need to fix this right now." Ethan gave Priya back her phone and pulled out his own. "Alright, future Mrs. Knight, let's make it official."

"Just like that? No PR strategy, no media rollout?"

"Are you backing out on me?"

"Not a chance."

Ethan snapped the picture just as Priya's grin broke through, her eyes crinkling with amusement. The ring wasn't in-your-face obvious, but it was there, subtly catching the light. He took a few more, playing around with angles, before leaning in to press a quick kiss on her jaw.

"Which one do you like?" he asked, scrolling through the images.

"All of them," she declared. "They're definitely an upgrade from my red-carpet debut."

"Then I say we post them all." But instead of uploading them, he tucked his phone away. "Tomorrow," he murmured, brushing his lips against hers. "Tonight, I want you all to myself. No interruptions."

Priya sighed contentedly, her fingers grazing the back of his neck, playing with the ends of his hair. But she knew the clock was ticking: In a few days, he had to leave.

"I'm going to miss you," she whispered, pressing her forehead to his.

Ethan's arms tightened around her. "Me too," he said, his breath warm against her skin. "But we'll figure it out," he promised. "Maybe get a place in both cities. One here, and one in

L.A. Your app's blowing up and everyone wants a piece of you. You can work from anywhere now, Pri. Even join me on location." He tucked a strand of hair behind her ear, his fingers lingering against her skin. "But right now, I have a better idea. How about a midnight ride?" He flashed that signature grin, the one that made logic and reason entirely optional.

"Shouldn't we at least change first?" Priya gestured toward their evening wear—her lavishly embroidered salwar khameez and his crisp dark suit.

"Want to throw on your trending pajama pants instead?" Ethan teased, plucking Priya's jacket off the hook and holding it out for her.

"You're never letting that go, are you?"

"Not a chance."

"Fine." With a mock sigh, Priya shrugged into her jacket. "But if we get spotted, you're explaining to TMZ why Bollywood Cinderella and James Bond are joyriding at midnight."

"They'll just assume I'm rehearsing for my next spy thriller—*Mission: Irresponsible.*" Ethan tossed over her helmet and locked the door behind them. "Hop on, hotshot. I know just the place."

The night was crisp with the smell of damp autumn leaves. The low growl of the engine echoed through the stillness as they coasted along the train tracks, then slipped onto winding back roads. Towering trees gave way to vast open fields, moonlight spilling over everything like liquid silver.

Priya let out a breath as they passed the campground site from her high school field trip. She caught glimpses of the lake through the trees, moonlight dancing across the water like drifting fireflies.

Suddenly, they were on *that* road. The road where Ethan had taken her on their first motorcycle ride. The moon loomed ahead—round, glowing, and impossibly large—as if they could ride straight into it.

Priya loosened her grip and raised her arms, her pulse thrumming with exhilaration.

"Whoooo!" she shouted, grinning as her voice carried through the night.

"Having fun back there?" Ethan called.

Their laughter mixed with the wind as the bike propelled forward. Priya wrapped her arms around him again, her cheek pressing against his back. Here, with Ethan, there were no limits, only the road stretching endlessly ahead—where the earth rose to kiss the sky and two worlds melted seamlessly into each other. Priya's heart filled with a quiet, thrilling certainty. The universe was wide enough and wild enough to hold every possibility, and their story was playing out on the greatest screen of all, right there beneath the stars.

GLOSSARY

Aarti: A devotional practice in Hinduism that offers light to a deity or sacred object, typically with lamps or candles, as a gesture of reverence and adoration.

Arey: An exclamation that can convey various emotions depending on the context and tone of the speaker, including frustration, affection, surprise, annoyance, or disbelief.

Atta: A type of whole wheat flour commonly used in South Asian cooking, especially for making flatbreads like rotli.

Baap re: From the word *baap*, meaning father. The phrase is commonly used to express surprise, astonishment, or amazement. It can be loosely translated to "Oh my goodness" or "Wow."

Bajra no rotlo: Millet flatbread.

Ben: Sister. Also, a respectful form of addressing a woman, similar to *madam*.

Beta: A term used to refer to a son (as opposed to *beti* for a daughter). However, it can be used to affectionately refer to either.

Bhagwanji: Bhagwan means God. The suffix *-ji* is a respectful honorific to denote reverence.

Bhajiyas: Also known as pakoras or fritters, they are made by deep-frying a batter-coated mixture of vegetables, spices, and gram flour.

Bindi: A decorative mark or dot applied on the forehead between the eyebrows.

Chaniya: A flared skirt worn by women in parts of India, especially Gujarat and Rajasthan. It is often paired with a *choli* (blouse) and a *dupatta* (scarf), forming the traditional outfit known as *chaniya choli*.

Chevda (or *chevdo*): A crunchy snack mix made with flattened rice flakes (*poha*), pulses, nuts, raisins, and spices. It typically blends salty, spicy, and slightly sweet flavors.

Choli: A fitted blouse that is usually paired with a sari or *chaniya*. It is often short, exposing the midriff, and comes in various designs and styles.

Daal: Various types of dried, split pulses (legumes) such as lentils, peas, and beans.

Dalit: A term used to describe individuals belonging to the lowest stratum of the traditional Hindu caste system, historically designated as "untouchable." The caste system was officially abolished in India in 1947, with the constitution providing for equal rights and prohibiting caste-based discrimination. However, many Dalits continue to face social, economic, and political challenges.

Dandiya: A traditional Indian folk dance from the state of Gujarat, performed with decorated sticks called *dandiyas*. It is normally performed in pairs or groups during festive celebrations.

Dhokla: A savory snack made from fermented batter primarily consisting of gram flour and/or semolina, often mixed with rice flour and yogurt. The batter is spiced with ingredients such as green chilies, ginger, and turmeric.

Dishoom-dishoom: The sound of punches being thrown in a Bollywood movie.

Diya: A traditional oil lamp, typically made of clay or brass. It consists of a shallow bowl with a spout for pouring oil and a cotton wick. The wick is soaked in oil and then lit, producing a small, flickering flame.

Dosa: A thin and crispy pancake commonly made from a fermented batter of soaked rice and *urad daal* (black lentils). It is a staple dish in the South Indian states and is typically served with a variety of accompaniments like *sambar* (a spiced lentil soup) and different kinds of chutneys.

Dupatta: A long rectangular scarf or shawl, typically worn with traditional attire such as a *salwar khameez* or *chaniya choli*, as part of a complete outfit.

Fafdas: Crispy snacks made from dough primarily consisting of gram flour, turmeric, black pepper, carom seeds, and other spices. The dough is rolled out into thin flat strips and deep-fried until crisp.

Ganthias: Crunchy snacks made from gram flour and spices. The dough is rolled into thick ropelike strands and deep-fried until golden brown. Ganthias come in various forms, including thick, chunky, or thin.

Garba: A traditional Indian folk dance originating from the state of Gujarat, characterized by its vibrant and rhythmic movements. Participants move gracefully in a synchronized manner, forming concentric circles or spirals while clapping their hands.

Ghee: A type of clarified butter.

Gujarati: The people, language, and culture associated with the state of Gujarat, located in the western part of India.

Hai Ram: An exclamation or an expression of surprise, shock, or astonishment. It is a colloquial way of invoking or referring to Lord Rama, a revered figure in Hinduism.

Holi: Also known as the Festival of Colors. It is a time of merriment, playfulness, and the triumph of good over evil. The main highlight of Holi is the exuberant throwing of colored powders and water; participants playfully drench each other in a riot of vibrant hues.

Jalebi: A sweet spiral-shaped dessert made by deep-frying a wheat flour batter and soaking it in sugar syrup.

Jiju: A respectful and affectionate term for one's brother-in-law.

Kadhi: A tangy yogurt-based curry.

Khakhras: Disk-shaped savory crackers made from a combination of wheat flour and other ingredients such as spices, sesame seeds, fenugreek leaves, or cumin seeds.

Khichdi: A soft, mushy dish of rice and lentils cooked with various spices and seasonings.

Laal: Red.

Lassi: A yogurt-based drink with sweet or salty flavoring.

Laxmi: In Hindu mythology, Goddess Laxmi is the goddess of wealth, prosperity, and abundance.

Masi: Refers to one's maternal aunt in Gujarati.

Mehndi: A paste made from henna leaves, used to create decorative designs—typically on the hands and feet—for festive or ceremonial occasions.

Muthiyas: Steamed or fried dumplings made from shredded vegetables, chickpea flour, semolina, and spices.

Narak (or Naraka): Refers to the underworld or hellish realms of existence. It is believed that the souls of the wicked and sinful are sent to Narak after death to undergo punishment for their deeds. Narak is often described as a place of intense suffering, where souls are subjected to various tortures and agonies. However, the concept of Narak varies across different Hindu traditions and texts.

Paneer tikka: Marinated cubes of paneer (Indian cottage cheese) grilled or roasted, often served with chutney.

Patras: Popular snacks made with colocasia or taro leaves. To prepare patras, a mixture of gram flour, tamarind pulp, jaggery, and various spices such as turmeric, red chili powder, coriander, and cumin is applied to the colocasia leaves. The leaves are then rolled up tightly and steamed or shallow-fried until cooked.

Pendas: Sweet and fudgy confections made from a mixture of milk solids and sugar, often flavored with cardamom and/or saffron.

Pooja: A sacred ceremony in Hinduism where devotees engage in prayers, hymns, and offerings to gods and goddesses, typically including rituals like lighting incense and/or lamps, presenting food, and chanting sacred verses.

Potla: A cloth bag or bundle. It also refers to a specific type of small cloth bundle filled with aromatic herbs, spices, or medicinal ingredients for Ayurveda, naturopathy, and home remedies.

Potu: A cloth or rag used to soak up water or cleaning solution to mop the floor.

Prasad: A sacred offering, often food, given to a deity during Hindu worship ceremonies, which is then shared among worshippers, embodying the devotee's acceptance of divine blessings and grace.

Pulao: A fragrant rice dish cooked with spices and often mixed with vegetables or meat.

Puri: A deep-fried bread made with dough shaped into small circles and fried until it puffs up and becomes golden brown.

Rotlis: Also known as rotis. They are a type of unleavened flatbread made from whole wheat flour, salt, and water. The dough is rolled into thin circular disks and cooked on a hot griddle until they puff up and develop light brown spots.

Salwar khameez: A two-piece outfit that consists of a *salwar* (trousers) and *khameez* (a long tunic).

Samosas: Popular savory snacks of crispy triangular pastry shells filled with various ingredients including vegetables, cheese, onions, beef, chicken, and spices. Samosas are typically deep-fried until golden brown and served with chutneys or sauces.

Sangeet: Derived from the Sanskrit language, it translates to *music* or *musical.* A *sangeet* ceremony is a lively event that takes place before Indian weddings, specifically within the context of Hindu, Sikh, and Jain traditions.

Sev puri: A popular street food snack made from crispy *puris* (deep-fried dough) topped with potatoes, onions, chutneys, and *sev* (crunchy noodles made from chickpea flour).

Sev tameta nu shaak: A tangy and spicy curry made with tomatoes and *sev* (crispy chickpea flour noodles), often cooked with onions, garlic, and a blend of spices.

Seva: Selfless service or volunteering. It embodies the concept of offering assistance or aid without any expectation of personal gain.

Sherwani: A coat-like garment worn by men, typically knee-length or longer. It is a popular choice for formal occasions, weddings, and cultural celebrations due to its regal and elegant appearance.

Shrikhand: A creamy dessert made from strained yogurt, sweetened with sugar, and typically flavored with cardamom and saffron. Sometimes garnished with nuts or fruits.

Tawa: A flat or slightly concave griddle traditionally made of iron or steel, commonly used in Indian cooking for preparing flatbreads like rotlis and parathas, as well as pancakes like dosas.

Theplas: A popular Gujarati flatbread, similar to rotlis but with a distinct flavor and texture due to the addition of various spices and ingredients. They are typically made from a dough consisting of whole wheat flour, yogurt, spices, and oil. Traditionally, theplas are flavored with spices such as turmeric, red chili powder, coriander, cumin, and carom seeds.

Tilak: A mark of devotion, cultural adherence, and/or protection against negative energies, typically made from a variety of materials including, but not limited to, ash, sandalwood, vermilion, clay, kumkum, or turmeric.

ACKNOWLEDGMENTS

This story wouldn't be what it is without the many hands, hearts, and minds that helped shape it into being.

Amy Tannenbaum, my tireless agent and steady guide—thank you for navigating this journey with me, from draft to deal and every step beyond. I'm endlessly grateful to have had your calm expertise and quiet encouragement along the way.

Bhavna Chauhan, my brilliant editor—you championed this story from the moment it landed in your inbox. That it found its way to you through a string of happy accidents still feels cosmic—truly cast in the stars! Your clarity of vision, sharp eye, and immense heart helped shape this book into what it was always meant to be. What an extraordinary gift it's been to work with you.

Megan Kwan—how lucky can one writer get? Not just one, but two amazing editors! Thank you for stepping in so seamlessly and guiding this story through its final stretch with such grace and kindness.

To Crissy Boylan, my sharp-eyed copyeditor, and Alison Strobel, my equally meticulous proofreader—your attention to detail and thoughtful insights were invaluable in giving this story its final polish.

To Talia Abramson—your design work, from the elegant interior layout to the stunning cover, breathed visual life into every page. Thank you for capturing the heart of this book so beautifully.

To the powerhouse team at Doubleday Canada—Amy Black, Maria Golikova, Carla Kean, Val Gow, Kaitlin Smith, Keara Campos, Taylor Rice, and Chalista Andadari—my heartfelt thanks for the care, insight, and expertise you brought to every stage of this journey. Your behind-the-scenes brilliance helped carry this book into the world, and I'm so deeply grateful.

To Hetal Patel, Faiza Daudo, Abir Fátima, MamaSita, and Soulla—thank you for your early reads and honest feedback. Your input gave me the clarity and insight I needed to continue.

To every friend, reader, writer, and behind-the-scenes cheerleader, including those whose kindness arrived after this page was written, please know you are seen, and deeply appreciated.

To my best girlie, Lyla—thank you for being a small but mighty presence by my side, every day.

And to my husband and son—thank you for the space to write, and for the love that holds me through it all.

I feel incredibly lucky to do this work—and even luckier to be surrounded by people who believe in me.

LEYLAH ATTAR is an award-winning Indo-Canadian author. Her self-published work has appeared on bestseller lists in *The New York Times*, *USA Today*, and *The Wall Street Journal*. A recipient of the Writer's Digest Award and the IndieReader Discovery Award, Leylah writes stories that reflect her diverse influences and heritage. *Caste in the Stars* is her traditional publishing debut. She lives in Toronto with her husband, their son, and the most adorable Yorkshire terrier on the planet.

leylahattar.com
IG: @leylah.attar
FB: leylah.attar